For my brothers: Patrick, Robert and Francis

After She Fell

MARY-JANE RILEY

An imprint of HarperCollins*Publishers*
www.harpercollins.co.uk

Killer Reads
An imprint of HarperCollins*Publishers*
1 London Bridge Street
London SE1 9GF

www.harpercollins.co.uk

This paperback edition 2016
1

First published in Great Britain by

HarperCollins*Publishers* 2016

Copyright © Mary-Jane Riley 2016

Mary-Jane Riley asserts the moral right to

be identified as the author of this work

A catalogue record for this book is

available from the British Library

ISBN: 978-0-00-818110-9

Set in Minion by Palimpsest Book Production Ltd, Falkirk, Stirlingshire

Find out more about HarperCollins and the environment at
www.harpercollins.co.uk/green

DECEMBER

Hunched against the wind that knifed through him, and trying to avoid the spray stinging his weathered cheeks even more, he didn't see the body at first.

He had pulled his battered old overcoat tightly around himself, shifted his carrier bag of belongings from one hand to the other, watching as his feet sank into the sand, each footprint filling with water then draining away. He raised his head and, in the early grey half-light, saw what looked like seaweed in the ebb and flow of the sea on the shore. He squinted. Not seaweed, but hair, floating in the water. He moved closer. A girl, and a young one at that, pale face pummelled beyond all recognition and part of her scalp missing. Her body was at an awkward angle to her head – one eye gazing sightlessly up to the dark sky – lying like a broken puppet. Poor lass, he thought, poor, poor lass. He looked up and thought he could see a figure on top of the cliff where the end of the road had fallen into the sea. He thought he could see someone, but he wasn't sure. A seagull wheeled and mewled above him.

FIVE MONTHS LATER

Daily Courier

The daughter of a top politician took her own life after a history of depression and eating disorders, an inquest has heard.

The body of Elena Devonshire, the 17-year-old daughter of MEP Catriona Devonshire, was found in December at the foot of cliffs in Hallow's Edge, North Norfolk, close to the school where she was a pupil.

A post-mortem examination revealed Elena died from multiple injuries consistent with a fall. Toxicology tests also showed a small quantity of cannabis in her system.

Yesterday's inquest was told that, between the ages of fourteen and sixteen, Elena had suffered from depression, coupled with an eating disorder.

PC Vic Spring from Norfolk Police said a text from the teenager to her mother had been discovered on the teenager's phone, found in her bedroom at The Drift – the private boarding school she attended – which 'strongly indicated' she had intended taking her own life. 'There was no suspicious evidence leading to her death and no neglect of care exhibited by the staff at her school,' he said.

Norfolk coroner, Sarah Knight, recorded a verdict of suicide.

After the inquest Mrs Devonshire said, although her daughter had been treated for depression and an eating disorder in the past, she had since made a full recovery. 'My daughter was looking forward to getting home for Christmas,' she said.

Ingrid Farrar, one of two head teachers at the co-educational school, said, 'Our hearts go out to Mrs Devonshire and Elena's stepfather, Mark Munro, at this difficult time. The school has a robust pastoral care policy and we are more than satisfied we helped Elena all we could.'

Catriona Devonshire was elected to the European Parliament for the South and East on an independent ticket eighteen months ago. She has already proved an able campaigner in the area of human rights.

CHAPTER 1

May

Despite the heat of the day, the window of the room was closed tight. Alex Devlin's sister sat in her chair, staring through the glass. Outside, trusted patients were standing around smoking or sitting on the benches at the edges of the grass. One woman was talking animatedly to her nurse, who nodded, looking into the middle distance. The garden was lovely at this time of year – the lawn lush and green, roses blooming in the sunshine, the silver birches coming into full leaf, and Alex could almost smell the honeysuckle that climbed through the hedge of bamboo at one end of the garden. Birds chattered and hopped from branch to bird table and back to branch again. She badly wanted to be out there, away from the stifling air and atmosphere of Sasha's room.

'Sash? Would you like me to take you into the garden? It's a beautiful day.'

Alex had been in the room for fifteen minutes and so far her sister hadn't said a word. She damped down a sigh. It was really hard going to keep on chatting when the person you were talking to didn't respond in any way at all. Not a sign she'd heard anything Alex had said. Not a flicker of expression.

She looked around the room. It was, considering the circumstances, a homely place, decorated in soft pastels. The bed had her sister's own patchwork bedspread thrown over it. There were two pictures on the walls, both with the glass removed, of course:

the first, a scene of beach huts and seagulls; the second, a small photograph of Sasha's twins forever caught in a time of sunshine and ice creams. The shelves were full of Sasha's favourite books, from Enid Blyton to Kate Atkinson. Did her sister need anything? The soap she'd bought last time was still in its wrapping. Not that, anyway.

She tried again. 'Love, it's gorgeous out there and really, really warm, even for late May. You remember how you love the summer?'

'Harry and Millie loved the summer.' A tear trickled down Sasha's face.

Alex's heart twisted, pain blooming in her chest. Words, at last, but words that contained so much hurt. She went to hug her sister, but Sasha pushed her away.

'I want you to go now,' she snarled.

She had to try. 'Sasha, please, let's go outside. Have a walk. Feel the sun on our faces. Enjoy being together, if only for a few minutes.'

'Enjoy?' Sasha's voice was low; she didn't move from her position at the window. 'I can't enjoy anything, Alex. You know that. I've got nothing left. Millie. Harry. Jez. Nothing.' She gave a sigh that shook her whole body. 'Please go.' Her voice was the merest whisper.

'Haven't you punished yourself enough, Sasha?' pleaded Alex. 'Let's go outside. Just this once.'

Silence. Sasha kept staring through the window, her shoulders tense. Alex knew there would be nothing more from her today. She bent down and kissed her sister's cold cheek. 'Bye, Sash. I'll come again as soon as I can.'

Nothing.

Alex shut the door quietly and leaned against it. Was this a better visit than last time? At least, Sasha had spoken to her. Most of the time when she came to see her, Sasha didn't say anything, so she supposed even a few bitter words were progress of a sort.

But she could hardly bear the pain that was almost tattooed on Sasha's eyes. Alex couldn't imagine what it must be like to live inside her sister's head, to know that you had killed your own children. She thought of her own boy – eighteen years old but still her boy – and how he had coped with the last few years. She was proud of him. She couldn't even contemplate life without him.

'Ah, Alex, I wanted to catch you before you left.' Heather McNulty, the matron of the unit, bustled along the corridor towards her. A well-groomed woman a little older than Alex, Heather always had a cheerful expression on her face even though she was surrounded by unresponsive or troublesome patients. She didn't wear a uniform, and today had a long skirt made of some sort of floaty material festooned with printed roses, teamed with a crisp white shirt. Alex liked the fact the staff wore their own clothes; it made it less of an institution, and made her feel better about Sasha being incarcerated there on the orders of the judge. Two years before, the judge, old and wrinkled but with a kind-looking face, had decreed that Sasha had suffered enough: for more than fifteen years she had lived with the knowledge that she had been responsible for drowning her own 4-year-old twins. But she would have to have treatment in a secure unit. Jez, Sasha's police officer husband, hadn't been so lucky to escape the wrath of the judge. He was jailed for weaving a tissue of lies and misinformation about what had happened on the fateful night, and for being responsible for the imprisonment of two people who had been wrongly convicted of murder. So, yes, Alex was grateful for Leacher's House. A secure unit it might be, but it could have been such a lot worse.

Alex frowned and rubbed her forehead. 'Is everything all right with Sasha? She hasn't started to self-harm again has she?'

'Not exactly. I only need to have a chat. Come with me to the office.'

Alex followed Heather down the corridor, transported back

more than a quarter of a century to when she was a schoolgirl following the straight back and sharp shoulders of her head teacher to the office for a telling-off. She felt that same degree of apprehension now: stomach knotted, wanting to drag her feet, wanting to get it over with.

'So, sit down, Alex.'

Alex sat.

Heather went round to the other side of her desk and neatly lowered herself into the chair, folding her hands in front of her. She took a deep breath. Fear rose in Alex's throat.

'Is Sasha ill?' She laughed nervously. Shut up Alex. 'I mean, more ill than normal?'

Heather clasped her hands together. 'Sasha has not been responding to treatment as well as we would like.'

'What do you mean?'

A small frown crossed Heather's face before the sympathetic smile was in place once more. 'Sasha has been suffering from, um, delusions, lately.'

Alex blinked. 'Delusions?'

'Sasha believes she murdered Jackie Wood.' Heather's voice was kind.

Alex caught her breath. Jackie Wood was the woman who had been imprisoned for fifteen years for what was then thought to have been her involvement in the murder of Sasha's children. It was only after she was let out on a technicality that the truth about the children's deaths began to unfold, and Sasha finally confessed. But before Jackie Wood could be exonerated she was murdered, and the murderer had never been found. There had been a time when Alex had wondered whether her sister had killed Jackie Wood, but now she refused to entertain that thought.

Heather was still talking. 'And obviously, we don't want her to regress further, so we feel – that is, her team feel – she needs a different regime.'

'Regime? What does that mean? And what sort of treatment?

She can stay here in Leacher's House, can't she?' Alex heard her voice rise. Oh God, oh God. She had visions of her sister being force-fed drugs by a Nurse Ratched figure or being forced to undergo ECT and Sasha becoming a shell, losing her personality, any sense of identity and—

'Alex.' Heather's voice was firm. 'I can see the panic in your face. Sasha is in good hands.'

'But she will get better, won't she?'

'As I say, she is in good hands. The best possible. Please don't worry; this sort of review is part of an ongoing process, and this is the twenty-first century, you know.' Her face was kind. 'Things are very different now.' Heather stood. The meeting was clearly over. 'You will be kept informed every step of the way.'

Alex stood. 'Thank you,' she said. Though for what, she wasn't quite sure.

Review. Ongoing process. Regime. Jackie Wood. The words went round and round in Alex's head as she pushed open the door and went out into the fresh, warm air, trying to shake off the chemical floral smell of Leacher's House. She took a few deep breaths to steady herself. The sun was bright and the sky was blue, like a children's painting. A perfect day. It was at times like these Alex found herself thinking of Harry: drowned by Sasha, brought to the shore by Jez. She thought of Millie who'd been taken away by the North Sea, and wondered if her body would ever be found. She still looked for Millie in crowds of young people, just in case.

Walking to the car park, she glanced back to see Sasha still sitting, still in the same position, still looking. She had always known her sister was not right and had needed proper help, but over the years she had been so blinded by her grief over the twins and the guilt she carried around at having an affair with the man who was imprisoned for killing Harry and Millie that she hadn't been able to see beyond her own feelings. She had let Sasha down. Now she was trying to make up for it.

Alex raised her hand and waved, and was rewarded by the tiniest of finger movements. The nearest she had come to a wave for a very long time. Love for her poor broken sister swelled in her chest. She couldn't let Sasha down again.

CHAPTER 2

The small mews house was a stone's throw away from Harrods and the moneyed part of Knightsbridge. Alex could smell the cash as she found the right address. Blood-red door flanked by two rose trees in square pots. The petals were a blush pink and when Alex bent to smell them they gave off a cloying scent. The woodwork of the windows was in the same blood-red, as were the garage doors. The other houses in the row had either the red or dark green wood. Three storeys of perfection. Not bad for a set of buildings that was once a line of stables.

She knocked on the door.

The woman who answered looked as though she hadn't slept for days. Heavy make-up couldn't disguise her grey skin and sunken eyes, the black shadows underneath. She was dressed in jeans and a tee-shirt, diamond studs in her ears. Her perfume was expensive though overlaid with the smell of cigarette smoke.

'Alex. Thank you for coming.' The woman held onto the door as if by letting go she would fall down.

'Cat,' Alex said, reaching out to hug the woman who had once been her closest friend. 'Of course I came.'

There had been no question about her going to Grosvenor Place Mews, even though she should have been hunting for stories, chasing commissions, chasing the cash.

She'd been in her news editor's office pitching an idea for looking into a story about people being trafficked for illegal organ removal when he'd leaned back in his chair and looked at her from under unruly eyebrows. 'I had a call this morning.'

'Right,' said Alex, not sure what that had to do with her.

'Someone looking for you.'

'Right.' Typical Bud, he liked to think he was being mysterious, building up the tension – all it succeeded in doing was to make her impatient. Even so, she wasn't going to give him the satisfaction of winning the game. 'Anyway, Bud, about the organ removal story. It's early days, but I heard from a reasonably reliable source—'

'Don't you want to know who it was?'

She looked at him: sitting in his cubbyhole in a dark corner of the office 'so the bean counters can't find me'; overweight, paunch almost resting on the desk. Computer pushed right to the back; the front of the desk piled high with editions of *The Post* going back years. And a higgledy-piggledy heap of press releases, cuttings, jottings, and God knows what. Coffee mugs littered the desk too, dark slime at the bottom of some. All Bud Evans needed to complete the 'I'm an old-fashioned editor and I don't take any nonsense' look was a green eyeshade. Bloody rogue. But he'd been good to her: employing her when nobody else would after it had all come out about Sasha and she felt she needed to leave Sole Bay and lose herself in the anonymity of London. Having taken her under his wing once in her life – when she was a raw recruit – Bud had come to her rescue again. She owed him.

She grinned. 'What if I said no?'

He made a gruff noise, somewhere between a snort and a cough. 'You want to know. Of course you do.'

She rolled her eyes. 'Go on then.'

'A Member of the European Parliament,' he said with a flourish. 'Asking for you personally. Said she was an old friend of yours. Didn't know you moved in such illustrious circles. Or have you gone native on me? Hobnobbing with the enemy?'

'An MEP?' Her heart began to beat faster. There was only one such person who could be asking for her personally: Catriona Devonshire.

She and Cat Devonshire had been inseparable through primary school and on into high school. Cat had been the sister to her that Sasha hadn't been. They had shared secrets, problems, worries. They swore to look out for each other forever. They went their separate ways to uni, but they still kept in touch. When Gus came along, Cat made no judgements, but left her new husband, Patrick, at home, put her fledgling political career on hold and came to stay. Her presence had been a soothing balm on Alex's soul.

And then the twins had been murdered and Alex's life had been consumed by guilt and the need to look after Sasha. Her world began to narrow; she had no time, no room in her head for anyone but Sasha, so she excluded everything and everyone else from her life, including Cat. And when Cat's daughter, Elena, had been born, a few short weeks later, Alex had broken off all contact.

'But I want you here,' Cat had pleaded. 'I want you to be Elena's godmother.'

'Cat,' Alex kept her tone deliberately without emotion, 'you have your family. Your career. Any association with me would spoil both those things. We need to put distance between us.'

'But Al—'

'No, Cat. I have to be with my family.' And then the sentence that had sounded the death knell on their friendship: 'I don't need you any more, Cat. I've got Sasha to look after. Gus. They are my family. They are the ones I need to look after now.' It had almost killed her to say the words, to know that she was losing Cat's friendship, but she didn't want the events of her life to taint Cat's. It had to be done.

And Cat had removed herself from Alex's life.

But Alex had followed Cat's career. Had felt proud of her friend as her political star rose and rose. Had grieved for her when Patrick died suddenly, and grieved even more when Elena was found dead at the bottom of the cliff. She'd wanted to go to Elena's funeral, but had been in Spain chasing a story.

Now Cat was getting in touch with her again. Alex felt something shift inside her. Perhaps here was a chance for her to mend their relationship, for Cat to forgive her for pushing her away. Whatever the reason, Alex knew she'd been given a second chance.

'Alex? Alex? Did you hear what I said?'

Alex blinked. 'Sorry Bud. What were you saying?'

'MEP? Wants to talk to you? Hasn't got your number? Said she might have a story?'

'Of course, the MEP—?'

'Catriona Devonshire. Is she a friend of yours, then?'

'She was.'

'She was talking about an exclusive. For the paper. The paper you work for.'

Clever.

'So you've got her number?' Alex asked, as casually as she could.

'Yep. Personal number, she said. Though God knows why she trusted me with it.' He gave his bark of a laugh. 'She must be desperate to talk to you.' He picked up his e-cigarette, beginning to suck hard on it. 'Bloody hell I hate these things,' he said gloomily, vapours of steam curling up into the air. 'Why does the sodding government have to spoil it for the rest of us?' He took it out of his mouth and looked at it soulfully. 'Nothing like the real thing.' He put it back between his lips.

'But we're a lot healthier in this office, aren't we?' Alex said sweetly. 'Now, Cat's number?'

'Cat is it now? Hang on. I wrote it down here somewhere.' He began to sift through the papers on his desk. Not a chance, she thought. Her shoulders sagged.

'Hah! Here we are.' He waved a piece of paper triumphantly.

'Thanks Bud.' She breathed again as she plucked it from his fingers and turned to go.

'And Alex?'

'Yes?' She tried not to laugh. Him and his e-cigarette just didn't look cool.

'She sounded desperate. Don't know what she wanted, but stories involving corrupt MEPs always sell. Better if it's a sex scandal. Didn't she marry that much younger man recently?'

'Mark Munro?'

'That's the one. Some city whizz-kid.'

'They got hitched about this time last year. Whirlwind romance and a summer wedding abroad.'

'And he's younger than her.' Bud looked thoughtful. 'Maybe—'

Alex raised her eyebrows. 'I thought *The Post* was a serious paper, not given to *Hello!*-style splashes or sidebars of shame reporting. And no one gives a toss if a man marries someone considerably younger than himself.'

'Ach, cut your feminist whining. And in these days of falling circulation we'll take anything.' He grinned. 'Almost anything. As long as you write it in the right way. So, if there's a story there—'

She grinned back at him. 'Don't worry. You'll be the last to know.' She winked before closing the door, knowing the story about organ trafficking would have to wait until she'd seen Cat.

So the next day Alex found herself sitting on the white leather settee inside the Devonshires' mews house. It was a house furnished for comfort: deep pile carpets, squashy sofas, one of those artificial fires that hung on the wall and cost a fortune. Tasteful paintings, from emerging artists she presumed, covered the neutral walls. A table here, a large pendant lamp there. A desk in the corner that was covered with bits of paper (rather like Bud's, Alex thought) was the only discordant note in the room. But there was no mistaking the atmosphere of deep sadness; the grief like a weight pressing down and squeezing out the air.

Catriona Devonshire perched on the edge of the settee, sucking on a cigarette as if her life depended on it. The fingers that held the cigarette trembled. The nails were bitten, nail varnish chipped. Her husband, Mark, tall, dark-haired and with the boyish good looks of a thirty-something film actor, stood by the floor-to-ceiling window, his shoulders tense with … what? Worry? Anger? It was difficult to tell. She could still remember the snide headlines in the papers about cradle snatching and toy boys. His expression, as he looked at his wife, was one of concern. It must have been difficult for him – headlines when he married Catriona – head-lines when her daughter died.

'Coffee?' said Catriona, suddenly leaping up, manically stub-bing her cigarette out in an ashtray perched on the arm of the settee. The ashtray wobbled, but stayed put.

'I'm fine, thank you,' said Alex who could have done with something, but the preponderance of white around her made her certain she would spill it. 'But you have one.'

'I've already … ' she indicated a table by her side. 'Everyone who comes makes me coffee. Even Mark makes me coffee. As if coffee could help.' She sat down again. 'Thanks for your letter, by the way. About Elena.' Her eyes glistened.

'It was the least I could do. I'm so sorry.'

'Yes.' She stared at nothing, twisting her hands together. She turned her head and looked directly at Alex. 'I've missed you.'

'Cat—'

'You weren't here when I needed you.'

'I'm sorry. I'm so sorry.' Alex wanted to say more: to explain about Sasha, about how her life had been, about how much she had missed her best friend. But today wasn't about that, wasn't about her. It was about Cat and what she, Alex, could do to help. She blinked away tears as she leaned forward. 'Cat,' she said gently, 'you asked me to come here.'

'Yes.' She began tapping her foot.

'Against my better judgement.' This from Mark, who turned

to give her what Alex could only think of as a sorrowful look mixed with annoyance. Interesting.

'Mark, please—'

He sighed. 'Oh Cat, you know my views on this.'

'I do. But I have to try and understand, don't you see? She was my daughter.' Catriona scrabbled down the side of the leather cushion and brought out a rather squashed packet of cigarettes. Taking one out, she lit it with shaking hands. Alex caught Mark's frown of disapproval. Surely he couldn't begrudge her this?

He looked directly at Alex. 'But to bring a journalist into the arena is asking for trouble.' His voice was calm.

Alex wondered what arena she had been brought into. Was she here as a friend or as a journalist? It was obvious which side of the fence Mark thought she sat on. She shifted on her seat.

Catriona looked pleadingly at Mark. 'She can help. She's my oldest friend. I trust her.'

Mark shook his head. 'Oh, very well, Cat. I can see you're not going to budge.'

Catriona smiled sadly at Alex. 'Mark doesn't think I should be talking to you; he says we should go to the police. But I really don't think they'll do anything. When it happened, when Elena died … ' her voice faltered, 'I told them it was impossible for Elena to have killed herself. She wasn't depressed or anorexic or bulimic. She would have told me. She was looking forward to coming home. We were going skiing in the New Year with another couple and their two daughters. She was thinking about university. Everything. She had everything to live for.' More desperate sucking on the cigarette. 'She didn't kill herself. I know she didn't.'

Alex tried to keep her expression neutral. So this was what it was about: Catriona's daughter. She had seen the results of the inquest and knew the verdict had been suicide.

'Cat,' she said. 'The inquest—'

Catriona leapt off the sofa, knocking her cup over, spilling the coffee. 'Fuck the inquest,' she shouted.

The three of them watched as the brown liquid spread across the white leather. Alex wondered if it would stain and how much it would cost to get out.

Catriona looked out of the window. Alex knew she wasn't seeing the London street, but was seeing her daughter, her beautiful 17-year-old daughter. 'Fuck the inquest,' she said, quietly this time.

'Was it an accident?' Alex kept her voice neutral.

Catriona rubbed her eyes with the heels of her hands.

Mark stood impassively. He sighed. 'My wife thinks Elena was murdered,' he said.

CHAPTER 3

ELENA

May: twenty-nine weeks before she dies

It starts halfway through the summer term.

Wednesday at two o'clock in the afternoon. For weeks after, I knew I would remember the exact moment when I felt someone watching me. Stupid really. I thought it was bollocks when people said the hairs on the back of their neck stood up, but that's exactly what I felt right at that moment.

I am plucking the petals off a daisy: 'Knob.' Pluck. 'Dick.' Pluck. 'Knob.' Pluck. 'Dick' … What does it matter? My mother's husband, my new stepfather, is both of those – and more. I throw the daisy on the ground. How could she have done it? Replaced Dad like that? And he's younger than her, for Christ's sake. I want to cry.

I look around, take the scrunchie off my wrist and gather my blonde hair away from my face and up into a ponytail. I am sitting on the grass by the tennis courts revising for my AS levels. All four of them. That's the trouble with this damn school – they push and push and push until you feel as though your head is going to fucking explode. Surely your brain can only take in so

19

much knowledge? The trouble with my brain is that the knowledge goes in and then bleeds out. I like Art and English, but I know my teachers want me to take Physics and Maths to A level. What the fuck for? I don't need Physics and Maths. I need English and Art. I want to take English and Art, no matter what my teachers or my mother and new stepfather say. My new stepfather. Even as I think it I still can't believe it. What did Mum do that for? Was it for the sex? Eeugh, please. Too much information. Mark Munro makes pots and pots of money. Some sort of banker wanker. And the bloody headlines when they got married! Jeez! You'd think no one in the world had ever married anyone younger than themselves. But there was such a lot of crap written and spoken about it all, especially as Mum is well-known and a bit older. There are times when I feel quite sorry for them. But, still ...

'Get your exams then you'll have choices,' Mark said to me just after he'd married Mum, when he thought he could get away with trying to be something like a dad to me.

I wanted to tell him to get fucked. You aren't my dad.

And it always makes my insides curl up when I think about my real dad: dead from an asthma attack when I was only ten. But I can remember him, I really can. And the good times, like when we went to the seaside together – just me and him – leaving Mum to network or phone Obama or something. We paddled and swam and built sandcastles and had ice cream and fish and chips and ate them sitting on the harbour wall, watching people go by.

He wouldn't have made me come to this school.

I shade my eyes from the sun. The Queen Bees are lying some fifty metres away, stretched out sunbathing, shirts tucked under their bras, skirts hitched as high as they dare, books discarded by their sides. Looking like razor shells in a row on the sand. They don't seem to care about revising. Lucky sods. The line shifts, sits up, looks around. Queen Bee Naomi Bishop's plump lips (courtesy of a so-called doctor in a clinic on Harley Street) are moving and I guess she's talking about catching the rays and the glories of having a tan. Or perhaps she's whining about something more meaningful like what colour to paint her nails at the weekend, and, of course, the acolytes are breathing in every word. When I first arrived at the school, full of simmering resentment because I felt Mum had listened to Mark and had pushed me away, I was courted by the Queen Bees.

'Come on, darling.' Queen Bee Naomi always manages to make every statement sound like a command. 'You want to be one of us. We know the best hot men to shag, the purest smack, and the best high living. You know it makes sense. We don't ask everybody, you know. Only girls like us.'

I remember I gave them what I hoped was a cool look (Tara said later I had looked cool), even though my heart was beating, like, really, really fast, and said, 'No thanks'. Just like that.

Naomi laughed, but I thought at the time it sounded a bit strained, you know?

'You will so regret it,' warned Jenni Lewis, Naomi's right-hand bee. 'You can't survive on your own in this dump.'

'I'll try,' I said. But I'm not one for cosy confidences, giggling late at night, sneaking out for sex with one of the sixth form boys. Not my style.

As I watch them, trying not to look as though I am another of the Queen Bees, Natasha Wetherby sits up, looks around, flicks her hair off her face. She smiles over at me and blows me a kiss. Yeah, right. I roll my eyes massively. Helen Clements, the mousy one of the group with hair that hangs like a pair of curtains and eyebrows thicker than Frida Kahlo, giggles: a high-pitched noise that carries over to where I'm sitting.

A second group of girls is over the other side of the tennis courts, laughing and talking. Two from my year sit on a bench, revising. Actually revising. Bloody hell. And further away, under a large oak tree, three or four boys from the Lower Sixth are lying down or are propped up on their elbows, chatting. One of them – Felix – is trying to smoke a cigarette, all cocky looks and holding it by his finger and thumb, but sort of looking around as if he's frightened of being caught. Another of the boys is Theo, in skin-tight jeans and gun-hugging tee-shirt: the current Queen Bees' heart-throb. I don't like either of them that much. Felix looks a bit, I dunno, angry all the time, as though it wouldn't take much for him to explode. He has a mean look in his eye. And Theo? Smarmy. Knows he's buff, got half the girls here thinking he's gorgeous. Doesn't do a lot for me.

And Max is with them. He should be doing games or homework or something with his mates from Year 11, not hanging around with guys from the sixth form. They treat him as a sort of mascot for them, get him to run their errands. I sigh as he catches my eye. Mistake. He smiles that wobbly, tentative smile of his that makes him look as though he's about to be hit with a big stick. He's had a bit of a thing about me ever since I found him being pushed around by the likes of Naomi and Natasha. They'd ambushed him in the changing rooms and were pulling his clothes off him, taunting him, laughing at the size of his dick, that sort of thing. He's a boy that invites taunts. But I couldn't let it happen and I managed to get him away from them. Since then he's had a bit of a thing for me.

Now he glances around to make sure no one's looking at him – no one is, they never do – and he gives me a little wave. I smile back. What else can I do?

'Hey, Lee,' Naomi calls across. 'Whatcha doing? Come over here.'

My best mate, Tara Johnson, who is trying to find a blade of grass wide enough to make a squealy-farty noise, looks at me; almost pleading with me to get up and join them so that she can follow too. She desperately wants to be part of the club. I sigh. I understand Tara's feelings, I really do. She likes to belong, be liked, to be part of the gang. Always wants to but never quite manages it. Laughed at for being fat and frumpy, for not being pretty enough, fashionable enough or interesting enough. At our old school I felt sorry for her and could protect her, but here at The Drift, life isn't so easy. Tara has to swim in a sea of piranhas. I mean, I do my best to defend and shield her, but it's tough. Tara does not fit in. At all. Any more than I do, but I can pretend if I have to. Tara tends to wear her heart on her sleeve. But she's a good and loyal friend sticking with me through thick and, quite literally, thin. Tara knows most of my secrets. Knows about my depression, my bouts of anorexia; knows the hard protective shell I'm growing after Mum's marriage to Mark. The shrinks said the eating thing and the depression were because I didn't grieve properly when Dad died. Mum went to pieces. I had to be strong. There was only her and me at that time, until Mark Munro came along. Then Mum got her life back on track and I was the one who went to pieces. Because I couldn't control my environment, they said. The only thing I could control was my eating.

They had a point.

And it was so easy to shut myself in my room and devour pro-ana sites and think all that shit was real. Poor fuckers. I was lucky. Mum got me help and I came out the other side. I think it made me stronger. What doesn't kill you and all that.

But then Mum's job became more important; she became more important, and everybody wanted a piece of her. She'd get invited to all sorts of things, and at some fundraising event for a cancer charity she met Mark, and boom! that was it. I ceased to be the most important thing in her life and dropped down to third. Plus, I don't know what Mark's real motives are for marrying Mum. He's a bit too young for her so I reckon he's in it for the reflected glory or something. And I think he was quite pleased when Mum came up with the idea of sending me to The Drift. 'It's a good school and you're really clever,' she said. 'And I don't want to leave you on your own when I'm away, and I can't expect Mark to look after you.'

Guess not.

And she said she'd spoken to Tara's mum (who writes the most salacious bonkbusters and has made a fortune) who was looking for a new school for Tara, and they both agreed The Drift – in the back of beyond and then some – was a good idea.

So now I'm here.

Sometimes I want to blame Mark for it all, and hope that one day Mum'll see sense. Sometimes I think Mum really believes she has my interests at heart. Sometimes I think she and Mark really do love each other. And sometimes I see pigs flying.

But I long for my old London school in the middle of the city: a vibrant centre, full of life. I miss the constant noise, colour, and the different mix of people. I like the never-ending procession of traffic, the street lights that block out the sky, the green parks that give areas of calm among the madness; whereas here it's dark nights, starry skies, hooting owls, and spoilt rich kids of fading TV stars or blockhead footballers. And the rich kids, who all seem to have been together since day one at the school, and often before that – attended the same prep school, darling – are obsessed with looks and fashion. Tara doesn't stand a chance. And I don't want to be a clone. A drone. A Queen Bee. After all, I've been there, done all that dieting stuff and it almost killed me. Never again. And as for boys, I can't see what all the fuss is about. And that's the problem. I have naff all in common with the Queen Bees, or with any of them. Nor does Tara, but she can't see that.

'Come on Lee, come over here. Leave fatso where she is.' Naomi laughs, and the other members of the gang sitting with her dutifully follow suit.

'No thanks, Naomi,' I shout back. 'I want to stay with my friend. She's more interesting than you.' And I grin like a mad woman.

Naomi waves, not fazed by or bothered by the sarcasm. 'Suit yourself.'

I look at Tara, see her bottom lip wobble. 'Come on, Tar, they're not worth it.'

'Easy for you to say,' sniffs my friend. 'You could go and be at one with the Queen Bees any time you like. I haven't got a fucking chance.'

'Tar. Haven't heard you swear before.' I am admiring.

'Now you have.' She is grumpy.

My phone pings.

hi gorgeous.

I look around again. Heart-throb Theo is looking straight at me. It must have been his eyes I felt on me. He smiles.

Oh God, I can do without this. As I say, neither he nor any of his mates interests me. No time for them. He might be the hottest dude in town but, you know, the Queen Bees can have him. I am about to fling my phone down on the grass when I think of something – it might be worth a flirtation just to piss off the Queen Bees. Yeah, could be fun. I text back, hiding a smile.

hi.

I don't have to wait long for his reply.

wanna hook up later?

Nice chat-up line.

maybe

the old summerhouse?

Original in his destinations too. He sure knows how to woo a girl.

maybe

'bout 8?

maybe. If I can get out

course you can. see you then.

Actually, I feel normal doing that. Not that I have any intention of going. I look across at him. He gives me a small wave and then turns back to talk to his group of mates.

They are laughing, and my face burns.

The skin on the back of my neck prickles. I know someone is watching me. And it's not Theo.

Hey you, it's me.

That was when it first started, wasn't it? You … lying there on the grass, long, tanned legs stretched out in front of you, talking to Tara, texting that boy. And there I was. Looking at you. I couldn't stop it you know, looking and wondering about you. Thinking, you don't know how gorgeous you are. Wondering if you would let me get close to you or if you wouldn't want to know. That's when I thought: I will try. I couldn't waste the opportunity. You see, I thought my life wasn't going anywhere, that I was trapped. But I was frightened, worried about how you might react if I made a move. Then I told myself I shouldn't worry about it, that I should go slowly and test the water. I looked at you again. You felt me looking at you, didn't you? You even turned and looked at me, but didn't see me.

But you didn't know then that it was me.

CHAPTER 4

June

Murdered.

The blunt word hung heavy in the air.

'Cat,' began Alex, her voice still gentle, 'is that right?' She'd had plenty experience of living with the thought that someone you loved had been murdered. It was something that never left you: that feeling of helplessness; the useless 'if only' thoughts that came in the depths of the night. Alex was still trying to live with all of that.

Catriona sighed long and hard, then sat up straight, her mouth in a determined line. 'Yes. It is. I feel it in here.' She thumped her breastbone with her fist. 'Elena wouldn't have done that to me. We went through a lot together, especially after her dad died. She wouldn't leave me this way.'

Alex nodded and thought back to what she knew about the 17-year-old's death. The teenager had been found in the early morning at the bottom of cliffs not far from her very exclusive boarding school, only days before the school broke up for the Christmas holidays. Alex could imagine what sort of Christmas the Devonshires would have had. She'd been through many of those when her sister's children had disappeared. She frowned. 'Cat, forgive me but the police found a text on her phone, didn't they? To you from her?'

'Yes, there was no doubt about that. But—'

'And she had been depressed and anorexic or bulimic or both,' Mark Munro cut across his wife.

'No, she had not been either of those things.' Cat balled her fists. 'She was well. Completely well.' The strain on her face deepened the lines around her eyes.

Alex frowned. 'What made you think she was ill, Mark?'

'I—' His eyes darted around the room.

'Mark?' Cat's voice was sharp.

'Catriona. Can we do this when we're alone, please?' He had regained control and his voice was stern.

Cat looked at him then shook her head. 'No. I want Alex to help me. Us. I don't want to hide anything from her. But if you're hiding something from me—'

He stared at Cat for a few moments before wiping his face wearily with one hand. 'Very well. If you must know I spoke to her. A couple of weeks before … before she died.'

'What? You never told me that.'

'I didn't think it would get this far.' He went over to a cupboard in the corner and took out a bottle of whisky. 'Drink?'

'Mark, you can't solve this with a drink.' She let out a hiss through her teeth.

'I'm not, Catriona. I just want a whisky, that's all. It's not a crime.' He banged a tumbler down on the top of the cupboard. 'Alex?'

'Not for me, thank you.'

'Mark.' Cat again, pain naked on her face. 'What do you mean you spoke to her? Why didn't you tell me?'

'I didn't want to upset you.'

'And did she say she was ill?' interjected Alex. She had to get a grip on this, see what she might be getting herself into.

Mark poured himself a drink then drank it down in one swallow. 'Not in so many words, no.' He poured himself another couple of fingers.

'What does that mean?' demanded Cat. 'What the hell does

28

that mean? And why didn't you say something sooner? Why didn't it come up at the inquest?'

'Nobody asked me, and as you know, I didn't go to the inquest. I was abroad at the time and it wasn't thought necessary to call me. You know all this,' he said simply. 'And I didn't want to make things any worse than they were. The text had been found and that was that.'

He was too smooth.

'So you thought,' said Cat, bitterly.

'Mark,' Alex made her voice firm, 'what made you think Elena was ill?'

He shrugged. 'Just the way she was talking. A bit lost, a bit helpless. She said things hadn't been going well at school. I suggested she talk to her housemother or whatever they call them at the school, that's what they're there for.'

'That's what I'm here for,' said Cat, a break in her voice. 'I'm her mother.'

'But you weren't around, darling, were you?' her husband said, gently. 'You were in Brussels. Some high-level meeting or something – I can't remember now – Elena said she had tried to speak to you but your mobile was off all the time.'

How could the man be so cruel? thought Alex. Did he realize what he was doing to his wife?

'The migrant crisis. All those displaced people. That's what it was. I wanted to help. But I—' Cat looked bewildered. 'If she'd left a message or something I'd've got back to her. She knew that. I always did.'

'But she phoned me instead,' said Mark.

'And you didn't tell me?'

'We thought it best not to. You were busy, had a lot on your plate; we thought it was best you weren't worried.'

'My daughter was feeling suicidal and you thought it was best not to worry me?' The fury was etched deep on Cat's face.

Mark shook his head. 'No, no, you're not listening.' He kept calm. 'She never said she was suicidal, only that things weren't going well and she wasn't eating properly.'

'But—'

'Mark, Cat.' Alex knew if she didn't bring the conversation back to the point the two of them would be going round and round in circles and they wouldn't get anywhere. 'We can look into Elena's state of mind just before she died. What I want to know is why you, Cat, think Elena was murdered?'

Cat let out a deep breath and leaned back into the cushions. 'You will help, then? You are interested?' She reached out and took Alex's hands, squeezing them tightly. 'I knew you would understand. That I could trust you. We still have it, don't we? That tie, that closeness?'

Alex nodded. It was true. It was as if they had spoken only yesterday.

'And you know what it's like to lose people close to you. You know how I feel.'

'For God's sake.' Mark's calm veneer suddenly cracked. '*I* know how you feel. Don't leave me out of this.'

'I'm not leaving you out of this, Mark, but you still think she killed herself. I don't.' She looked at Alex. 'The inquest was last week.' She visibly winced. 'It was horrible. Having to relive it all, listen to the lies about Elena. The details. The pitying look from the coroner as she told everyone Elena had thrown herself from the cliff. The reporter scribbling down the details in his notebook so they could fill a page of their grubby little paper.' Cat's eyes were glistening. 'And that text. The one they found on her phone. I never got it.'

'Are you sure?'

'Of course I'm sure. I'd have remembered if I'd got a text like that. We were always texting, you see. The last time I heard from her was about ten days before she died. But I deleted it.' She began to cry and rock herself backwards and forwards. 'I deleted it because the storage on my phone was almost full.

I deleted it. I keep texts from my secretary, but I deleted my daughter's texts.'

Alex put a hand on her arm. 'Cat, it's all right.'

'No it's not all right.' Gulping sobs escaped her.

'Tell me what the texts said.'

'Do we have to drag all this up?'

Cat jerked her head up. 'Yes we do, Mark.' She looked at Alex. 'She said she was looking forward to coming home. Said there were things going on at the school that she had to tell me about, worrying things, she said. She said … ' Cat gulped back tears, 'she said she had to talk to me. I asked her to tell me there and then but she wouldn't.' She looked at Mark. 'But nothing about not eating or being depressed.'

Out of the corner of her eye Alex could see Mark trying to catch her eye as if to say, '*See, no definite proof.*'

'And you don't know what she was referring to?'

'No. But then I got this.'

Suddenly she had her mobile phone in her hand and she turned the screen towards Alex. 'Here. Look.'

Alex looked. It was a Facebook tribute page – she had seen quite a few of them in her time when she'd written stories on young people who had died – a special page dedicated to that person. She took the phone from Cat and scrolled through the page. It was full of the usual: '*I love you hun RIP; You're the best, we'll miss ya; You'll be an angel in heaven now.*'

She looked up at Cat. 'It's great your daughter's friends cared, but—'

'Oh for goodness' sake.' Cat snatched the phone back and scrolled down, her finger moving at a frantic pace. 'There. See.' She thrust the phone at Alex.

Elena did not kill herself

The comment was prefaced by a picture of a silhouette – standard practice when people didn't want a profile photo – and the name 'Kiki Godwin'.

'And again. Look, underneath that message.' Cat's eyes were bright, feverish, her hands shaking. 'Another one.'

It's true. Elena did not kill herself.

Again, the same silhouette picture, the same name: 'Kiki Godwin'.

'And if you look, everybody else posted their messages just after Elena died and in the following few weeks. These two were posted four days ago, after the inquest.' Her excitement was palpable.

Alex clicked on Kiki Godwin's name. It took her to a Facebook page that echoed the silhouette but had no details about Kiki Godwin. She took her own phone out of her bag, opened the Facebook app and found Kiki's name herself. Then she sent her a friend request. Let's see if we get any reply to that, she thought.

'I'm guessing', said Alex, putting her phone away, 'you don't know who Kiki is?'

'No. Not at all. I presume it's one of her friends, but then, why doesn't she have a profile?'

'And have you shown this to the police?'

Cat met her eyes. 'No. Not yet. I don't trust them like I trust you. Them and their great size thirteen boots. No finesse, no subtlety. All they'd do is scare everyone off. Nobody would talk to them, least of all Kiki Godwin, whoever she – or possibly he – might be. Anyway, they wouldn't believe me. Even my own husband doesn't believe me. No, I want you to look into it, Alex. Please.'

'But Cat, the police have resources, know-how, manpower and all that.'

'That's what I keep telling her,' said Mark, now onto his third – or was it fourth? – whisky. 'Let the coppers handle it. Show them that message. Though personally I think it's one of those trolls. You get them all the time on these sorts of pages. We're lucky it hasn't been worse. Sometimes there's all sorts of filth there too. You can't believe what people can be like.'

'Mark, please.'

'I'm sorry Cat, but it's true. It should be in the hands of the police.'

'Who think she killed herself.'

'But you won't have it.' Mark tossed more whisky down his throat.

Alex thought of the articles she should be pitching, the money she should be earning. How Mark could well be right and it was a troll. It did happen; not so long ago some inadequate youth had been jailed for mocking the death of a teenager who'd thrown herself in front of a train.

She tried again. 'Cat, you should tell the police. That's the best. Let them deal with it. You're a politician; it'll go to the top of the pile.'

Cat gave a deep sigh and sat back on the settee, a steely look in her eyes. 'They have closed the case and they won't want to reopen it. Look, go and take a look around for me. Spend a couple of days up there, spy out the ground. Please. You can ask the right questions; I know you can. That's all I'm asking. A few questions. You're good at that.'

Alex looked at her helplessly. 'Cat, I don't know … '

All at once Cat smiled gleefully, like a little child, her eyes feverishly bright. 'But I do. I know you can help. And your editor – Bud, isn't it? – he thought there could be a good story in it. He was interested.'

Of course he was. He'd said as much to her. But he didn't have to come and see the raw emotions on Cat's face, the amount of hope she had.

'Look,' her friend continued, 'we've even got a little cottage up there where you can stay; it's one we use when we go – used to go – to see Elena on her free weekends. We rent it out, but the couple who were supposed to be staying there at the moment cancelled. Wedding or something. Please, Alex. I'm begging you. Two weeks – one week – and if you're getting nowhere then call

33

it a day. I'll try and accept it … Elena's death. I'll show the Facebook thing to the police and see if they'll do anything. Though I know they won't.'

'An offer you can barely refuse, hmm? Free accommodation and story you could sell anywhere,' said Mark, looking at Alex with a barely concealed sneer.

Alex bridled.

'Mark, stop it. Please, Alex, say you'll do it?'

'I'll have to think about it, Cat.' Did she, though? Here was a chance to help her friend – her oldest friend – find out the truth about her daughter's death, even if that truth were unpalatable. And if she found out that Elena did throw herself off the cliff then at least Cat would know for sure. She wouldn't live a half-life like she, Alex, had done. And she hated seeing the pain Cat was in. Perhaps she could do something to make that a little better. Then there was Elena. A beautiful girl who'd had a bright future in front of her. A girl similar in age to Gus. A girl who had grit and determination and who'd coped with the death of her father and a debilitating eating disorder. Elena deserved her help too. And she knew if it had been the other way round, if she was asking Cat for help with Gus, Cat wouldn't hesitate.

And what about the mysterious message? The reclusive Kiki Godwin? Alex's fingers started tingling, a surge of adrenaline in her gut: sure signs she was getting excited about a story. What if Cat was right? What if Elena's death wasn't suicide and this Kiki Godwin had some information?

'It could be a good story, Alex. And I know you'll be truthful, not sensationalist. It'll be an exclusive. And you can have an interview with me and Mark, whatever you find out.'

'Oh, count me out, Cat,' said Mark, anger evident in his voice. 'I can go so far but not that far, thank you. I'm not subscribing to this charade any longer.' He took a few breaths, which seemed to calm him. 'Please, Cat, let it go. You'll make yourself ill.'

Cat stood and walked purposefully across to her husband. She took his hands in hers. 'I have to do this, please Mark, please. I need your support.' She leaned into his body.

Alex watched as Mark's anger subsided. Tenderly he tucked a lock of Cat's hair behind her ear and planted a kiss on her forehead. 'For you, Cat. For you.'

Cat turned to Alex. 'One other thing that makes me think – no, know – that Elena didn't throw herself off that cliff. She was scared of heights. Terrified. She wouldn't even go to the top of the slide on Brighton beach last year, that's how terrified she was. She wouldn't have gone anywhere near that edge.'

CHAPTER 5

It was no wonder Cat Devonshire was described by the broad-sheets as an 'up and coming' Member of the European Parliament with a sharp brain and incisive mind, thought Alex, as she drove along the M11 towards East Anglia. Once Alex had agreed she would go and look into Elena's death, Cat had gone into overdrive: organizing the house in Hallow's Edge for her, making sure she had enough cash, promising to email over any documents that could be useful. And the last few days had been a whirlwind, what with preparing to leave her tiny ground floor flat (with garden) in West Dulwich (Tulse Hill, if she were honest), making sure the cat would be fed for however long she was to be away, telling Bud she was going up to North Norfolk and, yes, there could be a story in it, and managing to get custody of a company credit card. Bud had been rather begrudging about that, it had to be said. She did have to come back with a story of some sort now.

The only downside was that it had been difficult to explain to Sasha that she didn't know when she was going to be able to visit again. But tell her she had, and she even thought she had seen tears in Sasha's eyes as she left.

The heat was building, layer upon layer, the sky a pale blue as if the sun had bleached the colour out of it. The air vents were blowing warm air around the car and for the umpteenth time she wished she'd had the air-conditioning seen to. The motorway was long and boring and she still had a way to go.

She pressed the CD button and David Bowie's voice filled the car. That was better. Now she wouldn't think about Sasha, or about her own 18-year-old son who was somewhere in Europe trying to find himself. She hadn't heard from him since he'd got the ferry to France two weeks earlier.

'I'll be fine Mum,' he'd said as he heaved his rucksack onto his back ready to catch the bus to Dover. 'I need to get away, you know that. Exams can wait. And I'll FaceTime you.' Then he gave her a kiss on her cheek and went out of the house – whistling. Whistling! As if last night's quarrel had never happened.

It had started after supper when she took his clean washing into his bedroom for him to stuff into his rucksack.

'Mum,' he said, 'I know you don't like talking about my dad, which is why I hardly ever ask about him, but—' He stopped and began to chew his lip.

'It's okay,' Alex said, unnecessarily refolding a tee-shirt and admiring the way she spoke so calmly. 'I understand. I just thought we had each other all these years and we were a unit. A family.' And she had never wanted to go into details about how Gus had been conceived during a drunken, drug-fuelled one-night stand in Ibiza.

'We are. A unit, I mean. You are my family, Mum, and you've been bloody brilliant. It's just that I want to know where I come from. Who I am.' He didn't look at her as he carried on packing.

Alex tried to smile. 'Darling, you are a wonderful person and—'

'Mum. Who is he?'

'Gus.' How she so didn't want to do this. 'What's brought this on?'

'Tell me. You see, when I was younger I figured he was probably a Premiership footballer, or an actor, or a rock star.' He laughed. 'But then as I got older I thought maybe he was a murderer or a kiddie fiddler.'

'His name was Steve,' she said, smoothing the tee-shirt flat.

'Steve who?'

'I don't know.'

He turned to look at her. 'You must.'

She shook her head. 'No, I don't. I was in Ibiza on a newspaper jolly. We went to a club. He was the DJ there. I was young; it was my first taste of freedom; I didn't know what I was doing – there was free alcohol, some drugs – and I ended up going back to Steve's place.' Every word made her feel ashamed.

'And you never wanted to find him?'

'No.'

'Not even for my sake?'

'No.'

'That's so selfish, Mum, so bloody selfish.' She could see tears in his eyes.

'I'm sorry Gus; I never wanted to hurt you. I thought it was best left alone.' She wanted to cry too.

'And you wouldn't have said anything, even now, would you? Even now that I'm eighteen and about to go off travelling. Unless I'd asked.'

'Gus—'

'Well, I've got news for you. I'm going to find him.'

'How?'

'With the help of a friend,' he said coldly, before turning away from her.

She left his room.

Now she turned up the volume on the CD player, drumming her fingers on the steering wheel in time to Bowie, singing along with him, loudly and tunelessly: determined not to worry about Gus. He was a grown-up now.

Merging onto the A11 she began to feel she was in East Anglia proper, for the first time in two years. She thought about Cat, about Mark, and about Elena. At first sight, Elena's death seemed such an open-and-shut case. The coroner had thought so, too. A teenager for whom everything had got too much. A teenager with problems. Was that what had made her take her own life? But why so close to Christmas? And what about the text that had been found on her phone?

Mum, I don't think I can do this any more.

On her phone but not sent. Why?

She'd been depressed in the past. Had suffered from anorexia. Alex drummed her fingers on the steering wheel. Christmas – the lead up, the day itself – was always stressful, always the time when domestic violence increased, marriages broke up, people killed themselves; why shouldn't it be the season when Elena felt she couldn't go on? She'd crept out of school in the middle of the night (how easy was that these days? In all honesty, Alex's experience of boarding schools was Enid Blyton's Malory Towers books with their jolly midnight feasts and Harry Potter and magic goings-on – not exactly an in-depth knowledge), found her way to the end of the road that ended abruptly, falling away to the beach. Then she'd apparently thrown herself off the cliff road and down onto the rocks below before the tide had come in and dragged her poor broken body out, then in again; leaving it on the shoreline waiting to be found. What a waste.

According to the newspaper article about the inquest, it was an open-and-shut case. And, of course, her mother couldn't believe her beloved daughter would do such a thing, would reach such a deep and dark place that she could see no other way out.

Yet Cat's absolute conviction that it wasn't so open-and-shut had begun to chip away at Alex. Who had Elena spoken to in those last days, hours? Had the school noticed anything amiss? Had she become depressed and anorexic again, or was that just a convenient excuse trotted out by the school, the police, the authorities? The inquest seemed to exonerate the school of all blame. But still. Wouldn't they have noticed something about her behaviour in the days leading up to her death? Shouldn't they have noticed? Would you pay the thirty-odd thousand pounds to the school if you didn't expect some modicum of pastoral care? And she knew how much Cat regretted sending Elena to the boarding school. 'It was because I was away so much,' she'd told Alex, as if wanting Alex to absolve her from some mortal sin. 'I – we – thought it was best. And I had just got married.' She'd looked shamefaced. 'So selfish. Now I wish I could have all that time back with her, all the growing up I missed. All the worries she must have had going to a new school. And what did I do? Texted her. Some mother I am.'

Through Thetford and after – the tall conifers at either side of the road reaching up to the sky, and David Bowie changed for Lou Reed. She ought to try and get into some of the new music, but she liked the old rockers. Always had since hearing them on her father's old record player as a child.

The road stretched on as the sun became even higher in the sky. Skirting round Norwich – a city she loved and had missed – then up to the flat of The Broads, passing farm shops, bed and breakfast places, garden centres, a huge solar farm that went on for miles, and churches, always churches, some with the unusual round tower. Then on to the busy town of Wroxham, teeming with early summer visitors who spilled from the paths onto the narrow roads. As she went over the little bridge she glanced at where the boats were moored and thought about how she had never taken a boat out on The Broads. Maybe, she mused, she would rectify that this summer. Perhaps take … who? With a lurch she realized there was no one she could take. Gus would be away for the whole summer, and Sasha? Well, Sasha wasn't likely to be out on day release or whatever they called it anytime soon.

Her mind drifted back to her friend.

'Would you like to see Elena's bedroom?' Cat had asked.

Alex nodded. Of course she would; it might give her a bit of an insight into the teenager she had never known.

She followed Cat upstairs, and stood for a moment on the

threshold of the room. She wanted to get a sense of her daughter, a feel for her. What sort of girl had she been? She knew how difficult it was being a teenager in this day and age – Gus proved it – so she had sympathy with both Elena and Cat as far as that was concerned. It was hard growing up in a world that expected you to be perfect, expected you to either succeed well or fail badly; there seemed to be no middle ground.

It was obvious Cat had changed nothing since Elena had left for the start of the Christmas term the year before. Alex had a sudden flashback to Sasha who hadn't been able to give away Harry and Millie's clothes and toys for years. Eventually Alex had stepped in and taken all the stuff to the Red Cross shop in Sole Bay. It had broken Sasha even more.

Elena's room was that of a typical teenager, though maybe less messy, as she hadn't been there the whole time. Posters of bands Alex hadn't heard of were Blu-tacked on the walls. A flowery vintage cover on her bed. Poetry books, Harry Potter, The Twilight series, Judy Blume books were lined up on the shelves. Adult books too: Belinda Bauer, Lee Child, Antonia Honeywell, Jojo Moyes. An expensive iPod dock and computer sat on a sleek glass desk. A laptop made up the triumvirate.

'I presume she had a computer at school? And phone?' asked Alex.

'Oh yes,' said Cat, sitting on the bed, her hands absent-mindedly brushing the duvet cover, tears not far from her eyes. 'The laptop on her desk there, that's what she used. The police took it away but couldn't find anything. The phone's in her drawer. I didn't want to look through it.' She swallowed. 'It seemed too much like prying.'

'Hmm.' Alex knew that if there was no suspicion of foul play the police would have had only a cursory look at Elena's electronic stuff; they didn't have the resources to do a thorough job unless it was absolutely necessary.

'I come and sleep in here sometimes,' Cat's voice was faint.

Unbearably sad. 'To be near her. I won't let anyone wash the sheets. I can still smell her, just. I don't want to lose that smell. Sometimes, if I don't look at a photograph of her I feel as though I might lose what she looked like. Forget her face. The scar on her knee from where she fell off her bike trying to ride it without stabilizers for the first time. The birthmark on the inside of her wrist. The way one ear sticks out more than the other. Stuck out more than the other. Then I can't stop crying.' She looked up at Alex. 'That's the trouble. I can't stop crying.'

'I know. I understand.' Alex nodded.

'I know you do. You had to help Sasha through everything, despite what happened at the end. And you've got Gus. I know you would do anything to keep him safe. I couldn't keep Elena safe, that's why I'm begging you to help me. Please.'

There was no way, Alex knew, she was not going to help Cat now.

'Would you mind if I took the laptop and phone away with me? To have a look, see what she was doing at school?'

For a moment her friend looked panicked. 'I don't know … I'm not sure … '

'It might help me get a picture of her life, that's all,' said Alex gently, knowing the tremor in Cat's voice was, after all she had said, due to the possibility of losing something of her daughter's. 'I won't do any harm, or destroy anything, I promise.'

'But her passwords?'

'Leave that to me,' said Alex.

'She wanted to be an artist, you know. She was good enough too,' said Cat, her face sad. 'That's one of hers. It's Hallow's Edge.'

She pointed to a painting on the wall. Oil. A landscape. A beach, the sea, white horses, groynes, all painted as if the artist was sitting on the beach. And in the corner, on the edge of the cliff … was that a tiny figure? Alex moved nearer to peer at it, but the picture dissolved into a mass of paint blobs. She moved away, further across the room, and the blobs morphed into a figure that seemed to be wearing a long coat and scarf. It could have been anybody.

'She painted that in her last term; it was part of her Art A level. They let me bring it home. It's lovely, isn't it? I think it's somewhere near the school, but—' Catriona looked as though she was about to cry.

'Who's the figure in the top corner?'

Cat shook her head. 'No idea.' She got up and stood next to Alex. 'I hadn't noticed it. I didn't look closely enough. I didn't take enough interest. Not then.' She gulped back a sob.

'Cat … ' Alex hesitated, not wanting to appear intrusive. 'Would you mind if I took a photograph of the painting?'

'No. If you think it'll help in some way, any way, then please do.'

Alex snapped the painting. 'And do you have a recent picture of Elena? I'll give it back to you, I promise.'

Catriona nodded and went out of Elena's bedroom, coming back with a photo frame. 'This is the most recent one I have of her.' Her voice broke. 'It was taken during the summer holidays. We managed a couple of days in Dorset. Lovely little village called Kimmeridge. She seemed relaxed for the first time in ages.'

Elena had been strikingly beautiful. Long blonde hair framing a heart-shaped face with angular cheekbones. Dark brown eyes. A slight smile curved a rosebud mouth.

'That's odd,' said Cat, peering at the picture. 'I hadn't thought about that before.'

'What's that?'

She pointed at the photo. 'See? The ring?'

Alex looked. Elena was holding one hand up to the camera. She might have been waving or telling her mother not to take the picture. On the fourth finger of her right hand was an oddly shaped silver ring. 'Looks like one of those his and hers eternity rings. Seems as though there should be a partner to it, doesn't it?'

'That's what I said to Elena when I saw it. I think she was given it by somebody for her birthday. She gave me one of her mysterious smiles so I backed off. Didn't want to interfere. I wish I'd asked her more.'

Oh, Alex knew all about not interfering. Sometimes, though, you had to. 'And?'

'She was wearing it all summer holidays, wouldn't take it off. And she kept stroking it when she thought I wasn't looking. It was obviously very important to her. The thing is … ' she paused, 'there was no sign of it in any of her stuff they gave back to me.'

'Maybe she lost it.' Or perhaps it had come off her finger as her body was battered by the sea.

'Maybe.' Cat was thoughtful. She traced the outline of her daughter's face. 'I had the impression it was something she would keep through thick and thin. As I say, something really important.' She shrugged. 'Oh well, maybe it's nothing. Maybe she did lose it.'

The traffic was heavy now as she passed through some of The Broads villages before arriving at the real flatlands of Norfolk and she knew she wasn't too far away from Hallow's Edge. She could feel the lightness of air, the big sky above, the space around her, and she remembered why she loved East Anglia so.

After saying goodbye to Cat and Mark, Alex made a call and then went to Streatham, to an ordinary residential road. The house she was looking for was halfway up and part of a row of terraces with each tiny front garden having at least two wheelie bins. Number 102 had a decrepit armchair as a garden feature as well. A blanket hung across the ground floor window in place of curtains. She walked up the path and knocked.

A tall thin woman of about twenty-five whose pallor indicated she hardly ever saw daylight opened the door. She was wearing faded jeans and a tee-shirt with the dates of a long-gone music tour inscribed on it.

'Hey, Honey,' said Alex.

'Yeah. It's early, y'know?'

Alex grimaced. 'Sorry, I do know. But I wanted to get it to you as soon as.'

Honey rubbed the top of her head making her ginger crop stand up in spikes. 'Sure.' She yawned, widely, showing two sets of perfect teeth. 'I'll do my best.' She held out her hand. 'Give it here.'

Alex handed over Elena's laptop and phone. 'I need them back in pristine condition, Honey,' she warned.

'Come on, Alex, you know me. No one will ever know I've been in there.'

Alex smiled. She really did trust this hacker who'd somehow almost managed to stay below the radar of the authorities since she was sixteen. The one (and seemingly only) time she'd come a cropper was when Alex had found her after a tip-off for a story she was doing at the time about cyber security, and she'd managed to get Honey off the hook with the coppers in return for information. Honey had been grateful ever since.

She was on the road that wound along the Norfolk coast, sometimes going near enough to the sea, most of the time winding through flat acres of fields. Eventually she saw a signpost for Hallow's Edge and turned into the narrow road with hedges either side. For about half a mile there was nothing, then she spied a farm set back from the road, a couple of flint cottages and a modern bungalow. It really was as if she was entering a time warp. She drove slowly, praying she wouldn't meet a tractor coming the other way, and stopped the car by a curved flint wall before getting out. The heat hit her like a sledgehammer.

There it was. The Drift. Elena's school. A school for the privileged. Beautiful. It was at the end of a long gravel drive, lined with lime trees, that swept up to the front of the house. Two of the four brick and flint wings of the house made a graceful curve. Large wooden front door in the middle. Magnificent thatched roof. Heavy on the insurance. Alex knew there were two other wings curving at the back with beautiful views over the coastline and the sea. Shaped like a butterfly, it was built during the Arts and Craft movement. She knew all this because she'd looked it up online, and the pictures had been fantastic. She'd had to look up about the Arts and Craft movement, but, hey, that was what Wikipedia was for.

Alex breathed in deeply. East Anglian air. More specifically, North Norfolk air with its taste of salt and freedom and sense of space. There was a reason why everybody talked about the wide East Anglian skies – the world seemed to go on forever. She closed her eyes, continuing to breathe in the air that, despite its heat, felt cleaner and fresher than the diesel, spices, and dirt of London. She had missed this. For all the ghastly events of two years ago, she had missed this. Of course, this trip to find out more about Elena's death was another burst of conscience easing, but, who knew, maybe some good could come of it, if only to help Cat.

'Hi.'

She turned towards the voice and found herself looking at a boy – teenager, a young man – who could only be described as beautiful. Thick dark hair was brushed away from his forehead, cheekbones were sharp, top lip was slightly fuller than the bottom. Chocolate-brown eyes that were fringed by long, girlish lashes appraised her. He held a cigarette loosely between his fingers. For a moment Alex felt awkward, gauche even. Then she told herself not to be so silly. This was an adolescent. A beautiful one, but one who was about Gus's age. Younger. 'Hallo,' she said, smiling.

'Did you want some help? Only … ' The boy raised his eyebrows. Looked her up and down, slowly.

She felt discomforted. 'Only what?'

'You looked … lost, that's all.' He smiled back at her. Dazzling.

'No, not lost,' she said. 'Only looking. It's a beautiful building.'

'What?' He followed her gaze. 'Oh, yeah. That.' He shrugged. 'It's school, that's all I know.'

'You a pupil?' Though she had guessed this, and not only because she could see books protruding from the rucksack slung over one shoulder.

'Yeah, just. Exams. Then I'm outta here. Maths. Do you want to know where to go? Directions? That sort of thing?'

She shook her head. 'No. Really, I'm fine, thank you.'

He stared up the drive. 'Y'know, I never really look at the building. I know it's beautiful; a great example of some sort of architecture yadda yadda, but hey, to me it's school. Even if I live in a sixth form house and can wear my own clothes, go out at lunchtime, even smoke.' He grinned. 'As long as they don't find out, of course; it's still school with all its petty rules and regulations. I'm so past it.' He threw the butt down and ground it under one trainer-ed foot. 'But you don't want to know that, mystery lady. Good to see you.'

'And you.'

'Name's Theo, by the way.'

'I'm Alex,' she said.

'Yeah.' He sauntered off, lifting a hand as he went. 'Ciao.'

Ciao? Didn't that go out in the eighties? And what did he mean, 'yeah'? Had he recognized her? But it was two years ago, and the newspapers had not only wrapped fish and chips but would have been used as compost by now. So what? She couldn't worry about that. More likely it was a teenage tic.

She went back to the car and drove slowly past the entrance, peering up the drive. Theo was standing motionless, staring at her. For some reason, she shivered.

47

CHAPTER 6

She found the Devonshires' holiday home pretty easily with the directions she'd been given. The car had wheezed and bounced down a long rutted track that looped and curved down a hill until she reached the flint cottage that stood stark against the sky. Alex had to walk round the cottage to find the front door. She could see why. Whoever had originally designed the cottage had wanted visitors to marvel at the view. The sea, less than a hundred metres from the door, was grey and endless. She could have been at the house at the end of the world. The only sounds were the screams of gulls above her and the crash of the waves onto the shore. She looked to her right: grass and open fields with the beach below; to her left, in the distance, she could see cliffs, rocks, sea defences, the beautiful building that was The Drift.

Somewhere along there Elena had fallen.

The key was where she had been told it would be: under the stone pig guarding the front door. Marvellous, she thought, people still left their keys the first place a burglar would look. She felt comforted by the thought that the world up here hadn't changed much in the last couple of years that she'd been living in London, where, if you left your key under a stone pig, you'd more than likely get back to find your house stripped bare.

The air in the hallway was pleasantly cool and the rooms of the cottage were large and tastefully furnished: polished rosewood tables juxtaposed with modern settees. A cracked leather sofa. An old-fashioned upright piano and a couple of Ghost chairs. The kitchen had what she thought must have been the original pamment tiles, but there was every mod con, including a rather alarming-looking coffee maker. In the fridge she found a cold chicken and a bowl of salad as well as milk, eggs, butter, and a bottle of wine. Cat had been true to her word and had asked her housekeeper to stock up the fridge with essentials so she wouldn't have to go shopping straightaway.

She brought her case in from the car and took it upstairs to the main bedroom, which was furnished with an iron-framed bed, a dressing table, chest of drawers, and a door through to a small bathroom. Again, everything tasteful and charming. Cat had come a long way since their schooldays. Peering through the window there was that view again: endless sky and sea, the sun high and unforgiving. She was conscious of the sweat on her forehead. Fresh air, that's what she needed.

A cooling breeze was coming off the sea as she walked along the stretch of beach below the cottage. She'd walked across the grass to shallow steps that had been cut into the cliff enabling her to scramble down. She stood for a moment, imagining she was the only person in the world, for that's what it felt like, then she turned to her left, walking along the shoreline in the lee of the cliffs.

After ten minutes of walking she reached the section of cliff where the road above had been swept away in the ferocious gales and sea surge of the previous year. As she looked up she could see the remnants of blue and white police tape fluttering in the breeze. She imagined Elena standing at the edge of that road, looking down onto the beach and the rocks below. What had been in her mind that dark, cold December night? Had she been frightened? Or calm; sure of what she wanted to do. How unhappy must she have been to overcome her fear of heights? It was a long way to fall, but then it took only a split second decision to jump, and once that decision was made, you couldn't go back.

If she had indeed made the decision for herself.

Alex looked around and saw the rocks that Elena had most probably landed on, the seaweed draped over them like throws on a chair. Nearby, a family was picnicking, their red and blue tartan rug spread out underneath them, two boys – one aged no more than two – digging in the sand. A short distance from them, a young man and a woman lay on two towels soaking up the sun. Near to where the sea sucked at the shore, a woman was throwing a stick into the waves for her retriever to fetch. The scene was summertime on an English beach. Pity it was a beach where a teenager's broken body had lain for an old man to find.

She looked up again, along the clifftop. A chalet bungalow teetered right near the edge, gripping the last of the land for dear life. It looked as though it only needed a wisp of wind to send it toppling onto the sand below. It was weather-beaten and abandoned, with a broken door and smashed windows. Alex imagined the owners had given up the fight.

Suddenly a missile barged into her legs almost knocking her over. As she regained her balance, she saw the now very wet retriever sitting at her feet, a stick in its mouth. It dropped the stick, looking hopefully up at her, wagging its tail across the ground, distributing sand everywhere. Alex laughed, bending down for the stick before throwing it as far as she could.

A woman hurried up to her. 'I'm so sorry about Ronan. Are you okay?' She frowned, looking worried as she pushed dark corkscrew hair off her face.

'I'm fine,' laughed Alex, brushing sand off her clothes. 'I love dogs and he's a beauty.'

'He still hasn't learned obedience, however many classes I take him to.'

Ronan bounded up and dropped the stick at Alex's feet again. She picked it up.

'He'll be having you doing that all day if you're not careful.

And he loves going into the sea.' The woman had an open smile, though there was a sadness around her eyes and what looked like a wariness in them. She was wearing a smart, short-sleeved shirt and dark linen trousers, rolled up over her calves. She was bare-foot and carried sensible sandals in her hand. Alex saw a small tattoo of an angel's wing on her ankle. Alex smiled back.

'I might be tempted myself.'

'Oh, I wouldn't if I were you. North Sea's freezing even at this time of year. It's almost acceptable in September. If you're a masochist. My feet are like ice blocks.'

Alex threw the stick again. 'You live here then?' Alex's question was, in fact, disingenuous, as she had recognized the woman as a teacher from The Drift. It hadn't been a waste of time trawling through the school's website and imprinting the faces of the teachers on her mind. This was Louise Churchill, English teacher. And another thing she knew about the woman, thanks to Catriona, was that she had been Elena's English teacher.

'For my sins.' A flicker of sadness crossed Louise Churchill's face before she smiled again, though this time there seemed to be more effort behind it. 'No, it's a great place to live. I'm a teacher, though. That makes it hard.'

'Really?' said Alex. 'A teacher. That is a tough gig. I admire you. I don't think I could stand up in front of a class of kids and make them listen to me.'

She called to her dog. 'Ronan, come here. Don't go so far out.' Ronan continued to paddle, stick in his mouth. 'Oh, it's not so bad. It's not as if I'm at some inner city school or failing academy. The students are supposed to be the cream of society. Moneyed society, that is.' She pointed upwards and there, in the distance, The Drift stood: imperious, looking out over the sea. 'That's where I am. The Drift. Posh boarding school for posh kids.'

'Nice.'

'It is, mostly. What makes it hard is living in the village, but I guess I'm luckier than some who have to live in the grounds.

They never get away from it. It's not a bad place to teach, though it took a while to find my feet.' She looked at her watch then clapped her hands. 'Ronan. Here. Now.'

Alex thought about what Cat had told her about the young teacher. She and her husband had moved to the school and started in the January of the year Elena died. Her husband taught Maths. Or was it Physics? Some subject Alex was useless at anyway. She thought they might have had young children. Twins? Damn, her brain was turning to mush; she wasn't concentrating enough. There was a time when she wouldn't have forgotten any of those facts.

At that moment, Ronan bounded up to the pair of them and shook vigorously, splattering drops of seawater over the two women.

'Ronan, stop it.' Louise turned to Alex. 'I'm sorry, that dog really has no discipline.'

'It's okay,' said Alex laughing. 'It's quite refreshing in a funny sort of way.' Ronan began to bark at the waves, running in and out of the water. 'Now look at him,' she said, not sure whether she was glad or sorry the subject of what she was doing in Hallow's Edge had been avoided, 'he's loving that.' Probably glad, as she wanted Louise to trust her before they spoke about what had happened to Elena. It had been a stroke of luck to find her on the beach.

'You're right about that.' They both stood looking at Ronan for another few moments. 'Are you on holiday? Where are you staying?'

'A cottage over that way.' Alex waved her hand in the vague direction of the cottage. She didn't want to be too specific in case Louise knew of the Devonshires' place. Unlikely, but it was better not to take any chances. 'It's a beautiful spot, this.'

Louise looked around. 'It is.' Then she looked at her watch and groaned. 'God, lunchtime's almost over and I've got to get this one home, and then get back to school.' She bent down and clipped the lead onto Ronan. 'Can't be late. I'll bring the wrath of the heads on my shoulders. They don't like us to be a minute over time. If they could have a clocking in and out machine, they would.'

'Two heads?'

'One for the girls and one for the boys. The Farrars. A dastardly double act. But don't tell anyone I said that, will you?'

Alex smiled. 'Of course not.'

Louise hesitated. 'Perhaps I'll see you again? Are you up from London? I miss the city. This place can be quite lonely sometimes.' There was a vulnerability on her face that struck a chord with Alex.

'That would be great. I'd like that.' And Alex found that she meant it.

'Okay. I'll be here with Ronan tomorrow over lunch. I'm not on dinner hall duty this week, thank God.'

'Lovely. I'll try to make it.'

She watched as Louise strode across the sand to the slope that would take her up to the path above. At the top she stopped, looked round and waved at Alex. Alex waved back.

CHAPTER 7

The long evenings, that's what Alex loved about the month of June. She tried not to think that in not much more than two weeks' time it would be the longest day and then the evenings would start to draw in. But for now the light was soft and the air balmy. She was glad she had been able to eat her solitary dinner outside on the terrace.

But now she was feeling restless.

She had tried and failed to raise Gus on FaceTime.

What was he doing and why hadn't he answered his phone? This is where she could start to get worried and think about corrupt policemen and drugs mules. But Gus was sensible, she told herself. He'd had to grow up fast and had become quite streetwise these last couple of years in London. She had to trust him. And the ferry from Dover to Calais wasn't exactly the drugs route to the west. But where the hell was he? Please God this hare-brained idea about trying to find Steve was just that. An idea.

She washed up her plate and cup and left them to dry on the drainer. How pathetic they looked. Then she prowled round the house, picked a couple of books off the bookshelf in the sitting room: a thriller with a lurid cover and a Terry Pratchett novel. Who read what? she wondered. She opened a couple of drawers in the desk in the corner of the room but found them empty with the exception of a few drawing pins and paper clips. She went upstairs and into the second bedroom. Like the main bedroom, it was simply furnished: a double bed with an iron bedstead, a wardrobe, and a chest of drawers. In the corner was an antique washstand – Victorian, maybe – with a white roses washbowl and pitcher. But the photograph in a silver frame on top of the chest of drawers was what drew her eye. She picked it up. Elena, standing on the beach below with her arm around Cat, laughing; her long hair whipped around her face by the wind; looking as though she hadn't got a care in the world. When was it taken? How could she go from a girl who looked as though she loved life to one who threw herself off a cliff?

'She was a clever girl. And resilient,' Cat had told her in that dull, defeated voice as they sat in Elena's bedroom. 'She had depression and anorexia after her father died.'

'How did he die?' Alex was ashamed that she didn't know. And hadn't bothered to find out.

'Asthma attack. Elena found him. Her illnesses were a way of controlling her grief, they told us. But she beat it. She's – she was – strong. I know she was strong. She told me she never wanted to go back to that dark place. Never ever. She started making plans. She wanted to go to Art college, you know.' She smiled. 'She was good enough, too. She wanted to paint. She wanted to sculpt. She wanted to design. She could have had the world at her feet.' She put her head in her hands and began to weep. After a few moments she lifted her head up. Her face was crumpled with grief. 'She was doing well at school – and then I married Mark.'

'Did she like Mark?'

She frowned. 'Not much. I was hoping the Christmas skiing holiday would be a chance to bond. He'd been the one to persuade me to send her away to school, said it would be better for her and for my career.'

'And what did Elena think about that?'

'She seemed okay, at first. But I knew she hated it. I would have tense calls or abrupt texts. Then, in the summer term, the term before she died, she sounded, I don't know, happier I guess. More settled.'

'Boyfriend?'

'I don't know. I was so pleased she seemed to be settling in that I simply accepted it. I didn't bother to find out. I didn't bother to try and get to know my daughter.' She looked around the room. 'And now, this is all I know of her. Cuddly toys, boy bands she'd grown out of, and a dubious taste in literature.'

'Cat,' said Alex, 'I will find out what happened. I will get to the truth, though you may find you won't like it.'

Cat grabbed her hand. 'The truth. That's all I want.'

Alex hoped to God it was. She knew how much the truth could hurt.

Putting the photo frame down, she crossed to the window and looked out over the sea to the endless horizon, suddenly realizing what it was she was feeling. Lonely, that's what it was. Her son was halfway across the world, okay, maybe an exaggeration, but that's what it felt like; her sister was in a mental institution; her parents were old and frail and didn't want to know: there was no one in the world who cared where she was or what she was doing. Except Bud, maybe. He had always looked out for her and took her on as a freelancer at *The Post* when she'd fled Suffolk for London two years ago. She'd gone from writing profiles about the good, the bad, and the dangerous, to more investigative stuff: she had that instinct; the ability to nibble away at a story looking at all the angles: digging into its core. She hadn't had time to feel lonely, to seek out companionship, someone she could talk over the day with.

Not to say she hadn't had offers, but sharing a bed with another journalist was not for her: too much shop talk. No, she preferred brief encounters, a bit of fun, bit of a laugh then goodbye before anybody got hurt. At least, that was the theory. Didn't always work. One brief encounter had produced Gus, so that was a bonus. But two not-so-brief encounters had brought her nothing but heartache. The most recent had been with someone she thought she could love, and had even begun to trust: he'd moved in, got to know her son. But he had betrayed her. Since then, she had kept dalliances short and sweet.

Moved in. Getting to know her son. And the two of them had got on. Very well. What had Gus said about finding his father? That a friend was helping.

A friend.

Bloody buggering hell. Malone. Her erstwhile lover. The undercover police officer who had almost – not quite – broken her heart after she had allowed herself to fall in love with him. Scratch that. He had broken her heart. Malone had wormed his way into her life and into Gus's life. Then she found out, quite by chance, he was married. And what was worse, had got married as part of an investigation he was running. What did that say about his attitude to women? She hadn't spoken to or heard from Malone since she'd found out that special little nugget of information and had thrown him out of her life.

Her hand shook as she thumbed through her contacts on her phone. There it was. His mobile number. She wondered if it still worked or if he'd had to change it because of being chased by women. She stabbed the button.

It rang.

'Hallo?'

It was his voice: she would know it anywhere.

'Malone.'

'Who is this?'

'You bloody well know who this is, Malone. Alex.'

'Well, it's been some time; you can forgive a man for not recognizing your voice.' He sounded amused. 'How are you doing?'

She felt irrationally upset to realize that her name had not come up on his phone. She pushed the feeling aside. 'Have you been talking to Gus about his father?' The silence at the other end of the phone told her everything. 'Malone, what the fuck do you think you're doing interfering? How dare you? How dare you?' She found she was shaking. 'It's up to me to tell him about his dad, not you. I will tell him about his father when I see fit. Is that clear?'

'But you don't know much about him, do you? You told me that. Gus came to me and asked for help. Look, I'm fond of the boy and I've got the contacts.'

'So … ' she spluttered, 'so frigging what? I should never have said anything about him to you.'

'You didn't tell me much.'

'I don't know much, that's why,' she shouted down the phone, his calm voice making her even angrier.

'I know. But his first name and where he worked at the time was a good start.'

'Malone. It still has nothing to do with you. Nothing. Do you understand? You are Out. Of. My. Life.'

'Well, I have been for the last couple of years. Tell me, how are you keeping?'

'Nothing to do with you.'

'Work?'

His quiet tone – as if nothing had happened between them, as if he hadn't broken her heart, as if she hadn't kicked him out – made her see bright, bright, angry red. 'Work is fine, thank you. Absolutely fine.'

'What are you doing, Alex? Writing about pop stars? Reality TV? Fashion features?'

She heard the sneer in his voice and the mist became even redder. 'I'm looking into a possible murder, actually. The daughter of an MEP.' The words were out before she could stop them. Why did she respond to his goading so?

'Just be careful, Alex.'

'Oh … just fuck off. And leave my son alone. I forbid you to have any more to do with him.'

She stabbed the off button.

God but she needed a drink.

Snatching up a cardigan, she had just reached the front door when she heard a ringing from inside the house. A landline. Ignore it, she told herself, it wouldn't be for her. But the ringing continued: insistent, compelling.

Bugger. It was like a Pavlovian reflex: the need to answer, just in case there was a story at the end of it.

She went back into the house towards the sound of the ringing and found the phone in the corner of a windowsill in the dining room.

'Hello?'

There was silence at the other end.

'Hello? Who's there?'

Still silence, though she thought she could hear the soft sound of breathing.

'Look, I know there's someone there. Do you have something to say?'

There was a click as whoever was on the other end of the line put the phone down.

She looked at the receiver in her hand. What was that all about?

On the piece of well-kept grass outside the Green Man, people were sitting at picnic tables with pints of beer and glasses of wine. A lighthouse painted with red and white bands dominated the skyline a couple of hundred metres from the pub. A couple stood outside smoking. The place looked welcoming: an open door and buzz of voices spilling out onto the street, hanging baskets and tubs of tumbling early summer flowers – petunias, geraniums, busy lizzies – Alex's horticultural knowledge stopped there. Honeysuckle scrambling over a fence scented the late evening air.

The walk had calmed her; the red mist had receded. She was not going to think about Malone any more. The fresh air had been just what she needed to shake off the phone call to him and then the odd one with no one on the other end, and a drink would be bloody helpful too. Plus, the village pub was a good place to start asking around, quietly, about the school.

'You can go on in, love. They won't bite.'

Alex looked at the grizzled old boy in a thick pullover grasping his pint with dirt-encrusted hands. 'Thanks,' she said, smiling. 'You don't always know, do you, whether you'll be welcome or not?'

The old boy chuckled. 'This in't one of yer fancy London pubs: all fur coat and no knickers. This is a right real place. Tony keeps a good pint, even if he has prettied the old boozer up a bit.' Cackling, he went back to his pint.

The bar was full and the aroma of food, drink, and fun swirled around her head. Couples, friends, men and women were sitting round tables, some eating, some merely drinking, and the bar was lined with people. In one corner was a pool table with two teenagers engrossed in a game. Probably underage. Gus managed his first pint at fifteen in a pub with a pool table.

She pushed her way up to the bar.

'Hi.' A woman of about thirty-five with a pierced lip, crop top, and bleached blonde hair smiled at her.

'Hi. Glass of dry white wine, please.' She perched on a stool that had become free.

The barmaid went to the fridge took out the bottle and began to pour the wine into a glass. She had half a dozen silver bracelets on one arm that clinked as she poured.

'Thanks,' said Alex, as she handed over the money. 'Nice pub, this.'

The barmaid grinned. 'Bit fancy these days but the punters are good-hearted. Loyal, too. You on holiday?' She proffered Alex the change.

Not fancy prices though. 'Keep that. Buy yourself one.'

'Ta.' The barmaid poured herself a glass of wine too.

'Oi, Kylie.' A man came out of what Alex presumed was the

kitchen carrying two plates of fish and chips. 'Get your arse into gear.'

'I'm on my break, Tony, okay?'

Tony rolled his eyes as he weaved his way through customers to find the right table.

'He could do with employing more sods like me, then I'd be able to have a proper break,' the barmaid muttered.

Alex smiled and took a sip of her wine. Cold. Slightly sharp but nicely alcoholic. 'Not exactly. On holiday, I mean.'

'Oh?' The barmaid leaned on the bar, obviously up for a chat. 'I'm Kylie, by the way.'

'Alex. I'm here looking into the death of the girl from the school. The Drift. For the family. Get some closure. They're in bits.'

Kylie drew back, a guarded look on her face. 'What, you're some sort of private detective? Or copper?'

'Nothing like that. A friend of the family who's good at asking questions. Her mum wants to make sure she knows everything.' Alex leaned forward. 'She doesn't trust coppers.'

'Who does?' Kylie said. 'And I'm thinking you mean the girl from the nobby school who topped herself just before Christmas? Yeah, I heard about that. Poor kid. Poor family.'

'Did you ever see her? I mean, in my day we were always trying to get into the local pubs when we were at school, y'know? Thought it was cool.'

Kylie nodded. 'Yeah, they do try. The local kids come to play pool – as you can see – and the posh kids come to hang about and pretend to be slumming it. Think we don't notice them but you can always tell the posh kids. Designer clothes and trainers however much mud they like to splatter on them. Most of the time they leave quietly when they're told, or they are eighteen, but occasionally—'

'Yeah?'

'They make a bloody song and dance and then the landlord has to sort 'em out. When he's not downing the profits, of course.'

'What about the school? Do they come down heavily on them? Punish them?'

'I think it's punishment enough being up at that place,' she chortled. 'They lose some of their privileges, apparently.' She rolled her eyes. 'As if they didn't have enough already. But the diehards always come back again. It is funny, though, when there are teachers in here and the kids come in. They usually turn tail and run fast.'

'Teachers come here?'

'Don't sound so surprised,' said Kylie in mock horror. 'Only pub in the village,' she said, putting on a dodgy Welsh accent.

Alex remembered Gus liking *Little Britain* and smiled at the joke.

'Besides,' Kylie went on, downing her drink, 'there's nowhere else to go. Not in Hallow's Edge. Unless you count the teashop, and that's not licensed. Have to drive to Norwich for entertainment. Or, I suppose, Cromer or Sheringham, if you're desperate. And believe me, some of those teachers are that desperate to get out of that place. Another?' She pointed at the glass that was empty, though Alex couldn't remember drinking it.

Alex nodded, pushing her glass across the bar. It was a fine line to draw: wanting to be friendly and encouraging without getting totally pissed. 'And one for you?'

Kylie looked around the bar and shrugged. 'Why not? The punters can drink a bit more slowly.' She grinned before pouring two more glasses when someone came to the bar and ordered a round of drinks. 'Hang on a tic, I'll be back in a mo.'

'Busy tonight,' said Alex, when Kylie came back. 'The pub.'

Kylie sniffed. 'It's not bad, I suppose. Gets better when the summer kicks in proper.' She nodded over to a corner. 'Look. Talking about having kids from The Drift in here, there are a couple over there.'

Alex turned slowly, trying to appear nonchalant. Sure enough, in the corner were two boys. One of them she had seen when she stopped at the school when she first arrived. What had he said his name was? Theo, that was it. The other lad was cut from the same mould. Square jaw, blue eyes, tanned skin, silver stud in his ear. He caught her eye and raised his pint.

Alex turned back to Kylie. 'So,' she said, 'why are the teachers desperate to come here?'

'Huh, that's easy. Being cooped up at the school is, I am reliably informed, shit, pardon my French. You know, driven by results and all that, and rich kids' parents wanting their little darlings to succeed. You have to feel sorry for the poor sods: kids and teachers. Drives them all to drink.' Kylie took a bar towel and started to wipe down the bar. 'But, you wanna know more about that kid, that right?'

'Elena Devonshire.'

'Because? I mean, she killed herself didn't she? We haven't had no coppers in here since she was found at the bottom of the cliff that morning. I don't think old Reg has recovered yet, poor bugger.'

Alex remembered the name from some of the press reports. 'Reg Gardiner? He found Elena?'

'That's right.'

Suddenly, thought Alex, Kylie was remembering a lot more than she had when she'd first walked in. Perhaps the wine had loosened her tongue.

'Lives in a tumbledown caravan that's about to drop into the sea, and spends his time walking at all hours with his dog.'

'Is he the old boy sitting outside?'

'Reg? In the pub? No, my love, you won't find him in here. He likes to drink on his own in the caravan. Bit of a loner.' Kylie leaned over the bar to whisper conspiratorially in a loud voice. 'There've been rumours that he was inside a few years back, but nobody's sure what for. He's not quite right in the head, if you know what I mean?'

'Must have been awful for him.' Alex took the photograph of

Elena that Cat had given her out of her bag. 'Did you ever see her in here?'

Kylie blew air through her pursed lips. 'Not in here.'

Alex nodded, not quite sure what she was hoping for.

'I did see her around the village sometimes. They're allowed out on Friday evenings and at weekends. She ran with a crowd; you know, the sort of girls that all look the same? Well-groomed, designer clothes, long, straight blonde hair.' Kylie poured them both another glass of wine, pushed the glass towards Alex. 'I say she ran with them, but it was odd. She never really seemed a part of them.'

'Was she ever with a boy. On her own?'

Kylie thought for a minute. 'Maybe. I dunno.' She shrugged. 'To be honest, as I say, I can't tell one from another. Anyway,' she drank some of her wine, 'you sure you aren't some sort of private detective?'

Alex shook her head. 'No. I really am a friend of the family. And a journalist.' She saw Kylie's eyebrows rise to her hairline. 'Like I said, I just want to get to the truth,' she said hurriedly, before Kylie thought to throw her out. 'If there is another truth. Maybe she did throw herself off the cliff, but her mum wants to be sure, you know?'

Kylie nodded. 'Yeah. I guess.' She looked at her watch. 'Anyway, my break's done. Nice to meet you, Alex.'

'If you hear anything or can help in any way—' Alex took a card out of her bag. 'My mobile number's on here.'

'Cheers. Best get on.' Kylie turned to serve some more customers, and Alex wondered whether her quick dismissal was to do with the fact she was a hack and thus intrinsically untrust-worthy. Still, she wanted to make a few waves, see if anyone came out of the woodwork, and a barmaid as voluble as Kylie was bound to spread the word that there was someone asking questions about Elena Devonshire's death.

She went out into the still warm summer evening where the

light was only just beginning to fail. She was restless, slightly on edge, and didn't want to go back to the cottage straightaway. Now, she judged, would be as good a time as any to see where Elena had fallen to her death. The walk from the pub to the headland shouldn't take her long – blimey, by the time she went back to London she would be as fit as a butcher's dog with all this exercise.

There it was – the road that ended in a sheer drop down to the beach. A huge slab of concrete partially blocked her way but it was easily skirted around. Had that been there when Elena had come along the road? And why would she even have been on this bit of tarmac if she hated heights so much? She must have known where it led.

She walked along it. There was no barrier. Nothing to tell her of the danger at the end of the road. Only police tape that must have been put up after Elena had died. That's what she had seen from down below. Not that a piece of flimsy tape would stop anybody from falling over the edge. She went closer to the edge and peered over. 'Bloody hell,' she said to herself, 'that is one steep drop.' Below were the large black rocks, some naturally there, others looked as though they had been brought in as sea defences. As she inched further forward, she sent small pieces of stone and tarmac skittering down to the beach below. She steadied herself. There was nothing between her and that drop. She stepped back from the edge feeling a little dizzy. How easy would it have been to take that final step? Would anything be going through your mind, or would it be a spur of the moment decision?

She looked around and there was the chalet bungalow and, further along the path, the caravan that she'd seen earlier from below, also teetering on the edge of the cliff, both looking like they had been abandoned by their owners years ago. Although, as she got closer, she could see there were signs of life in the caravan, even though two of the windows were boarded up. There was an electricity cable of sorts running from goodness knows where and into the caravan. Old and holey socks were pegged to a makeshift washing line at the side. There had even been an attempt to cultivate the patch of earth by the caravan steps. Must be Reg Gardiner's place, she thought. Perhaps he had seen more than he had let on. If he had a criminal record he wouldn't have been willing to talk to the coppers. She filed the thought away.

Walking past the caravan, she came to the chalet. Unloved. Uncared for, definitely empty. She hopped over a small wall, ignoring a scrawled notice that said 'Keep Out'. On the tufty grass lay Coke and beer cans, cider bottles, empty crisp packets; the wrapping from a couple of sandwiches, broken glass. A leggy yellow rose together with a rosemary bush tried to survive in the dry earth. She went over to the chalet and pushed the door. It lurched open. Without stopping to think, Alex went inside.

It was the acrid smell that got to her first: fetid, feral, unwashed bodies. The light coming through the windows was dim, so she turned on the torch on her phone and shone it around. In the corner of the room was a frayed and crumpled sleeping bag. Several cigarette packets lay discarded on the floor together with more empty Coke cans, crisp packets, glass from the broken windows. In a small mound of blackened wood and paper there was evidence a fire had been set. A pile of newspapers teetered on the floor, which was covered with cracked and rotting lino. There was an old stool with three legs, a couple of tatty chairs, and a small table that had seen better days. A mound of plaster and rotten wood was scattered on the floor. She looked up and saw broken struts from the bedroom floor above. On the table were what looked like a couple of atrophied bread rolls and an empty can of baked beans, mould growing in the leftover tomato sauce at the bottom. Had someone actually sat at this table and eaten something? Threadbare curtains fluttered at the windows.

She tried to breathe through her mouth so the sharp, sour smell didn't catch at the back of her throat. Somehow she didn't think this was a meeting place for lovers. Surely even hormonal kids wanting a fumble or more would be more discerning? Especially if they came from The Drift. Ha. If they came from The Drift they would have the run of Mummy and Daddy's second home somewhere along this coast. Not for nothing was it nicknamed Chelsea-on-Sea. Local kids, would they come to a dive like this? Unlikely. There must be better spots. What about junkies? Alex looked. Sure enough, a couple of syringes lay discarded on the floor. Being careful where she stepped, she went over to the sleeping bag, picked it up by one corner. A couple of discarded syringes rolled out and clattered onto the lino. Then a belt and a bent, discoloured teaspoon. Sadness washed over her. Drugs were everywhere. It was a popular misconception that those in the country or in nice seaside villages didn't have a problem with drugs, that it was confined to urban jungles. So wrong. It was everywhere; many driven to it by the boredom, loneliness, and the isolation brought about by living in a place where there was nothing to do and no public transport.

The atmosphere was oppressive, bearing down on her shoulders. It was time to get out; there was nothing else for her here.

She took a last look round, shining the phone torch into dark corners, and saw something dully reflecting the light. She went over and picked it up. It was dusty and grimy so she wiped it on her jeans. An oddly shaped ring, silver probably. An eternity ring perhaps? Alex's heart beat faster. Could this be Elena's ring? The one Cat had said was missing? And if it was, what was it doing in a dump like this?

And who had the other one of the pair?

CHAPTER 8

ELENA

End of May: twenty-eight weeks before she dies

Is this how it begins? A few snatches of conversation here and a few there: conversation that feels all secret and special. It is intoxicating. Liberating.

I'm lying on my saggy old bed in an old tee-shirt and scuzzy shorts looking round the room I share with Tara. The posters on the wall: One Direction, for God's sake; The 'Desiderata': *'No doubt the universe is unfolding as it should.'* Really? Maybe it is, now. Strings of fairy lights carelessly winding around the headboards. Our two desks piled high with books and papers; photographs of family and friends Sellotaped onto the walls above. Clothes discarded on chairs, spilling out of the two small wardrobes; shelves jam-packed with books, soft toys, pieces of memories of friends. This is my life on the surface. It doesn't show the dark side. The you-know-what. The depression. The anxiety. The anorexia. And in recent times, the anger that Mum had to go and marry someone so unsuitable: that's the word, isn't it? Unsuitable and young, for fuck's sake! I mean, what's that all about?

I've always known I'm different. I don't surround myself with besties, don't wear friendship bracelets, don't want to go to boy band gigs. Apart from the you-know-what, I am happy in my own skin. As I say, just wanting to get through it and out the other side.

But now.

But now things are changing. Really changing. I thought that wouldn't happen until I'd left this dump, gone to uni, gone on a gap year, done something, lived a little. But it's happening now. Right here, right now. I hug the knowledge to myself, wanting to get each moment out of my head and look at it. Hold it up to the light. Twist it around and around and examine it, watch it sparkle. Is it really happening? Is love really happening?

There's a knock on the door.

I find Max waiting outside, shuffling from foot to foot and blushing. Of course.

'What do you want?' I ask, not unkindly coz I know he fancies me. A lot. Even if he can hardly bear to look at me.

'I... I... I ... ' He looks down at his shoes.

I try not to sigh. He can't help his stammer. 'Come on Max, I've got to get back to an essay I'm trying to write. And you shouldn't be here anyway.' He would get into real trouble if any of the prefects found him in the sixth form building at this time of day.

'I know.' His face is anxious. 'I just ... '

Now I am getting pissed off. I have things I want to do and it doesn't involve writing an essay.

'I saw you with Theo the other day,' he blurts out. 'Coming from the summerhouse. He talks about you to his friends. He's really horrible.'

'I know that, Max. Don't worry about it. I don't.'

'You should. What about me?'

'You?'

'Me.'

The silence is painful as it dawns on me what he is asking. 'Max.' I try to sound even kinder than before. 'I can't – you're too – it's just … '

His eyes are wet. Then he thrusts something at me. 'Here. For you.' Then he runs off.

A box of chocolates. A frigging box of chocolates. Oh, Max.

I throw the box of chocs onto my desk before locking the door. Tara is doing prep in the library and won't be up for hours. I look at my clothes. I pick a pair of skinny jeans up off the floor, pull an electric blue shirt off a hanger and dress quickly. I won't have much time to do this. I go to the chest of drawers and find my eyeliner and mascara. Finally, I rub some gloss over my lips and give my hair a quick brush. Rummaging around in my bag, I find my phone and open up Facebook. I hardly ever do this, but I'm happy. I post. Then thumb through to the camera, pressing video then record. The red dot comes on. How long have I got? God, I should have found that out. Never mind. I can go on until it stops. Can't I?

I sit cross-legged on the bed and brush the hair out of my eyes. I smile. That's easy. I feel like smiling all the time now.

'Hello, it's me. Elena,' I say to the screen. Awkward! I cough, not sure what to say next. This is new territory for me. A private video. I run my tongue around my lips, tasting the stickiness of my lip gloss, then smile at the screen. 'Did you mean what you said? That you found me beautiful? That you wanted to hear what I had to say about things? That you … ' I hesitate for a moment, 'were really interested in me? As if what I thought matters? As if I matter?'

I pause the recording. That's what I miss about Mum since she got married: she didn't seem to have any time for me, to listen to me. What with Mark and the job I might as well be invisible. There is a prickling at the back of my eyes. I blink the tears away. Enough of that. I've got someone who understands about that. Who said the same thing had happened to them –

Mum married someone younger and was busy with work – so understood what I was going through. I could forget about Mum with her job that physically took her away and her new husband who mentally took her away. I take a deep breath and smile again before pressing record once more. 'You said you hadn't met anyone like me before. Anyone as beautiful. Did you mean that? You did, didn't you? I could see it in your eyes.'

I press stop. It's all too exciting – talking about what could be seen in each other's eyes. Or is it soppy? Stupid? I press record.

'The eyes are a mirror for the soul, you said. Well my soul overflows with you. With the thought of you.'

Too much. Too wanky. Sounds like something a bad poet would say. I delete it. Clear my throat. Press record. 'I know you said you wanted to hear from me; you wanted me to send you a vid, but I'm not sure what to say. It's all so … new.' And exciting. And bad. I know it's bad. Haven't we had all that stuff drummed into us about responsibility and abuse of power and all that crap? But I'm sixteen, almost seventeen, for fuck's sake: I know how it works. Or think I do. A kernel of doubt enters my head. Am I being taken for a ride? No. I do know how it works.

There is a loud knocking on the door and the handle rattles. 'Hey, Lee, what you doing in there? Why's the door locked?' Tara sounds petulant. 'Come on, Lee, I wanna come in.'

I quickly turn my phone off and open the door.

'What you doing in here, Lee?' Tara looks around the room, eyes suspicious. 'Is there someone with you?'

'No.'

'Why are you dressed up? Make-up and everything? Didn't I hear you talking?' She pounces on the box of chocolates on my desk. 'Ooo, who are they from? Not Theo. Not his style.' She undoes the red ribbon, takes off the cellophane and dives in. 'Let me guess. Max? I'm right, aren't I?' She gives me a chocolate giggle.

I shrug. We have laughed about Max fancying me but I don't

want to laugh now. Now I can understand how raw his feelings must be.

'Whatever,' she says, and takes another chocolate. 'So?'

'So what?'

'You didn't answer my question.'

'I was talking to myself.' Now I blush. That's when I really hate myself and the way my body lets me down. 'And I'm not dressed up.'

'You so are. Is it Theo?' Her eyes light on the phone on the bed. 'Were you talking to him? How's it going?'

How is it going? Nowhere, really. He is a good cover, that's all. Though how long I can keep up the pretence, I'm not sure.

It happened like this.

I get a text from him – Theo – and manage to sneak out of school and meet him in the old summerhouse at the very edge of The Drift's grounds. We aren't supposed to go there: it has been condemned as unsafe, but I know it is the place he and his friends take their girlfriends to smoke skunk and shag. It's known in the sixth form as the 'knocking shop'. The boys stay the same – Theo, Felix, Lucas and Ralph, occasionally Ollie – it is the girls who are interchangeable.

'Sssh,' says Theo as he opens the door. We go in, the torch on his phone lighting the way.

'Where did you get the key?' I ask.

He grins, tapping the side of his nose like some detective in a bad cop show. 'Don't you worry about that, sweetie. Come on.'

He goes around drawing the tatty old curtains before sitting down on one of the wicker settees that still has life in it. It actually does have cushions on it, almost making it inviting, as long as you don't look at the broken weave sticking out ready to pierce your arse. The shadows cast by the harsh light of the phone dip and dance around the room, giving it an eerie quality. During the day, I know, the sunlight streams in, illuminating the dirt and the dust.

Being here at night feels uncomfortable and strange. It smells musty and of something sweet. There is also the definite tang of dead mouse.

'Won't anyone find us here?' I whisper.

He gives me an amused smile. Probably thinks he looks sophisticated. 'Never been here before?'

I shake my head. Of course I haven't, you stupid bastard, is what I want to say. What sort of girl do you think I am? But of course I don't say that.

'You don't need to worry. It's far enough away from the school that the teachers won't see us, and anyway, I've booked it out for us tonight.'

'Booked it out?' What's that all about?

'Yeah. We have a book. Literally. Reserve our place. Sometimes there's more than one couple, but I've managed to get it just for us tonight. Great, isn't it?'

I almost want to laugh. No, not almost. I really do want to laugh. How many girls have lost their virginity in the salubrious surroundings of the old summerhouse? More than one couple at a time? Jeez. Doesn't seem romantic somehow. And where do they do it? Sitting upright on a broken wicker settee? Lying on the wooden floor?

'Okay?' He takes a blanket out of the rucksack I don't realize he is carrying and spreads it out on the floor. 'Here,' he says, as he lies down on the blanket, propping himself up on one elbow. He lays his phone carefully down beside us, angling the light away. 'Lie down with me.'

Now what? Here I am with Theo Lodge, the pin-up out of all the guys in the Upper Sixth. Rugby, cricket, big guns, fit. Looks good in anything, particularly tight jeans and sharp shoes. Holidays on Necker Island … and he wants me to lie down with him. I feel a bubble of giggles in my throat. I swallow them down and sit next to him, arms hugging my knees.

God, this is romantic. Not.

'Do you want one?' Theo says, as he takes out his tobacco tin and starts to roll a joint.

There is the explanation for the sweet smell. I shake my head. 'No.'

'Go on, give it a try. You might like it. Or I can do better than this. I've got some Charlie if you want it? Gives you a great high.' He looks at me and I think he's probably already had a couple of lines.

'I don't. End of.'

Theo shrugs. 'Okay.'

He takes a deep toke and then puts his arm around me, pulling me down so I am lying beside him. My hip digs into the floor. I want to giggle. He blows out smoke then pulls me in for a kiss. His stubble is soft against my cheek, his tongue probing my mouth like an anxious worm. He tastes of tobacco and cheap drink. He smells of sweet cannabis and floral aftershave.

I feel nothing. Zilch. Nada. Nothing.

'And?' Tara bounces down on the bed beside me, waiting for an answer.

I shrug. 'And, nothing.'

'Was he fixing a date? Just now, I mean?'

She makes a sudden lunge for the phone, but thankfully I get there first, snatching it up and hugging it close to my chest. 'None of your business.' But Tara looks so crestfallen that I feel bad. 'Actually, yes, we are fixing a date. Another one.' The words rush out of my mouth. Stupid.

Tara's eyes open wide. 'Really? Cool. Do you like him?'

Now there's a question. 'He's okay.'

'Okay?' squeals Tara. 'Okay? He's hot.' Her shoulders slump. 'You are lucky.'

'How do you work that one out?'

'I wish I had someone who was interested in me. I mean, you might not see your mum much, but at least she knows you're

74

there. She's married to a younger guy and you're going out with Theo who is hot. And buff.'

'Yeah, I'm lucky,' I say. Not thinking of Mum, or Mark, or Theo.

Yeah, I am lucky, I really am.

Hey you, it's me.

I feel as though I've known you forever, and yet I've been looking for you for so long and then, suddenly, you were there. Quite literally. Standing in the corridor with your rucksack on your back looking at the noticeboard. I tapped you on your shoulder; do you remember? And then touched your elbow, gossamer light. And you turned round and those beautiful brown eyes looked straight into mine. That's how it felt. What did we talk about at first? Probably something mundane like schoolwork. Or a prep paper or the exams. I can remember you were wearing a little skirt with thick black tights; your hair was loose around your face. You were wearing earrings in the shape of hearts. I wanted to reach out and touch them, but of course I didn't. I had to talk normally to you, gain your confidence. I think I made you laugh and your whole face lit up and I remember watching your lips and wondering then what it would be like to kiss them. I let you go then because I could see you were looking around, trying to see if your friends were near; you didn't want to be seen with me, and I understood that. I was prepared to wait.

CHAPTER 9

June

Alex let herself into the cottage and grabbed a glass of water and a couple of paracetamols to try and ward off the headache that was threatening before going to sit on the terrace. The evening was still balmy. The moon and stars had come out, casting a pale glow onto the water below. She listened and, in the distance, could hear the pull of the sea on the shore. It was so peaceful; a world away from the traffic roaring around the South Circular in London and the light pollution that meant you never saw the sky properly. She felt soothed.

Fumbling in her pocket she took out the ring she had found earlier in the derelict chalet and began to rub it with an old cloth to bring up the shine. It was beautiful. The design of half a heart etched into the silver had to be one of a pair. Someone, somewhere had the other half of the heart. She caught her breath and went inside to fetch her laptop and the photo of Elena that Cat had given her. She peered at the photo. Stared at Elena's hand. Then at the ring. She was right. It was definitely the same ring.

Pulling her laptop towards her she quickly found the police file on Elena's death Cat had sent to her; it had been released to the MEP by order of the coroner. The facts fitted with what Cat had told her. Elena had fallen from where the narrow road had crumbled due to sea and wind erosion. There were marks at the edge where she had fallen, but as it rained on the night she died, there were no conclusions to be gained from that. She might have changed her mind and tried to rein herself back from the terrible momentum. Or they might be nothing at all. Police had noted the gorse bushes on one side of the road had been flattened, some branches broken, but again, had come to no firm conclusions. The post-mortem had shown a small amount of cannabis in her system.

'Matter' – such a terrible word in the context of a young girl's death – and parts of her clothing were found on the rocks below. The sea had then claimed her and washed her clean.

There was no mention of any ring being found.

The file contained a photograph of Elena as she was: caught in time at the age of seventeen. Cat had told her it was another taken during the summer holidays before she died. 'Quite an odd time,' she'd said. 'Some days she was as happy as a singing lark, and others as miserable as I don't know what.' The photo showed Elena in the countryside, walking down a path with trees either side and sunlight dappling through the leafy canopy. Her back was to the camera, but she had turned her head and was smiling over her shoulder. Her long blonde hair glinted with sunshine. She looked carefree, young, eager to start living. Gus was like that, wanting to seize his chances, experience life.

The post-mortem shots were another story. They were more than hard to look at. She could only do it if she viewed them dispassionately, as part of a story of someone she hadn't known. She schooled herself not to think of the life that had been cut short. Elena's face was battered and crumpled beyond recognition; the jagged rocks had torn off long strips of skin. Some of her hair was missing. The damage was extensive, but she knew Cat had insisted on seeing her daughter's broken body. Alex knew there would have been little they could have done in the mortuary to make Elena look better. It must have taken all of Cat's strength, and then some, to see her daughter like this.

There was nothing to suggest Elena had taken her own life, but equally, nothing to suggest she hadn't.

Alex leaned back in her chair wondering what she had learned from reading the report yet again. Nothing new, that was for sure. Nothing out of the ordinary. Girl fell, girl died. Nothing to suggest the police didn't do their jobs properly; nothing to suggest they went that extra mile.

Nothing.

She pushed her laptop away and picked up her phone. There was a message from Honey, her friendly hacker, to call her.

'Hey,' she answered. 'How's the back of beyond?'

Alex laughed. 'It's lovely, peaceful.' She imagined Honey in her airless house in Streatham with the constant buzz of traffic rolling by not far away.

'Too quiet. And I bet the internet connection's crap.'

'Internet's not too bad; mobile signal's not great. I have to come outside for that. Listen.' She held up the phone for a few seconds. 'Did you hear the sea?'

'Mum took us to Southend once. That was enough for me. Full of sand and people eating candyfloss. And I wasn't allowed my Nintendo.'

Alex smiled. 'So, what have you got?'

'Something.' Even from a couple of hundred miles away and with a dodgy signal Alex could tell her tone was serious. 'Whose phone is this? I mean, I know whose phone it is, that's easy enough, and there's no lock on it, but why have you got it?'

'That doesn't matter.'

'User's got a serious selfie habit. Or did have.'

'And by that you mean—'

'Selfies? Y'know, when people, mostly young people, take pictures of themselves—'

'Honey. Don't be patronizing. I know what selfies are. I meant the serious habit bit.'

'Okay.' Alex heard Honey take a deep breath. 'On first look there's not much different about the stuff on there. Facebook, a bit of Twitter, an Instagram account. Email: personal and a school

78

address. A few other apps. All easy enough to get into. The one thing there isn't a lot of is the usual pouting pictures or the self-obsessed chat. Why do they tell the world everything? Don't they know how easy it is to have your identity stolen, your—'

'Honey. Please.'

'Oh, yeah. Anyway, I dug about a bit and found the – um – selfies.'

'Why didn't the police find them? I know they only had a cursory look, but still … '

The impatience in Honey's sigh travelled easily down the phone. 'There's an app, right, where you can hide pictures. It's dead simple. It looks like a calculator. I mean, it is a calculator, but punch in a four-digit number and the equals sign and there you have it.'

'There you have what?' Alex was confused.

'A secret place to store documents, pdf files, text files, and jpegs. That's where she kept the pictures. Presumably, from the look of them, she sent them to someone first. Could have been via Snapchat or something similar.'

'Snapchat?'

'Yes.' She spoke slowly, as if to someone of limited intelligence, which she probably was compared to Honey. In the IT department at least. 'You send something by Snapchat and it deletes itself in a few seconds. Of course, she could have sent them via WhatsApp and deleted the history, or—'

'Honey.' Alex needed to stop her before the conversation descended into a discussion about technology that would baffle her. 'Who did she send them to? Elaborate, please.'

'That's where she was clever, actually. She didn't use Snapchat or WhatsApp, or if she did it was for—'

'Please. Get to the point.'

'Okay, okay. Just want you to know how much is out there. And I haven't even started yet.'

'Honey—'

'Right. They were actually sent to an email account that I had to do a fair bit of digging to find. But, it wasn't that hard.'

Alex had to allow Honey a certain amount of self-satisfaction. 'Elaborate.'

'There's the thing. It was an email account, but every message was in draft, so the other person only needed the account name and password to see the messages. That way they can't be traced. There's no trail out there on the internet.'

'Why would she worry about her emails being traced?'

'Er … I'll send the file to you. Let you make up your own mind.'

Was she imagining it, or did Honey sound embarrassed? 'Okay, do that. And maybe we can talk more later.'

The line went dead and Alex thought for a moment. An app to hide pictures behind. An email account that went nowhere. It was just the sort of thing she'd known Honey would find easily. And the sort of thing the cops wouldn't bother about as they believed Elena had killed herself. For them, it was an open-and-shut case, and with money tight they wouldn't bother going any further with it. Even being leaned on by a politician didn't have any currency these days.

She finished her water while she waited for Honey's email.

From: BlackOps
To: Alex Devlin
Re: Elena

Hi. I've put the stuff I found in a file to save you trawling through it. The email account was called You and Me, if that's any help.

The file began to come through immediately but, due to its size and the slow Wi-Fi connection, was taking an age. Then, at last, it was there. She tapped the trackpad.

Alex let out a low whistle. There was Elena wearing nothing but a pair of white lacy knickers and a matching push-up bra. She was draped suggestively over an upright chair (in school?), looking over her shoulder, an embarrassed expression on her face, her bottom thrust towards the camera. There were a dozen more photos, at least, some showing Elena in her underwear, a few of her with no clothes at all. In some she was posed over the chair; in others she was lying on her bed in her student room. In the background Alex could see school textbooks, a poster of One Direction tacked to the wall. What was it all about? What on earth would possess her to take half-naked and naked pictures? Was Elena some sort of prostitute? One of those girls earning a fast buck titillating men over the internet? No, they were surely only going to that draft folder. So who were they going to?

Her mobile chirruped.

'Honey.'

'Got them?'

'Yeah, I just … ' She rubbed her forehead. 'I don't understand what she was doing. If she was sending them to an email address, then that suggests they were just for the other person—'

'Or people.'

'Good point. Or people who can access that address. How could she take them on her own?'

'Come on, man, where have you been? On her phone; I know that much. Maybe with a selfie stick or more likely with the delayed action you get on the phone cameras these days.'

'Right.'

'So?'

'What?' Alex was trying to think. Should she tell Cat about the photos? What should she do?

'Anything else you want?'

'Look,' said Alex, an idea blooming in her head, 'can you put a message in that draft folder?'

'Sure. What?'

'I don't know, something like, "what happened to Elena? From a friend."'

Honey laughed. 'Sounds like something out of a bad spy movie.'

'Maybe,' she said testily, 'but it's all I can think of at the moment. I just want to draw him out.'

'Coolio.'

'And Honey—'

'Yeah?'

'Let me know when you've got an answer.'

'Sure.'

'And Honey … '

'Yeah?'

'Passwords?'

'Sure. *Happiness* for Facebook. *Happinessis* for Twitter. *Wantadog01* for her public email account. Poor kid. I don't suppose she ever got one?'

'What?'

'A dog?'

'No.'

'Oh well. And *lpg01£20pjkM* for that very private email account.'

'Crikey. That's a one.'

'Probably let the computer choose that one when she set it up. Not easy to guess.'

'You could say that again.' Alex wrote the passwords down on a piece of paper, getting Honey to repeat the one for the email account.

'And the account for the Kiki Godwin person,' said Honey, 'was set up on a school computer. The Drift, in the back of beyond. Near where you are now, yeah?'

'Yes. Can you find out any more about Kiki Godwin?' Alex heard Honey suck air through her teeth.

'Sometimes it's the simplest things that can be the hardest nuts to crack, if you see where I'm going.'

'Er … yes,' said Alex, who didn't.

'Like, the account was set up on a school computer.' She spoke slowly again to Alex. 'So that means anyone who had access to one of the school's computers could have done it.'

'Right. So it could have been anyone at The Drift?'

'Yeah.'

Great.

'Okay, Honey. Thanks for your help.'

'No probs. I owe you.'

Alex was just about to say goodbye when Honey spoke again. 'The Drift.'

'What about it?'

'That's where this Elena was at school, yeah?'

'Yeah.' Oh, bloody hell. 'What about it?'

'Posh. My mate's uncle teaches there.'

'What?' Alex wasn't sure she heard correctly. 'Your mate's uncle?'

'Yeah, Sy. My mate. Lives here. With me. I mean, we're not an item or anything like that because, you know, I don't have time for that sort of crap but I do have mates and—'

'Honey, whoa, slow down. Let's back up a bit.'

'Sure.'

'So your friend Sy has an uncle who teaches at The Drift?'

'That's what I'm trying to tell you. Hang on.'

Alex heard the clunk of the phone being thrown onto a table, then silence. After a couple of minutes, Honey came back.

'Sy says he'll tell him you're looking for info on this Elena girl. Unc likes a bit of excitement, a bit of putting two fingers up to the system. He finds life a bit boring. Used to be a mountaineer until he fell down one.'

'I'm not—'

'Sy says to watch out, he can be a bit of a player. Though he is good to Sy. Takes him out for a meal once a month when he comes to London.'

'Honey, tell me who it is then I can introduce myself to him—'
But she was talking to thin air. True to form, Honey had rung off without any sort of goodbye.

Conversations with Honey always verged on the surreal, and this had been no different. She laughed. Somehow it didn't seem strange that Honey knew someone who had a relative who taught at Elena's school. Honey knew a lot of people; Alex had found that out when she had worked with her. Now she would have to wait. Or maybe she could ask around, do a bit of digging. Couldn't be too many ex-mountaineers on the staff. She went inside and opened up Facebook, checking that Kiki Godwin hadn't got back to her before logging in using Elena's password. Some three hundred friends; not many in comparison to other teenagers. Alex knew what their Facebook pages could be like. She had trawled through a few. And had even occasionally been allowed to look at Gus's page (Eight hundred friends and counting). Usually some unsuitable but funny video. She wondered how many real friends these kids had. It was funny how teenagers lived their lives online these days, lived in a virtual world. Did that mean they lost their grip on reality? And anyone could be a Facebook friend. Even Kiki Godwin with the faceless avatar. Alex scrolled down looking for status updates. They were few and far between and had completely petered out in the weeks leading up to Christmas. Most of her posts consisted of pictures of holidays, London landmarks, Norfolk seascapes. One photo was familiar. Alex zoomed in. Yes, her hunch was right. That was the one from which Elena had done her painting that Cat had got back from the school, but there was no figure in the photo. Then one status update: '*I am happy*'. And below an interesting comment: '*Who's the lucky guy? Spill the beans babes!!!*' from a Natasha Wetherby. Then she looked for Kiki Godwin who had posted on the RIP wall. No sign. Unsurprising.

Elena's Instagram account didn't yield anything interesting, and again – photographs she had posted of the beaches, more

London landmarks, her mother skiing the year before – stopped in the middle of October. Her emails and her Twitter account told the same story. So, something happened that term that made her stop using social media altogether. Or maybe it was a question of not wanting to use social media at the time? Maybe her secret email account – and the person who she sent all the pictures to – kept her busy? Had Natasha Wetherby hit the nail on the head?

Alex closed the lid of the laptop. She'd had enough of staring at screens. She went outside again into the fresh air. What had she gained with trawling through Elena's life? Not a lot really. Some online friends, a bit of teenage chit-chat, photos she turned into art, no sign of the mysterious Kiki Godwin, and a distinct lack of interest in her online life from October onwards. Was it because she was depressed and ill? Or was it, as she had thought before, because something or someone more interesting had come into her life?

Alex shivered, suddenly chilly, though the evening was warm. She went back inside and poured herself a glass of wine from the fridge. She knew she'd already had too much, but now she needed to think what to do about the photos Honey had sent over. What was best to do? She could go to the plods with the info that Elena was posting nude pictures of herself to some secret email address, but would they do anything about it other than shake their heads ruefully at some kid who had been so stupid as to take them? And then it would get out and Cat would be devastated. Police stations were like leaky sieves, and despite Leveson, tip-offs to the red tops still got sold. It would be all over the *Daily Mail* before you could say 'public interest'. Because that would be the justification. Cat was in the public eye and anything she or her family did was in the public interest. There had been plenty of publicity when Elena died as it was. No, she owed it to them, to her friend, and even to Mark for that matter, to see if she could find out what Elena had been up to in the last months of her life. If she found out the pictures had any bearing on her death, then she would go to the police.

Probably.

CHAPTER 10

Alex found herself humming as she drove along the track from the cottage and onto the coast road. A cloudless sky boded well for another beautiful day. She had slept well, waking up only once to hear the screech of an owl in the distance, then the bark of a fox. And, with the sun rising in the sky, she had gone for a run along the beach, flirting with waves as they rushed into the shore. It had felt good to draw the fresh sea air into her lungs rather than diesel fumes and the dust of the people of London, to feel her heart pumping and her leg muscles crying out for relief. Back at the cottage, she'd eaten her cereal (Coco Pops: a childhood habit she couldn't break), drank an instant coffee (not quite feeling the love for the futuristic machine on the worktop), and left the cottage, heading for The Drift.

As she drove, she wondered about Elena's pictures and who they had been for. Had he asked her to pose naked, or was it something she had decided to do for herself? Obviously she thought the app on her phone had been enough protection and that nobody would find them. And that must be another pointer to the fact that she didn't expect to end up dead. Surely she would have deleted the photos before she killed herself?

The school looked just as impressive as it had done the day before – more so – as she drove slowly up the drive, seeing the extensive grounds: a tennis court, cricket pitch, and was that the sun glinting off water? A school that charged upwards of thirty thousand pounds a year was bound to have an outdoor swimming pool. Probably an indoor one, too.

What would it have been like to have been able to send Gus to a school such as this? Would he have come out more self-assured, believing that success was his right and that when he left school the world owed him a living? She laughed at herself. There was no point in thinking about those sort of what-ifs – far too late for that. Besides, she could never have sent him away. And it hadn't done Elena Devonshire much good. What pressure there must be to succeed at such a school.

After checking she didn't have lipstick on her teeth and giving herself a spritz of perfume, she left her car in the visitors' car park and followed the signs to reception, hoping her uniform of smart trousers and jacket, white shirt and kitten heels was the right sort of thing worn by those hoping to send their child to a school such as The Drift.

Would this work? Or turn out to be one of her more ill-conceived ideas? Time would tell.

Her footsteps crunched on the gravel.

Pushing open the heavy front door she found herself in a cool tiled hallway. The mullioned windows let through shafts of light, which picked out the bare threads in the ancient rug covering some of the tiles. On the walls were oil portraits of former head teachers – mostly men – and a polished wooden board giving the names of past head boys. In the last fifteen years, there were head girls on there too; testament to the fact the school had become co-educational. Keeping up with the times.

Alex could smell polish and that distinctive undercurrent of school dinners. For a moment she could hear the screams and jeers from her own schooldays. The pushing and the shoving, the disrupted classes, the despairing teachers, the classrooms with their dodgy radiators and posters peeling off damp walls. Having to pretend not to enjoy class, not to be clever, having to protect

Sasha from the bullies. She blinked hard and came back to the privilege of The Drift.

'Can I help?' A woman on the wrong side of forty with tendrils of hair escaping from a loose bun and glasses perched on the end of her nose peered at her through a window. Reception. Alex had been expecting comfy chairs and someone with manicured nails and a uniform to greet her: something more in the style of a spa than a school.

Alex gave her a friendly smile. 'Alex Devlin. I have an appointment with Ingrid and Sven Farrar.'

'Ah. Prospective parent.' Said with a wide beam.

Alex matched the beam. 'That's right. Hoping to enrol (was that the right word, she wondered?) my son in the school.'

'Of course.' Could the beam get any wider? 'And an excellent choice, if I may say so. Though The Drift is, ah, selective in its choices.'

'As am I,' said Alex with a little laugh.

'Of course. It's so important, don't you think? The right education for one's offspring. To give them the correct start in life.'

'It is indeed. Of course. Absolutely. Correct start in life and all that.' Oh Lordy, was she giving the right impression? What was the right impression?

'Absolutely.' The woman nodded, bringing a book out from under the counter. 'If you could just sign here', she pointed to a dotted line, 'and then I can give you an identity badge. Please wear it at all times.' She frowned. 'We do take security very seriously. Well you have to, don't you?' Now the woman smiled at her. Professional. Sharp.

'You do,' said Alex, signing on the dotted line and timing and dating her signature. 'There we are. All done.' She hoped she sounded duly impressed with the security arrangements.

'Even the students have to do it now just so we know who is supposed to be in the building and who isn't. Never used to be like that. That's the twenty-first century for you, I suppose.'

Alex exchanged the book for a badge.

'I'm Patricia, by the way. Pat. I suppose you'd call me the school secretary.' Pat pushed a few of the tendrils of hair away from her face. There were beads of sweat on her forehead. Alex smiled in sympathy.

'I've never known it so hot, though the building is lovely and cool isn't it?'

Pat nodded. 'Mostly. The windows in these old buildings keep the heat out and the thatch is supposed to keep the temperature down. But stuck in this little office … well, it's jolly warm.' She took a hanky out of her pocket and mopped her brow as if to press home the point.

'It must be.' Alex injected as much sympathy into her voice as she could. 'And I expect you don't get much of a break. From the office, I mean. All those demands of the children and the teachers.'

She gave a little laugh. 'You're not wrong there. Goodness, the stories I could—' She peered at Alex over the rims of her glasses. 'You're not going to get me there, though. Telling tales out of school, as it were.'

Alex smiled. 'Of course not. I wouldn't expect you to. But I think it's important to get to know the people who really run schools: people like you.' Alex watched Pat practically preen herself. 'After all, I expect you're more than a receptionist. I mean, you must know what goes on at The Drift.'

Pat nodded. 'Oh, I do, that's for sure. I haven't quite got the ear of the headmaster and headmistress, but I do keep my eyes open, hear a lot of what goes on.'

'I'm particularly looking for excellent pastoral care in a school. I think it's important, don't you?' said Alex.

More nodding. 'Most important. And, of course, The Drift has excellent care. That's why, as well as having a head teacher for the girls and a head teacher for the boys, we have the house system with a housemistress and master and personal tutors …

why am I telling you all this?' She gave a little laugh. 'Ingrid and Sven will take you through it.'

'I gather a girl died last year just before Christmas? That must have been quite shocking?'

'Um. Yes. Ingrid and Sven don't really like us talking about it.' There were beads of sweat on Pat's forehead that were not because of the heat. 'I'll ring through to them now. Let them know you're here. They don't like to be kept waiting. Do take a seat.' There was a touch of nervousness in her smile now. Alex sensed she wasn't going to get any more from her for a while, but Pat was certainly someone worth cultivating.

Alex did have a good idea about how the school worked: Catriona had taken her through it. In the sixth form there were four houses: two for boys and two for the girls. Elena was in Britten – named after Benjamin Britten, of course – and her housemistress was one Zena Brewer. A nice woman, Cat had said, but a bit timid, easily intimidated. Easily controlled, perhaps? Zena Brewer had told the police that Elena had not been herself since the beginning of the Michaelmas term, possibly even before that. She believed it was a reoccurrence of her illness and depression, but Elena had refused all help. 'The woman said she had tried to contact me several times,' Catriona told Alex, 'but I never got any messages. Nothing.'

Alex flicked through the brochure about the school that had been left on the table, feeling as though she was waiting for the dentist: that slight knot of apprehension in her stomach, wondering how bad it was going to be. But she also had that tell-tale flutter of excitement again; the possibility of a good story opening up in front of her.

'Mrs Devlin?'

She looked up. A boy – youth – of seventeen or eighteen stood in front of her, dressed in jeans and a tee-shirt; a silver stud in his ear, and fuzz on his chin. The boy from the pub. 'Hello,' she said.

He showed no signs of having recognized her. 'I'm here to take you to Sven and Ingrid. My name's Felix.' He stuck out his hand.

Alex stood and shook it. A firm handshake. Held a little too long. He looked her in the eye and smiled, a bright, white smile. Still, she was impressed. She wasn't used to this from teenage boys, more the shifting from foot to foot, the inability to look you full on, the monosyllabic chat. A spike of loss twisted in her gut. Where was Gus now on his great adventure? She would talk to him soon, hopefully, hear about what he was doing. She blinked. Concentrate.

'So you want your son to come here,' said Felix as he led her out of the reception area and up a magnificent flight of stairs with a chandelier hanging down over them.

Alex raised an eyebrow. 'News travels fast.'

'Of course. Nothing's private here.' He grinned. 'Everybody knows everything about everyone. Especially if you're a Senior like me.'

'That sounds a bit grim. No privacy at all?'

'Oh, you can be private if you want, but it doesn't happen much.'

'I thought you teenagers liked to have privacy. You don't want adults to know all your business.'

'Maybe.'

At the top of the stairs they turned down a long corridor, their footsteps echoing on the wooden floor. Glum portraits of past heads hung on the walls. There were numerous doors. Offices or studies? she wondered. 'And a Senior?'

'Upper Sixth. Special privileges and all that to help to keep everyone else in line. There are about eight of us.' He smiled that white insincere smile again. 'You have to earn it.'

Alex was intrigued. 'Earn it? How? By being good?'

'Something like that. But now I'm only here to finish my A levels and then I'll be free.'

'And what are you going to do with your new-found freedom?'

He turned and looked at her. 'Haven't worked that out yet. I'm sure I'll think of something.' His eyes seemed to flick over her body. Or had she imagined it?

They passed a group of girls in the heavily carpeted corridor, all sporting short skirts, little tops, ankle boots, and clear skin. Most had tans and wore the aura of money. There were giggles as they went past and a couple of the girls fluttered their eyelashes at Felix. He stopped outside an open door and knocked. 'Anyway, here we are. Just go in. I might see you later?' He raised an eyebrow, touched her elbow, and walked away.

What was that all about?

Alex took a deep breath, but before she could cross the threshold into what she thought was going to be the lion's den, a young boy came rushing out of the room, barging into her.

'Steady,' she said.

The young boy looked up at her. His face was red and his hands were clenched. 'Sorry,' he muttered.

She smiled down at him. 'That's okay. Are you all right?'

'Yeah. Sorry and all that.' The boy wiped his face with one hand. Wiping tears away, Alex thought. He was frowning. 'Thanks,' he said, then he scuttled away, but not before being caught by Felix.

'Max Delauncey. Walk, don't run.'

'Ow, stop it Felix; you're hurting me.'

'Walk nicely,' said Felix.

Alex stood watching until Felix looked at her and smiled. It was not a nice smile. Max was like a frightened rabbit, thought Alex, as she went into the office.

'Mrs Devlin.' A tall, lean, even cadaverous, man with grey hair cropped close to his head strode across the floor and took her hand in both of his. 'Good to see you. I'm Sven Farrar and this,' he turned to an equally tall woman standing behind a desk dressed in what must have been a designer peacock-blue skirt and jacket and high heels. Her blonde-silver hair was done in a smooth chignon and pearl studs were in her ear lobes. She was sleek and pale. 'Forbidding' was a word that came to Alex's mind. '… is my wife Ingrid. Do sit down. Coffee?'

Alex sat in a comfy armchair in the window, forcing Ingrid Farrar to leave the safety of the desk and sit in one of the two armchairs opposite. 'That would be lovely, thank you.'

'So, Mrs Devlin—'

'Ms. There is no mister.'

'Of course.' Ingrid Farrar inclined her head and gave a chilly smile that didn't reach her pale blue eyes. 'Ms Devlin. You wish to enrol your son at The Drift.'

Alex nodded. 'Yes. I'm looking at one or two schools to see which is the best fit for him. You know how it is.' She wondered about customer service: neither head teacher was making her feel at all comfortable or as if they wanted her child here. Or maybe The Drift was such a sought-after school they didn't have to be warm and approachable.

'We do.' Sven Farrar sat down and steepled his fingers under his chin. 'Of course, we do have selection criteria for our pupils, but we can look at that later, if necessary.' He smiled and it changed his whole face, making it seem warm and open. 'I expect you'd like to know a little bit about the school. And maybe a tour?'

'That would be good, thank you.' Alex tried to look like a prospective parent. She smiled and nodded appreciatively.

Ingrid Farrar leaned forward. Her smile, on the other hand, did nothing to transform her face. 'Have you sufficient funds for The Drift, Ms Devlin?'

Wow. Straight to the point and no mistake. Alex smiled easily. 'I wouldn't be looking at the school if not.'

Ingrid Farrar sat back and looked at her. 'Do you think we came down in the last rain shower, Ms Devlin?'

Alex was taken aback. 'I beg your pardon?'

'Ingrid.' Sven Farrar frowned at his wife. 'I thought we agreed to—'

'Oh for goodness' sake, Sven. What's the point?' She drew a breath. 'Ms Devlin, we know you are not looking at this school as a possible place of education for your 18-year-old son.'

Alex winced. Rumbled. Some fake sheik she would be.

'We know you are a journalist.' She spat it out as though it were a dirty word, and slapped a computer printout on the table. 'So I think we can terminate this meeting, don't you?'

Alex looked at the printout. It was a copy of the article she had written about the rise of gangs in suburbia, clearly bylined and with a nice, clear picture of herself.

'And this.' Another piece of paper was deposited on the desk. *Journalist exposes police cover-up.*

'All about your sister and the death of her children by her own hand. And your part in getting her husband put in jail.'

Alex would not show the emotion she knew Ingrid Farrar wanted to see. She refused to give in or be intimidated. She looked up at the head teacher. 'As you so rightly say, I am a journalist and I have no intention of enrolling my son here.' She gave a humourless smile. 'He's over the other side of the world at the moment anyway.' Poetic licence.

Sven Farrar rubbed his temples. 'And you are here because?'

'I think you know why.'

Silence hummed in the room.

'*Ms* Devlin,' began Ingrid Farrar, the chill in her voice lowering the temperature by several degrees, 'we would like you to leave. Now.'

The two of them stared at her, unblinking. If they had auras, she thought, they would be malign.

'Elena Devonshire,' she said. 'That's why I'm here.'

'More gutter press ramblings?' sneered Ingrid Farrar.

'No. I'm here because Mrs Devonshire, who is, as you know, a respected MEP with a great deal of influence, wanted me to come and ask you some questions about how her daughter met her death. And I think it would be in your interests to help me.'

Ingrid Farrar gave a laugh that sounded like the cross between a bark and a honk. 'Oh, really.'

'Ms Devlin,' said Sven Farrar in a smooth tone. 'The school has been completely exonerated over Elena Devonshire's death. There was absolutely nothing more we could have done to help her. And we do not succumb to blackmail.'

'But surely, if she was ill you would have got her treatment, let her parents know, maybe?'

Sven Farrar interlaced his fingers. 'Of course. And her housemistress would be her first port of call. But these teenagers are very adept at hiding all manner of things from those in charge. You surely must realize that with your own son.' His lips thinned as he smiled.

She chose to ignore the jibe. 'You must have seen some signs? Somebody must have seen something? Friends maybe? Her stopping eating, getting thinner?'

'Ms Devlin.' Ingrid Farrar took over the reins. It was obvious to Alex where the power lay. 'The police and the coroner are completely satisfied that Elena Devonshire took her own life. It's very sad and our hearts go out to Mrs Devonshire and her husband, and may I also point out that at no time was it definitely said that Elena was ill; it was mere supposition. Her housemistress, Ms Brewer, suspected something was wrong, but could not get Elena to seek help.'

'And the drugs? Cannabis in her system?'

Ingrid Farrar wanted to let go. Alex could tell by the woman's clenched fists and the muscle twitching in her cheek. She wanted to tell her to piss off, at the very least. 'Ms Devlin. Of course we do not condone any type of drug in this school. If any are found, then the students concerned will be asked to leave. It's as simple as that. Zero tolerance.'

'Nevertheless—'

Ingrid Farrar held up her hand. 'Nevertheless, Elena had obtained cannabis from somewhere, I agree. From where, I can only speculate. But that is the danger of the freedoms we encourage all our students to explore. And some will push those freedoms to the limit. Some will find problems wherever they go.' She stood. 'Now, I believe we have helped all we can so I'll wish you good day.'

Alex knew when to stop flogging a dead horse. Sven and Ingrid Farrar were too much of a practised double act to let any interesting snippet drop, so she stood and offered her hand. Ingrid Farrar looked at it for a few moments, then took it as though it were contaminated.

But she wasn't finished. 'And, Ms Devlin, we don't like journalists here. We have a duty to protect our students from people like you. They have suffered a great deal of upset and need time to grieve. You are not welcome here, and you have tricked your way in. We would be within our rights to call the police, but have elected not to do so. But mark my words, we will have no hesitation in doing so if you set foot on the school grounds at any time in the future.'

Alex wondered how Ingrid Farrar's expression would change if she told her about the naked pictures Honey had found on Elena's phone.

There was a knock on the door and a large woman with a shelf for a bosom bustled in with a tray of coffee. There was a plate of biscuits, too. Alex took a deep breath. Shame she wouldn't be getting any of it now. Nor a tour. Oh well. She smiled brightly. 'Thank you for your time, I appreciate it.' Then she swept out.

'So will you be sending your son here?' Pat called to her as she passed the reception desk.

'I very much doubt it, Pat.' She stopped, unpinned the visitor's pass from her blouse and put it on the desk.

Pat looked disappointed. 'Shame. The school could do with more parents like you. Oh well. Nice to meet you.'

'And you, Pat. Thanks for your help.'

She strode out into the sunshine, breathing in the fresh air. That was better. The air in the Farrar's office had been heavy and claustrophobic making her feel hemmed in. Here, the beach and the sea beckoned. Then she would gather her thoughts and see which way to go next.

'Alex Devlin.'

Alex had just opened her car door and tossed her bag onto the back seat when she heard her name being called. She looked around and saw a tall man dressed in tee-shirt and paint-splattered jeans coming towards her, walking with a pronounced limp and a smile that said he knew how good-looking he was despite the livid scar that ran from the corner of his eye to the middle of his cheek. His face hadn't seen a razor for at least a couple of days.

'Yes. Who's asking?'

'Jonny Dutch.' Another disarming smile.

She waited.

'Sy Temperley's uncle.' Now there was the slightest irritation in his voice.

Alex was impressed. Honey's friend had actually come up with the goods. 'Right. I really didn't think—'

'Really didn't think what?' He smiled again. Alex swallowed.

'When Honey said that Sy would ask his uncle to get in touch to maybe try and help me, I didn't think he would.'

'Have you ever met Sy?'

'No.'

'Then you wouldn't know that one of Sy's traits is that when he says he's going to do something, he does it. Persistent bugger. Anyway, he asked me to talk to you. So here I am. But in about ten minutes I have some little sods to teach how to draw.' He rolled his eyes.

Alex looked round, sure that the head teachers were somehow

watching her to make sure she left. 'Mr Dutch. I'm not exactly welcome here and I think if I don't get away from the school grounds the Farrars might well have me escorted off. Could I see you later, perhaps? In the pub?'

'In the pub. Sure.'

'Um, okay. Is there a time that's good for you?'

'Anytime with you is a good time for me.' Another disarming smile.

'Right. Later today?' She wanted to tell him to lay off with the smiles.

'Sure. Or … where are you staying?'

'The cottage on the headland. It's—'

'I know it,' he interrupted. 'The Devonshires' bolthole. Holiday home. I'll come there. More intimate than the pub. Less chance of being overheard.'

He walked away, whistling, leaving the air around Alex disturbed and just a bit irritable. She shook her head and opened her car door, risking a glance up at the school building.

Ingrid and Sven Farrar were standing in the window of their office looking directly at her. Like statues in a museum.

CHAPTER 11

That all went well, didn't it? Trying to do her undercover bit with the Farrars. Pretty useless, really. Wouldn't win her any prizes that was for sure, and the other thing that was for sure – Bud Evans would think she had done a poor job. She could hear his voice in her head now telling her she hadn't been prepared enough, hadn't been tough enough. Look, he'd be saying, look how well you've done in your investigative reports before. How could you let a couple of establishment teachers get the better of you?

All true.

Disconsolately, Alex stirred the coffee that had been set down in front of her by a woman in her sixties who obviously didn't sample the array of cakes and pastries on the front counter.

She looked around. It was like being in someone's front room. Actually, that's exactly what it was: the front room of one of the terraced houses on the street down from the school given over to a teashop of questionable comfort: Formica tables and wooden chairs. An ice-cream chest pushed into one corner, charity posters stuck to the windows, dog bowl with water just outside the door. Alex approved of that. But it was bloody hot, in spite of the door being propped open. No air-conditioning here.

She had felt in need of caffeine after her 'interview' with the Farrars and her – what? – run-in with Jonny Dutch and thought Hallow's Edge Tea Parlour would be just the place, despite its unprepossessing frontage. An old car on blocks with its tyres missing, two wheelie bins – one for rubbish and one for recycling – weeds growing through the cracked concrete path. On the plus side there were a couple of picnic benches on the grass outside and large terracotta pots crammed with white, red, and pink geraniums. And the sign on the door said 'open', and she was thirsty.

So, she thought, taking a sip of her coffee, which was surprisingly good, what had she managed so far? Annoying the head teachers. That, she could count as a success. Yes. Even Bud would think that was a success. She had wanted to ruffle feathers, cause them to be suspicious of her, wary of her. And if they hadn't been doing their job properly as far as Elena was concerned, then she hoped she'd really given them something to think about. Okay, so she now wouldn't be able to go poking around the school – not without help – but she had wanted to see what the Farrars were like. And she had found out. An odd couple, cold and narcissistic. It was clear that Ingrid ruled the roost. Sven had certainly deferred to her during her 'interview'. She didn't think they were only trying to protect the reputation of the school. She got the feeling they were trying to protect the school's reputation at the expense of the pupils. No one likes a child to die on their watch, but they seemed to have smoothly and successfully swept it under the carpet. She stirred her coffee absent-mindedly. Would be good to do a little bit of digging into their pasts.

Then there was Jonny Dutch. A bit of a player, Honey had said. She supposed he'd be a good contact, but she wasn't sure how much she wanted to meet him again.

'Cake?'

Alex looked up. A young teenage girl with a pierced lip, eyebrow, and a large black earring that enabled Alex to look through the hole in her lobe stood over her, pencil poised over her pad.

'Er ... '

'Coz we got lemon drizzle, coffee, passion cake, and double chocolate chewy choc chip brownies. Fancy any?'

'I'll have the chocolate chewy brownies, please.'

'Double chocolate chewy choc chip brownies?'

'That's the one.' Alex smiled.

'Good choice,' said the girl. 'My nan makes them and they're proper gorgeous.'

'Chocolate's good for lifting the spirit, I always think.'

The girl frowned. 'You're not wrong there. Are you on holiday? Because if you don't mind me saying so you don't look as though you're having a great time.'

Alex smiled. 'I'm sort of on holiday. I'm a journalist.'

'Ooo, really?' The girl sat down opposite, putting her pencil and pad on the table. 'I've always wanted to meet one of them.' She flicked a long mousy plait over her shoulder.

Alex couldn't help laughing. 'Are we some sort of strange species or something?'

'What? Nah. It's just … nothing ever happens around here. When it did, me nan wouldn't let me out to talk to them journalists that came sniffing around. Said it might lose her business. I said I'd get them in here to have some cake and stuff, but she wasn't having it. Didn't want 'em here, she said. Said they were scum. Said they would just hoover up the story and bugger off back to London.' She stuck her hand out. 'I'm Georgina. George to me mates.'

Alex shook George's hand. 'Nice to meet you, George. My name's Alex.'

'So what are you doing here?'

'Looking into the death of Elena Devonshire, the girl from The Drift.' She thought she might as well come clean with the no-nonsense George.

'Threw herself off the cliff, didn't she? Those journalists were only around here because it was a posh girl at a posh school. Wouldn't have cared less if it had been someone who actually lived here. I mean, look, say it had been me who'd done it? No one would have given a toss.'

'I'm sure your mum and dad would've.'

George waved a dismissive hand. 'Oh yeah, well, I wasn't talking about family. I was talking about everybody else. London newspapers, for instance.'

'Now, I'm sure—' Alex stopped. George was, in all probability, right.

'You know it's true.'

'George.' The woman who had taken her order bustled over. 'Stop bothering the lady.'

'Oh, she wasn't at all,' said Alex.

'She's here to work,' said the woman. 'If she can't be bothered to go to school—'

'Nan, I told you, I've got no lessons today—'

Nan fixed her with a gimlet eye. 'If you can't be bothered to go to school of a morning then you must do some work. Now, what is it the lady's ordered?'

'Brownie.' George was sulky.

'Go and fetch it.' Nan turned to Alex. 'Sorry about that.' She began to wipe the table around Alex's coffee cup.

'You on holiday?'

'More or less.'

'Heard you were a journalist.'

Alex looked at her, startled. The woman laughed. 'You don't get away with nothing round here. Heard you were staying in that posh second home along the way.'

'News does travel fast.'

George's nan lowered herself into the chair opposite Alex. 'I'm teasing you, m'dear. I cook and clean for the Devonshires when they're here. Keep an eye on the house too; get it ready for when they come and stay.'

'Ah, so I've got you to thank for the chicken and salad. And the milk and stuff?'

George's nan waved her hand in dismissal. 'Glad it's all come in useful. Now, Mrs Devonshire – such a lovely lady – said you were here to find out a bit more about what happened around the time Elena died, is that right?'

Alex nodded.

'A bad business, it was. She was a lovely girl, you know. Not like some of them up there who treat you like you're something they've picked up on the bottom of their shoe. I know she'd had her problems, what with her eating disorders and all that, but that was before she came up here.'

'And you didn't see any signs of it?'

'Her not eating or making herself sick you mean? No. None at all. Not that I saw her very much, though she did come in here and have the odd bit of carrot cake. Her favourite, that was. Last time I saw her she seemed happy enough, if a little distracted, I suppose you could say, and George said she thought that might have been because there was a boyfriend in the picture.'

'George said?'

'Yes. She knows a couple of the lads from the school. I don't like her running around with them, but what can you do? Anyhow. I know you're a journalist and I know Mrs D wants you to ask questions, but can you please not do too much raking up of dirt? It's bad for business.'

'I'll do what I can, Mrs—'

'Bartram. Marilyn Bartram. Call me Marilyn. If you like. Mind you,' she said, 'I always thought they didn't ask enough questions after the poor girl died.'

'What do you mean?'

She frowned. 'Well. We had all the vultures up from London, if you don't mind me saying, and our own lads from the local rags, but the fuss died down pretty quickly. The police were around for a while, but didn't hardly talk to any of the people round here. They seemed to accept that she threw herself off that cliff.'

'And you?'

'Like I said. She seemed happy enough to me. Last time I saw

104

her she said she was looking forward to going skiing at Christmas. Mind you—' Marilyn frowned.

'Yes?'

'What she wasn't looking forward to was having to share her mum with the new "Mr Devonshire". She called him her mum's toy boy, though he wasn't that much younger than Mrs Devonshire. Still … That's what she told me anyway.'

'That's interesting. Thanks, Marilyn.'

'I hope I haven't been speaking out of turn?' She looked anxious.

Alex shook her head. 'No, not at all. I think Cat knew Elena was having a hard time accepting Mark.'

'Yes. Well.'

George came over with the brownie and set it down on the table.

Marilyn stood up stiffly, holding the small of her back. 'I'd better get on. And please, with all your questioning and the like, don't go involving George, will you? She's precious to me, she is.' She ruffled her granddaughter's hair.

'I understand. Thanks, Marilyn.' Alex bit into her cake, which had just the right amount of chocolateyness and gooeyness. She watched as George cleaned a couple of the tables with a cloth. In fact, she thought, George would be the ideal person to talk to about Elena, particularly if she was friends with some of the kids from The Drift.

Alex finished the last of her coffee and resisted the urge to lick her fingers clean of the chocolate heaven that had been the brownie, wiping them on a napkin instead. She put some cash on the table. 'Bye George,' she said, giving the girl a smile.

George waved to her and Alex stepped out into the sunshine, blinking, as she went from the gloom of the Hallow's Edge Tea Parlour into the bright light.

'Hallo again.'

Alex squinted at the face behind the voice. It was one of the

boys from The Drift – Felix – smiling at her, teeth dazzling. 'Hi.'
She tried to step to the right, round him. He blocked her way.
She stepped to the left. He blocked her again.

'Oops. Having a bit of a dance,' he said, winking at her before
stepping out of her way.

She gave him a tight smile. 'Yes.'

'Well,' he said.

'Nice to see you again.'

'Felix.'

'Yes. Felix.'

'And you, Ms Devlin.'

Insolent.

She nodded to Felix and made her way down the path and
onto the road, aware of him standing and staring at her.

Her back prickled.

CHAPTER 12

If anything, the day was getting hotter. Alex had been back to the cottage to change out of her school visit outfit and to collect a towel so she could sit on the beach. Now, dressed in shorts and a tee-shirt and after a bit of a paddle, she turned her face up to the sun to enjoy its warmth on her face. She closed her eyes, trying not to think about Felix and the odd way he had turned up at the teashop. Of course, there was no reason why he shouldn't have been there; it just felt a bit … strange. Made her uneasy.

The sound of panting interrupted her thoughts and then her face was being enthusiastically licked by a long, rough, slobbery tongue.

'Ronan,' she said, pushing him away, laughing, 'that is not nice. Yuck.'

The dog stood there wagging his tail, looking as if he were smiling at her.

'I'm so sorry.' Louise panted up to her, bending over, hands on knees to get her breath back. 'It's a sign he likes you.'

'What? Slobbering all over me?' Alex grinned, wiping her face with a bit of tissue she had found in her pocket.

Louise grimaced. 'Sorry.'

'And you were right. I had a paddle, but there's no way I'm going swimming. Would take a bit of planning, I think. You have to gear yourself up for going in the North Sea.'

Louise threw a ball for Ronan. He splashed into the sea and the ball made a squeaky noise as he caught it between his jaws.

'You've been to this coast before then.' She whistled to her dog. True to form, he ignored her.

'Yes.'

Then Ronan deigned to come back, ball in mouth, which he dropped at Alex's feet. She threw it into the sea again for him.

'I know who you are.' Louise looked out to sea.

Alex waited.

'You're that journalist. The one whose sister killed her twins.' She still didn't look at Alex, and her voice had a hint of aggression. 'I remember I saw it in the paper. Your picture. I used to read your *Saturday Magazine* features. I realized when I got back to the school yesterday. I thought I recognized you, but I couldn't think where from. Then it came to me.' She put her hands on her hips. 'Look at that dog. As disobedient as they come.'

Ronan was now hopefully offering his ball to a fisherman on the shoreline, his tail sweeping a patch of sand. Louise turned and looked at Alex at last. 'And I heard you're here about Elena Devonshire? That was the reason you started talking to me yesterday, wasn't it?' Having been ignored by the fisherman, Ronan dropped the ball at Louise's feet.

Alex didn't say anything. She bent down, picked up the ball, and threw it once more. At this rate she'd be getting tennis elbow. Ronan raced after it again. 'Her mother is a friend of mine,' she said eventually. 'Elena was in your class, wasn't she?' Alex held her breath, wondering if Louise would answer. Small waves broke around her ankles. She was aware of the pebbles beneath the soles of her feet.

'I'm sorry. For your friend, I mean. Elena's mother. I can't imagine … I can't imagine what it must be like to lose a daughter.'

'Thank you.'

Ronan began to chase his tail. Round and round and round. Until he caught it and promptly fell backwards. A couple went past, rucksacks jiggling on their backs, wiry legs and sturdy shoes declaring their intent for serious walking. They nodded hello.

'She was a – good – pupil.' A noticeable hesitation in her voice.

'Meaning?'

Louise shrugged. 'Just that. Good. Fairly intelligent, fairly attentive, worked hard. She would have done quite well. I teach English.'

'Yes.'

'Of course, you would know that.'

Alex sensed there was more to be said. 'Was it a shock when she died?'

'Of course it was a shock.'

'I'm sorry. Stupid question. I didn't mean—'

'I know. What you meant was, had she been ill. Depressed. All that sort of thing.'

'And had she?'

'I think she was unhappy, and yes, I think she had started … wasn't eating again. I watched her at meals; we eat with the students in the evening, usually.' She made a face. 'God, it's so dull. With those students from morning till night. Thank God, I get let out occasionally to put my own children to bed.' She looked at Alex. 'I've got two. An 8-year-old and a 9-year-old. Quick succession. I wouldn't recommend it. Anyway, I could see she was doing that classic thing of playing with her food, pushing it around the plate, hiding peas under potato, that sort of thing. She looked as though she was getting thinner too.'

Alex knew she had to be careful or Louise Churchill might clam up completely. 'So, what happened with Elena?'

'What happened? Did I tell anybody you mean?'

'Yes, I suppose I do mean that.'

Louise sighed. 'I tried. Her housemistress.'

'Is that Zena Brewer?'

Louise raised an eyebrow. 'You are well-informed. Yes, that's right. Bit useless if you ask me; not up to the job. Can't see things going on under her own nose. I think the Farrars keep her on because they can push her around. She said she would talk to Elena, but I don't think she ever did. Told me she would talk to her "soon".

So I tried to have a chat with Elena, but she said there was nothing wrong, that she was coping with things and not to worry.'

'Couldn't you tell her parents?'

Louise gave a harsh laugh. 'You're joking, aren't you? There's a strict protocol to be observed. A chain of command, if you like, and woe betide anyone who tries to circumvent it. No, it had to go to Zena and then up to the Farrars. They would then say whether or not the parents were to be contacted.'

'But surely, if it's in the interests of the child—'

Louise snorted. 'This is The Drift we're talking about. Expensive. Private. Most parents put their children there because they've got their own lives and they don't want them interrupted. The last thing they want is to deal with a situation. That's the school's job.'

'Do you know what was making her unhappy?'

The silence stretched and Alex wondered if Louise had heard the question. She spoke, finally. 'Some of it was the normal teenage angst, you know: what am I going to do with the rest of my life, that sort of thing. She hadn't done particularly well in June's AS levels. Distracted by her mother's marriage. And then there was the visit from her stepfather.'

'Mark did mention he'd visited a couple of weeks before she died.'

Louise turned and looked at her. 'Couple of weeks? Couple of days, more like.'

'I must have misheard.' Alex made a mental note to pin down exactly when Mark had visited Elena. It might not be important, but then … 'What did he want?'

'She wouldn't tell me.' Louise turned to Alex. 'There was no reason for her to speak to me about personal stuff, not really. I wasn't her form tutor, or housemistress, or anyone of significance.'

'Who was her form tutor?'

She grimaced. 'David Vine. He's left now. Only young and couldn't stand the pressure. Lucky sod. What I wouldn't give for

Paul to realize the pressure wasn't doing us any good, and then we could go too.'

'If you hate it so much, can't you persuade your husband to leave?'

'Leave? Paul?' She laughed. It wasn't a pleasant sound. 'He loves it here, you know, the whole private school thing: the sports, the society, the famous people, the influential people. That and the thought of a private education for the kids … couldn't contemplate that in the real world. I don't want to contemplate it now, not really. I'm not sure I want my kids to face the pressures of The Drift. But I don't think I'll have much of a say when it comes to it.'

'Why not? They're your children as much as his.'

She shrugged. 'There are things … anyway, no, I can't drag him away.' She kicked at the sea like a petulant child. 'I'm stuck now. And anyway, it was hard enough to find this job.'

Alex's ears pricked up. 'Oh? Why?'

Louise gazed out to sea. 'Just a bit of trouble with a pupil. It was all a misunderstanding, but Paul felt we had to go.'

'What sort of misunderstanding?' Alex thought she could guess, but she wanted to hear Louise say it.

Louise chewed her bottom lip. 'Nothing. Forget I said it.'

Alex felt sorry for the woman; her voice and her manner were so bleak, as if there really wasn't a way out. And there was definitely more to their move to The Drift than she was willing to say. But now Alex wanted to turn the conversation back to Elena. 'Do you think she killed herself?'

Louise crouched down, began to sift through the pebbles on the shoreline. 'You know she was found not far from here?'

'I did know, yes.'

'Poor old Reg. I don't think he's got over it. Said it was the worst thing he's ever seen. Early morning it was.' She straightened up. 'And to answer your question, all the evidence points to it, doesn't it? And the police and coroner said so.'

Alex could have been mistaken, maybe it was a reflection of the sun, but she thought she could see tears in Louise's eyes. Elena's death had affected pupils and teachers alike.

'What about a relationship?'

'What do you mean?'

'Was there any boy trouble that you know of?'

'There could have been. Teenagers and hormones and stuff. And they do go on in the school. Relationships between pupils, I mean.'

'I see. There was a painting—'

'Painting?'

Alex shrugged. 'I'm not sure it means anything really. One of her paintings – and I believe she was a good artist – has a figure in the corner. I wondered if it is significant?'

'I couldn't tell you. As I said, she didn't talk too much about personal stuff to me. It's possible, I suppose. I mean, maybe it was a tribute to Jonny.'

'Jonny Dutch?'

'She was one of his star pupils. You know.'

'Just that?'

Louise looked at her. 'As far as I know.'

Alex felt she was stonewalling. Louise was far from the friendly, eager woman she had met on the beach yesterday. Was it just because she now realized she was talking to a journalist? Time to bring out the big guns. She was taking a chance bringing it out into the open. 'The other reason I think there may have been someone special in her life is the photographs.'

'Photographs? What do you mean?' Now Louise turned the full force of her stare onto Alex.

'Look, Louise, can I rely on your discretion?'

'Of course,' she answered, almost irritably. 'I'm a mother myself. And as a teacher I'm used to discretion.'

'Okay. The photographs were a bit compromising, you know? Of Elena.'

'What? Like sexting?' She shook her head. 'Surely not. It's something that's covered in PHSE lessons. They know better than that at The Drift.'

'Okay.' Alex wondered what made The Drift teenagers exempt from the perils of the internet compared to teenagers at state schools. 'But the pictures would have put Elena at the mercy of unscrupulous people. It's not hard to start spreading them over the web, and I wondered if that had happened, if you'd heard anything?'

'Hang on a minute, how did you find out about these "compromising photographs"?'

Alex was not imagining it; Louise was on the alert. 'I'm not at liberty to say.'

'And how have you got hold of them?' Louise narrowed her eyes.

'As I said, I can't really say. Sources and all that.'

'Seems to me that's very convenient.'

Unwittingly, Louise had, as they say, hit the nail on the head. 'But they do exist,' said Alex, ignoring her hostile tone. 'You don't know anything about them?'

She shook her head. 'No. I don't believe it.' The answer came quickly. 'Or else it was one of those stupid things those arses of boys had something to do with.'

'Which boys?'

'Oh, what does it matter now?' She bent down and picked up a large stone, hurling it into the sea. 'She's dead, and all this talking about her isn't going to get her back.'

'Louise.' Alex decided to try the gentle approach. 'If you do know anything—'

'Then I shall tell the police, of course.' She whistled for her dog. 'Ronan, come on, time to go.'

The dog bounded towards her and she clipped the lead onto his collar. 'I don't know where you got the idea about those photos, but I wouldn't rely on your "sources" if I were you. And

I don't think there's any point in you "looking into things", as you put it; there really isn't anything for you to look into. And I shouldn't really be talking to you, not about this. They wouldn't like it. Nice to meet you again, Alex.' And with that she turned and walked away.

Alex watched her go.

CHAPTER 13

ELENA

June: twenty-three weeks before she dies

The sound of sobbing startles me awake.

I roll over, squinting at my watch. It's five-a-frigging-o'clock. I sit up.

Tara is lying curled up, foetus-like, in her bed. The sobbing is coming from her. Don't think I've ever heard someone so miserable.

'Tara,' I say, 'what's wrong?'

The sobs carry on.

So I left Tara on the beach yesterday, early evening. It had been hot and bright and we'd been sitting there drinking horrid Helen's dad's champagne, celebrating – and I say that loosely – the end of the AS exams. Queen Naomi had been quizzing me about Theo, about how into him I am, how often I see him, what we do together, etcetera etcetera – as if I was about to tell her any of that. I got tired of their questions, of Helen's drunken giggling, of Jenni's obsession with painting her toenails orange while sitting on the sand – stupid cow – and tired of Tara's hangdog look because she so wants to be part of the gang and they just don't want her. Me? I can't be arsed. Don't care.

As the afternoon drew on the boys came down to the beach after their cricket match and then it got really, really dullsville. It was all flirty here and giggly there, and I thought, what the fuck do you know? So I was bored and came back to school. The teachers seemed to be turning a blind eye to us lot down on the beach – a blind eye, or they just don't care; take your pick – and I reckon they were having their own party, so when I got back to my room I watched a bit of catch-up TV on the iPad and then closed my eyes to dream.

I never heard Tara come back.

And now she's crying big snotty tears; trying to muffle it all with a pillow but not succeeding. Tara can be a real grade 'A' drip sometimes: always going on about how fat she is, how many spots she's got, how she wants a boyfriend but nobody ever volunteers for the role, and she doesn't half moan on, but she doesn't normally cry like this. Not like this.

I sigh and push back the duvet. Luckily the sun is up and it's pretty warm already. I pad over to her bed and get in beside her, trying to cuddle up to her. She curls up even more. 'Come on Tar, you can tell me about it. Did someone try to snog you? Someone you don't like?' I pull the pillow away from her head.

She looks awful. I mean, like, really, really awful. She's pale, great black rings around her eyes – and it's not just mascara – though that's in tracks down her face. There is a bruise on her cheekbone and her lips look sore. There are bites on her neck.

Whoa! Bites?

I sit back, horrified. Tara sobs even louder. I notice then that she has her clothes on and they are torn and dirty.

'Tara, you must tell me what happened.' I'm frightened for her now.

She shakes her head. Hard.

I feel desperate. 'You must. Please.' I bite my lip. I have to ask the question. 'Were you attacked or something?'

She shakes her head. The sobs have stopped, but the tears still fall.

'Tara, I'll go and fetch someone if you don't tell me what's happened to you.'

She grips my arm. 'No. no, you mustn't do that, please. It's my own fault.'

'What's your own fault?'

'This. The bruise. The bites, the sores, the everything. And I hurt. All over, Lee, all over.' The sobbing begins again. I can't bear it. Tara is my best friend, however stupid she is, however naïve. My best friend.

'Tara, please?' I feel a bit desperate.

My friend nods slowly. 'All right.' A deep, shuddery breath. 'It was fun, at first. We were all talking and laughing and drinking. Nat and Helen were smoking something – not sure what it was. The boys had joined us. Theo. Felix. Max.'

'Little Max?'

'Yeah. He was the one who had to go and fetch more stuff from the sixth form—'

'Stuff?'

'Booze and some cocaine. Bit of skunk. I dunno. They kept making him go. I was hoping he'd get caught, but either there were no teachers around or no one took any notice of him … ' She shrugs. She is so sad, so sad. 'Anyway, I was drinking too much and I had a smoke—'

'Oh, Tara.' I know my friend cannot handle that stuff.

'And I was drinking more and smoking, and I dunno, I began to feel sick and woozy and dizzy and—'

'Did someone give you roofies?' If they're floating around the school, we're in all kinds of shit.

Tara shakes her head. 'Don't think so. I sort of know what happened. I sort of let it happen, though it was like it was someone else, y'know? I was, like, in the sky looking down. Out of myself.'

'Was it Felix?'

117

'Felix?'

'Who had sex with you? Come on, Tar, I know it happened.'

She nodded, miserably. 'Not just Felix,' she whispered. 'Hugh and Ivan. I let them.' Her face twisted. 'I'm so ugly and dirty.'

I have never felt rage like it. They know Tara is an innocent abroad. They knew what they were doing when they gave her all that crap. They knew. I feel my fists clench. I have to think about my breathing, keeping it steady. I'm not going to be any good to Tara if I lose it. 'Tar, are you on the pill?' As I ask I'm running through scenarios in my head – we were going to have to get to Mundesley, get to a chemist, get the morning after pill – then I will have to look after her while …

'Yes. Mum thought it would be a good idea.' She starts crying again.

It takes a while but I manage to get Tara to the bathroom and into hot water. I gently soap her all over. More bruises are blooming on her skin. There are scrapes on her knees and elbows, small grazes on her back. I get her out of the bath and wrap her in a towel, taking her back to her bed.

'You won't tell anyone, Lee, will you? Please? Please?' She cries some more.

What could I do but promise her I wouldn't tell anyone.

As soon as Tara is asleep, I fling on some jogging bottoms and a tee-shirt and let myself out of Britten. I manage to hug the edge of the building before darting across the lawns over to Nelson House.

It is early and quiet except for the chattering and singing of birds.

'Hallo.'

I stop, heart literally in my mouth, no shit.

Max is sitting on the bench outside the door. He is wearing yesterday's clothes. At least, I think that's what they are. They don't look too fresh.

'Max – what the fuck? You gave me a heart attack.'

He shakes his head miserably. 'Sorry, Elena.'

'What for?' Though I think I can guess.

''Bout Tara. It was horrible.'

I take his cold hands in mine. 'Max, don't ever take that stuff, will you?'

He looks up at me, pupils dilated. Too late. 'Who are you? My mother?'

Fuck. I let go of his hands.

I let myself in the side door with the key Theo has given me and creep up to his room that he shares with Felix.

I am so, so angry with them.

I go into their room and immediately wrinkle my nose.

It stinks of boy and sweat and sex and dirt and vomit and fuck knows what else.

'Hey, Theo,' I say, not bothering to keep my voice low and shaking his shoulder hard. He opens his eyes and looks at me blearily. Felix just carries on snoring. He is so out of it. 'Theo, you bastard.'

'What do you want, Lee?' He smiles a bit. 'Come for an early morning—'

I slap him. 'You fucking dickhead. Why did you do that to Tara?'

'What?' For a moment he looks confused then a smirk spreads over his face. 'Oh, that.'

'Yes, that.'

'She loved it. Every second. She was gagging for it.'

I slap him again. And again. He catches my hand. 'Come on, Lee. You want it too, don't you?'

'No I do not,' I hiss. 'And this is my friend you're talking about. And if she "loved it" like you say, then why is she lying in bed covered in bruises and scratches and crying all the time? My friend. You gave her so much crap that she didn't know what she was doing and you all took advantage of that, didn't you? Didn't you? I'm going to go and tell Farrar about this and then I'm going to find that moron Bobby from the village or whatever the fuck his name is who you keep getting the stuff from and I'm going to—'

Now Theo Lodge slaps me. Hard. I look at him in shock and put my hand up to my cheek and feel the heat of my skin.

'First of all,' says Theo in a low, hard voice, 'you go nowhere near Bobby. He's a really nasty piece of work and *I* supply *him* for the rest of the village, you stupid arse. He'd cut your face before you could say sorry. And don't you dare go to the Farrars or else … '

I understand the meaning of the phrase 'a face as black as thunder' coz that's the sort of face Theo has. He looks as though he is about to hit me again and again and harder and harder. I shrink back.

'Or else what, Theo?' My bravery is fading. If I'm not careful I will start to shake. I am going to have to tell someone. Sven Farrar. Jonny. A teacher. Someone.

Then his expression mellows a little bit. 'Just don't do it, Lee. Don't do it, for your own sake. And mine. Please.'

I stand up straight. I see Felix propped on one elbow, looking at me. He gives me a slow, mean smile.

I leave.

Hey you, it's me.

So everyone was grounded after the after exam so-called celebrations. No one really knows what went on that night on the beach, or, if they do, they are keeping it to themselves, but it did get out of hand, didn't it? I am glad you didn't get mixed up in it all … God knows where that might have led.

Thanks for the video. You look beautiful. I keep playing it over and over again. Perhaps some pictures next time, do you know what I'm saying? I want to see all of you, every last piece of you so that I have something to look at, to remind me how gorgeous you are over the long summer holidays. Will you do that for me? Will you?

CHAPTER 14

June

Alex settled herself on her rug behind an outcrop that gave at least a little shade and unwrapped her sandwiches. She began with the cheese and tomato, following it up with swigs from the bottle of water she had brought with her. Living the dream, she thought. She smiled. The ham and mustard sandwich went down well too, followed by a peach and more water.

What was that all about with Louise? She wasn't the friendly person she'd been yesterday: eager to make friends, eager to please. No, today she was like a completely different woman. Clammed up over any mention of Elena. Alex had seen her shoulders stiffen. Was she frightened? And then there was that odd remark about Elena's stepfather coming to see her just before she died. Mark had said it was a couple of weeks before. Maybe it was nothing, just different memories. Still it was something else for her to look into. She thought she had better talk to Mark on his own about it. Just in case.

The sun was making her sleepy. She put down the book she had been intending to read and lay back, eyes closed, trying to empty her mind of the Devonshires, The Drift, the Farrars, Louise Churchill. Everything. The sound of the sea slapping onto the pebbles on the shore and dragging out again was soporific.

She must have drifted off because the next thing she became aware of was voices nearby, drifting along the warm air.

'So what was she doing, asking you questions or what?' A man's voice: young, well-spoken.

'No. She was just having a cuppa.' A girl. Younger.

Alex recognized that voice: George from the café. Perhaps she could collar her and have a chat about The Drift and how it fitted in with the local scene. Or how it didn't. She began to get up, but heard the man speak again.

'She must have said something.' Something in his voice – threat? impatience? – made Alex sit back down again.

'No.' Whiney voice from George.

'Look. You're supposed to be keeping your eyes and ears open for me.'

'Yeah. Well. Not always easy with me nan on me back all the time.' Sulky this time. 'Anyway, I didn't know you wanted to know about the journalist woman.'

'Anyone who's asking questions they shouldn't be asking. That's who I want to know about.'

'But that could be anyone.'

'That's the point, you daft bitch. I want to know about anyone.'

'But—'

'Oh, fuck off, George.'

'But you promised me … '

A rustling noise. 'Here you are. Just take it.'

'Do you still love me?' Desperation.

'You know I do.' Tenderness in the voice now. A silence. 'Now fuck off.'

'When can I see you again?'

'When you've got some information for me. And remember, I want the money from your mates this time. I don't want to wait any longer.'

Alex thought she could hear them walking away: a crunch of shells, a rattling of pebbles. She shuffled forward and risked a look around the rock. The youngsters she'd heard talking were walking away from her. Yes. Definitely George. The plait of hair down her back and the slouchy way of walking confirmed it. She seemed to be trying to lean into the youth, who was tall with an effortless stride. Trousers, a shirt. A pupil from The Drift, perhaps? He looked vaguely familiar. It was frustrating, but without standing up and giving herself away, she couldn't be sure. But there was obviously something going on, and her being in Hallow's Edge was definitely ruffling feathers. And what information did he want? She waited a few more minutes before peering around the edge of the rock again. There was no sign of the boy, but she could see George hurrying up the path from the beach. Quickly, she folded up the rug, gathered her rubbish, and went after her.

George walked a short way along the cliff path then turned down the beach road. Alex kept her distance behind her, thinking she was going back to her grandmother's café. But she walked past that, head down, shoulders hunched, obviously trying not to be seen.

The road was narrow, the hedgerows dense and high. The only way she could hide if George turned around was to throw herself into the foliage, and by the look of it, she would get scratched pretty comprehensively if she did that. Fortunately, George seemed intent on getting to wherever she was headed. Too intent. Alex was beginning to feel the sweat trickle down her back. The heat was relentless.

George turned left off the road and down a track. Heading towards the lighthouse. Here, the landscape was flat with fields of oilseed rape stretching in every direction. The crop had lost most of its dandelion yellow colour and was now coarse and pale green and was as high as she was. It was like a scene from a children's picture book, though Alex thought a red-faced, sweating adult walking quickly after a plump teenager was not necessarily the thing fairy tales were made of.

If George turned around, there was nowhere to hide.

She didn't.

The white lighthouse with its three red bands stood in the middle of a field surrounded by a brick wall and beech hedge. There was what looked like farm buildings to one side and a small cottage to the other side. An old keeper's cottage perhaps? It all looked deserted. The oldest working lighthouse in East Anglia, it was open to the public on certain days of the year. Thankfully, today was not one of those days.

She saw George stop, so she crouched down in the oilseed rape just in case the teenager looked around. Sharp stalks scratched her legs and irritated her skin. Sure enough, George glanced over her shoulder as if worried she was being followed. Alex crouched even lower, praying she wouldn't be seen. There was no feasible excuse for her to be half lying down in the middle of a rape field.

After counting to thirty and trying to combat the cramp in her calves, Alex peeked above the stalks. She laughed at herself. What in God's name was she doing playing at this cloak-and-dagger stuff? Hadn't she got better things to do? For all she knew, George could be going for a walk, clearing her head. She watched as George went through the gate and into the grounds of the lighthouse, before quickly walking up to the surrounding wall herself.

She found the gate and opened it carefully. It made a groaning noise. Bugger. The lighthouse loomed above her, and she had lost sight of the teenager. She made her way across the grass towards the derelict farm beyond where she heard voices.

'Have you got it?' A male voice. Not the cultured tones of someone from The Drift – more local.

'He wants paying. Says you owe him.' George's voice, a slight wobble in it.

'He can fuck right off. Posh boys.'

'He said … he said I shouldn't give you any unless you can pay him.'

'He doesn't need the money.' Another voice.

'Nah. Just give it us, George.' A girl's voice this time. More conciliatory tone.

'I can't. I told you, he wants the money. Said not to give it to you unless you paid me.'

'Well, he can't have it, can he?' First youth, aggressive. Alex thought she was destined to hear out these conversations while she was in hiding. 'Just hand it over.'

'I can't.' She sounded frightened now.

'What you come here for then?' The girl again, tone less conciliatory this time.

'Felix said—'

'Felix. Fuck him. Fuck Felix.' The first boy laughed. 'We don't care about him. We just want the shit.'

'No.' George, standing her ground.

Alex was afraid for her.

'Yes, bitch.'

'Ow. Ow' A scream from George. 'Stop it, Bobby, you're hurting me.'

'Give it here.'

'I can't. He'll … Please stop.' She was crying now. 'Please don't. Please. Here, have it.'

Alex leapt up; she couldn't let this go on. 'Hey,' she shouted. 'Leave her alone.'

Two youths and a girl turned to look at her. 'Who the fuck are you?' asked the tallest and oldest of them who had hold of George's wrist. Must be Bobby.

Alex couldn't think of anyone less deserving of the name Bobby. She had known a Bobby when she was at school. He'd had fair hair, milky skin, and glasses with very thick lenses. His smile had been gentle and he was totally unthreatening. This Bobby had black hair cut close to his scalp and small, mean eyes. He was wearing jeans and a vest and his muscles and tattoos were impressive. 'Doesn't matter who I am, leave her alone. Now.'

'Oooo, Georgie girl, brought your mum along have you?' he sneered.

'Go away.' George wiped her face with her hand, leaving dirty smears on her skin. 'I don't need you.'

'I know, George,' said Alex, calmly, walking towards her. 'I was just wondering what was going on. I heard shouting.'

'Nothing's going on, is it Georgie?' said the youth called Bobby.

'No, nothing, that's right, isn't it?' This from the girl. The second boy nodded like a nodding dog and bounced on the balls of his feet.

'That's right,' muttered George. 'Nothing's going on. I don't need you.'

'We was just going,' said Bobby, pushing past George. 'Come on.'

The girl curled her lip and the second youth nodded even more frantically and followed Bobby. Alex watched them go. Bobby turned and flipped them the bird, grinning. Alex wanted to return the favour, but resisted, knowing she would only look childish. She watched them as they went around the side of the lighthouse.

She turned back to George. 'What was that all about?'

George shrugged and looked down at the ground, poking the dirt with the toe of her shoe.

Petulant teenager alert.

'George?'

'What were you doing following me?' She sniffed, rubbed her nose with the back of her wrist. The skin around her lip piercing looked sore and inflamed.

'I thought—'

'What?'

The sun was still high, the blue sky cloudless. The air weighed down on Alex's shoulders. 'I don't know. I saw you on the beach. Heard you talking to someone—'

'Felix. So what?' There was defiance in her eyes. 'And you still haven't said why you followed me?'

Alex looked for the right words. She decided to be honest. 'I thought you might be in some sort of trouble, that's all.'

'Well I'm not, okay? I can do what I like. It's a free country.'

'Shouldn't you be in school?' Oh God, she really was sounding like a prim and proper adult.

'Study period. Anyway, once you've signed in for the afternoon they don't know where you are. They don't care. And what's it to you?'

'But you were with your nan this morning?'

'Yeah. Well. Had those free periods didn't I? But she sent me back this avvo.'

They stood in silence, broken only by the sleepy buzz of bees on a nearby bush.

Alex tried again. 'I was worried because I thought Felix sounded—'

'What?'

'Mean, I suppose. Is he your boyfriend?'

'He says he loves me.' She shrugged. 'I dunno, though.' She frowned. 'Why do you wanna know? It's got nothing to do with that girl who topped herself. Elena.'

'I didn't say it had.'

'Is that why you followed me? Something to do with her? I know my nan liked her. Thought she was polite and stuff.'

'No, George. I told you, I was worried.'

'If you were that worried why didn't you say something before I got here?'

Fair question and one Alex couldn't answer with any truth.

'Anyway, Felix said—' She stopped as if she had said too much, her tongue playing with her piercing.

'What did Felix say?'

George shrugged again. Some sulky teenager she was. 'He said you – journalists – only want to wallow in other people's shit. Is that right? And me nan doesn't want me talking to you.'

Alex smiled. 'I know she doesn't. Is Felix from The Drift?' She tried to feign indifference. Felix, the golden youth who had shown

127

her to the Farrars' office. Smooth. Confident. But something not quite right about him.

'What of it? Think he's too posh for me?'

'No,' Alex said gently. 'Not at all.'

'Wondering why he hangs about with me?'

'No.'

'Liar.' Her face was sulky.

'Well, maybe just a bit. Can't imagine your nan liking him.' She smiled to take the sting out of her words.

'Fuck no.' She turned and looked at Alex, eyes wide. 'You won't tell her, will you?'

Alex shook her head. 'Not if you don't want me to, no. But, George, is he—'

'What?' Defensive now.

Alex didn't know what to say. She didn't want George to know she'd been spying on them, but on the other hand she felt a responsibility for the child. Whatever Felix was into, she knew in her gut it wasn't good. After all, she'd been through it herself when Gus was very nearly expelled from school over drugs and joyriding. It was only thanks to the sensitivity of a forward-thinking head teacher that he was allowed to stay in school.

'Is he what?'

George's belligerent voice brought her back to the present. 'Taking advantage of you.'

George went red, then laughed. 'What's that supposed to mean? Taking advantage of me? That's something my nan would say. Anyway, I told you. He loves me, like, loads. So.'

'So?'

'No. I'm not that soft.'

Alex nodded. 'Okay.' God, she would have to do something about her choice of phrases: she didn't want to be classified in the same age bracket as her nan.

'Anyway, why do you want to know about that Elena?'

'Because—' Alex considered her words. Having heard what

she had just heard, she knew whatever she said would get back to Felix. 'Because her mum doesn't think she killed herself.'

'What's that got to do with you?'

Fair question. 'I'm her mum's friend, and she asked me to come to Hallow's Edge to dig around a bit, ask some questions to see why Elena might have wanted to kill herself.'

'She was anorexic and all that, wasn't she? They said so.'

'Who said so?'

George sniffed. 'Felix. His mates. They said.'

'I'm not sure whether she was or not, George. But it's something I want to find out. Did they say anything else about her?'

George shrugged. 'She was going out with his mate, Theo, for a time. She dumped him. He didn't like that. I think they were angry with her and were going to teach her a lesson. But they've never said what. And they said ... ' she hesitated.

'Yes?'

'I think they thought she might have been going out with someone local – but I've never heard nothing – or someone really, really secret.'

Alex found her heart beating fast. 'Like a teacher?'

George shrugged and her face closed up. End of conversation about that, she thought.

'Okay,' said Alex, thinking she had better tread carefully and change the subject – not that this particular subject was any easier – 'what did those kids take off you?'

George's back stiffened. 'None of your business.'

'It is if it was drugs. Is that what the package was? George. Please. Is Felix dealing drugs? Selling them to the local kids?'

'No. Anyway, I told you, none of your bloody business,' the girl shouted at her, before turning and running away.

Great.

CHAPTER 15

By the time Alex reached the path to the Devonshires' cottage she was tired, hot, and cross. The afternoon was still sweltering. What had she hoped to achieve by stalking a teenager like a detective in a telly drama? It had got her absolutely nowhere. Nowhere at all. Was it drugs supplied by Felix that George handed over to the local lads? Maybe it was something else entirely. But if it was drugs, then she did have an obligation to do something about it. The package would be long distributed by now. There was one question niggling at her: if it was skunk or coke or, God forbid, crystal meth, where had Felix got hold of it in the first place? Somehow she would have to find out more about it. And she hadn't even asked George why Felix was interested in knowing what she, Alex, was finding out about Elena. What questions he didn't want people to be asking. Which again was a big fat nothing. Some bloody investigative journalist she was. Investigate bollocks. Useless. She should probably stick to celebrity gossip and show business and reality TV stories. And she had a headache. Probably dehydrated.

'Well, hello again.' A tall figure stepped out onto the path in front of her. There was no mistaking those muscles and tatts.

'Bobby,' she said, wondering if she could find a branch or something to use as a weapon. He was clenching and unclenching his fists.

'Remembered my name. Well done.'

'How could I forget? Now, if you don't mind, I'd like to get home.' He was so close to her she could smell his sweat, mingled with a meaty smell.

'Not your home though, is it? Your home's in London, and if I were you I'd get back there now.'

'Really?' She folded her arms, thirst making her more irritable than frightened.

'Yeah, really. Go back and forget you've seen anything.'

'What did I see, Bobby?'

He stepped forward. She stayed where she was. 'Nothing. You saw nothing. Because you don't want to end up like that posh bitch who tripped over the edge, do you?' Then he turned and jogged away.

Shutting the front door behind her she went through to the kitchen to pour herself a glass of water, trying not to notice her hand was shaking. She would not be intimidated by Bobby. She would not. She leaned back against the sink as she drank, closing her eyes with relief. She pushed thoughts of the encounter right away. A small-time thug was not going to stop her from helping Cat. She put the glass down, knowing she should write down what had happened today and see if she was getting anywhere. It would help clarify her thoughts. It was how she always worked, how she liked to work. But she could do that out on the terrace. In the sunshine. And with a bit of luck the sea breeze. Then later she would try and get hold of Gus. In fact, she would keep trying until he answered his bloody phone, otherwise she really would begin to worry.

She went upstairs to get her laptop and notebook, and changed into her bikini, then she went downstairs and through onto the terrace.

'Hello.'

Alex stood stock still, heart beginning to beat furiously. 'What are you doing here?' She was pleased at how calm she sounded, despite wishing she could cover herself with a sarong or a long tee-shirt or something to make her feel less vulnerable, and despite wishing people would bloody well stop catching her unawares.

Jonny Dutch raised an eyebrow. 'You said you wanted to talk to me.' He drew deeply on a cigarette and blew three perfect smoke rings into the air. He leaned back in the chair and stretched out his long legs in paint-splattered jeans, still watching her. He was wearing scuffed trainers and she had a glimpse of a bare, brown ankle. All at once she realized why the Victorians found that part of the leg sexy. And now she was going to have to step over his legs to reach the table and claim a chair for herself.

'Shouldn't you be in school?' The second time she'd asked that today. But it had been a very long day so far.

'At this time?'

She looked at her watch. 'Don't you have to supervise home-work or prep or dinner or something?'

'Not today. And I thought you'd be pleased to see me.'

'I can't imagine why. I hardly know you.' She moved towards the table with as much dignity as she was able to. He obligingly moved his legs out of the way. 'Thanks.' She put her laptop and notebook down and then sat in a chair, looking out over the sea. The breeze cooled down her face. She didn't know how she felt. 'How did you get in?'

'Door was open.'

Alex thought about when she'd come back earlier that day to pick up her sandwiches. She was sure she had locked the door behind her. Absolutely sure. And she'd taken the key with her, not left it under the stone pig. The slight unease that had been plaguing her since seeing Felix at the teashop intensified.

'Cool here,' he said.

'Yes.'

'Been bloody hot.'

Should she offer him a drink? Tell him to come back another time? Ask him what the hell he thought he was doing arriving unannounced like this?

132

Dutch smoked some more. 'So, are you going to offer me a drink?'

No. 'Lemonade? Water?'

'I was hoping for something stronger.' He gave her a half-smile.

'Too early.' God, she sounded prim.

'A not-before-six girl, eh? Lemonade it is then.'

She looked at him.

'Please.'

She went back inside and ran upstairs to fetch a kimono before pouring out two glasses of lemonade, feeling irritated. What was that all about? She'd met the man for approximately ten seconds outside the school. Maybe it was the sheer effrontery of him turning up without any warning. More likely, it was that he had somehow got into the cottage.

When she went back outside, Dutch was in the same position, still smoking, looking out at the sea.

'Great place, this,' he said.

'It is,' she said.

'So?' he said.

He was here now. 'Sy, well, that is, Honey, thought you might be able to help me.'

He raised an eyebrow.

She stifled a sigh. God, what was it with her and enigmatic men? She thought she'd done with them after Malone. Okay, best thing to do was to see if Dutch could be of any help to her, then she could get rid of him.

Alex sat down. 'I need someone on the inside.'

'On the inside?' Dutch gave a short laugh before he took a gulp of the lemonade and grimaced. He knocked out a cigarette from a packet and lit it. 'Sorry. Forgot my manners.' You don't say, she thought. He pushed the packet across the table.

Alex shook her head. 'No thanks.'

'And are you sure you haven't got anything stronger than lemonade?'

The way he said the word made it sound like she was giving him poison to drink. Which was tempting.

She went inside once more and came out with a bottle of white wine, and a can of beer she found in the back of the fridge. He nodded at the beer and she tossed it to him. He popped the can and began to drink. 'That's better,' he said, when he had finished the can. 'Now I can think a bit more clearly.' He grinned and the skin around his eyes and mouth crinkled making him look softer, more approachable. 'So, a bit of spying?'

Alex poured herself a glass of wine and watched the condensation form on the outside of the glass. Too early really, but what the hell. 'Something like that.'

'Hmm.' Dutch crumpled the beer can with one hand, cigarette stuck in the corner of his mouth. She wondered if this can-crumpling was some sort of macho showing-off thing from him, or something he did as a matter of course. 'Because Honey is his housemate, Sy wants me to help you,' he said, putting the crumpled can on the table. 'Any more where that came from?'

'No,' said Alex. 'I have to say—'

'You find it odd that an old lag like me is a teacher at a thirty-thousand-a-year boarding school for very posh kids?'

'Something like that.'

'Quite simple really.' He rested an ankle on a knee. 'I needed a job; they needed an art teacher for a year. Maternity leave or some such nonsense. I trained as a teacher after university, and also do my own painting. Perfect fit, really. Oh, and it helped I knew the chair of governors of the school.'

'I thought you were a mountaineer?' Something made her want to know more about Jonny Dutch.

'I've done many things.' His face closed up. 'That was a hobby that became a compulsion. Didn't end well. That's the other reason I'm here. Main one really.' He picked up the beer can and looked at it as though he was hoping there would be more in it. 'So, what do you want me to spy out? Does it involve creeping around corridors and going into dormitories after lights out?'

'No, it does not.'

'Shame.'

'I want to know more about Elena Devonshire.'

He nodded. 'She was a good artist. Could have been a great one. Shame she's dead. It's usually bloody dull teaching rich kids how to paint. They think they know it all, that's the trouble, because they've been to all the art galleries, the museums, the cultural stuff. Been to them all but with zero appreciation. Elena was the exception.'

Alex leaned forward. 'I've seen one of her paintings. And look at this.' She got her phone and scrolled through the photo album until she found the picture of Elena's painting she had taken in her bedroom. 'See this. Do you know anything about it?'

Dutch leaned forward and peered at the screen. 'I remember her doing that in the Michaelmas term as part of her course. It's good, isn't it?'

'What about the figure in the corner?'

'What about it?'

'Do you think it's significant?'

'Of what?'

'I'm not sure, but something tells me it's important. She took a photo of the scene, presumably before she started to paint it—'

Dutch nodded. 'Standard practice. Sometimes they go and sit with the easel and stuff, draw it first; sometimes they work from a photograph. I think Elena did both with this one.'

'And then she painted a figure into it. One that wasn't there originally.'

'So?' Dutch looked baffled.

'So, is it significant?'

'Significant?'

'Yes. Does it mean anything? That's what I'm asking you.'

'How the hell should I know? I'm just her teacher. Who do you think it is? A boyfriend or something? And even if it is, there's no way you're going to make out the face. I don't think you're going to be able to identify a boyfriend she may or may not have had from that.' He laughed. 'You're probably adding two and two and making thirteen.'

'Maybe.' Alex wasn't so sure.

'So what do you think happened to Elena? Presumably some dark deed, otherwise you wouldn't be here now.'

Dark deed. That was one way of looking at it. 'I'm not sure her death was as straightforward as everyone keeps saying.' Alex put the phone away and sighed. 'I guess you're right about the figure. It's just that something makes me think it's important.'

'No point if you can't make out who it is, though. Ah, damn, she was so good. Creative. Good at English Lit and Lang for that matter. Graphic design, all sorts. She could have got into art school if she'd wanted to.'

'And did she? Want to, I mean?'

He sighed. 'I think part of her did. But there were so many pressures on her. And the school wanted her to concentrate on more academic subjects for her A levels. All very well to dabble in Art and English for AS, as long as you back it up with Maths and Physics.'

'I failed Physics,' said Alex.

'That's why you ended up as a journalist.' He gave her a wry smile to take the sting out of his words.

They smiled at one another, and a tiny spark leapt across the room. Oh, no, thought Alex, I am not going anywhere near this. No way. And besides—

'I met her English teacher,' she said to break up the sudden shimmering tension in the air.

'Louise?'

'Yes. She said you and Elena were close. Very close, in fact.'

'Really? I was her teacher; she wanted to go to art college; I wanted to help her. Why? Do you think I was involved with her? Screwing her?'

Alex shook her head, the scorn in Jonny Dutch's voice making her feel stupid. That was exactly what she was wondering.

'Good. Louise Churchill can be a bit fanciful, shall we say. Imagines all sorts.'

'Right.' Alex tried to relax her shoulders, which were up around her ears. 'The second time I met her she went all weird on me. Clammed up.'

'Found out you were a hack.'

Alex nodded. 'For some reason, when people find out what I do they back off.' She grinned.

He smiled back. The air shimmered; the tension dissipated. 'Look, can I have a glass of that wine if there isn't any beer left?'

Alex went and got him a glass. She needed to do something.

He settled back in the chair again having downed half the wine in one go. His drinking habit looked even worse than hers. There was some comfort to be gained in that. He lit another cigarette.

'I don't believe Elena killed herself.' As Alex said it she realized that was exactly how she felt. Call it intuition, instinct, whatever.

'Is there any more wine?'

Alex saw the empty bottle and went to get another from her dwindling supply.

'So, why do you think Elena didn't kill herself?' asked Dutch, when he had a full glass in front of him.

She frowned. 'I wasn't sure at first. Maybe I'm not totally sure now. But certainly when I first spoke to Catriona – Elena's mother – I thought she was in denial. The police thought she'd killed herself, the coroner, the school: they were all convinced. I thought I'd come here, poke around a little, and go home with the difficult job of telling Catriona it was time to let Elena go.'

'But?'

Alex closed her eyes. A good question. What was the 'but'?

'Since I've been here I've got a feeling, an instinct if you like, that all isn't what it seems. Maybe she did throw herself over the cliff, but even then I don't think it's straightforward.'

'Presumably you've got more to go on than just "instinct"?' He made it sound like a dirty word.

'Maybe not.' She felt herself prickle. 'But I'm not satisfied. For a start the Farrars struck me as very odd. Louise Churchill practically warned me off—' She was about to tell him what had happened between George and Felix and the local youngsters this afternoon, but something stopped her.

'Ah, the lovely Louise.' He poured himself more wine, lit yet another cigarette.

'Yes, the lovely Louise. Tell me about Louise Churchill and Elena.'

He leaned back in his chair, his body suddenly seeming to fill the terrace with its maleness. 'She's a good teacher. Inspires the kids, even the ones who don't want to be inspired. The ones who don't care about Shakespeare or Fitzgerald or modern poetry; she has a way of making it relevant. And she used to say how good Elena was, talented and all that. She would *enthuse* … ' He frowned. 'I think that's the right word. 'Enthuse about her. Different to her husband.'

'Paul.'

'Yeah. Paul. Now he is a strange one. I don't think he could even look up the word "enthuse".'

Alex rather thought that was a bit of the pot calling the kettle black there, but she let it go. 'In what way? He teaches Maths, doesn't he?' She knew that very well, but wanted Dutch to talk.

Dutch nodded, then frowned again, this time, at the fact the second bottle of wine was empty. How he kept *compos mentis* after that amount of drink, Alex didn't know.

'He's very uptight, desperate to do the right thing. Licks arses, but at the same time is aloof and you don't hear much about his kids and home life. Louise doesn't talk about life chez Churchill either. Strange,' he mused, 'I hadn't thought of it like that before.'

'Louise mentioned he liked being at the school, wanted to stay in the job. They've been at The Drift for, what, about eighteen months?'

'About that. I gather he's an old acquaintance of Sven Farrar's: one reason why he got the job. And, of course, rumours followed him from his other school.'

Alex sat up. This is what Louise had intimated too. She wanted to see what Dutch knew. 'Oh? What rumours?'

Dutch shrugged. 'The usual where male teachers and students are concerned. Especially if the teacher concerned has to make a quick exit.'

'You mean he was involved with a girl at his old school?'

'As I say, rumour, speculation.' He stubbed his cigarette out under his foot, picking up the stub end between his thumb and forefinger.

'Where did they start? The rumours, I mean?'

Dutch frowned. 'That's a good point. I don't know. A whisper here, a bit of small talk there. There was certainly some shadow that followed him, though not necessarily the shadow of sex with a pupil. Still, who knows?'

'Someone must have said something. Perhaps that's something you could look into? Please?'

'Spying over the coffee in the staffroom. Okay. I'll see what I can get.'

'So, if they're true, these rumours,' Alex said, thoughtfully, 'then maybe that's why Elena was acting strangely in those last few months. She was having an affair with Paul Churchill.'

'Hmm. Possible, I suppose. Anything's possible. And he is good-looking. But teaches Maths.'

'So?'

'Very unsexy, don't you think?' He smiled.

Alex looked out over the sea. The evening was still bright and warm. She could hear voices carrying on the sea air: people on the beach nearby, laughing, calling to their dogs. 'I think she was involved with someone before her death.'

'Elena?'

'That's who we're talking about,' Alex replied, a touch irritably.

'And your money's on me or Paul Churchill?' He gave her an amused look. 'I don't know whether to be flattered or angry.'

Alex blushed.

The landline began to ring.

'Are you going to get that?'

Alex blinked, her palms suddenly sweaty, then went into the dining room and answered the phone. 'Hello?'

Breathing. Then a little laugh.

'Who are you? Damn you, tell me who you are.'

The line went dead.

'You look a bit pale,' said Dutch when she went back outside.

'Do I?'

'Bad news?'

'No. Nothing like that.' They looked at one another without saying anything.

'Let's have another drink. It'll relax you,' Dutch finally said, getting out of his chair. 'Where do you keep it?'

She rolled her eyes. 'I haven't got any more. You drank it all. And I don't need relaxing.' Condescending sod.

He looked at his watch. Expensive, Alex noted. 'Have to be the pub, then. It'll be open by now. Why don't you get some clothes on and we can walk down there? Only take about twenty minutes. Could get something to eat. It'll soak up some of that lemonade you've been drinking.' He grinned down at her.

'It's not me who needs food to soak up the booze,' she muttered as she went up to her bedroom to change. 'It's you, mate.' She sighed. What was she doing? He couldn't hear her anyway.

They walked along the road to the pub in silence, the evening bathed in a golden light. Alex tried to decide if it was a comfortable silence or not. Certainly Dutch didn't seem to be fussed about talking, striding out ahead of her. Striding out with a limp she rather thought he was trying to disguise. The air was still warm, scented with the sea and the heat and something else. Something decaying.

'Did you always want to come to North Norfolk?' she asked Dutch, genuinely interested.

He grunted.

Oh great.

'Not really,' he said, eventually. He stopped and took a deep breath. 'I did want to be in a wide open space, preferably near mountains.'

'Er … Norfolk?'

He glanced over at her and gave her a brief grin. She felt that small electric charge again. 'Stupid, I know. Friends thought I was mad. One of them didn't think there were any trees here, never mind mountains.'

'We have trees,' she said.

'We? I thought you were from London.'

Alex let the silence sit for a minute. 'No. I was born and brought up on the Suffolk coast. A Suffolk swede as opposed to a Norfolk turnip. But I love East Anglia. I know what you mean about the space. Not hemmed in by people or traffic.'

'Or your thoughts.'

She nodded. 'Yes.'

'What made you leave and go to London then?'

'Oh, you know. Job, better life, that sort of thing.' She didn't know him well enough to rip the plasters from her wounds. 'What about you?'

'Military. I was a soldier. Afghanistan. Seemed a bit more exciting than teaching. Then came out. Climbed mountains. Fell down one and couldn't climb any more.' He slapped his leg. 'I was lucky I could walk again, never mind anything else. Ironic, really. All the way to Afghanistan and back, seeing your mates blown apart, lose their minds, and I come home and fall down a mountain. Stupid.' He turned and looked at her. 'Perhaps that's why I came to Norfolk. Can't fall down anything.'

She didn't know whether to smile or not.

'I trained here too.'

'In Norfolk?' She was surprised.

'Yep. Thetford.'

She nodded again, understanding what he was talking about. 'The mock-up of Afghan villages. I remember reading about that.'

'Yeah, well. It's one thing fighting the Afghans in Thetford forest, quite another in Helmand Province.' A bitter note to his voice. 'And now here I am. Teaching rich kids.'

There didn't seem to be a lot she could say to that.

She was almost sorry to see they had reached the pub. Dutch had been talking freely out in the open with no one around, and now that they were about to join the crowds in the pub she thought he might clam up.

'Hey, Tulip, how are you doing.' Kylie winked at them from behind the bar as they walked in.

'Tulip?' Alex looked at him quizzically, suppressing a smile.

'Dutch, ergo Tulip.' He gave another of his brief grins. Now Alex could see how it changed his whole face, from hard and uncompromising to open and engaging. He shrugged. 'It fits. I don't mind. Wine?'

'Yes, please.'

'I'll get a bottle.'

Of course he will.

'So,' said Dutch, settling down with the wine and filling both their glasses with a flourish, 'what makes you think Elena was involved with someone before she died? Oh, and I hope it's okay but I ordered fish and chips as well. I'm starving.'

'It'll have to be.' Alex couldn't work out whether or not she was irritated at Jonny Dutch's assumption she would like his choice of food. Oh well.

She looked around the pub to ensure they couldn't be overheard. She took a sip of her wine. It was fairly decent. 'Okay. Honey found some pictures on her phone that suggested—' She stopped, not really wanting to go on. Was she saying too much?

'Ah,' he said. 'From the uncomfortable look on your face I think I can probably guess the sort of pictures.'

'You're right.' Alex was grateful she didn't have to spell it out.

'They're all at it these days. Naked selfies. They don't realize how easy it is for them to bite them on their arses in the future.' He smiled. 'If you forgive the pun.'

'Louise Churchill said the opposite. That the dangers about sexting were all laid out in the PSHE lessons.'

'Ah, the dreaded personal, social, health and economic education. No one takes any notice in those classes, I can tell you.' He poured himself more wine. 'Anyway, the taking of naked selfies doesn't necessarily mean she was involved with someone.'

'Oh, come on Jonny. You don't take selfies for yourself, particularly those sort.'

He shrugged. 'I wouldn't know. But why are you here, snooping around?'

'Hardly snooping.'

'Yes, but surely the coppers should be involved if you think there's been foul play.'

Sighing, she put her chin on her hand. She had to be careful; all this drinking was going to her head even though it didn't seem to noticeably affect Dutch. By rights he should have been on the floor by now. 'Cat – Elena's mum – doesn't want the police involved until absolutely necessary and, as I don't have any hard evidence, I don't think it is absolutely necessary.' Was she beginning to slur her words? 'Can I have some water please?'

'Lightweight.' But Dutch went to the bar and came back with

a bottle of water for her. 'Horrible stuff,' he said, as he poured it into her glass.

'I thought you'd be one of those people who drank litres of water a day.' She downed a glass, realizing how dry her mouth was.

'Used to. When I was fit and healthy. Now I just paint.'

'And teach it, and teach it well.'

'What would you know?'

'Elena's painting was great.'

'Yeah. I guess. But that's more down to her natural talent. I merely guided her through.' He shifted in his seat. 'So, back to the matter in hand. No police.'

'No police,' she said firmly. 'Another reason: I wouldn't want the photos getting out into the media.'

'Not until you want to publish your story.' He raised his eyebrows.

Alex gripped her water tightly, wondering whether or not to throw it at him. 'The photos will never get published if it has anything to do with me.'

'If you print a story, then—'

'We'll see. If I do print a story, it'll be with Cat's blessing, and it'll tell the truth.'

Dutch raised his glass and gave her a smile she could only think of as ironic. She damped down her irritation.

'Here you go.' Kylie put two plates of fish and chips down in front of them together with several sauces and some cutlery. 'Enjoy.'

The smell of freshly cooked food made Alex realize how hungry she was. They both started to eat and there was silence for a while.

'So, what else do you want from me?' Dutch ate like he drank: fast.

Alex leaned back in her chair. 'I guess I want you to keep your eyes and ears open around school; let me know if you come across anything interesting.'

'How will I know what's interesting?' Now he was mocking her.

'I'm sure you'll work it out. I have every faith in you.' She looked directly at him.

'Really? That's dangerous,' he said, draining his glass. 'Come outside. I want a smoke.' Without waiting, he strode away. Alex clicked her tongue in frustration and followed.

Before she could get to the door, her way was blocked by a girl in jeans, trainers, and a hoodie. Alex thought she must be too hot.

'Excuse me,' said Alex, trying to squeeze by.

The girl put a hand on Alex's chest. 'You're not wanted here, you know.'

'I'm sorry?'

'You will be if you keep interfering. Leave George alone. What she does isn't anything to do with you.'

Alex peered at the girl, whose face was partly obscured by the hoodie she was wearing. Recognition dawned. 'You're the girl that George met at the lighthouse. With Bobby and the other lad.'

'That's right.' Aggression oozed from every pore.

'Look, I've already been warned off by Bobby-boy; I don't need you as well. Overkill, I'd say, wouldn't you?' And she neatly side-stepped the girl and went out to join Dutch, leaving the girl with an open mouth.

Dutch was sitting, sideways on, at one of the picnic benches in the garden, rolling what looked suspiciously like a joint. He lit it and inhaled deeply, taking the smoke deep into his lungs. 'That's better,' he said, looking up at the sky. He saw her looking at him. 'Purely medicinal.'

'Where do you get it from? The cannabis?'

He shrugged. 'Here and there.'

'Only, I wondered … how do the kids at The Drift get on with the kids in the village?'

He laughed. 'Not at all. The kids in the village think the kids

145

at school are posh bastards and the kids at school think the village kids are just bastards. Simple. Why?'

God, the night was still warm and all that drink hadn't helped her cool down. Maybe some more water. Should she say anything about George and Felix now? Her mouth made her mind up for her. 'I think there's a lad called Felix from your school who's distributing drugs. I don't know where he's getting them from, but I think he's dealing to the locals.'

'Felix Devine. Mmm. Very likely I would say. Thinks he's God's gift to women. Mind you, a lot of women agree.'

'And the drugs?'

He shook his head. 'I don't know anything about that. Besides, he's officially left school now and is merely hanging around, making a nuisance of himself.'

'Perhaps that's why he's hanging around. To deal.'

Dutch let out a long breath. 'As I said, I don't know about that. I have my own source and obviously I don't do it on school premises.'

She raised an eyebrow. 'Obviously.'

'Anyway, enough of you making judgements about me—'

'What? I wasn't.'

He laughed. 'I can see the disapproval written right across your face.'

She shrugged. 'Not disapproval exactly … ' She thought about Gus and how his life could have been difficult to get back on track if his drug-taking hadn't been nipped in the bud, and thought about her night in the club in Ibiza and how drugs had made her life choices for her. 'They're not the answer, are they?'

'To what? Life and the universe? They're the answer for some.' He opened his eyes. 'We didn't come here to debate the rights and wrongs of drug-taking though, did we? As I remember we were talking about what I could do for you in school. Anything else?'

She thought for a minute. 'What about Paul Churchill's former school. Do you know where it was?'

He took another deep inhale of his spliff. 'Yes.'

'And?'

God, the man was annoying.

'Cambridge.'

'What was it called?'

'No idea. I'll find out.'

That was all she was going to get. 'Thanks.' She looked at her watch and got up from the bench. 'Time I was going before it gets dark. And I appreciate your help.'

He waved his hand, smiling; more relaxed now from the effects of the drug. 'No problem.' He stood up, swaying ever so slightly. 'If you hang on a sec while I have a slash, I'll walk you back.'

There was an offer she could refuse easily. 'I'm fine thanks. It's not far.' She looked at him and grinned. 'I think it's you who needs walking home.'

'Are you offering?'

'No.'

'Okay.' He began walking to the pub entrance, when he stopped. 'And Alex?'

'Yes?'

'I'm doing all this for you.'

'Yes, and I'm really grateful—'

His eyes glittered. 'The question now is, what are you going to do for me?'

CHAPTER 16

The sun was setting as Alex set off home along the coastal path, casting crimson, ochre, and golden light across the sky. There was no one around, just her and a few seagulls. She tried not to think of Dutch's parting remark or what it meant. Would he think she owed him something? Perhaps she did. It was a tall order to ask a virtual stranger to be her spy in the camp. He would want some sort of recompense. She could sort out a tip-off fee for him, but she knew that wasn't what he was talking about.

And what about that girl who'd tried to threaten her in the pub? Although Alex had been able to stand up to her, the girl – Bobby's mate – had managed to unsettle her. And, Alex asked herself, what had the girl and the nasty piece of work that was Bobby got to do with Elena Devonshire, if anything?

She didn't register the footsteps until it was too late.

She was grabbed from behind, an arm around her throat. Alex drew breath in to scream, but a hand was clamped over her mouth and the scream couldn't get out. Oh God. What was happening? Who were they? What did they want? Was it some sort of joke? No, not a joke. Bobby? She could hardly breathe. Black spots were dancing in front of her eyes and she felt the oxygen leaving her brain. Was she going to be raped then left for dead? Here, on a path in a village in Norfolk?

No she bloody well wasn't.

She began to twist and turn, grabbing at the arm around her

throat. She found the thumb, grabbed it, bent it back, further and further and—

'You fucking bitch.'

The arm wasn't around her throat any more and Alex gasped, trying to get air into her lungs. Her throat was sore, so sore. She started to run.

'No you fucking don't.'

A punch to the side of her skull. Her head jerked to one side. Nausea. Dizzy. Blackness.

This time her arms were pinned to her side and she was being pushed further and further forward off the path toward the scrub and the edge of the cliff. She tried to dig her feet in, but she was only wearing thin sandals. Her heels were soon scraping the earth. She could smell sweat – her own and someone else's – and fear. Her own? A male voice in her ear; breath stinking of beer and fags hot on her cheek.

'Look down there, bitch.' Her head was forced downward and she thought she could feel the sea spray on her skin.

She tried not to – tried to keep her eyes closed – but fear made her open them and she found herself staring at rocks on the beach below.

'Did you think I didn't see you? Stay away from us,' said a male voice. 'Go back to London.' Whoever was holding her pushed her forward even more. She thought she was going to stumble over the edge. Fall onto the rocks. Smash her head open. Break all her bones. Then be swept out to sea where she wouldn't be found for weeks or months, if at all. Swept out to sea like … never to be found. Gus wouldn't know what had happened to her. The waves crashed onto the rocks, the sound filling her ears. Salt and seaweed smell in her nostrils. She was going to die.

She was pulled back from the brink. Her head spun. She was thrown into the bushes, thorns scratching her arms and legs; her head striking the ground, hard. More nausea. A hand around her arm. Hurting.

Then.

'Come on mate, that's enough.'

'I just—'

'I said enough.'

The grip on her arm loosened. Fell away.

She knew those voices. Had heard them recently. Who were they? Who were they?

She welcomed the blackness.

The first thoughts Alex had when she opened her eyes were that her bed was hard and for the first time in what seemed like weeks she was cold. And her head hurt, really hurt. She blinked hard at the moon high in the sky, realization dawning that she was outside, lying partly in a gorse bush and partly on shale.

And it was dark.

She sat up slowly, head pounding, aware of scratches on her hands and arms. There was grit on her palms. Her head started throbbing even more. She tasted blood in her mouth. Then the nausea rose up and, turning her head to one side, she vomited up the drink and fish and chips she'd had in the pub.

She looked around, tried to get up on her hands and knees. The nausea rose in her throat again. She retched, but there was nothing left. She fell back onto the ground.

Then she heard stumbling footsteps on shale; a voice calling out, 'Who's there?' Familiar voice.

Relief swept through her. 'Jonny. It's me. Alex.'

'Devlin? Is that you? It sounds like you. Though what you're doing out here at this time, I haven't got a fucking clue.'

Jonny Dutch stopped when he saw her, taking in the scratches on her face, on the back of her hands and the blood on her tee-shirt. 'Lord woman, you look ghastly. What's happened to you?' He swayed on his feet.

She looked at him. Even in the moonlight she could see the glassy look in his eyes; the sheen of sweat on his skin. His tee-shirt was bunched at the top of his jeans as if he couldn't make up his mind whether to wear it loose or to tuck it in. There were dirt marks on the knees of his jeans, suggesting he had fallen over at one point. He wasn't in any state to help her.

Dutch knelt awkwardly down beside her and took her hand. He shook his head and breathed deeply, throwing off his drunkenness, gathering himself together. His skin was warm, his hand comforting. 'You look all beaten up, girl.' Softly, he traced the line of a scratch down her face and then stroked away the tears with his thumbs. 'Jesus. Can you stand?'

'I'll try.'

He bent down and put an arm around her, helping her to stand. Her head swam and she stumbled against him. He held her close. Tight. She began to cry.

An hour later she was sitting in the cottage with a brandy in her hand. She'd cleaned the worst of her scratches and put on some antiseptic cream. A bruise was blooming under her eye. The back of her head had been sticky with blood. Dutch had cleaned it with cotton wool for her.

He came into the sitting room, rubbing his hair dry, a towel wrapped around his waist. 'Thanks for the shower,' he said.

Alex smiled weakly, trying not to look at the livid scars running down one side of his chest, the scattering of dark hair that tapered under the edge of the towel. 'It's the least I could offer you. I couldn't let you go home covered in my blood and tears. And dirt.' She waved over to the corner cupboard. 'Help yourself to brandy.'

'Any idea who did this? And why would they attack you?' He went over to the cupboard and poured himself a drink. He had long fingers with blunt, square nails that she found oddly fascinating.

She cupped the brandy glass in her hand, swirling the amber liquid. Obviously she'd been thinking about it. Her first thoughts had been that the attack had something to do with Bobby. Maybe he'd been lying in wait for her. But then she heard their voices in her head again. 'I think it was boys from The Drift.'

He raised an eyebrow. 'Why?'

'Why did they do it or why do I think they were from The Drift?'

'Both.'

'Their voices. Young. Posh boys.'

'Who?'

She shrugged. 'Not sure.' For some reason she couldn't fathom, she didn't want to tell him yet. It had to be Felix: she was sure she recognized his voice from earlier. And one of the other boys could have been Theo. Of that she was less sure, but … 'Unhelpfully, they didn't shout out their names. Just told me to stay away from them. Oh, and called me a bitch.'

'Nice.'

'I suppose it's something to do with drugs.'

He looked at her.

'Come on, I've told you about this before. And I know the village kids are involved.'

He sighed. 'You're right. There is a culture of drugs. The school runs a policy of zero tolerance, but they still come from somewhere. The kids are good at hiding it, though. No one's been caught or expelled for a couple of years.'

'Zero tolerance or just turning a blind eye? I can't imagine the Farrars having much of a policy on anything. They just do what they want. And anyway, you're no role model.'

'Told you. It's for the pain.'

'Hmm. Not a good example, though, is it?' she retorted.

'No one knows.'

'Are you sure about that?'

He tipped the rest of the brandy down his throat. 'Yes.' His voice was firm.

'Okay, but how can you be holier-than-thou when you're using,

152

too? How do I know they're not your supplier?' She knew she sounded curt. No, worse. Censorious. She was obviously starting to feel better.

'Some booze and a bit of puff is hardly going to bring the full force of the law down on me now, is it? And it's not much, just enough to keep the bastard pain away.'

She tried not to look at the towel; or worse, imagine what was beneath it.

'So,' Dutch said. 'What makes you think it's about drugs and not Elena Devonshire?'

Alex sipped her brandy, trying to stop her hand from trembling and ignoring the deep aches in her muscles and the stinging from her cuts and grazes. It burned its way down her throat. She had to focus: that's what she was here for. 'It could be about Elena, I suppose. Perhaps they're related. Elena and the drugs. Maybe she'd found something out? Whatever it's about, they don't like having me around asking questions, and that just makes me want to dig even deeper.'

'Are you going to report it? The attack, I mean?' asked Dutch.

Alex studied her drink as if hoping to find an answer at the bottom of the glass. 'I should.'

'Perhaps. But then—'

'What?'

'You've no real idea who it was.'

'No.'

'Let me ask around a bit. See if I hear anything. If we get something concrete, then we can do something about it. I'll wring the little shits' necks.'

'Yes. I guess you're right,' said Alex. 'Not about wringing their necks, but about trying to find out a bit more about who it might have been. Otherwise it'll be a hassle.' Was there another reason Dutch didn't want her to report it? After all, it was lucky he had come along when he had. And why was he on that path anyway? It was the opposite way to the school.

'Look,' she said, trying not to wince as she adjusted her position on the chair. 'I really want to talk to Elena's housemistress. Can you sort that for me?'

He gave a brief smile. 'Ah, the redoubtable Zena. I expect so. She has a bit of a thing for me. So I reckon I can sort it.'

Alex jumped as a loud knock sounded on the door. 'Who the bloody hell's that at this time of night?' Keep calm, she told herself.

Dutch caught hold of her arm. 'I'll answer it. Just in case.'

More knocks.

Alex looked at Dutch. 'What? So you're going to defend my honour in a towel?'

His mouth twitched. 'It might frighten them away. Look, if it's those kids, take my word for it, they will fuck right off when they see me.' He got up and tucked the end of the towel in a little more firmly before striding down the hallway to the front door. Alex heard it flung open, then a voice.

'And who the fuck are you?'

'Jonny Dutch. Who the fuck are you?'

That voice. Alex didn't know whether to let her heart sink or soar.

'Malone, that's who I am. Now get out of my way.'

He hadn't changed then.

CHAPTER 17

ELENA

August: seventeen weeks before she dies

So I arrive much earlier than I need to and push my way through the summer crowds, through the swing doors and into the department store, trying not to look like a loser as I rock onto my toes to see which floor the restaurant is on.

My phone pings. A one-word message.

Bitch

Another one comes.

You'll pay

I sigh, knowing full well who sent it, and I'm really pissed off with it all. Theo can't accept that I've dumped him. Unceremoniously. I don't think that's happened to him before. Tough shit. I finally came to my senses and realized I couldn't keep stringing him along. It wasn't fair to him or me. When he touches me my skin crawls, and it isn't only because I don't want him. It's really because I want someone else; I am consumed with someone else.

But that wasn't the only reason.

So, on the last day of term, I tell him it's over and to leave me alone.

'It never even began for you, did it Elena?' he said then, his mouth twisting with bitterness and referring to the fact he couldn't get me in his little book. I had refused him everything.

I didn't know what to say. I was sick of pretending and, after the incident with Tara on the beach, I was sick of him.

'And.' He jabbed me with his finger. 'Don't you go sneaking off to Farrar or anyone about you-know-what.'

'The drugs?'

'Keep out of it. Remember, I told you, Bobby is a nasty piece. And I won't hesitate telling him about you if I have to.'

I pushed his finger away. 'Fuck off,' I said.

Now he keeps sending me messages, nasty ones at that. But you know what? I don't care. Because on the last day of term I got a present. Somehow it was in my locker – don't know how it got there or anything – but it was there when I cleared it out. A beautiful silver eternity ring engraved with half a heart. I knew who had the other one. And there was a note with it.

Happy Birthday
Meet me in London
And there was a date. A time. A place.

It made the summer holidays back with Mum and Mark just about bearable. Mum had to fly to Brussels for a couple of days, leaving me with Mark. Oh joy. Then he said he wanted to take Mum away 'for a delayed honeymoon'. Vomit. I said I'd be okay on my own, would probably get a couple of friends to stay while they were away. Mark took this at face value: took the Eurostar to Brussels and then they went somewhere. Fuck knows where. I can't remember. But I was happy because it meant I could go to my … what would you call it? Assignation? Romantic or what? Anyway, I could go without having to lie or pretend, and if the opportunity came to spend the night away, well, there's nothing stopping me. Though there is a part of me, a large part of me I admit, that wishes Mum would be there for me. Just for once.

Actually, that's not fair. Mum always says if I need her she'll be there. But that kind of got lost after she married Mark.

So I'm here. I'm flicking through dresses hanging on padded hangers that I neither want nor have the money for. Should have sorted that out really. Mark would have given me any amount of cash just so he could go and shag Mum in peace. Anyway, there you have it. I didn't ask.

A rake-thin woman with a heavily Botoxed forehead and a bad facelift asks me if I need help. Heaven save me from snooty shop assistants. I look her up and down seeing the signs of anorexia. I don't need that now. I feel in control of my life and future. In control in a good, rollercoaster-y sort of way. I guess that's what love does for you.

I give up with the dresses and go to the ladies in desperate need of the loo. Staring out from the mirror as I wash my hands is a young woman with a faint blush on her cheeks and happiness in her eyes. It's me; it really is me. I smile. I lean into the mirror and put on some more lipstick. Just a little. Then perfume on my wrists and in my cleavage so I smell of rose and honey and mandarin and something less identifiable. The eternity ring reflects prisms of light. I stand up straight. I am wearing a maxi dress with a subtle rose pattern and a pair of sandals. My toenails are painted in the latest Kate Moss colour, so are my fingernails. I feel good. Excitement fizzes in my belly.

I look at my phone. It's still too early, so I wander to the beauty hall and glide past the make-up counters with face creams and body washes, all sorts of unguents, and an array of goodies in stylish packaging that promise eternal beauty. I ignore immaculate-looking men and women offering me a spray of musky perfume. Then through to bags and scarves where I run my hand across dark buttery leather and let silky soft rainbow colours trickle through my fingers. I can't concentrate on anything and I realize I am nervous. We haven't met outside Hallow's Edge before. Could it be awkward? Is it a mistake? What will we talk about? Will we be able to be alone with each other? Then I stroke my ring and my heart calms. It will be all right.

It has to be.

The restaurant is busy, noisy with the clatter of cutlery and voices, smelling of food and perfumes and face powder. Am I really supposed to be here? I'm seventeen. I should be in Topshop or Primark or H&M, shopping for bright, disposable clothes, joining the chattering parakeets in the changing rooms, not here in the stuffy restaurant in a stuffy department store: somewhere Mum would have brought my grandmother. Is there a table reserved for us? I ask a waiter who consults – with a degree of pomposity – a large, fat book. He shakes his head. No, but there is a free table in the corner by the window. Wonderful views of London, he says. I swallow my disappointment and nod and the feeling of being special slips ever so slightly. That will be fine, I say, and follow him, dodging people and prams and waiters.

I order a glass of wine. He doesn't question my age.

I ask for the menu. He puts it down on the table with a flourish, together with the wine.

I sip the wine. It is fruity and smooth and caramel and cold. It is delicious.

I order a jug of water. I look at the menu but say I don't want to order yet as I am waiting for a friend. He gives me a 'look'. I giggle. He smiles. I feel so excited I can hardly sit still. It's that fizzing again. I never felt anything like this with Theo. Nothing.

I look at Facebook. Twitter. Instagram. Don't check in; don't update my status; don't post any pictures. Obviously. I check my emails, see if there is a message I have missed. I finish my wine; I drink my water. I start to chew my nails, something I haven't done for years. I stop when I realize it wouldn't take much to chip my nail varnish.

The restaurant is less busy now. The constant stream of people looking for a table has dwindled to a trickle. The waiter has stopped asking me if I want to order anything else, though I feel like more wine. I look around, trying not to seem like someone who is looking for somebody, even though I am.

The waiter takes away my empty glasses and the menu, clearly wanting me to leave so they can make the table ready for someone else. The fizz in my belly has turned to acid. It heaves and churns and bile rises in my throat. I am alone. No one is coming.

My phone pings.

Bitch

I get up and leave.

Hello you, it's me.

What can I say but I am sorry. Sorry, sorry, sorry; a million times sorry. I was all set to come to you. I had arranged it: no one knew where I was going, the real reason I was coming to London. A friend, I had said, wanting to tell the world you were more than a friend.

But.

It couldn't happen. I couldn't leave after all. Not because I didn't want to, but because I couldn't. An emergency. Please understand. If I had left there would have been questions, suspicious looks. You do understand, don't you? Please say you understand.

I will make it up to you. I cannot wait until we can be together again.

CHAPTER 18

June

'What's that man doing here dressed only in a towel?'

Malone. Only feet away from her. Had barged in as usual looking like a child whose wishes had been thwarted. He stood glaring at Dutch. Alex rather enjoyed his anger.

'And it's nice to see you, too, Malone, after all this time.'

'Is it?' he said, raising an eyebrow. 'Only, I rather got the impression you'd moved on.' He jerked his head at Dutch.

Alex laughed. 'Don't be so stupid. It's been two years, Malone. Two years since I found out you were married and—'

'I told you at the time I was getting a divorce.' His Irish eyes glinted.

'That wasn't the point though, was it?' She sighed. 'Look, I haven't got the stomach for this at the moment. And Jonny's a friend, that's all.'

'What friend hangs about answering the door at this time of night in a fucking towel?' He scraped a hand over his hair, which was cut short and close to his head. There was a small mole on his hairline she had never noticed before. 'And what the fuck have you done to your face?'

'I'll go and get my clothes and leave you to it, shall I Alex? Unless—'

'You get your fucking clothes and get the fuck out of here,' snapped Malone.

'Malone.' She shouldn't be surprised by his rudeness, but she was. 'Jonny has been helping me. I was attacked tonight—'

'Attacked? What the fuck?' He strode over to where she was sitting and gently took her chin in his hand. It was a shock to feel his warm skin on hers.

'Will you be okay?' This from Dutch, who completely ignored Malone.

Alex could feel Malone bristle as he softly stroked her skin, fingers probing the bruise on the side of her face. Bloody hell, they were like a pair of lions circling each other. No, not lions, that was too grand. Cockerels. Peacocks. That was it. And the irony was she didn't want to be fought over by either of them. She had enough to think about without having to deal with inflated egos.

'Of course she'll be okay. I'm back.' He didn't bother to look at Dutch.

Alex tried not to sigh. Malone was back, was he? Nothing from him for two years – not a call, not a text, not an email – then she calls to take him to task – all right, shout at him – about helping Gus find his dad, and now he walks in as though they'd seen each other only yesterday. How did she feel? That was the difficult question. There was no doubt that when he had first come into the room her heart had started to race. Then she remembered the animosity with which she had thrown him out and realized if she wasn't careful she'd be acting like a silly teenager.

'Ouch.' Alex batted his hand away. Malone had probed a bit too hard.

'Sorry.'

'Jonny, I'll be fine. Malone is … ' she hesitated, 'an old friend. He'll look after me. You go and get some sleep so you're ready to teach tomorrow. Call me about that other thing.'

'If you're sure?'

Alex nodded. She was so tired. 'I'm sure.'

'She's sure,' snarled Malone.

'Oh, shut up, Malone.'

'Yeah, shut up Malone.' Dutch came over and kissed her on the lips. Possessive.

She wasn't sure she liked it. 'See you later, Jonny.'

She heard the door close behind him.

Sighing, she shifted her body. Malone. She'd let him into her life and allowed Gus to think he would be permanent. She'd interviewed him as an undercover cop for the magazine she was working on at the time, and had fallen for him. She knew that by their very nature undercover police had to be good actors: duplicitous and verging on the sociopathic. She'd thought Malone was different. He wasn't. And he left when she discovered he had a wife he was still very much married to. It hadn't helped that he'd married Gillian 'as part of the job'. It had actually made it worse. She hadn't wanted to be with someone who could treat women like that.

But, God, she had missed him.

'So, now that guy in the towel is out of the way, tell me what's going on.'

'How did you find me?'

He grinned at her. 'Easy. Your phone call told me everything I needed to know. Daughter of an MEP who'd died? That wasn't hard to work out. Then a favour from a techie friend to find out exactly where you were from the coordinates on your phone.'

'Come to help, have you? Or say you're sorry?'

'Sorry?'

'Oh, I forgot, you don't know what that means.' The drilling was constant in her head. 'Go away, Malone. I don't need you.'

'I need you.'

Her eyes flew open in surprise. 'What?'

'Look,' he rubbed the top of his head again – he had to be very nervous – and that thought pleased her. 'I suppose I want somewhere to crash for a couple of days.'

'Crash?'

'You know, stay. Out of the way. You were the only one who I thought would put me up.'

She looked at him, exasperated. 'Put you up? Put up with you, you mean. Don't you ever stop to think, Malone? About how I might feel, what I might want?'

'Of course I—'

'No, you fucking well don't. I threw you out, remember? Two years ago. Two whole years.' She swallowed, controlling the anger that threatened to consume her. 'Fuck knows what you've been doing in that time. Probably got married about three times. So why in God's name would you think I'd want you to stay here now? What's wrong with a hotel?'

He raised an eyebrow. God he was irritating. 'I can help … with the Elena Devonshire thing.'

'She is not a thing.'

'Now you're deliberately twisting my words. I know you felt guilty about losing contact with Catriona Devonshire, you told me.'

She closed her eyes. What hadn't she told him?

'Come on, Al, I can help. Give me the details. What you know.'

Maybe he could. He did owe her, after all. So she took a few deep breaths and told him about Cat and Elena and why she had come to Hallow's Edge to look into Elena's death. How she wasn't sure at first, but because people closed up when she asked around, she had begun to think there was something suspicious about her fall from the cliff. She told him about the possibility of drug dealing among the village kids and pupils at The Drift and that Jonny Dutch was her spy in the camp. He snorted at this point. When she told him about being attacked and almost pushed over the cliff, the muscle in his jaw twitched. She knew it was a sign of his anger.

Malone kissed the top of her head. It took her back to happier times. 'You'll be okay, sweetheart. Nothing's broken.'

'I know. And Jonny helped disinfect some of the cuts.' She enjoyed telling him that.

'Jonny Dutch.' Was that a snarl in his voice? 'Your "spy in the camp". A teacher, is he?' He sounded dismissive.

Alex laid her head back. Exhaustion was taking over. 'Yes. But he's been in the army and climbed mountains. And fallen down them.' Her voice trailed off and she closed her eyes, her head beginning to throb.

'Alex.' She opened her eyes. Malone frowned. 'You might have concussion. What day is it?'

'Tuesday.'

'What's your name?'

'Alex Devlin.' She shut her eyes again. She wanted to sleep.

'Who's the prime minister?'

'Tony Blair.' She opened one eye. And laughed. Malone actually looked concerned.

He shook his head. 'Come on.'

From somewhere far away she heard a phone ringing, then she was lifted and taken upstairs. And that was all she remembered.

The drilling was still going on in her head when she woke up the next morning. She stretched her limbs gingerly, knowing the bruising would be livid on her skin and the scratches beginning to scab over. She pressed her fingers against her temples, trying to take the edge off the pounding in her head. She had to get up. She had to—

Malone. That's what else had happened last night. Bloody hell. What a time for him to turn up. The way he had marched in as if he owned the place, taking control. The cheek of him. Did he put her to bed? She looked. Pyjamas. That meant he must have undressed her. She groaned.

Alex managed to get herself out of bed and shower and dress with difficulty, the headache above one eye. If anything, every-thing hurt even more than it had last night. She dabbed a bit of make-up over the bruises on her face – not that it did much good – and went downstairs. Malone was asleep on the settee. Thank God. And was fully dressed. Thank God again.

He opened an eye. 'Coffee and toast would be good,' he said.

'Would it now?'

'Thanks, sweetheart.' He closed the eye.

'You're not worried I'm still concussed then? About to keel over?'

'You're still here, aren't you?'

She shook her head and for a reason she couldn't fathom went dutifully to make coffee and toast, calling out to Malone that she was taking it out onto the patio. Another beautiful day. Indigo sky. Sweet air. And somewhere out there two youths who thought it fun to frighten her, badly.

She began to cry.

'Are you that glad to see me, then?' Malone sat down opposite and picked up a knife to spread butter and marmite on his toast.

Self-obsessed as ever.

She wiped the tears away with the back of her hand. 'Overwhelmed, that's all.'

He pointed his knife at her. 'From the look of you they meant business.'

She smiled weakly. 'They certainly meant to frighten me. But I'm not letting them think they succeeded.'

'Any idea who they were?' He didn't look at her; he carried on spreading the marmite, back and forth, back and forth, as if he wasn't really interested in her answer.

But she knew that casual stance of his. 'I have a suspicion, but I'm not telling you.'

Malone stopped spreading. 'Why not? I can help. You know that.'

'I don't want you to, Malone. I can deal with this.' She could imagine him teaching those boys a lesson, and then she'd never get to the bottom of what was going on in Hallow's Edge, whether they had anything to do with Elena.

'Presumably the kids you were telling me about last night?'

She sighed, almost defeated. 'Presumably. But leave it Malone, please.'

'I don't want to leave it. And how many phone calls have you had with no one on the other end?'

'A couple. How did you—?' She remembered hearing a phone ringing before Malone took her upstairs. 'There was one last night, wasn't there?'

'Yep. Had to answer it, wouldn't stop ringing. Breathing. A silly laugh. I told them to fuck off. Gave them a fright, I think.'

She had to laugh, and for a brief moment thought how good it was to have Malone around. A brief moment only.

'Look … ' Malone hesitated; put his knife down on the plate. 'I know what you're trying to do.'

She narrowed her eyes. 'And what is that?'

'I know you want to help Catriona Devonshire because of what happened to Sasha.'

'So?' She was defiant. 'And anyway, not just Sasha but also because of Gus.'

'Gus?'

'More or less the same age, Malone. Imagine if something happened to Gus. I would want to know all the details. I would want to know exactly what had happened. I wouldn't rest. Cat wants to know, and I want to help. I have to do this, Malone.'

She became aware that Malone had his hand over hers. She removed hers. 'Where is he, Malone?'

It hurt having to ask him that. It hurt that Gus hadn't wanted to tell her he was looking for his father.

'Don't worry, he's in Europe. You know, it wasn't all about finding his father, this going away travelling. He wanted to spread his wings, reach out into the world a bit.'

'Thanks. That's comforting. Now I don't have to worry he's in some godforsaken country with no communications. And I know he wanted to spread his wings.' Alex was suddenly cross. 'I do know that. He is *my* son after all.' And she wanted to tell him that he'd lost the right to care about her son the day she turned him out of her house. 'So where have you sent him?'

'I haven't sent him anywhere.'

'Stop playing with words, Malone. You know damn well what I mean. Is he close to finding his father?'

'Steve Dann.'

'Steve Dann. I never knew his last name.' She let it sink in, wondering how she felt. Nothing. 'And have you found out where he's living?'

Malone nodded. 'It wasn't that easy because he left Ibiza shortly after you and he—'

'Met?'

Malone grinned. 'That'll do. Anyway, he led us a long and convoluted dance around the world as he's been working in clubs and bars from the Greek Islands to Brazil.'

'And now?'

'And now we think Steve Dann is back in Ibiza.'

'How much did Gus know before he left?'

Malone shrugged. 'Not much. We knew he was back in Europe. It was only yesterday we found out he was in Ibiza.'

The pounding in her head, the stinging of her cuts and bruises, and the pain in her heart all made her want to cry. 'And Steve, has he—?' She was going to ask if he was married, had a family, but all at once she didn't want Malone to tell her this; she wanted Gus to tell her. Where was he now? She had a sudden urge to see her son, to look at his face.

She opened up the Facebook app on her phone.

There he was. Four photos of Gus. In a bar. He had a big grin on his face and he looked relaxed and happy. In one of the photos he was grinning inanely, head next to a man with a goatee beard and wispy hair. Both of them wearing black grungy tee-shirts. Goatee Man had an arm slung across Gus's shoulder. Another photo showed him next to a pretty girl with dark curls and sparkly eyes, or maybe, that was just the light. They both looked happy in that one, too. For a moment her finger hovered over the screen, wondering whether she should 'like' one of the pictures. No, she told herself, don't interfere.

'See?' said Malone. 'He looks happy, doesn't he?'

'Oh, do stop looking over my shoulder,' she replied, irritably. 'Let me look at these in peace.'

Malone went back to his seat and began scraping butter onto more toast. That irritated her too. Everything about Malone was irritating her at the moment. As she drank in Gus's features she had to admit he did look happier than she'd seen him for a long while. Then she checked for what seemed like the hundredth time if Kiki Godwin had accepted her friend request.

She had.

There was a 'whooshing' noise telling her there was a message for her from Kiki Godwin, sent at that very moment. Her heart began to beat faster. Perhaps she was getting somewhere.

I can tell you more about Elena. Meet me in Karen's Kafe on the quayside in Mundesley. Today at one o'clock. Thanks.

And that was it. A stark message from this so-called Kiki Godwin. She looked at her watch. Plenty of time to get to Mundesley. It was only down the coast.

'Malone, I've got to go.'

Malone stopped mid-chew. 'I've only just got here.'

'You got here last night,' she pointed out. 'And I didn't ask you to come.'

'Don't you want to know why I'm here?'

Yes, she did. 'Apart from needing somewhere to crash? Not particularly. Save it for later. Lock the door behind you when you leave and put the key under the stone pig.'

Being in control felt good.

CHAPTER 19

The village was the slightly brasher sister of Sole Bay, thought Alex, as she walked along the beach road into Mundesley. An amusement arcade, one fish and chip shop on the front, and a couple of magnificent hotels built in the town's heyday as a seaside destination, all made her feel as though she had stepped back forty years. It was a good feeling. Safe. There was a shop selling touristy stuff: buckets, spades, windbreaks. Another café for tea, coffee, snacks. There was the odd boarded-up building, too, showing that not everyone had weathered the recession. The air was salty, vinegary with an overlay of suntan oil. People sat outside bars and cafés or meandered along the path just looking, some trying to avoid the deadly combination of hot parents and irritable children.

Alex stopped on the pavement for a moment, drinking it all in. She loved the seaside, particularly the seaside in East Anglia. There was nothing like it. Yes, it was hot, bloody hot at the moment, but this was the east coast and the winds from the Urals would soon be in evidence.

During the past two years of living in London, she had been desperate to escape the grimy air, full of diesel fumes and human skin. It was so crowded, sometimes she felt unable to breathe, so occasionally had gone to Brighton. That wasn't much better. Packed, as it was on warm days, where you sat shoulder to shoulder with a stranger on the pebble beach. That was not what she had been looking for. She had been looking for solitude and for certainty that whatever happened the waves would push and pull unceasingly along the shoreline. She didn't find the solitude, though the certainty from the sea was there. But she missed her home town; she missed the sunsets and the sunrises – she had stopped looking at the sky in London – and knew she would have to go back there one day, if only to slay the dragon of her continuing guilt. For now, the coast of North Norfolk was a good substitute.

The sudden ringing of a bell as a bicycle bore down towards Alex made her jump back onto the pavement. Bloody hell, danger from all sides. She was eager to find the café – or Kafe. There were side streets off the main drag, most of which were dead ends, ending at the promenade wall. The expanse of beach and sea below was magnificent. The sands stretched for miles, broken up by groynes that crept out into the water.

Then she saw a fingerpost pointing toward Karen's Kafe, down a street away from the beach. Soon she came to some ramshackle lock-ups – some not so locked up – with yawning doors showing piles of wooden crates and plastic boxes. A sign stuck on the steel side of a garage gave the speed limit as five miles per hour. There were fishermen's nets, old buckets: all kinds of paraphernalia. A couple of men were loading vans with old fridges and ovens, pieces of scrap metal. A shirtless young guy with impressive tattoos winding around his chest and down his arms and with even more impressive muscles was scooping up what looked like engine parts into his arms. He reminded Alex of Bobby.

She shivered despite the warm air, and looked over her shoulder. Did she imagine it, or did she see someone dodge out of sight around the corner? She shook her head. She was letting her imagination run away with her.

She saw the café in the distance. A young boy standing outside. Waiting for his mates? His mum? As she drew closer, she saw the boy was wearing a sweatshirt despite the heat of the day, and jeans that had seen better days. He was painfully thin: wrists sticking out from the too-short sleeves. His hair, greasy and unkempt, needed a good cut. He was vaguely familiar.

'Alex Devlin?'

The boy, who looked about sixteen, seventeen perhaps, blinked furiously at her.

'Yes. Are you—?'

He turned beetroot. 'Kiki Godwin. I know it seems silly, but yes that's me. I didn't want anyone to know it was me who was posting on the Facebook page so I thought that, not only would it be good to have a different name, but if I posted as a girl—'

'Shall we go into the café? Get a cup of coffee or a cold drink?' Alex said, wanting to stop the verbal diarrhoea.

'No,' said the boy, looking like a frightened rabbit about to bolt at any moment. 'I thought there wouldn't be anyone around here.'

'Well, there's hardly anybody. Just a couple of men in white vans. The odd fisherman picking up his nets. That's all.'

'Can we go for a walk? Perhaps find a bench?' The boy tried to pull the sleeves of his sweatshirt down over his hands as if to ward off the cold. He didn't manage it. He didn't look Alex in the eye.

Eventually they found a formal patch of grass with long, tidy beds of summer flowers that reminded Alex of the tiny plastic toy flowers she used to push into their plastic flowerbeds as a child. There were, luckily, plenty of benches, some under wooden pagodas; one was occupied by a couple eating fish and chips, probably to keep out of the way of the seagulls circling around. At the end of the park was a square tower: the coastguard lookout, Alex had read on the village information board earlier. The boy sat on a bench overlooking the promenade and the sea. The inscription on it made Alex smile: 'This bench is dedicated to Albert Kings who hated Mundesley and all the people living here'. The flat sea slopped lazily to shore. Alex tried not to wince as she sat down, her damaged muscles protesting.

'What have you done?' The boy pointed at Alex's face as he jiggled his legs, the fingers of one hand beating a tattoo on the thin material at the knees. Alex noticed his fingernails were bitten right down, the skin by the sides of his thumbs ragged and red.

Alex grimaced and put her hand up to the bruise on her cheek just under her eye. It was sore and turning from a deep purple to green and yellow. When she had caught sight of herself in the mirror that morning she thought it looked like the colours of a Suffolk sunset.

'Altercation with the foot of a youth.'

The boy looked horrified. 'Was it Felix? Or Theo?' he whispered.

'What makes you think it was either of those two?' Alex asked in a mild tone.

'Sort of thing they'd do.'

Alex remembered where she'd seen him before. 'I saw you coming out of the head teachers' office didn't I? The other day? It's Max, isn't it?'

The boy nodded. 'I ... '

Alex put a hand on his arm. She felt the bone through the sleeve. So thin. 'It's all right, Max. I want to help, I really do.'

Max sniffed, rubbing his nose with the back of his hand.

'Were you a friend of Elena's?' she asked, gently.

He sat perching on the edge of the bench, ready to run at any moment. Alex knew she had to tread carefully.

'Yes. She was good to me. Not like Felix and Theo and that lot. Or those bloody Queen Bees.'

'Queen Bees?'

'Naomi and Natasha and Jenni and Helen. That lot. They all treated me like their pet.' He began to chew the side of his thumb. 'That's all I was to them, really. A pet. To do their bidding. And I did, too. I wanted to belong. Like her friend Tara, and that awful day—'

'What awful day was that, Max?'

Alex knew she had to keep it calm, friendly.

'I don't want to talk about it,' he muttered.

'Was it to do with drugs?'

Max's head jerked up.

'I know there's a problem, Max. There is everywhere. And I've come across Felix and Theo. And someone called Bobby.'

'They are fucking awful,' he said, quietly. 'Dregs of this world, I reckon.'

'Why don't you tell someone, Max?'

'Elena did. She shouldn't have done because they said they would hurt her if she did.'

'So Elena tried to do something about the drugs in the school?'

'That's what I said, didn't I?'

'Did the people involved – the dealers, the pushers – did they have something to do with her death? Did they kill her, Max?'

Max blinked hard. 'She wasn't killed.'

Alex looked out over the sea. A family of three grown-up children and their parents walked past, chattering, bickering, one of them carrying a bag from the fish and chip shop. Overhead, a man paragliding rode the warm air currents while gulls flew around him. An elderly man in shorts, socks, and sandals walked slowly by with a greying collie on a lead. For one moment Alex wished she was at home in London, writing an article and frantically trying to hit a deadline; Gus out somewhere playing football with his mates. Instead, she was here, sitting on a wooden bench in a formal park looking over sand and sea with a young and troubled lad. And her son was somewhere in Europe. She rubbed her forehead.

'I loved her.' Max's voice was quiet. 'I loved her, but she didn't want to know. Not really. Oh, she was kind enough to me and all that, but I was in the year below and I'm not exactly a great specimen, am I?' He smiled sadly at Alex. She looked at his pinched face, greasy skin and hair, at his thin limbs, and her heart twisted in sympathy.

'Tell me about Tara.'

'I can't.'

'Max. Please?'

He sighed heavily. 'It was after the exams. They were all celebrating. Elena went back to the school, but they kept on celebrating. There was drink and cocaine and skunk and God knows what. Tara got wasted. I was there as someone they could boss around.'

Alex guessed what had happened. 'And she was raped.'

'Not raped. Not really. I mean, she was totally out of it.'

'It was rape, Max, and you know it.'

He hung his head. 'Maybe. She left school before Elena died.'

'Why?'

'Dunno.'

Alex thought she knew the reason and made a mental note to check it out.

'You say Elena wasn't killed, Max, but you posted on the Facebook tribute page. That's why we're here. You said she didn't kill herself.'

'I—'

'Why did you post it if you didn't mean it? Come on Max, help me out here.'

'I don't know. I don't know.' He chewed his lip and Alex saw beads of blood appear at the corners of his mouth. 'Maybe I just wanted to say something. To be part of it. But Elena did kill herself. She threw herself off the cliff.'

'How do you know?'

'What?'

'How do you know she threw herself off the cliff?'

'I … well … I saw it.'

'You saw it?'

'Yes. I was there.'

'Why?'

'Why?'

'Why were you there?'

'I had followed her to talk to her and then I saw her go over the edge. It was deliberate.' His answer was delivered in a monotone, almost as if he had rehearsed it.

Everything was telling her, every journalistic instinct was screaming at her, that Max was lying. She would not entertain the thought that Elena had taken her own life. It didn't feel right. And she wasn't going to go back to Cat without answers. She wasn't going to let her down again.

'I don't believe you.'

Max didn't look at her. 'It's true.' Suddenly he jumped up. 'I'm telling you she was sad and not eating and under pressure and she threw herself off the cliff and I don't know why I said what I did on that Facebook page and I'm sorry, all right?' And he ran off as if the Hound of the Baskervilles were after him.

Still Alex didn't believe him. Something had made him post on that page. Something had made him want to meet her. And something, or someone, had put pressure on him.

'Well, if it isn't our favourite hack.'

Alex looked up to see Felix, Theo, and another boy swaggering towards her. Theo gave her what she could only think of as a wolfish smile. It made her feel sick. They were a far cry from the urbane, charming if shallow young men she had met when she first arrived in Hallow's Edge and had visited the school. Now they looked more like the thugs she knew them to be. She stood up to face them.

'Yeah,' said Felix, his hands in the back pockets of his jeans. 'Our favourite piece of shit.' He leaned in close. She could smell some sort of spicy aftershave. Expensive. 'Nice shiner you've got there.'

'How did she get that?' This from the third boy who looked to be cut from the same mould as the other two: floppy hair, faded jeans, muscle-hugging tee-shirt, trying to look menacing. He put his head onto one side. 'Looks like you bumped into a wall.' He grinned, showing even, white teeth that Alex wanted to push down his miserable throat.

'Must have, Ollie,' said Felix. He winked at Alex.

She narrowed her eyes. 'You little shit.' Clenching her fists, she heard children laughing; the fish and chip family talking loudly, laughing; a dog barking; the noise of a car engine. They were so cocksure, these lads with their sense of entitlement and their certain knowledge that the world owed them a living, owed them everything, that the bubble of rage and frustration burned in her gullet until it threatened to spew out in a lava flow of anger. She was sick and tired of being played for a fool. She stood, trying not to wince in front of the boys, then grabbed the neck of Theo's tee-shirt and yanked him in close to her.

'Listen up, you little prick.' She almost spat in his face. 'I don't know if you had anything to do with Elena's death, but if you did, know this: I'm going to find out about it. And what's more, you are going to pay for attacking me last night.'

'Attacking you?' This from Felix. He was laughing at her. Laughing. 'Where did you get that idea from?'

Alex pushed Theo away from her so hard that he stumbled into the bench and sat down hard. She turned to Felix. 'You are nothing but a coward.' She pushed at his chest. He stumbled backwards. 'A silly little boy who is nothing,' she pushed again, 'but a coward.' Another push. 'Probably a mummy's boy as well.' Another push, and he stumbled, tripped over a stone and fell onto his backside. She poked at him with her foot. He tried to scramble backwards. She pushed him harder. Theo and Ollie looked on, frozen in their astonishment.

'Fuck,' he shouted. 'What the fuck are you doing?'

The fish and chip family were staring at them, open-mouthed. They'd put ketchup on their chips, thought Alex. She smiled. 'A mummy's boy. No balls. Or very small ones. People like you find it hard to let go of the apron strings. A coward and a bully. You know it and soon everyone will know it.' She stalked off.

For the second time that day she felt good.

But now she ought to look for Max. She couldn't let him

wander around Mundesley in that state, and especially if Theo and Felix and – who was the other one? Ollie, that was it, Ollie – were hanging around. And especially after she had humiliated them.

She began to walk towards the centre of the village.

The place was busy. People, bicycles, cars were everywhere. Alex peered into shop doorways, the front of cafés – no luck. Then she saw a tall, thin man with grey hair coming out of a mini-market with a carrier bag. Something about his furtive movements made Alex look twice. Sven Farrar. Too much of a coincidence? She hurried towards him, about to call out, when he climbed into a Range Rover parked on double yellow lines. And in the front seat was a boy with a scared white face. Max. What was he doing in the front of Farrar's car?

She shrank back against a brick wall as the Range Rover went past her. Farrar and Max were looking straight ahead. They didn't see her.

Now all she had to do was figure out why Max, Sven Farrar, and the lads from The Drift were in Mundesley — at the same time.

CHAPTER 20

It was mid-afternoon by the time she parked her car at the cottage.

The front door was wide open. Okay, so she had told Malone to lock up when he left. Did that mean there was someone in her house? Malone wouldn't forget to do as she'd asked. The side of her face ached; she had the beginnings of yet another headache behind her eye, and one of her legs was still stiff, the ankle swollen.

Could it be burglars? She stood stock still, trying not to think about the cottage being trashed or someone (Bobby?) going through her things or – she heard voices coming from some-where – the kitchen, she thought – and someone was whistling. She tiptoed around the house to the open kitchen window, crouching down so she couldn't be seen, clutching her phone in one hand and a large stone she had just picked up in the other. If bloody Theo or Felix had come to the cottage she would call the police, and wouldn't hesitate to hit one of them with the stone, if necessary.

No, it couldn't be them. They wouldn't have got back here before she did.

Slowly she uncurled herself until her eyes were level with the windowsill. The voices were louder. She could see the back of someone. Someone who had an apron tied around his waist and who was merrily cutting up tomatoes and cucumbers, putting them into the salad bowl as he did so. The radio was on, a programme about football blasting from it.

'Malone,' she said. Large as life and just as ugly; Malone was making up a salad and some sort of sauce was bubbling away on the hob.

Malone turned, dramatically clutching his heart and looking absurd in the Cath Kidston apron. 'Good God, woman. Don't be creeping up on people like that. I could have shot you or thrown a knife at you.'

'You're too busy playing bloody Mary Berry in my kitchen,' she said, furious with adrenaline.

'Strictly speaking, this isn't your house, and Mary Berry is more well-known for her cakes, not her sauce Puttanesca. This is the luscious Nigella.'

'Malone, will you stop going on about it. I don't care who's cooking what. I want to know what you're doing?'

'Cooking you supper, what else? Thought I'd get started early.'

'And I thought I would have some lunch, do some research, and try and speak to my son. So you can bugger off.' Adrenaline made her even more angry.

'Why don't you come inside rather than shout at me through the window? Or, better still, go round and sit on the terrace with your computer, and I'll bring you out some cheese on toast.'

'Malone,' she said, exasperated. What was he doing in the cottage anyway? What gave him the right to stand there in a stupid pinny cooking spaghetti and sauce? 'I don't want cheese on toast.' Actually, it sounded rather good. 'And I don't want your supper.'

'Or is your new friend coming for a visit? Because if he is, there isn't enough to go round.'

'New friend? What new friend?' Bloody headache was threatening her ability to think.

Malone's smile turned to a glower. 'The man in the towel.'

'The man in the … oh, you mean Jonny?' That man and his jealousy, not that he had any right to be jealous. None at all. Absolutely none. 'Now look, I am going to sit on the terrace and do what I want to do.' She stamped off, trying to ignore her stiff leg, feeling like a disgruntled teenager.

The terrace was peaceful with the sun sending golden slivers of light over the sea and the gentle swish of the waves on the beach below. Gradually her irritation at Malone seeped away. The warmth of the day was bringing out distant scents of honeysuckle and rosemary. She wondered when the heatwave was going to end. And she wondered about Max, why he'd been in the car with Farrar just after meeting her. The answer was obvious: Farrar had wanted her to meet Max. The question was why?

Max. She frowned, thinking back to when she had first seen him outside the Farrars' office. Max Delauncey, that's what Felix had called him. Delauncey. The name nagged at her. There had been a big story about a Delauncey a few years ago. She logged on to her computer, bringing up Google, and typed in the name. She hit return.

The search brought up the website of Delauncey Construction, as well as invitations to view the profiles of individuals of that name on LinkedIn. Even the website of a dancer of that name who seemed to specialize in exotic dancing. But there, near the bottom of the page, was what she wanted: a news article from the *East Anglian Daily Times*.

Tragedy strikes Delauncey family

The brother and nephew of Essex construction tycoon Edward Delauncey have died in a speedboat accident off the coast of Suffolk.

Henry Delauncey and his 18-year-old son Timothy died when their boat hit a wave and capsized off Lowestoft. His 12-year-old son, Max, survived the accident.

It is the second time the family has been dogged by tragedy. Henry Delauncey's wife, Amelia, was killed in a car accident in Spain three years ago.

She couldn't bear to read any more. That poor kid. He must be so angry with the world. Losing his whole family like that. Scrolling through more news stories she came across accounts of the investigation into the speedboat accident, the funerals of Henry and Timothy Delauncey, the inquest. Then a little footnote: childless Edward Delauncey was to be Max Delauncey's official guardian, and Max was to attend his father's old boarding school in Norfolk.

Alex looked at the words for a long time. Then she typed 'The Drift' and 'Police' into the browser bar. There it was, a BBC News Online story in March.

A teenage boy is being questioned about a stabbing of a teacher at a school in North Norfolk.

The victim suffered an arm injury when he was attacked at The Drift, a co-educational school in the village of Hallow's Edge.

She looked again, finding another story from the end of March …

Charges have been dropped in the case of a 16-year-old boy accused of the stabbing of a teacher at a school in North Norfolk.

Now all she had to do was to find out if the boy in question was Max Delauncey, and she had an idea how to do that. If it was, and Sven Farrar had managed to persuade the teacher in question to drop the charges, effectively covering up the whole affair, then Farrar could have some sort of hold over Max. Then she had to wonder whether Farrar would make Max talk to her, tell her Elena's death was not suspicious. How far would the head teacher go to protect the reputation of the school?

She found The Drift's website. 'Let's have a look round,' she muttered.

News. That's what she wanted. She scrolled through items about a science day at Norwich Castle (lucky them), new prefects, pupils raising money for the homeless (yes, well) quickly followed by an item about pupils enjoying a skiing trip to Canada. Then she found what she was looking for: an item about the opening of a new drama studio the year before. *With grateful thanks to His Honour Mr Justice Lodge for his very generous donation that enabled us to go ahead with the project.*

Surely that was no coincidence? Had to be horrible Theo's dad.

She then looked at the profiles of the Farrars. They had been at the school for the past five years, transforming it from a public school that struggled to attract pupils to one where many of the rich and famous wanted to send their children. And so a great deal of money had flooded into the school's coffers. 'And I bet they don't want to lose any of their wealthy parents,' Alex muttered. More money into the school equalled more salary for them. And more power. She read on until she saw something that made her pause: Ingrid Farrar, née Brewer, had been married to Sven Farrar for fifteen years.

Brewer.

Alex leaned back in her chair. Couldn't be a coincidence. Zena Brewer was Ingrid Farrar's sister. The woman who had told Cat she'd tried to contact her several times about Elena, but from whom Cat had never received a call or an email or a text. The woman Louise Churchill had described as a 'bit useless'. So in all probability Zena Brewer would get to stay on at the school whatever her abilities, and would have to dance to Ingrid Farrar's tune. Nothing like jobs for the relatives.

She needed that talk with Zena Brewer. But first things first.

She sent a text to Honey, wanting her to ask Sy for Dutch's number.

Her phone bleeped a few moments later. Great. Alex rang Jonny Dutch. Answerphone. Bloody things. Why couldn't people just pick up? 'Jonny. It's Alex here. Alex Devlin. Thanks for your help yesterday. And I'm sorry about Malone. Could you call me about Zena Brewer? Oh, and Paul Churchill and where he taught. Thanks.' She looked at her watch wondering if Kylie was on shift at the pub. She would go along later and test out her theory.

'Dutch? Why are you apologizing about me to him?' Malone put an espresso in front of her, made with that bloody complicated machine. Trust him. And then, with a flourish, a slice of cheese on toast. Topped with a tomato.

'Oh, shut up, Malone. Leave it. Get back to the cooking. I'm going to try Gus now.'

'That man's no good for you.'

'You don't know anything about him.'

'Yes I do. I checked him out.'

Alex looked at Malone. He had the ability to make her so angry. 'Well, you shouldn't have done.'

'Listen to me—'

Alex held up her hand. 'I am not going to listen to you. I'm going to eat this toast – for which, thank you very much – and try to get hold of Gus. I haven't spoken to him since he left; I've only seen a few pictures. I do not want to think about you or Jonny, so leave me alone.'

Malone stared at her, then turned and went back to the kitchen.

Best place for him.

Alex pressed Gus's number for the third time, swallowing the last of the cheese on toast, which, she had to admit, was pretty good.

She was oscillating between being annoyed and worried. He knew she would be wanting to hear from him: how he was getting on, where he was staying, who he had met. When he had proposed the trip around Europe she was just grateful he didn't want to go to the Far East or the wilds of Borneo or anywhere else where she would worry about bad company, about people slipping drugs into his luggage, about crooked police throwing him in jail. She knew she was being silly, but she couldn't help it. So Europe had seemed a pretty safe bet to her.

'You're to keep in touch, Gus,' she'd told him when she'd first agreed to him going travelling. Before she knew of his ulterior motive.

'Of course I will, Ma,' he'd said, giving her a hug. She'd noticed how he had to stoop down to put his arms around her, how his shoulders felt more broad. She knew he had been putting in time in the gym and going for long runs. Running, he told her, cleared his mind. All he thought about was putting one foot in front of the other and the way his body was moving, how he was breathing. He loved to feel the wind and rain and sun on his face. When he was running, he told her, he wasn't Gus Devlin, cousin of two 4-year-olds who were murdered by their mother, but he was plain old Gus. Alex could understand that. Even though they had made the move to London, the story of her sister Sasha and Harry and Millie followed them. Which was why, when he told her he wanted to leave school and travel somewhere where nobody would know him, she could hardly refuse. He needed to find out who he was.

'But what about your exams?' she'd said, bewildered.

He'd shrugged. 'They'll be there when I get back.'

'But—'

He'd turned away from her then. 'Mum. I have to do this. I'm going mental here. I need to get away. And don't tell me I'm too young, I reckon I'm older than most guys around here.'

The ringtone went on. Pick up, Gus, please.

Anything could have happened to him. He could be lying dead in a gutter somewhere. Dead in a field. In an alleyway. He could be—

'Hey, Mum.'

There he was. He waved at her, grinning. He looked tired but relaxed. His shoulders weren't all hunched up around his ears and he didn't have that worried frown that had been part of his expression for some time. He also looked as though he could do with a good bath. And was he a bit thin? She did hope he was eating properly and not existing on … oh, listen to yourself, Alex. Shut up, for goodness' sake. He was in some sort of bar. She could see bottles on the wall behind him. Crowds of people standing, sitting. The lighting was low. There was a lot of laughter and chatting and clinking of bottles in the background.

'Where are you, sweetheart?'

'Spain.'

Of course.

'I met a guy called Dave.' On cue, the guy called Dave came into view, gurning for the iPhone. At least he wasn't the guy with the goatee beard she'd seen in his Facebook photographs. She couldn't trust a man with a goatee beard. Gus pushed Dave out of the way. 'He says his cousin can get us some hotel work for a few weeks. It'll be awesome.' His smile grew even wider. 'I need to earn some money. I'm thinking of going to the Greek islands in September so need to get some cash in.' He looked happy and well.

No you're not, my darling, thought Alex. If you find your dad, you'll be staying in Ibiza.

He frowned. 'What have you done to your face, Mum?'

Her fingers went involuntarily up to the bruise around her eye. Damn. She'd forgotten to cover it up. 'That? Walked into a wall, literally. Stupid, I know. But never mind me, as long as you're happy.'

'I'm happy, yeah.' His eyes darted from side to side and he pulled on his eyebrow with two fingers, a sure sign he was uncomfortable.

'Gus—' Alex wanted to ask him how the search for his dad was going, whether he had an address, knew where he was going. Whether he'd managed to get in touch with him. 'Gus, when you left you said you were going to look for your dad.'

'Yeah.'

Alex swallowed hard. 'I've spoken to Malone. He says he's been helping you and—'

'Yeah?' His face brightened. 'You've spoken to Malone? That's cool, Mum, really it is. And you're not mad at me?'

She looked at him. Her boy. She smiled. 'No sweetheart, I'm not mad at you. I just want you to be happy and if this makes you happy then how can I be mad at you?'

'Thanks, Mum.'

'The hotel work—'

'It's on Ibiza, Ma.' He turned his head slightly away from the phone. 'It's just my mum. She worries about me.'

185

To his credit, he didn't roll his eyes. Not that she could see, anyway.

'Gotta go now, Ma. Some serious drinking to be done.' He laughed as he shook his head. 'I know what you're thinking, and yes, I am eating properly. Talk to you later. And watch that alcohol intake. I don't want you walking into any more walls.' He waved.

'When—?' His picture disappeared and she was left looking at her own face. Too late. Good job probably. She mustn't keep trying to pin him down.

Alex sat down, still holding the phone, as if putting it down would mean finally letting him go. But then she'd done that already, hadn't she? Let him go. Her boy in a maroon Babygro. All her life she had tried to protect him from things: from Sasha, from the horror of the twins' murders, from negative publicity. She had seen that as her job. Perhaps it was time to let him go properly. She rubbed her temples.

'So, did you get through to him?'

'I did.'

'How's he doing?'

'Fine.' She wasn't going to make this easy for him.

'Thought you might like a glass of wine.' Malone put a full glass of red in front of her. 'So where is he?'

'Spain.'

He raised an eyebrow.

'He's going to Ibiza. I guess an Englishman of about forty-five called Steve Dann shouldn't be too hard to find.'

He took her hand. 'You're doing really well.'

Alex shook his hand away and took a large gulp of the wine. 'Don't talk to me as if I'm about nine. I'm not "doing really well". I'm fuming. I'm angry with Gus for wanting to find his father; I'm angry with you for helping him, and I'm angry with me for not wanting him to find Steve. And I'm sad that I'm not enough for him.'

'Alex—'

'Why did you have to do it, Malone? Why interfere?' She banged her fist on the table. Some of the wine slopped onto the cloth, staining it red. 'What are you doing here anyway? Where is your wife? Or have you conveniently forgotten about her again?'

'I told you, we are divorced now,' he said mildly.

'Oh, for fuck's sake.' Alex's chair fell onto the tiles with a clatter as she stood up. She leaned across the table. 'Gus is still a child.'

'He's eighteen.'

'He's still my child. And as a child he sees things in black and white; they don't see other colours.' The other colours that could be brought on by conflicting emotions and messy relationships. Messy, dirty, multi-coloured relationships. 'He won't understand.'

'Won't understand what?'

'What I did.' Furious, she blinked away tears.

'Alex. You had a one-night stand that resulted in you becoming pregnant. You had a baby. You brought him up. He's a great lad and you've done a great job. It's happened before and it'll happen again, so stop beating yourself up about it. He'll understand.'

She glared at him, hurt flaring in every pore. She didn't know which was worse: Gus getting in touch with Malone without her knowing, Malone telling him about Ibiza, or Gus wanting to find out about his father. Or, another voice said, Gus growing up and away from you. Not needing you.

'I've had enough of this. I need some fresh air.' She stood up straight.

'We are in the fresh air,' he pointed out in a mild tone. 'And you haven't finished your wine.'

'Oh, bugger off, Malone. And I don't even like red wine. I'd've thought you would remember that, at least.'

Alex marched away from the cottage wanting to put as much distance between herself and Malone as she could. He was an impossible man. Irritating. Infuriating. Pops up like a case of toothache just when you don't need him. Gus was her son, nothing to do with him.

Bastard.

Before she knew it she found herself at the end of the road where Elena had gone over the cliff. She stood and breathed in the clear air and wondered for the umpteenth time what she was doing there. Was she chasing a friend's dream? No, she had to see it through to the end, whatever 'it' was.

She turned to go, when she saw an old man shuffling along, pushing a pram and heading towards the dilapidated caravan.

'Mr Gardiner,' she called out. 'Can I talk to you for a minute?'

Reg Gardiner looked up, briefly, then pushed his pram faster. Alex hurried towards him.

'Mr Gardiner. Reg. I'm sorry; I only want to have a word with you about the young girl you found on the beach.'

Reg stopped. 'I only found her, you know.'

Alex nodded. 'I know. I was wondering if you saw anything else. When you found her, I mean.'

He squinted at her. 'What are you? Police?'

'No.' Something stopped her telling him she was a journalist.

'Only, I don't want no police around, not no more. I'm done with them. I did my time and I didn't do anything to that girl. Nothing. I just found the poor lass, that's all. That's all. Now leave me alone. I did nothing.'

Alex put her hand on his arm. 'Reg, I know that. In fact, it was wonderful that you found her before she was washed out to sea. Otherwise, her mum, my friend, would never have known what happened to her.'

'I was worried, you know, that them journalists would rake it all up again. Even though it happened years ago. Years.'

Alex nodded, hoping he was going to tell her more.

'It was my wife. She disappeared. Was never found. I was questioned over and over again, but I didn't have anything to do

with it. She'd just gone. That's all. I left my house and then … '
His filmy eyes watered. 'I just wandered. Ended up here.'

Alex patted his arm. 'It's all right, Reg. Really.'

Reg nodded, and started shuffling towards his caravan once more. Alex watched him go.

He stopped at its door. 'There was something,' he said. 'A figure. Small. On the top of the cliff. Couldn't see if it were a man or a woman. But they were there. Watching.'

Reg went back into his house.

That was interesting. Someone making sure Elena was found?

She was glad to see the pub was quite quiet when she arrived. No sign of Dutch or the boys from The Drift, or Bobby, or any of his mates. Christ, she was getting paranoid. But then, just because you're paranoid doesn't mean they're not out to get you. And Kylie was behind the bar.

'You're early,' the barmaid said, reaching into the fridge for a bottle of wine. 'The usual?'

Alex nodded, rather liking that she was becoming a bit of a local. Either that or a bit of a lush. 'One for yourself?'

'Ta.'

'Kylie—'

'Oh dear. Sounds like you're after information.' Her bracelets jangled as she drank her wine, leaning over the bar. 'Not getting very far with finding out about the girl, Elena?'

'No, I'm getting somewhere, I think.' Alex made herself comfortable on the bar stool. There was no one else around. 'Kylie, do you know anything about a stabbing? At The Drift? I think it was in March, so not too long ago?'

Kylie looked at her, and Alex thought she was not going to say anything. Then she smiled. 'Bloody hell, it was the talk of the village. I mean, I know we've got some rough ones here in Hallow's Edge, but, bloody hell, they're rougher up there.'

Alex didn't like to mention Bobby.

Kylie refilled their glasses. 'I know that nothing much happened in the end. We had the cops here, of course, but not much else. I think all the teachers were forbidden to talk about it or something.'

'Forbidden?'

'Yeah, so one of 'em said when I asked. In their contracts or something, I don't know.'

'But—'

'But not a lot gets past us.' She winked. 'What do you want to know?'

'Who was the boy?'

'Poor kid. I felt sorry for him. No family and cooped up at that miserable school. Name of Max Delauncey. My brother used to work for Delauncey down in Witham so I know all about his family all being dead. I don't think he really meant to hurt anyone. Though they do say he bought the knife in Mundesley and took it into school, deliberate, like. It wasn't that he took it in to show people and then something went wrong. No, I heard he'd planned it.'

'Can't have liked the teacher much.' Alex knew she had to let Kylie tell the story in her own time.

'That's for sure. I was surprised, actually. About the teacher.'

'Who was it?'

'Tulip. You know, Jonny Dutch. He's the one that got stabbed.'

CHAPTER 21

ELENA

September: ten weeks before she dies

I stand in the doorway of the canteen, my hand unconsciously stroking the silver ring on my finger.

Michaelmas term. Breakfast time at The Drift and the air is alive with the buzz of chatter; the volume and pitch rising ever higher as everybody tries to make themselves heard. Every one of them believing their opinion is more important than anyone else's. The teachers who struggle in, eager to show commitment, already look worn out with the noise.

I smell the bleach and polish; the aroma of bacon and eggs and burned toast is only starting to make an impression; later, the institutional mince and cabbage smell will layer the air. The boarders have been up for half an hour; roused out of their beds by the Larks: specially selected students who had to make sure everybody was up, washed, dressed, and ready for breakfast by eight o'clock.

Tara waves at me. I go over and sit at her table. 'You were throwing up again this morning,' I say.

She hangs her head miserably. Her skin is grey and she looks pudgier than ever.

'Tara, you've got to talk to me.' I grip her hand.

'I'm fine,' she says, withdrawing her hand. 'Just a tummy bug. Promise.'

I look at her and I know, pill or no pill, it is more than a tummy bug, but she won't acknowledge it. She doesn't want to acknowledge it. We have talked about what happened that day last term down on the beach, and she won't see that it was rape. 'I was all right. Honest. I knew what was happening and I wanted it.' And then she would start crying again.

She wasn't all right. Not at all.

I feel guilty stuffing myself with bacon and tomato as I watch Tara picking at hers, pushing it around the plate. 'You must eat,' I say.

She shrugs.

'Okay Tars?' Felix Devine stops at the table. 'We're having a bit of a party later. In our study room, if you're free to come?'

'Thanks, Felix.' Tara tries to muster a smile. 'I'm not sure.'

'All the boys'll be there: you know, all the ones you like.' He winks. Looks at me. Smiles. 'You're not invited.'

'Thank God for that. You had me worried there.'

He walks off.

'You're not going to go, are you Tars?'

'Dunno.'

'Oh, come on, you know they're only after one thing. And there's always drugs and stuff at those parties.'

'So?'

'It's not good for you.'

'So?'

Tara has lost it. Totally lost it.

I look across at Naomi. She is yakking on as usual and Helen and Nat and Jenni are hanging on to her every word. Probably talking about food and diets and pro-ana sites. I've been there, done that, got the feeding tube to prove it. I can laugh about it now, but having an eating disorder really is no joke.

'So, what's with the ring?'

'What?'

'The ring.' Tara points at me. 'On your finger, duh.' She nibbles on a piece of toast.

'Oh. That.' My hand goes to stroke the silver ring. It's like a talisman now. All will be well if I stroke it ten times in the morning and twelve in the afternoon. Don't ask me how I came up with those particular numbers; I just know it works. 'A birthday present. It's nothing.' *It's everything.* I'm lucky, but Tara …

I make a decision.

I stand up.

'Where are you going?' asks Tara.

'I've just remembered I've left my essay in our room and I've got to hand it in today. I'll see you later.'

I try not to run out of the dining room, but if I don't hurry I might change my mind.

I knock at the Farrars' door. I'm sweaty and shaky and when I am standing in front of Sven and Ingrid Farrar I wonder if I have made the right decision, but as I tell them about the drugs – what I think is happening in the school, that there is an inexhaustible supply, and who is behind it – a weight lifts off my shoulders. I nearly tell them about Tara, but know she would hate me forever. I am going to have to find some other way of getting her to face facts.

'So,' says Mr Farrar, 'Felix Devine and Theo Lodge are the main culprits, you say?'

I nod.

'Have you any evidence? Anything concrete?' This from Ingrid Farrar.

'No pictures or anything, only that I've seen them.'

'Where are they getting the drugs from?'

I shake my head. 'I don't know.'

The grilling goes on until I feel as though I am the one who is in the wrong. The Farrars want to know times, dates, places.

They want evidence. They want stuff that I haven't got. All I can say is that I've seen it with my own eyes. They seem unwilling to believe me. Eventually Mr Farrar smiles, well, stretches his thin lips.

'Thank you for bringing this to our attention, Elena. We will certainly be looking into it.'

And that's it.

I leave their office wondering if I have done the right thing. I know that Theo and Felix have families with influence, parents who give stacks of cash to the school: perhaps that's more important? But at least I've done something.

It's late in the afternoon and I am doing some work in the library. Theo and Felix swagger in. The three or four other people who've been working in the library alongside me pack up their books and leave hurriedly. Okay, so this is not going to be pleasant, but they can't hurt me. Not here.

'So you took yourself off to the heads and snitched, yeah?' This from Theo. It's unnerving; both him and Felix are smiling at me. 'What did you think would happen? That we'd get expelled? Suspended? Zero tolerance and all that?'

I say nothing.

Theo pushes his face into mine. 'They've hauled us over the carpet, yeah? We've had our privileges taken away, yeah? And our parents are probably going to go apeshit for a while. But that's it.' He smiles, waves his hand around the library. 'Who do you think paid for this? What would happen if me and Felix and Ollie and Ivan had to go? The cash for the school would dry up. They'd take my younger sister away too; Ollie's brother. Theo's baby brother wouldn't be sent here. Do you think the Farrars would want that? No they fucking wouldn't.' He pushes me. 'Keep your nose out of it, Devonshire. You've no idea what you're meddling in. None at all.'

They swagger off, Felix throwing me a smile over his shoulder.

I can't say I didn't expect that.
My phone buzzes.

Hallo You. It's Me.
Are you all right?
Come and see me.

CHAPTER 22

June

The heatwave showed no signs of abating. East Anglia hadn't seen the like of it for ten years, according to the local radio weather forecaster. Alex switched the radio off. She had woken early, her room too stifling for sleep. She dressed quickly and quietly, putting her swimming costume on underneath her dress, and crept downstairs, wanting to get out of the house without waking Malone. It was the second night he had slept in the cottage; the second night he had made himself comfortable on the cracked brown leather sofa in the sitting room, covering himself with the duvet from the spare room. He preferred to sleep there, he told her, rather than sleeping next door to her, just a heartbeat away. He'd grinned when he said that. Alex did not.

The air outside was still early morning bright and the sea even looked inviting, small waves with white horses making their way to shore. The beach was fresh and new. Slipping off her dress she ran into the water, gasping with the cold of it and shouting out loud as the salt got into her cuts and grazes. She dived under the waves and came up again shaking her head, breathless from the chill. She had been wrong all this time. Swimming in the North Sea was exhilarating. It washed everything clean, made her feel alive. She struck out towards the horizon with a steady rhythm.

She turned onto her back and floated lazily in the water, enjoying the feeling that she could be the only one in the world. There were no sounds but for the occasional cry from a seagull above. The water lapped around her body.

Flipping herself back onto her front, she realized she had drifted a long way from the shore. She began to swim, all at once feeling the tug of a current beneath the water. Cold began to seep into her bones. Stupid. So stupid not to have known she was being pulled out to sea. Stupid to think the sea was really that warm. She blocked out the fear that threatened to seep into her mind. She was a strong swimmer and she wasn't that far from land.

Arm over her head into the water. Hand. Scoop the water behind. Kick her legs. Ignore the water in her ears. Breathe. Ignore the water in her mouth. Breathe. Arm over her head into the water. Hand. Scoop the water behind. Breathe. Breathe. Kick legs. Breathe. Fight the current, the numbing cold.

At last she could feel sand beneath her feet. Exhausted, she stumbled ashore and threw herself down, and lay panting on her back with her arm over her eyes to block out the sun.

'Are you okay?'

Alex took her arm away from her face and opened one eye. She sat up, dusting the sand and small stones off her sides. 'George. What are you doing here?'

'I've got a free study period first thing.'

Of course she had. Alex smiled at her. 'It's okay. I'm not questioning you, I was wondering, that's all. And yes, I'm fine thanks. Swam out a bit too far.'

George hugged her knees, her hand brushing the sand and shingle by her side to and fro. 'I heard you'd been, y'know, attacked and that.'

'Who told you?'

'Felix.'

'What did he say?' She had to be careful here, ignore the surge of animosity that had risen in her throat. However sweet George was, she still thought the sun shone out of Felix's arse.

'Said you deserved it. An' he laughed.' Her voice was muffled as she lowered her head onto her knees. 'I told him he shouldn't laugh at that sort of thing, and he told me to eff off.'

'George, you know it was Felix who attacked me? And Theo and another boy?' Their voices were still in her head, those cultured mocking tones. And Felix was the sort of boy who thought he could control everyone in his orbit.

'No. No.' She banged her head on her knees.

'I can't prove it, not yet, but it was them. Look at me.'

George lifted her head and the expression on her face was tragic and tears streaked her cheeks.

'Look at this.' Alex pointed to the bruise on her face. 'And these.' She showed George the cuts and grazes on her arms and legs. 'They threatened me.'

Alex thought back to when she had confronted Theo and Felix and Ollie in Mundesley. The way they sneered. They mustn't be allowed to get away with it. But then, nor must she be allowed to be side-tracked from what she was here for, after all: to find out the truth about Elena's death. And there was no doubt there was a truth to be discovered; her talk with Max yesterday had proved that. And she would discover that truth.

'Threatened you? What do you mean?'

'Told me to keep out of things. They almost pushed me off the cliff trying to frighten me. Whether it was about the drug dealing or what—' she noticed George's horrified face. 'Come on, George. I saw you with that Bobby and his mates. At the lighthouse, remember? Anyway, I will find out what it's about.'

'No.' George jumped up with hands over her mouth. 'No. I don't believe you. Not Felix. I—' She turned and ran.

'George. Wait.' She didn't want to let her go, not like this. She pulled her dress over her still damp body, slipped on her sandals, and started running after the teenager. This was getting to be too much of a habit, she thought, as she panted up the incline, tired after her swim for shore; leg and face still aching from her beating at the hands of Theo and Felix. She saw George reach the top of the path then disappear out of sight.

A scream tore through the air.

George.

She ran faster.

George was standing at the door of the broken-down chalet, her hands over her mouth again. She screamed some more.

'George,' said Alex, taking hold of her shoulders. 'Stop it. Stop that noise right now.' She hoped her firm tone would get through to the girl who was rigid. 'What is it?'

'I can't … I can't … ' She was gulping out huge sobs. 'In there,' she said. 'In there.' She was staring through the chalet door. 'I went in and—'

'Stay here.'

She had to blink to get used to the gloom. The smell of decay and hopelessness was still there, but it was overlaid by a much stronger stink. The stink of urine and faeces. Of death and betrayal. Of despair. There was no air in the chalet.

Alex saw the stool first, overturned on the floor, and by the stool a boy, kneeling, feet bare, dirty jeans, head between his knees, arms by his sides. Held loosely in one of his hands was a syringe.

'Max.' Alex noticed the tips of Max's fingers were blue and he was making a gurgling noise. Alex shouted his name again. Nothing. No response. More gurgling. But he was breathing. Still alive. Right. Call an ambulance. Recovery position, first, that was it. She thanked God and Bud Evans she'd been sent on a First Aid course when she began writing for *The Post*. She rolled Max onto his side, turned his face that was as pale as milk to one side, then laid his head on his arm.

She ran outside where George stood shivering with shock. 'George,' she said, urgently, 'have you got your phone?'

'Alex? Who is that? Are they—?' There was a pool of vomit by George's feet.

'It's Max Delauncey from the school, and he's alive, just. But he won't be for much longer if you don't give me your phone. Now.' She tried not to shout too loud so as not to alarm the teenager, but Max had to have help and quickly.

George handed over her phone and Alex rang for an ambulance, then ran back inside the chalet to make sure Max was still breathing. He was, thank God. Alex stroked his matted hair. 'It's all right. You're safe now, Max. We'll get you help, don't worry.' She looked around. Same old mess on the floor: syringes, blackened foil, a couple of old spoons, a couple of empty energy drink cans, broken glass, the sleeping bag in the corner. What a shithole in which to try and end your own life. Unless it was an accident. Or attempted murder. God, no, surely not? She listened, hoping to hear sirens. Come on, come on. 'Don't you dare die, Max,' she said, still stroking his hair. 'Don't you dare.'

'Alex.' George stood in the doorway.

Alex beckoned to her. 'Come here, George. Come and talk to Max. We've got to keep him alive.'

'What's happened to him?'

'Drugs overdose.'

'Oh.' Her eyes were wide.

'"Oh" is right, George.' This was a hard lesson for the teenager to learn, but to see the effects first hand should surely push her away from the destructive path of drugs. Surely?

Then she heard the familiar screech of sirens. Thank God. Thank God. 'George. Stay here while I go and tell the paramedics where to come, okay?'

George nodded tearfully.

Alex ran outside to see an ambulance and a police car drawing up. Please God they weren't too late.

CHAPTER 23

'So the girl —'

'George.' Last seen shaking. Red-rimmed eyes and snot-filled nose.

'Yes, George', said Malone impatiently, 'didn't really know anything that important.'

Alex shook her head. 'Not really. The plods have taken Theo and Felix in for questioning and George has told them the two boys were selling drugs to the locals, but she didn't know more than that.'

'And we still don't know where they're getting them from.'

'No. I don't.' She pushed away the salad of peaches, mozzarella cheese, and Parma ham Malone had made for her. With mustard vinaigrette. She couldn't think about food. She'd been worried that George would see Max, curled up, almost dead, every time she closed her eyes. She was doing it herself. Violence like that, even if self-inflicted, did that to you. And, although she'd had a shower and changed her clothes, she didn't seem to be able to get the smell of decay and hopelessness out of her nostrils.

It had been a long few hours with the police wanting to take statements; having to wait for George's nan to arrive before a particularly bullish copper could ask her anything. And now all she wanted to do was close her eyes and be still. Not have Malone buzzing around her like an irritating wasp.

'Perhaps Theo and Felix will crack and say who's supplying them. Someone must be. Local at a guess.'

'I wonder if they will,' said Alex. She took a long drink from the glass of water by her elbow.

'Their golden futures are less assured now, though, aren't they?' He speared a piece of ham with his fork. Nothing stopped Malone from eating his food.

Alex snorted. 'I wouldn't bank on it. Theo's father is some barrister who is highly successful at getting criminals off, and Felix's father is a top judge. They'll probably get let off with a rap over the knuckles.'

'I suppose it depends on what the plods find.'

Alex shot him a look. 'I don't want you doing your usual stuff.'

'I don't know what you mean.'

He was so good at playing the innocent, probably the reason why he was good at his job as an undercover policeman. 'Yes you do.' She stared at him steadily, remembering how he had hidden the weapon that had killed Jackie Wood, the woman who'd been put away for the murder of Harry and Millie. 'And,' she continued, on a roll now, 'you haven't told me any more about Gillian or why you decided to see me after all this time. Oh no, wait a minute, you wanted somewhere to crash, didn't you?' She stood up, exhausted and tired of Malone, and hating that he reminded her of the time when her sister was really going downhill. 'I think you've had your time now. So if you could pack your bags and find somewhere else to "crash".'

'Sure I can't help you? You know, where those arses are concerned?' Unperturbed, he carried on eating.

'Absolutely not.' There was no way she wanted Malone to wade in with his size twelves, disrupting everything in his not-so-subtle way. Planting evidence or getting rid of it, that's what he was so good at.

'Any doubt the overdose was self-inflicted?'

'There's always doubt.' Her jaw was hurting: she was gritting her teeth so hard. Why couldn't he fuck off?

Malone sighed and put his knife and fork together on the plate. 'What's eating you?'

Alex gazed up at the pale blue sky and counted to ten. Slowly. 'Malone. I have just come back from seeing a young boy curled up on a dirty floor in a derelict building, minutes away from death. I've also had to comfort a 16-year-old girl who will always have that picture in her head. I want to know if all this – mess – is in any way connected to Elena's death and I'm not sure I'm doing a very good job. You're here for God knows what reason and won't tell me about Gillian.' She stood up and walked to the edge of the garden and looked down onto the beach. Out at sea a couple of yachts were scudding across the water looking as though they were racing each other. There was a lightship warning of a sandbank. Closer to shore, a windsurfer was skimming the sea with elegance.

Malone began to talk, voice devoid of its usual devil-may-care tone. 'My job was to infiltrate an environmental group. It wasn't one of those lentil-eating, tree-hugging, sandal-wearing groups—'

'You can be so judgemental,' she snapped.

'You know what I mean. Anyway. They were more into direct action; a bit like those animal rights activists in the late nineties, but more so. They weren't content with merely threatening the families of scientists they didn't agree with, or throwing bricks through windows; they would plant devices under cars or send them letter bombs. You must have covered stories about that sort of thing?'

Alex nodded.

'So you know the lengths some people will go to, just to make a point.'

'And Gillian?'

'Gillian was the leader.'

'And?'

'She fell in love with me.'

'You made that happen.'

'I did. That was my job.'

'And you? Did you fall in love with her?'

There was a pause. Alex turned to look over the sea, holding her breath. Waiting for his answer.

'No.'

She wasn't sure whether that made it worse or not.

'But … ' Another pause. 'There is a girl.'

'A girl?'

'I mean, a daughter. I have a daughter.'

The numbness spread through her body, followed by anger, denial, acceptance, all in quick, hot waves. 'How old?' Why did she feel like this? Why did she even care? This was Malone. Slippery, unreliable, dangerous. But she also knew there was another side to him. Charming, roguish and, yes, caring.

'She's six now and she's beautiful. But I rarely see her.' There was a depth of sadness in his voice that tugged at her heart.

'What's her name?'

'Marcia.'

'That's pretty.'

He shrugged. 'Yes. Well. Gillian's half American. But, as I say, I hardly ever see her, particularly now we're divorced and Gillian is in jail.'

'Jail?' She was confused.

'Yeah. That was sort of the point of the whole thing. When she rang that day when we were in Sole Bay?'

Alex nodded. That was when she had found out Malone was married. That was when she'd thrown Malone out of the house and swore never to have anything to do with him ever again. She cut him out of her life and didn't even consider the idea that Malone would come back into it, or into Gus's. She could see now that maybe it was being a parent himself that had prompted him to do that.

'It was to tell me she'd been tipped off that the police were about to arrest her. She wanted me to help her. But I couldn't, of course. I'd done my job. End of.'

'End of,' she echoed, wondering if he was as blasé about it as he seemed to be. 'So what about Marcia?'

A deep sigh. 'She is with her grandparents, Gillian's parents, and – no surprise here – they won't let me see her.'

'Can't you go to court?'

'Ha. That would be interesting, wouldn't it? You see, at the moment they don't know that I'm actually an undercover copper, only that I'm some wastrel. I was never identified in the court case against Gillian. I was a number. The only trouble is … ' His voice tailed away and Alex sensed he was getting to the heart of his story. 'Gillian's brother is also an activist, in Scotland, and he's got wind of the fact I'm not entirely who I say I am. In fact, I think he knows exactly who I am, because he spent some time in jail about ten years ago with someone I put away.'

Alex didn't know what to say.

'It's a small world, isn't it?' He smiled at her and she could see the pain in his eyes. 'And all this means I'll probably have to get a new identity and I'll never see Marcia again.'

There was such desolation in his voice that Alex wanted nothing more than to go over and put her arms around him; she had never seen him this vulnerable.

'But there's one other thing.'

'Yes?'

'Gillian's brother is trying to find me. According to the grapevine, he wants,' Malone made quotation marks in the air with his fingers, '"answers".'

Now she understood. 'That's why you're here, isn't it? Because of this brother. He's looking for you, and you've run to me. Putting me in danger and quite possibly Gus. If he's big in some terrorist-type organization then he'll be able to find out all about you and all about your friends. About me.' She could hear her voice rising. 'Oh my God, we're all in danger. No wonder you told Gus it was a good idea to go looking for his dad. You wanted him out of the way.' She thought a minute. 'Has this brother been looking for you all this time? And why are you here now? After two years? Why are you suddenly considering me and Gus? Is it because he's got close?' She looked at Malone and saw an expression on his face she had never expected to see, that of contrition. She felt sick. What was wrong with her? How could she get it so wrong the whole time? Gus's father. The man who'd been thrown into jail for killing Harry and Millie (no, she couldn't revisit that particular mistake: the guilt she'd almost thrown off would come back and suffocate her). Malone? Irish, roguish, compelling Malone. 'I'm right, aren't I? That's exactly why you're here?'

'Hey.'

At the sound of a male voice they both jumped. Alex felt a spike of fear pierce her back, then she saw who it was.

'Jonny,' she said, trying to ignore Malone's raised hackles. She could feel them from here.

'Hi.'

'What does that prick want?' muttered Malone, and Alex was grateful Jonny couldn't hear what he said.

'Shut up,' she whispered. 'Just shut up.' She thought about her conversation with Kylie in the pub and wondered again why Dutch hadn't ever mentioned being stabbed. She tried to smile at Jonny, but wasn't sure if it came out as a grimace. 'Great to see you. What are you doing here?'

'You rang me? I've been a bit slow getting back to you so I thought I'd take the opportunity to come and say hello and sorry and maybe cadge a drink or two, but I see you've got company.'

'No, no, come on in Jonny. Take a seat.' She brushed imaginary fluff off one of the garden chairs and pointed to it. What was she doing? Overcompensating, that's what.

'Yeah, come on in Jonny,' Malone muttered again.

Alex flashed him a look that she hoped said shut the fuck up and get out of here. He didn't take the hint.

'We've just finished eating, haven't we, Alex. So come in, come in.' The switch from disgruntled to that easy, fake smile of his. Alex wanted to ram it down his throat.

'Sure.' Jonny walked over to the table, his limp more pronounced today. He noticed Alex looking and grimaced. 'Bad day, that's all.' He sat. 'The police have been around asking about Max. God, I can't believe it.' He rubbed a hand over his head. 'I mean, he'd been on a bit of a downward spiral, but I didn't think he'd do that.'

'Do you know why?' asked Alex. 'When I saw him he was upset but I didn't think—'

Jonny looked at her sharply. 'What? You saw him?'

'Yesterday. In Mundesley.'

'Why?'

'Because he had some information about Elena.' She wasn't going to tell him the whole of it.

'Oh, right.' His face relaxed. Alex wondered what that had been about.

'You never told me that Max had attacked you?' Alex said casually.

It was barely noticeable but Dutch stiffened. 'You never asked.' He kept his expression neutral. 'And it hasn't got any bearing on all of this.'

'All of this?' asked Alex.

'Elena's death. It happened after that. A few months ago.'

'I know, but he was a friend of Elena's.' They were doing a dance around each other.

'He was in the year below; I don't think they were that friendly. And anyway, how did you find out about that? There were no charges, no names in the papers—'

'No, the school saw to that one.'

'That's the way they do things,' he said smoothly.

'I'd call it more of a cover-up,' said Malone.

Dutch flashed him a poisonous look.

'Why did he do it?' asked Alex.

'What?' Dutch was clearly irritated.

'Stab you. There must have been a reason.'

'None.'

'What, he just came up to you one day and stuck a blade into you? You were what, hanging around, shooting the breeze?' Malone was incredulous.

'Look. There was no reason. He had a blade. I was the nearest teacher. End of story.'

'And you didn't press charges?'

'No, Mr Malone, I didn't. It was a scratch and the kid had enough going on at the time, okay? Look, do you want to know which school Paul Churchill taught at before The Drift or not?'

'Couldn't you have phoned?'

'Malone. Don't be so rude.' It was like dealing with a teenage Gus.

To his credit, Jonny didn't look perturbed. 'Sure. But I wanted to see Alex.'

'Why?'

'Malone. For God's sake, lighten up. Please.'

If anything, Jonny Dutch was amused. 'Because I like her. Is that okay with you?'

'Not really.'

Oh, for God's sake.

'So,' said Alex, thinking the best thing to do was to ignore the exchange. 'The school?'

'Yeah, right,' said Jonny. 'Stratton School. In Cambridge. Now, how about that coffee? A real one this time. I could do with a good hit of caffeine.'

As Alex went to try to work the coffee machine from NASA she wondered at the atmosphere. Jonny, normally so relaxed he almost fell over, seemed to be more wary, more on edge. Malone, of course, couldn't bear to see another man on what he thought was his territory, though he couldn't be more wrong about that.

She flicked a switch and let the machine do its gurgling thing as she looked out of the window at the two men who were sitting saying nothing to one another.

She thought of George. Of what she had told her. The drugs that were rife in Hallow's Edge. Supplied by the boys at the school and distributed by young girls like her: duped into acting as couriers. Duped by the smooth-talking, fit, young Hugh Grant lookalikes, who inhabited their lives for a magical time. Girls whose alternatives were the acned youths of the village with no money and little imagination. To George and her mates, the lads from The Drift were like Greek gods: oozing wealth and privilege and a life they couldn't imagine. Alex sighed. She supposed in her situation she would be impressed by that, too. She hoped George had told the police officer everything they needed to know.

The pressing question now was where the boys got their supplies. And what, if anything, did this have to do with Elena falling off the cliff?

CHAPTER 24

ELENA

October: eight weeks before she dies

I don't know what's happening to me. I really don't.

Sometimes I feel as though my head is being squeezed in a great vice and will explode at any moment. I can't concentrate on my work. I can only paint. What I mean is that when I'm painting I can lose myself in that world. For a few hours it is only the smell of the paint and the thoughts in my head and the scene in front of me.

It's the afternoon and I'm out on the beach. Jonny has sent me out to get on with my project. I have taken a photograph of what I want to paint, eventually, but now my fingers itch to sketch it. I find a flat rock and sit with my pad and pencil drawing the sea and the sand and the sky and I feel in perfect balance for once. I have escaped the confines of school and just want to be on my own. I even had to escape Tara by telling her the painting was part of coursework. I am so worried about Tara: she looks so ill and it'll soon be too late for her to do anything about it. I think I'm going to phone her mum.

I pick up my pencil and make a few deft strokes on the paper. I like to think they're deft, anyway. Maybe I'm fooling myself.

But I must concentrate, otherwise all I'll do is doodle hearts and flowers and stupid things like that, and I can't afford to do that. I must concentrate on this. I want to make a good job. Jonny says I could be good enough to exhibit if I work hard. And I want to work hard. I want to please him, of course I do.

Pulling my coat around me and tying my scarf around my neck, I carry on drawing, the cold making my fingers clumsy. The wind knifes against my cheeks and I have to hold on to the paper. I can smell the brine of the sea. In the distance white horses roll to shore. I'm trying to capture the wildness of the sea, the expanse of sky, the crumbling cliffs. Dunno if I'll be able to.

I look up and see someone walking towards me. Big. Face obscured by a hoodie. Hands in pockets. I know who it is and my heart begins to pound. I have seen him lurking around the school. I know who he is. But this is a public place and there are people around. I can see fishermen in the distance, someone walking their dog, a jogger. Nothing can happen here.

Can it?

Bobby stands in front of me and spits. Smiles. He has a gold tooth. 'Bitch,' he says. 'Watch your back.' And he walks off leaving me more frightened than if he had tried to hit me.

It takes a few minutes before I can draw again.

I see Max walking along the beach. He looks strung out. He won't listen to me any more. Story of my life. Nobody wants to listen to me. I've asked him why he wants to put himself in debt to those tossers Felix and Theo. They don't care about him; does he think they do?

'Hi,' says Max, stopping in front of me. He looks cold in his too-short school trousers and blazer. He needs something warmer to wear. I unwind my scarf from around my neck. 'Here,' I say, 'take this. It's fucking cold out here.'

Max takes it and wraps it around himself.

I concentrate on my drawing.

Before I realize it, he's behind me, looking at what I'm doing.

I can't shift my arse else I'll lose perspective and all that crap.

'That's good. What's it gonna be?'

'A painting,' I said, not bothering to hide my sarcastic wit.

'Right.' He reaches out a finger and prods at it, leaving a dirty finger mark on the paper.

'Thanks.'

'Sorry,' he says, pulling his finger away. 'I wish I was like you.'

I give what I perceive to be a hollow laugh. 'You're the only one, then.' I think of all the times I'm alone in my study bedroom climbing the walls. Or when no one picks me for their lame sports team. Or I'm left to the end and know that no one wants me. About how conversations pointedly stop when I come near and carry on when I've gone. God, it was unbearable last term, but it's far, far worse this term, and I know it's all to do with splitting on Theo and Felix. I have Broken. The. Rules. Well, tough shit.

He stands and stares at me. I try to draw. I snuggle down more in my coat. I try to draw some more. Eventually, I can't stand it any longer.

'Max. What do you want?'

He shrugs and I see the tears on his cheeks. I sigh inwardly. I put down my pencil. I push my hair away from my face. Christ but my hands are cold. 'What is it?'

He dashes away the tears. I wait.

'Theo and Felix. They hate you.'

'I know.' I'm trying to be patient.

'All the teachers are watching everybody. The Queen Bees can't get their stuff. Theo and Felix can't sell it.'

'Good job.'

'They're going to get their revenge, you know.'

I shrug. I do know that. Something is coming, but I don't know what. Yet. I can only hope that I'll know just before the shit hits the fan.

'You're lucky.'

I go back to my drawing. 'How so?' I look up at the sky and

wonder if I'll be able to get the light in the sky right. The greys and the whites and the dull monotone. How to capture the slate of the sea? What mix in my palate to use? How to convey the salt air?

'Your mum loves you. Even your stepdad wants the best for you.'

'How do you work that one out?' I was still frowning, thinking of colour.

'The way you talk about them.'

I contemplate that one. Don't get it. I only ever diss Mark and don't talk about Mum that much. Yeah, I'm proud of her, of course I am; who wouldn't be? Powerful. She travels a lot. Sometimes I get to go with her. Most times I don't, but, yeah, I'm proud of her. 'Right,' I say because I'm not sure what else I should say.

'My mum's dead. So's my dad and brother.'

I nod. 'I know. That's shit.'

'It makes me so angry sometimes. I've got no one. No one. That's why sometimes it's easier to take something. To get rid of the pain.'

His voice is so desolate I don't know what to do. Life's unfair, I know that. It's not shit for me. A bubble of something explodes in my chest.

I am loved.

'Look, Max,' I feel awkward now and wish I could share some of what I've got. 'I'm sorry about your family—'

'But I love you, you know that,' he bursts out. 'If I had you I'd stop using. I know I would. It's only a bit of coke here and there. I could stop easily. For you.'

I shift uncomfortably on my rock. 'Max … ' Ah, fuck. 'Max, I'm happy as I am. On my own. And you should stop for you, not anybody else. And before it ruins your life.'

He wraps his arms around himself. 'I still love you.'

I watch as he walks off, hunched against the wind.

I go back to my drawing. I look at the beach, the sea, the sky. Then I turn and look at the cliff and my heart stops. A figure. I reach into my pocket for my phone so I can take a picture. Capture the moment.

It's not there.

Hello you, it's me.

I know you saw me there. On the top of the cliff. I had some free time and I heard you were going to the beach to draw.

Can I tell you again how happy you make me? Knowing that you feel the same about me as I do about you gives me so much pleasure. The thought of you being mine keeps me sane in this dreary world.

Because you are mine and I won't let anyone take that away from me.

CHAPTER 25

June

With its Victorian fountain and railings, and surroundings of the Guildhall and church of St Mary the Great, Market Hill in the centre of Cambridge was a magnet for tourists. Alex would liked to have lingered in the market, to explore stalls that sold everything from olives to rag rugs to fossilized dinosaur excrement, but Malone was ploughing on, looking at his phone for the directions to Stratton House: the school where Paul Churchill used to teach. Young people dressed in vintage tea dresses floated around and about, shouting to one another, mingling with stout ladies in crisp linen trousers and sensible shoes, and with men in shorts and tee-shirts that should never have seen the light of day. There was a vibrant buzz about the place and Alex wanted to stop and drink it all in.

'This way, Alex, come on.' Malone disappeared down a side street.

Alex dutifully trotted after him, wondering why she had allowed herself to be talked into letting him come with her. Actually, she knew why: his clout as a police officer, undercover or not, could actually help when it came to talking to the head at the school. It was also good to get out of the cottage and away from Hallow's Edge for a short time and the sad problem of Max.

They walked past one of the colleges for which Cambridge was famous. Its gates were open and Alex saw through into tree-lined quads, green grass, and yellow stone studded with mullion windows and gargoyles leering down from mini towers. Even from the street Alex could smell the newly mown grass and the tranquillity that lay between its walls. Probably not too tranquil for the students who had to slave away doing essays and exams, though, she thought. These beautiful colleges and their grounds really were wasted on the students, particularly in the spring and early summer when the cherry blossom was out and the days began to get longer.

'Here we are.' Malone stopped in front of an arched door set into a wall. A discreet sign told them it was the school they were looking for. Malone pressed the intercom buzzer and announced who they were. The door swung open.

Malone had rung Stratton School to make an appointment while they were on their way, driving through the flat Fenland. She had heard the surprise and possibly caution in the head teacher's voice over the loudspeaker in the car as he agreed to meet them. Now they were sitting in a cosy study facing Nigel Astley: white beard, leather patches on the tweed jacket that had to be too warm for the time of year, and eyes that twinkled. Polar opposite to Sven Farrar.

Alex looked around the room. Photographs of boys and girls on school trips were dotted around the walls. Piles of books teetered on top of chairs and magazines and papers were in an untidy heap on the floor. It reminded her of the deserted chalet in Hallow's Edge, but cleaner. She heard the sound of children playing in the distance, and the faint school dinner smell of shepherd's pie and cabbage floated on the air.

'Is this an official visit, Detective Inspector?' Astley looked at first Malone, then Alex.

Detective Inspector indeed. He'd kept that quiet.

Malone smiled. 'Let's say semi-official. My colleague and I … ' he indicated Alex, who nodded, but said nothing; she was leaving it all to Malone, 'are just making initial enquiries at the moment. Just trying to get the lie of the land.'

'Has there been a complaint about Paul Churchill?' Astley leaned back in his chair.

'No,' said Malone.

'Then I really don't see how I can help you.'

Malone spread out his hands. 'Let me put all our cards on the table. Certain rumours have reached us about Mr Churchill and we are looking into why he left Stratton House in the first place.'

Astley pursed his lips. 'Paul Churchill is a good teacher; I have no doubt about that, and I was sorry to see him leave.'

Malone nodded, leaving a conversational gap for the head teacher to fill. He duly obliged.

'I understood from him his wife wanted to move.'

'His wife?' Alex burst out, ignoring the irritated look from Malone.

Astley looked from one to the other. 'Yes. From what he said she was the one who wanted to go somewhere completely new. She was a fairly NQT – newly qualified teacher – and wanted to spread her wings. At first, I thought they might be going to an inner city comprehensive or something, but no, it was to a school similar to this. Up in North Norfolk. I believe Mrs Churchill has relatives up that way. Why is that so surprising?'

'Certain information had come our way that suggested a different scenario,' said Malone, in the smooth tone Alex knew had got many a person to divulge their secrets.

'Oh?'

'There were rumours – and I must reiterate they were only rumours – that Mr Churchill took more than a professional interest in one of his pupils and that's why he had to move.'

Astley looked appalled for a moment, then gave a hearty laugh. 'My dear Detective Inspector.' He spoke to Malone as if he were one of his recalcitrant pupils. Alex watched Malone's efforts to keep his composure, and wanted to laugh. 'Paul Churchill was – is, I should still imagine – an exemplary teacher, so I don't know where you got that idea from. Also, if any such rumours had reached my ears, then I can assure you the matter would have been thoroughly investigated. And if true, he wouldn't have got another job.' He shook his head. 'No. You have got that very wrong.'

'That was interesting.' Malone put the car into gear and pulled smoothly out of the tight parking place. 'Astley was very certain that Paul Churchill was a good teacher and it was his wife who wanted to move.'

'So why did Louise tell me it was Paul who wanted to leave his old school? And I hadn't heard anything about relatives in the area. I know I've only spoken to her twice, though.'

'True. But she was lying to you about Paul wanting to leave his old school. And if she was lying to you about that, then what else could she have said that wasn't true? And, why should she lie anyway?'

'She intimated that Elena had started starving herself again. She warned me off, too, which I know I thought was odd at the time.'

'Perhaps another chat with Mrs Churchill would be in order?' Malone glanced across at Alex.

'Yes. I also need to talk to Mark Munro about why he said he saw Elena a couple of weeks before she died when in fact it was only a couple of days. I mean, once he'd said that he'd been to see her before she died, why would he lie about the timing? There must be something more to it.'

'So you have to go to London do you?'

'I guess so. I seem to be going all over the bloody country.'

'Get him to come to you.'

Alex looked at Malone. Now that was a bloody good idea. No time like now. She scrolled through her phone and found his private mobile number. Answerphone. A–bloody–gain.

'Probably screening his calls,' said Malone, helpfully.

'Thanks.' She left a message asking him to ring her back. 'Malone,' she said, 'can we go via Norwich?'

'What? Hardly on the way, but, yes, sure. Why?'

'I'm on a roll now. I want to have a chat with Tara Johnson. One of Elena's friends – her best friend – Cat told me. She lives there with her baby.'

'How did you find that out?'

Alex laughed. 'Quite easily. Her mother's famous, writes books – not the sort you'd like—'

'What sort's that?'

'Not ones heavy with sex and shopping, that's for sure.'

'You think I'm some sort of stereotype?' He pretended to look hurt.

'Shut up, Malone. Anyway, her mother is very proud of her granddaughter. Put a birth notice in the paper. Then I rang a couple of contacts in Norwich and voila.'

'Good.'

'And later I want to wangle a dinner invitation or something to the Churchills'.'

'How do you propose doing that?'

'Jonny Dutch.'

'That wanker.'

'Yes, Malone, that wanker. He has his uses.'

'Stinks of cannabis.'

'Says it dulls the pain.'

A hollow laugh from Malone. 'Yeah. Heard that before. Are you shagging him?' He ground the gears. 'Damn.' Beeped the horn. 'Get out of the way you prick,' he shouted.

Alex smiled to herself. 'None of your business, Malone. Is that why you're so tetchy?'

He glowered. 'I can't imagine you would be. He's such a prick. Watch him, though.'

The speedometer climbed to eighty.

Red rag to a bull. 'Oh, and you're good partner material, are you?' She folded her arms. 'I don't think so. Interfering in my son's life; marrying someone because it's part of the job, and having a daughter with her. I don't think you get to hug the moral high ground, do you?' Exhausted, she leaned her head against the window and shut her eyes. 'Just keep driving, Malone.'

CHAPTER 26

Malone parked the car on a side road and switched off the engine.

'I'll wait here, shall I?'

'Please.'

They were the first words they had said to one another since Alex had feigned sleep. She hadn't wanted to talk to him at all; he made her so bloody mad.

Alex got out of the car and slammed the door and walked into the maze of roads and houses. Tara Johnson lived at thirty-two Newmarket Gardens, which, if she remembered rightly from looking it up on Google Maps, was down Burwell Road, then left onto Feltwell Avenue. Her destination should be further on the right. Perhaps she should have brought the satnav with her. Or used the one on the phone.

The Genesis Estate had been built in the nineteen twenties and was one of the first housing estates in Norwich. Over the years its reputation had gone from being an estate full of – to coin a politician's phrase – 'hard-working people', to an estate full of – another politician's phrase – 'problem families'. Problems mostly being lack of hope. Now the streets were clean, the gardens of the semis well kept, and children played in the green spaces between the streets.

And here it was. Number thirty-two. A wooden gate led into the shingle front garden. Pots of geraniums and petunias were dotted around. The solid brick house looked freshly painted and well-kept with venetian blinds at the windows and a satellite dish bolted to the wall. She thought she saw the blind twitch.

Alex knocked on the door. There was no noise from within. She knocked again.

The door opened.

'Sssh. You'll wake Jessica.' A girl with a round face and hair that looked as though it could do with a wash stood in front of her. She was wearing baggy jeans and a long tee-shirt. A muslin square had been flung over her shoulder. She looked tired but content. Tara Johnson.

Alex smiled. 'May I come in?'

'I'm not buying, I don't want to save my soul, and I don't vote. And I've just got the baby off for her nap so I was hoping to have a bath—'

'I'm not selling, I'm not religious, and I'm not a politician. I won't wake the baby. And if the baby does wake, I'll look after her while you have a bath. So now may I come in?'

'Why? Who are you?'

'My name is Alex Devlin and I'm a friend of Elena Devonshire's mother.'

'Elena?' Tears filled her eyes. 'I would have loved her to have met Jess.'

Alex nodded. 'I know, and that's why I'm here.' She reached out and touched Tara's arm. 'I want to find out the truth behind her death. For her mum's sake. You're a mum; you know how much you want to protect Jessica. Elena's mum is really suffering, so can I come in and talk to you. Please?' She looked around. Tara's next-door neighbour had come out of his house and was pretending to water his flowerpots while earwigging on their conversation. It would have been more convincing if he'd thought to fill the watering can with actual water, she thought.

Tara bit her lip. Then opened the door wide. 'Okay. I don't get many visitors so it'll be nice to talk to a grown-up for a bit.'

The house smelled of washing powder with an overlay of stale milk. An oversized settee filled the small lounge just about leaving room for the largest TV Alex had ever seen.

Tara saw her marvelling at it and gave a wry smile. 'Enormous, isn't it? If the teachers at The Drift saw that they'd be well fed up. All that posh teaching. But it's mine. And I like watching it. You know, things like Jeremy Kyle and all those toothless old people who are supposed to have got three women preggers. Makes anyone who watches it feel better. And after that, orange-coloured men running around flea markets and stuff. I mean, what a way to make a living. Makes me feel better. At least I've got Jess in my life. And it can be dull with a baby on your own.'

Alex nodded. 'I know that. I'm a single mum, though my son has left home. Gone travelling. But couldn't you be with your mum?'

Tara shrugged. 'Could of. But she's in LA. One of her books is being made into a mini-series, and I didn't want to go over there and just hang around with Jess, so I came here. It's mine. My haven.'

'What about Jess's father? Do you ever see him?'

A dark shadow passed across her face. 'No. Tea? Coffee?'

'No, I'm fine thanks.'

Tara nodded and sat on a small stool under the window. 'How did you find me?'

Alex smiled. 'Easy. Your mum put a notice about the birth of Jessica in the paper with quite a lot of detail. It wasn't too hard.'

Tara laughed. 'I didn't want her to do that, but she insisted.' Her face grew grave. 'So what about Elena? She killed herself, didn't she? That's what everyone said. It happened just after I left. I went to her funeral. It was horrible.'

'Tell me about her, Tara.'

Tara looked out of the window. 'She was good to me. Knew I was carrying Jess before even I could face it. Told my mum, who came and got me.' Tara smiled. 'She was strong, you know? I

223

didn't realize how strong until she died, I suppose. You see, at school there were the Queen Bees—'

'The gang of girls?'

'That's right. Naomi, Natasha, Jenni, and Helen, mostly. They thought they were the best. I did too.' Tara looked out of the window. 'I so wanted to be one of them. So much so I … ' She fell silent. Alex could hear a clock ticking somewhere. 'I tried to be one of them, joining in with the drugs and stuff. Did you know about that? The drugs around the place?'

Alex nodded.

'The trouble is, if you didn't join in then you were, like, out of it. You never got asked to anything, not parties or barbecues down on the beach or tea in the studies. You never got a decent boyfriend or anything. You had to belong.' She looked back at Alex. 'That's when I fell pregnant. A night on the beach. Trying to belong.' Her expression was pained. 'It was horrible. Elena said I should tell the teachers what had happened: how they'd given me so much stuff that I didn't know what I was doing. But I wouldn't. Elena was like that though, wanted things to be right.'

'Did Elena have a boyfriend?'

'Theo Lodge. For a time. But it wasn't real. Everyone knew that because Naomi was shagging his friend Felix—'

'Devine?'

'Yeah.'

Felix and Theo. Those names cropped up everywhere. Alex touched the fading bruise on her cheek.

Tara coloured. 'They had a book.'

'A book?'

'They rated the, um, girls from one to ten.'

'Rated the girls?' Oh, sweet Jesus. Impotent fury rose in her throat. 'Do you mean they rated their performance in bed, or wherever the shagging took place?'

'Yeah. But Elena wouldn't have anything to do with it. Said

Theo was a prick. Said he had a small willy. He didn't like that.'

I bet he didn't, thought Alex.

'The Queen Bees didn't like Elena either. She wouldn't conform. And when she told the Farrars about the drugs, they all had their privileges taken away for six months. You know, things like being able to go into the village in their free time. Lights out later, that sort of stuff.'

'So the Farrars knew what was going on, but no one was expelled.'

Tara shook her head. 'No. But the boys and the Queen Bees said they would get her back. I think that's why the pictures—' Tara clapped her hand over her mouth. 'I shouldn't have said anything about those.'

Alex reached out to her. 'I know about them. I've seen them.'

Tara looked at her sideways. 'But that's not all of it. It got much worse than a few pictures.' She bit her lip, drawing a small bead of blood. 'Somehow Felix found them. I don't know whether he hacked her phone or computer or it was something to do with AirDrop, but he found them. And posted them online.' She sighed and rubbed her face with her hand. 'Before you ask, it's a private website. You have to have a password to get onto it. That's what he sent round. I suppose that's one good thing. I mean, he could've, like, put them on Facebook or Twitter or something and they would have gone everywhere.'

'Someone sent Elena the password?' Of course they would have done: there would have been no fun in the so-called 'slut shaming' if the slut in question didn't know it was going on. Alex's heart ached for the dead girl. What must it have been like to know that your fellow students were looking at you, naked or half-naked?

Tara nodded. 'She was sent the link and password one day in the Michaelmas term. And then she could see that lots of trolling had been going on with people saying the most horrible, vile things about her pictures.' She swallowed hard. Alex knew she was trying not to cry. 'I guess she must have done the pictures for someone special, and now they were being seen as something dirty. To be ashamed of.' She looked at Alex as if trying to make her mind up about something. 'Here.' She took her phone out of her pocket. 'I took some screen shots. Just in case. I looked for the website after she died but it had been taken down. Felix or Theo, I guess. They wouldn't have wanted to be incriminated, you see. Wouldn't have wanted the photos to go viral, otherwise the trolling could have been traced back to them.' She handed the phone over to Alex.

Alex looked at the screen. There were the pictures; the same as those she had seen in the file Honey had sent, but what was different were the unkind, cruel remarks underneath them. *'Who'd want to fuck that?'* *'Who do you think you are?'* *'With a body like that you should kill yourself.'* Alex didn't want to read any more.

'And it goes on and on,' said Tara.

Alex handed the phone back to her. 'I can't imagine the effect on her that must have had.'

Tara gazed unseeing at the phone. 'It was horrible. But she was amazing. Elena, I mean. She just,' Tara shrugged, 'I dunno, carried on as though dozens of blokes hadn't pored like grubby old men over her pictures.'

'She rose above it.' How hard must that have been.

'Yeah. She did. I think she thought that it couldn't get any worse. I should get rid of them really. You know, she was great, Elena. She'd got through all her anorexia and stuff after her dad died and was a real support to her mum. She didn't deserve all this.' Tara put the phone down. 'What you said when you came in about looking into Elena's death. What did you mean?'

'I'm not sure she killed herself.'

Tara frowned. 'What, it was an accident?'

'Or someone pushed her.'

Tara looked as though all the air had been crushed out of her.

'Wow. Just, wow.' She shook her head. 'I don't know what to say.'

'It's okay.' Alex shifted on the settee. 'You said Theo wasn't a real boyfriend. What did you mean?'

Tara wrinkled her nose and took the muslin square off her shoulder. 'He was like a smokescreen. She did have someone, I'm sure of it. But someone she didn't want to tell us about. Whoever it was had given her this ring. Silver. She loved it. Kept pushing it round her finger, you know?'

'Do you have any idea who might have given her the ring? Who she might have been seeing?' Alex held her breath.

Tara sighed and looked at her hands. 'No. She kept it really, really quiet. She did visit the Churchills a few times, but she said that was for extra tutoring.' She laughed. 'You're not thinking it could be Paul Churchill, are you?'

'Why not?'

'He's a maths teacher. Christ, you don't get duller than that.' She looked thoughtful. 'I mean, most of the teachers were old and wet. Apart from Jonny Dutch, I suppose.' She looked out of the window. 'Busybody next door is still in his garden.' She rapped on the glass and made shoo-ing motions with her hands.

Alex kept her voice even. 'Jonny Dutch? The art teacher?'

'She loved art and she said Jonny Dutch was one of the few teachers interested in her. Max Delauncey used to follow her around a lot.'

'He was in love with her, wasn't he?'

Tara smiled. 'He'd do anything for her. But she wasn't interested. That's all I know really.'

'Max is in hospital,' said Alex. 'Overdose.'

Tara paled. 'How bad?'

'Pretty bad.' Alex had called the hospital earlier for a condition check, but all they would say was that Max was 'critical'.

'How do you know?'

'I found him. In that filthy deserted chalet, on the floor.'

Tara winced. 'Max was always … so angry with the world.

Elena was always kind to him, but she couldn't get him off the drugs. That stuff messes with your head.'

'What about someone like Zena Brewer? Couldn't she have helped? Or the school counsellor?'

Tara laughed. 'You've got to be kidding. They were about as useful as – I dunno – … '

'A chocolate teapot?'

She laughed again. 'I guess.'

'Who was supplying the drugs?' Alex thought she'd go for the straightforward approach.

'If you've been sniffing around The Drift and Hallow's Edge you'll have some idea. The boys. Felix, Theo, the lot of them. Loved to see themselves as some sort of gangsta dealers. Pricks.'

'But where did they get them from?'

'I don't know. Jeez. Max.' She shook her head. 'Will you let me know how he does?'

'Of course,' said Alex. 'When he's better you could go and visit him. Take Jess with you. Show him there is a future.'

Right on cue the sound of a baby crying came from somewhere above them. Tara shot out of the chair. 'Look, I better go and feed her; she doesn't like to be kept waiting.' She kept glancing up at the ceiling in the direction of the baby's increasingly desperate cries.

Alex stood. 'You go. I'll see myself out. If you think of anything, give me a ring. I'll leave my number here.' She put her business card on the windowsill. 'And good luck with Jess.'

'Thank you. You know, in spite of everything, school and that, Jess is the best thing that's ever happened to me.'

Alex nodded. She knew that feeling.

CHAPTER 27

ELENA

November: three weeks before she dies

It shouldn't be like this. Not like this.

I did it for love and now they're out there on that horrible site for everyone to see, to jeer at.

Lying on my bed I look at my phone again, the bright colours of the screen mocking the misery in my heart and my soul. Look at me, sitting naked on a chair, pouting into the webcam. And another: lying back on the bed – this bed – trying to be sultry. Slutty, more like. A whore. And the comments, the trolling. My hand trembles as I read the comments over and over again. *'Whore.' 'Prossie.' 'Who'd fuck that?' 'Ugly bitch.' 'I'd kill myself if I looked like that.'* And worse. Insults I can't bear to read. What have I done to deserve this? I have loved, that's what I have done. And I have done what I wanted to do, not what the Queen Bees dictated. Not been like them. They give it away for free, no emotional investment, no love. Just so they can get in that book and be rated by the likes of Theo and Felix and Ollie and Hugh. Like a gadget on Amazon or something. Arses. Dicks. The lot of them. They think it's somehow 'empowering' to sleep their way around the school. They're doing it because they want to, not because they are pressured into it. Yeah, right.

But now this. How can I explain it? How the fuck did they get hold of them, my most precious pictures? Then I remember. When I went to the beach to paint and I wanted to take that picture, I didn't have my phone with me. I'd left it in my room, and anyone could have gone snooping and found it. Found the pictures. I groan. But how did they know about them? I think about throwing my phone across the room, wanting to hear it smash and break. But doing that won't take the website away.

I curl up tightly and face the wall, never having felt so cold in all my life.

The room seems so empty since Tara went home. I rang her mum like I said I would, and she came flying in like an avenging angel, all clouds of Poison and cigarette smoke. She whisked Tara away, loudly declaring the school was 'shit' and 'whatever happened to pastoral care?' But as Tara refused to say anything about being pregnant or who the father was (don't think she knew) or how or even when it happened there wasn't much she could do. And Tara had sworn me to secrecy.

But how I wish she was here now. I so want to talk to her. The sentences are clogging my throat, screaming to get out of my head. But I've got to keep them in, stop them from falling, otherwise everything will come crashing down and I'll have no one. And I love having someone who makes me feel special and wanted and needed.

I sent the photographs because I had been asked to and I had given them willingly. I won't let the bastards get me down. I won't.

I can't say anything, or it will be over.

I press my fist into my mouth.

Then I get up and pad along the corridor to the bathroom.

Tonight's dinner is sitting heavily on my stomach. I almost smile; that is the phrase my mother always used when I got tummy ache. I had to force down tonight's offering of sausages and mash followed by French fruit tart: a fancy name for pastry with a bit of fruit and custard in it. And now my stomach is twisting and turning, forcing bile into my throat: the food like one big ugly, fat jellyfish writhing in my stomach.

I hang my head over the toilet bowl. My gag reflex is so well-trained I know it will hardly take seconds for the two fingers at the back of my throat to bring up that writhing jellyfish. I can almost taste the acrid vomit, almost feel it spew from my mouth. I think about sinking, panting, to the floor, mouth tasting foul, but stomach purged and clean; the vicious boiling settling down to an empty gurgle.

I stand up slowly. Perhaps that's all I need: to hang my head over the cold porcelain and remember what it feels like. Remember that feeling of being on a high because I had beaten the system, but also to remember that the high only lasted for moments. Then I feel dirty. Worthless. That I let everybody down. That I am not as in control as I think I am. That's what I remember.

I wipe away the thin film of sweat on my forehead. I have been close, but I haven't done it. It is the first time in years I have felt the urge to purge, but I haven't given in to it. I am strong. I allow myself a small smile. I lean against the cool tiles of the toilet cubicle and say it aloud this time.

'I am strong.'

For the first time like, ever, I know I can do without the happy pills, the counselling, the desperate need for approval. I can even deal with the fact Mum seems to have forgotten about me. I am strong. I am loved.

And now I have to deal with the fact the photos are out there for everyone to see, to ogle, to drool over.

Well. Fuck 'em.

It started with giggles and sly looks. People cutting off conversations when I walked into a room. At first I thought it was the usual silent bullying from Naomi and the rest of the Queen Bees.

231

Tara was still doing her lying around looking miserable act, but even she started to look uneasy around me.

'Tara. What is it? What have I done?' We were both in our study bedroom at our respective desks trying to work in between staring out of the window. I was unsuccessfully attempting to untangle some T. S. Eliot poetry and Tara was just staring out of the window, but she winced at my question. 'Come on, there's something. You've hardly been able to look me in the eye for the last twenty-four hours.'

'I don't know what you mean.' But Tara went as red as a beet-root and clicked her pen in, out, in, out. It was maddening.

'Have I sprouted hair from my nose? My chin? What?'

'No,' mumbled Tara.

'Then what?' Frustrating or what?

Tara shrugged.

'Tara. Please. I'm not going to stop pestering you until you tell me.' All at once I felt frightened. It had to be something really bad. Tara told me everything, absolutely everything; we didn't keep secrets – well only one, anyway – that wasn't the way we worked. So if she was reluctant to tell me about something, then it had to be really, really awful.

Tara slammed her book shut and blew air through pursed lips. 'Okay. Don't say I didn't warn you. You're not going to like it. I don't like it. I mean, like, how could you do it? What possessed you? Who made you? Who is he?'

I went cold. 'What are you talking about?' Please, no.

'This, this is what I'm talking about.' Tara thrust her phone at me. 'Look at this web page.'

I looked. At the selfies I had taken. I scrolled through. They were all there. Worse still were the remarks people had left underneath the photos. I felt the tears welling up. Someone had taken something beautiful and made it all sordid. Fuck. Fuck. Fuck. 'What is this site?' I asked, marvelling at how steady my voice was.

232

'It's private.'

'Well, that's all right then.' I hid my terror behind sarcasm.

Tara looked stricken. 'Sorry, sorry. But it's better than going on Facebook or something and then the whole world can see it. That would be much worse, surely?'

'Much worse.' I laughed bitterly. 'How did you get it?'

'I was sent a link and a password.' She shrugged. 'That was it.'

'So you clicked on it.'

'Of course I did. Wouldn't you?'

I looked at Tara. I suppose I was being unfair. If I'd got something like that in my inbox I would so have wanted to find out what it was all about.

'Look, I'm sorry. I wanted to tell you, but I didn't know how to.' Tara bit her lip. 'I really am sorry.'

'Who did this?' I whispered, looking at the screen. 'Who hates me this much?' Theo? Felix? Lucas? Who? 'Do you know, Tar?'

Tara shook her head. 'No. Everyone's wondering.'

'And someone's lying.' I know it's them. Aided and abetted by Naomi.

'What are you going to do?'

'What can I do? They're out there. As you pointed out, it could be worse; they could have gone viral. Around the world.'

Tara nodded. 'Thank heaven for small mercies.'

'One of your mum's sayings?' I spat.

'Don't be mean.' Tara began clicking her pen again. 'What are you going to do?'

'What the fuck can I do? They're out there now.'

I thought I had hidden them well. The innocuous phone app that no one would realize had photos behind them. Why had I kept them? Why not delete them once I'd sent them? I think it was, as usual with me, something to do with being in control. And I wanted to be able to see what I had sent. What I looked like. How I loved.

The feeling of being in control, of being grown-up, dissolves. I am a child again and I want my mum. It is shameful, but I need to talk to someone about it, and she is the person I want to talk to. But I don't think I can.

I leave the bathroom and make my way back along the dark corridor to my room. I slide into bed and close my eyes. Despite everything, I actually feel a sort of peace.

Hallo you. It's me.

Are you all right? You've seemed a little distant over the last few days. When I asked you what was wrong you just smiled and shook your head, but I am sure there were tears in your eyes. What is it? I'm afraid, you see. I'm afraid it's something to do with me and you are going to say we shouldn't see each other any more. But you're not going to say that, are you? You're not going to throw away this perfect love, this cocoon of happiness?

I want to see you now.

CHAPTER 28

ELENA

November: two weeks and three days before she dies

Hallo you. It's me.
What have you done?
What have you done?

CHAPTER 29

June

A simple sleeveless dress and jewelled sandals would do. Alex took the dress off its hanger and slipped it over her head. Looking in the mirror, she applied mascara and more than a few dabs of concealer over the bruise on her face. Then a slick of lip gloss. It was too hot for anything else. She thought of Malone, glowering downstairs. She could almost hear his bad temper. She smiled to herself. It had given her a lot of satisfaction to tell Malone she was going to a barbecue with Jonny Dutch. That he wasn't invited to the end of term bash at the Churchills'. That he wouldn't be welcome and he would have to lump it. The looks on his face had ranged from incredulity (he hadn't been invited) to frustration (she wasn't going to wangle him an invite) to anger (she was going with 'that prick Dutch'). Yes, very satisfactory. Though she had to admit she felt a certain amount of trepidation about going with Dutch. And she wanted to know more about his relationship with Max.

Jonny Dutch had called her when she and Malone had got back from Norwich the day before. Said he'd managed to get her an invitation to the barbecue as his plus-one, and, as an added bonus, Paul Churchill was quite keen to meet her. She hadn't known what to think about that. But she wasn't going to pass up the opportunity of seeing the Churchills. She didn't know quite how she felt about spending the evening with Jonny Dutch. Could he have been Elena's mysterious lover as Tara had suggested? She supposed she could use the evening to gauge whether that was possible. And naturally she also relished the opportunity of putting Malone's nose out of joint by going with Jonny.

There would also be the chance to meet some of the other teachers and staff. Perhaps there was someone else at the school who had been grooming Elena, someone she hadn't thought of. And she very much wanted to see Sven and Ingrid Farrar again. They were certainly not who they seemed.

And had Elena been involved in the drug dealing that had been going on? After all, at Elena's inquest it was revealed she had a small amount of cannabis in her system. Then there was her stepfather, Mark Munro. Where did he fit in with all of this? What had his visit to the school been for?

There seemed to be so many strands to Elena's story.

She looked at herself in the mirror. She'd do.

'Can I at least make up the bed in the spare room?' Malone had eyed her grumpily, arms crossed.

Alex picked up her bag and keys. 'I don't want you here much longer, Malone. You know that. You're putting us in danger.'

'Sofa again, then.'

'Actually, I'd like you to go.'

'I know you would.' He gazed at her, eyes boring into her. She felt a spike of lust that she managed to shake off. She was not going to go there, no way. 'But I'm not. Not yet. Don't worry, I've covered my tracks; you know I'm good at that.' He grinned and Alex found herself smiling back. Stop it, she told herself, just stop it.

Concentrate, Alex. 'I don't care. I don't want you here.'

That lazy smile. ''Course you do. You're not telling me you've still got the hots for the lying art teacher with a limp, have you?'

'None of your business,' she said, hearing a knock on the door.

He had that look, Alex could see it. He was metaphorically balancing on the balls of his feet ready to jump in and interfere in her life again. Except he didn't exactly interfere, did he? A small voice insisted on telling her. He helped her, didn't he? But she didn't want his help now. 'I don't want you gate-crashing this party. Okay?'

He nodded. 'Okay.'

He didn't mean it, she knew that. 'I don't want you there, understand.'

'I said okay. But—'

'But what?'

'You might need a bit of help. Looking around.'

'Malone. I do not need any help at all. Right?'

He studied her, his expression serious. 'Be careful, Alex. I told you I'd been looking into Dutch and—'

Alex held up her hand. She didn't want to hear this, not now. Probably not ever. 'I can look after myself.'

'I know.'

'Right then.'

There was a second, more impatient knock on the door. Malone raised his eyebrow. 'Don't keep lover boy waiting.'

'Malone,' she said through gritted teeth. 'He is not lover boy.'

'You're so easy to goad.'

She pointed at him. 'You had better be gone when I get back.'

'Ah, you would cast me out into the not-so-gentle night.'

'Oh, for goodness' sake. We're in a heatwave. You're not going to freeze to death. So bugger off.' She went to the front door. 'See you, Malone.'

'See you.'

She didn't look back.

The barbecue at the Churchills' terraced house in a road just outside the centre of the village was in full swing by the time they arrived. Alex's mouth watered as she smelled the charcoal and the sausages and beefburgers on the air. They hadn't talked much on the way – Jonny had asked her if Malone had minded her coming to the barbecue with him, and Alex had replied – rather tightly, she realized on reflection, that it was no business of Malone's what she did. Jonny had been a bit surprised.

'I got the impression you two were an item,' he said.

'No.'

'He certainly thinks so.'

'No.'

'Right.'

She couldn't help but notice the small, smug smile on his face and it slightly irritated her. 'I am not interested in being an item in anybody's life,' she said.

'Right.'

Good.

Following their noses, they went down the alleyway by the side of the house and into the back garden.

It was full of people laughing and chatting in the warm evening. Jazz played softly in the background. The garden was a riot of colour: along the back fence roses of every shade and hue jostled for space with white and yellow jasmine and blowsy clematis and graceful hollyhocks. Terracotta pots of daisy, geraniums, and trailing petunias were scattered here and there. There was a slate patio area and in the middle was a mosaic of a Grecian urn made of white and pink and grey pebbles. Were they from the beach? Probably not. There was bound to be some sort of law preventing everyone from stripping the beach of stones. She thought back to her tiny garden in Sole Bay and how it had looked neglected for most of the year. Then to her tiny garden in London, just a square of grass really, but enough to sit out on.

She pushed away thoughts of her garden and looked around to see who was at the party. Couples were chatting easily to one another; more people stood around in groups. Was that Pat, the receptionist? The tiny garden was packed.

'Jonny, good to see you.' A man in a striped pinny wielding a large pair of tongs welcomed them. 'And this is Alex, yes?'

'That's right,' she said, holding out her hand. 'The journalist.'

He smiled. Not threatening. Paul Churchill was an ordinary looking man. Pressed jeans, polo shirt, sandy hair going a little thin on top. A well-groomed close-shaven beard and moustache, pale, pale blue eyes. Pleasant smile. Unremarkable. Could Elena have fallen in love with him? Been seduced by him? By the fact he was a teacher and took more than a passing interest in her? Was he the sort of man who didn't care he was the adult and Elena the child? Was he the sort of man who couldn't keep it in his trousers?

'Hello.' He took her hand. Firm, not limp. 'I'm Paul. And Louise mentioned she'd met you on the beach. Said you'd got on like a house on fire. Ronan took a liking to you, I gather.' He smiled. 'I've been looking forward to meeting you.' He let go of her hand, and she noticed healed grazes on his knuckles. Strange.

At that moment, Ronan bounded up to her, greeting her with vigorous tail wagging. She bent to pat him. He rolled over onto his back.

'Up you get, Ronan; Alex doesn't want to spend all evening patting your stomach.'

'I don't mind,' she said. 'He is so beautiful.' His fur was silky soft. She straightened up. 'You've got a gorgeous garden here. And all these people.'

'Thank you,' he said. 'The garden is really Louise's passion.' He looked around. 'I don't know where she's gone, probably something to do with the children, but she'll be so pleased to see you.'

'Oh yes, you've got two, haven't you?'

'That's right.' His face softened. 'Rowena and Charli. They're lovely. That's who I do it all for. Anyhow, I must away, sausages call.' He waved the tongs about in the air. 'Do help yourself to a drink, please. They're on the table in the corner.' His face closed up as he nodded at Jonny. 'Nice to see you.'

'And you.'

Was there a bit of coolness between the two of them, she wondered? And if so, why?

'You and Paul not the greatest of friends?' she asked as they made their way over to a table bowed under the weight of bottles. Wine, spirits, beer, soft drinks, they were all there so that even Jonny might have difficulty in drinking the Churchills dry.

'We're all right,' he said, pouring her a white wine from a bottle with an indeterminate label, and popping the top off a beer for himself. 'Just a bit of a misunderstanding. In the wife department.'

'Oh?' She thought she could guess.

'Didn't realize they were married when I started at the school. So, you know.' He didn't look in the least bit embarrassed.

Alex rolled her eyes. 'I can guess.'

'She wasn't interested anyway,' he said. 'Pity. I don't think she's happy.'

Alex looked at him. Interesting thought; the same she'd had when last she spoke to Louise on the beach. Perhaps Jonny had more redeeming qualities than she'd thought.

'Ms Devlin. I didn't expect to see you here. Still around?' Alex was caught about to take a big swallow from her plastic glass of wine when Ingrid Farrar addressed her, steely stare in place. Jonny melted away.

'So it seems,' she said, smiling widely and refusing to be intimidated.

'I trust you have come to the right conclusion in your, shall we say, rather unorthodox way of doing things?'

'Ingrid, I don't know what you mean. I haven't finished yet. All I want to do is establish the truth behind Elena's death.' She saw with satisfaction that Ingrid Farrar's fingers were white as she clutched her drink.

Ingrid Farrar leaned in close. 'You know what happened,' she hissed. 'She was ill. She killed herself.'

'Who are you protecting, Ingrid?' Alex said, almost enjoying herself. 'The school? Or yourself?'

The head teacher drew herself up to her full, thin height. 'The school has an impeccable reputation and I intend to keep it so.'

'Yet you have Elena Devonshire who may or may not have killed herself, and Max Delauncey critically ill after an overdose. Not a good track record, is it, Ingrid?'

Ingrid Farrar's mouth churned, as if she was desperate to spew out words she would later regret, before turning away. 'Is it appropriate to bring this up here? We are supposed to be celebrating the end of a successful year and term.'

'Are we? Glad you can put it all behind you. I doubt Elena's mother feels like celebrating. Nor Max Delauncey's family. Oh, and I understand Max was involved in the stabbing of one of your teachers, wasn't he?' God, how do these people become head of so-called prestigious schools? 'And what about Felix and Theo being questioned about drug dealing? That certainly doesn't reflect well on the school and there will be some adverse publicity about that.' The newspapers were already circling.

Ingrid Farrar narrowed her eyes. 'I think you'll find that Felix and Theo were easily led astray and I'm sure the police will find the real culprits. And as for the incident with poor Max, I don't know how you found out about it, but that was swiftly dealt with and no harm done.'

Alex raised an eyebrow. 'You don't let anything touch the reputation of the school, do you Ingrid?'

'I don't know what you mean?' She was gripping her glass so hard that Alex thought it might crack.

'I mean all those generous donations made by various parents. Hush money, it's called in some circles. In fact, I think you're very good at hushing things up.'

'Now you're deluded.'

Alex smiled tightly. 'Every time a pupil goes off the rails you get a big donation from their parents or relatives. And what happens to the pupils? A smack on the wrist, that's all, and maybe a request for them not to do it again because, after all, you wouldn't want the parents to pull the children out of the school and lose all that lovely money, would you?' Ingrid Farrar opened her mouth to speak. Alex jumped in first. 'Does that money all go to the school? And then there was the cover-up over the stabbing of a teacher. My, my, Ingrid, you have got a lot of skeletons in your closet.'

'And you want to be careful. Slander could cost you a lot of money.' Ingrid Farrar moved away.

Alex watched her. How she hoped the Farrars would get their comeuppance. Though they were probably Teflon-coated.

'Alex. I didn't know you were coming.'

Louise Churchill stood in front of her dressed in an above-the-knee skirt and short-sleeved shirt. She wore flip-flops. She pushed her fringe away from her forehead. There was a wary look in her eyes and the air around her shimmered with tension.

'I came with Jonny,' Alex said.

'Ah.' The wariness increased.

'Yes. I am aware he likes to think he's a hit with the laydeez.'

Louise laughed and some of the wariness disappeared. 'Look, I'm sorry about last time,' she said. 'On the beach. I said some stupid things. Caught me unawares. You know, those questions about Elena. I'd been feeling guilty because I had wondered whether there was more I should have done for her – could have done. I was too … ' she was searching for a word, 'dismissive, I think.' She peered at Alex's face. Frowned. 'What happened to you?'

Alex touched the bruise. Obviously hadn't used enough concealer. Or maybe the wrong shade. 'Fell in with the wrong crowd,' she said.

'You need to watch yourself.'

Was it her imagination, or was there a warning in that sentence? 'I will,' she said. 'Look. I know you think I'm just some scummy journalist here to cause trouble, but all I want to do is get to the bottom of what happened to Elena. For her mother.'

'I understand that, of course, and I hope you're able to help Ms Devonshire find some sort of peace. It must be difficult.' Her eyes looked everywhere but at Alex.

'Yes, it is. Louise … ' Alex hesitated, 'forgive me for asking, but are you happy?'

Louise's laugh was a brittle tinkle. 'What an odd question. I know Paul has his faults and I think you caught me on a low ebb the other day, but really, we're very settled here.' She looked around. 'And now I must mingle.' Her smile was bright, bright. 'See you later. Have some food. Enjoy.'

Alex watched as Louise moved off and disappeared among a group of people. She was a difficult one to fathom. Settled. That wasn't the question she'd asked. She poured herself another drink. Prosecco this time, always slipped down easily.

'Here you are. Burger in a bun.'

Jonny appeared by her side and thrust a paper plate into her spare hand. 'Thought you might like to soak up the alcohol.'

'Thanks.' She took a bite. Mayonnaise and ketchup. Fried onions too. She looked at Jonny and nodded appreciatively. 'This is good.'

'I pride myself in sussing out a woman's tastes.' He grinned at her, obviously pleased with himself.

Alex wanted to laugh but had her mouth full of burger and bun. Really, the man was incorrigible. 'Jonny, tell me why Max stabbed you?'

'It was a nick, nothing more. Now can we stop talking about it?' He nudged her arm. 'Zena Brewer. Over there. I'm just off to get another beer.'

Alex knew a diversionary tactic when she saw one, but nevertheless she looked and spied a small woman, probably in her early forties, dressed in an unflattering calf-length skirt and a tee-shirt that outlined the rolls of fat around her waist. Elena's housemistress who wouldn't return her calls. She was deep in conversation with Paul Churchill. The teacher put his hand to her cheek and let it linger there. Zena Brewer seemed to lean into it. Her eyes closed. Interesting.

244

Paul Churchill moved away. Alex marched over.

'Ms Brewer?' Alex stuck out her hand. 'Alex Devlin. I've been trying to get hold of you.'

'Ah. Right.' Zena Brewer looked hunted, her eyes darting around as if looking for an escape route. 'If you'll excuse me.'

'Please don't leave. I only want to talk to you about Elena.'

'Elena.' Alex could see her thinking about what she should say. 'Elena Devonshire was a very troubled young woman,' she said, suddenly firm.

'Did she talk to you?'

'Sometimes. I tried to help, but—'

'When you say she was troubled, was she depressed? Not eating?'

'Not to my knowledge,' she said, her posture all at once stiff and unrelenting. 'I knew she had things on her mind, but she didn't want to talk to me. And if a pupil doesn't want to open up, then there's nothing more to be done.'

'Couldn't you have referred her elsewhere?'

Zena Brewer looked at her as if she were a dimwit. 'If she wasn't going to speak to me, then she wasn't going to speak to anyone else, was she? She wouldn't be "referred on" as you so helpfully put it.'

'Why did you say you tried to get hold of her mother several times when it was quite obvious you didn't try at all? Did you lie about trying to contact her because your sister, Ingrid Farrar, told you to lie?'

She enjoyed the astonished look on Zena Brewer's face.

'Yes, I know you're sisters, and I think you lied to the inquest because you and Ingrid knew you should have rung her mother. There were things going on in the school that were worrying Elena, who was not in a good place, but you are so incompetent that you didn't do anything about it.'

Zena Brewer gaped like a goldfish. 'I don't understand what you mean,' she said eventually. 'And anyway, her father came to see her. Stepfather,' she corrected herself. 'Just a couple of days before she died.'

'And you didn't think it was odd?'

'Odd? What, that she died two days later? No, why?' She blushed. 'You're not suggesting ... oh no, Mr Munro is a very respected businessman. He has an office near The Shard.'

'Right.' Obviously the height of propriety.

'And I don't appreciate being interrogated by the likes of you when I'm at a party,' she spluttered. 'Enjoying myself.' She glared at Alex. 'Now, if you'll excuse me, I have to go.' And with that, she pushed past Alex and marched off.

'Any luck?' Jonny appeared by her side, making her jump.

'Not really,' she said, thoughtfully, watching Zena Brewer as she marched down the alleyway, leaving the party.

CHAPTER 30

The evening wore on, the sun casting a pink glow around the edges of the sky as it set. Soon, there were flickering candles in jars throwing small shadows in the garden. Fairy lights twinkled among the leaves of a Russian vine. Music floated lazily on the air. The evening was still warm. Alex had exchanged small talk with any number of teaching staff, trying to avoid being seen as the evil hack wanting to publish their deepest, darkest secrets. Some of them wanted to talk about Max, express their anger and sadness, but also keen to point out he was a troubled teen. There was an ongoing investigation, of course, and maybe something would come to light, but it wasn't their fault. They were tight-lipped about the stabbing, of course. The Farrars certainly had a hold over their staff. And if she brought up the question of drugs, they recoiled in horror. Felix Devine and Theo Lodge? Well, they hadn't seen that coming, as if such a thing wasn't possible. No, not possible at all. If there were drugs, it would have been stamped on. Hard. Must be local lads.

Alex looked around. Most people were well oiled by now and wouldn't be inclined to notice if she slipped into the house. 'Here,' she said to Jonny, thrusting her glass into his hand. 'I need the loo.'

'Through the kitchen then top of the stairs and turn left. Don't barge into the children's bedrooms.'

'I'll try not to.'

The brightly lit kitchen was a mess – plates of half-eaten food were piled on top of oven trays crusted with pastry that had been tossed carelessly on top of the work surfaces. Glasses were strewn around, sticky with wine deposits. A pair of oven gloves was on the floor. Alex hung them up on a hook. Everybody was outside. No one was in the kitchen at this party. She went through to the hallway, which was lit by a dim bulb – one of those you put in for children who don't want the night to be pitch-black.

She climbed the stairs, wondering if Louise's children were watching television or playing on a computer. Surely they wouldn't be asleep, not with a party going on downstairs? She thought of Gus and how she could never settle him as a young boy if she had people coming round. He always wanted to show off and generally make sure she couldn't relax for the whole evening. If she managed to get him into bed, she would more often than not find him on the landing, legs dangling through the banisters, wanting to know who was there, what was going on. At the time she thought she couldn't wait for him to leave home. Now she couldn't wait for him to come back.

The children's bedrooms were easy to identify.

Rowena's Room. Keep Out. That means You.

and

Here lives Charli. Enter on Pain of Death

Alex's lips twitched. So that was clear then.

She tiptoed past an open door and glanced in. A tastefully decorated bathroom with a claw-foot bath in the corner. Alex had always wanted one of those. A piece of paper Blu-tacked to the door declared it was the loo for guests. She pulled it off and crumpled it up in her pocket.

Further down the landing there was a closed door. She pushed it open, the sound of the jazz music in the garden following her. A bedroom. Louise and Paul's bedroom. She could smell powder and a light, floral perfume mixed in with something deep and spicy. A small light on the chest of drawers in the corner cast a deep shadow. There was a picture of a large nude over the king-size bed. Make that a large picture of a nude over the king-size bed. An overstuffed sofa sat fatly under the window.

She jumped, startled by her own reflection in a mirror above a dressing table. Looking over her shoulder, she hurried towards the dressing table. What was she looking for? What did she expect to find? An incriminating note, perhaps. Something Paul Churchill had left lying around pointing to an affair with Elena. Of course, just because he was having an affair didn't mean he killed her. But she might be further along the path if she could confront him with that fact.

The top drawer was full of pins and empty jewellery boxes and discarded tubes of hand cream. Alex rummaged around for good measure. Nothing. The drawer next to it was much tidier. Paired and rolled socks. Bloody hell, who did that these days? She thought of all Gus's orphaned socks and made a mental note to try harder. She opened the next drawer. Tee-shirts, thin jumpers, a skirt. And the next: men's jeans, jumpers, polo shirts. Nothing out of the ordinary. She tried not to think what she was doing was distasteful, grubby, even; the equivalent of a Sunday tabloid hack rooting around in a person's recycling. No, what she was doing was helping Cat. She had to help her get to the bottom of what happened to Elena; there were too many people not saying anything. Someone, somewhere had to know more. A girl like Elena did not just jump off a cliff to her death, she was sure about that. Call it a hunch, call it intuition, but from everything she'd heard about her, she just didn't think it would happen.

She looked around again. She really ought to be getting back to the party before she was missed. There was a door in the corner. The en suite, perhaps? It was. Stylish shower room: the shower head was large and round like a dinner plate. She opened the cabinet on the wall. It was packed with the usual bathroom stuff: paracetamol, athlete's foot spray, a bottle of pills that looked like … she took the half-full bottle out and checked the label.

Antidepressants. Thanks to her sister she knew every antidepressant on the market. The label said they were for Louise Churchill.

Something glinted in the corner at the back. She moved the athlete's foot powder, the antiseptic cream, and full tube of toothpaste and there it was: a silver ring with half a heart engraved on it. Alex looked at it, her own heart beating fast. She thought back to the ring she had found in the deserted chalet and knew, beyond the shadow of a doubt, that she had found the companion ring. She glanced over her shoulder and listened carefully. Nothing. She picked up the ring and held it up to the light. It was beautiful and so delicate.

'What are you doing in here?'

Alex shoved the ring into her pocket, grabbed the bottle of paracetamol, and turned around. 'I'm sorry,' she said, smiling with apology and holding up the bottle. 'I couldn't find the bathroom, but I found your en suite.' She smiled and shrugged her shoulders. 'I had a bit of a headache.' To illustrate the point, she opened the bottle and shook out a couple of pills, swallowing them dry. Careful, she told herself, don't gabble on, don't explain. That's a sure sign of guilt.

Paul Churchill looked at her for a moment as though he wasn't sure whether or not she was telling the truth, then she saw his shoulders relax. 'That's okay. There was a sign on the door but it has gone missing. Guess I had better do another one.'

'Yes. Good idea.' She made for the doorway, but Paul continued to block it. She couldn't get past him. 'I, er … ' she indicated to the landing. 'I'd better get back to the party. Find Jonny.'

'Jonny Dutch. Painter extraordinaire.'

Alex could now see from his sway and glazed eyes that Paul was drunk. There was a sweaty sheen on his face too. Very drunk.

'He's an arse, you know that, don't you?' Slurring his words.

'Is he?' she said, carefully, wondering if she could squeeze past him without touching him. Probably not.

'Tried it on with Louise.'

'Ah.'

He laughed, but not in a good way. 'Stupid sod. Thinks he's such a ladies' man. He doesn't know the half of it.'

'No, I don't suppose he does.' Agree with him, Alex, just nod and agree and try and get past him. For some reason she felt, not frightened exactly, but unsure of her ground, didn't know what to expect from him. 'Now, excuse me, I'd better be getting back to the party.'

'Stay with me.' He grabbed her wrist as she tried to get past; leered at her. 'You're very—'

'Paul,' she said, firmly, removing his hand from her arm. 'You're drunk and not helping yourself here. Let's go downstairs and get some water, shall we?'

'I'm not a child, you know.' He looked petulant.

Bloody hell, they were all the same. Liked to think they were the centre of everyone's universe. 'I know that. But Louise wouldn't be happy to find you up here. With me.'

He laughed. He looked manic. 'I don't suppose she'd give a fuck.'

Alex looked at him. She put her hand in her pocket and felt the smooth edges of the ring against her fingers. Thought about who could possibly be Elena's lover. Who could have had a grudge against her – enough to push her off the cliff? The same person, or two different people?

And things began to make sense.

CHAPTER 31

ELENA

December: five days before she dies

The worst has happened – i.e. someone (Felix or Theo, that I do know) has distributed my photos, my private photos, around the school. Oh, I thought I knew about technology, enough to hide them, but it only takes a simple thing to hack into a phone and get photos, especially if they got hold of my phone. That's all it needs. Whatever. There they are. On a fucking website. But I've coped. I didn't sink into depression. I didn't start vomming all over again. I've been eating properly: as much as you can with what's on offer. And it's because I have someone to keep well for. Last time it happened, in those dark, dark days after Dad died, I felt as though no one cared. I s'pose, deep down, I knew Mum did care, but she was so wrapped up in her grief that she didn't have any time for me. I get that, I really do. They had been (and this is where I try not to gag) childhood sweethearts, so it was obvious she was going to miss him. She didn't shop or eat or talk or even cry. I was that bit younger and wasn't sure what to do to help. I went to the shops, but came back with all the wrong stuff, and that seemed to make her even sadder. I lived on toast for a while. Till she got better anyway.

I look over to my desk and sigh. The books are lying open ready for me to write that damned essay. As if I give a flying fuck about Philip Larkin. The only decent poem of his was the one about being fucked up by your parents. But we're going to have mocks straight after Christmas and I don't want to fail them. Think of the grief Mum and Mark would give me.

There's a knock on my door.

'Yeah?' I say. Then swing my legs off the bed really quickly and try to look as though I'm doing something because it's the useless housemistress. Zena Brewer.

'Elena, your stepfather is here.'

'Here?' I know I sound stupid, but what in arse's name is he doing at my school?

'Yes. Here. He's in the office, says he hasn't got long. Chop-chop.'

Chop-chop? Yeah, right. Then I think, for one heart-stopping moment, that perhaps something's happened to Mum. But then I think, no, she'd be dripping with sympathy and have a pathetic expression on her face.

'Okay, thanks,' I say, pulling on a jumper. 'I'll be there in a sec.'

'Don't keep him waiting. He's a busy man.'

And I'm not? I look over again to the books on my desk. I suppose not.

I go into the office. Chintz curtains with tie-backs and pelmets, deep pile carpet, big mahogany desk with a comfortable leather chair behind it. A couple of armchairs grouped around a glass table. Mark is standing with his back to me, looking out of the window. He turns as I close the door.

'Elena. Good to see you.'

He is always so polite. He is wearing his dark navy three-piece suit, and his pointed leather shoes had been shined until they, well, shone.

'Is Mum okay?' I ask.

He frowns. 'What? Yes, yes of course she is. She's at a conference in Brussels. Migrant crisis again.'

'Only, I thought … '

His face clears. 'I see. I'm sorry.' He nods. 'You thought there could only be one reason why I'm here on my own at four o'clock on a December afternoon. I understand that.'

'Great.'

'Elena—' He looks as though he is pleading with me.

I hold up my hands. 'Okay, okay, I'm sorry.'

'Look. I think we'd better sit down.'

'That bad?'

'Sit down, Elena. I've had to cancel meetings to get here; bribe that Brewer woman not to saying anything so that it doesn't get back to your mother, so just do as I ask for once. Please.'

It's the 'please' that gets to me. I sit.

He paces, prowling around the room.

'If I'm sitting, how about you sit down too?' I ask.

He does. Then looks everywhere but at me.

'Mark, you're beginning to worry me now. What is it?'

He swallows, finally lifts his eyes to mine. 'Look. I know it wasn't easy for you when I married your mother; I know you miss your dad and that I'm no substitute.'

You can say that again.

'But, know this, I do love your mum. Really love her.'

I nod, wondering where all this is going.

'And I don't want anything to hurt her. Anything I do … ' he swallows. 'Anything you do.'

Riiight. I draw the word out in my head. I try not to shiver.

'The thing is … the thing is … ' He runs his hand over his hair, pushing it away from his face, looks away, out of the window into the gloom.

Suddenly I know what this is all about. 'You've received a link to a site where there are photos of me.' My voice is flat, but inside

I'm burning up with embarrassment. Anger. Shame. Bastards. Sending it to Mum.

Mark nods. To his credit, he looks uncomfortable.

'So you're here to … ?' For a second I feel hopeful. Maybe they care, both of them.

A brief smile. 'It can't get to your mother. I don't want you telling her, pouring out all your troubles to her.' He is all business now it's out in the open. 'From what I can tell, it's a closed site, only open to those who have the link and password.' I nod, but he's not looking at me: he is looking anywhere but at me. Probably sees me naked when he does. 'Luckily, as I said, Catriona is away; the email came to our home account. Obviously this person who sent out the link doesn't have access to my private address or your mother's. And I intend it to stay that way. If she finds out about this, she will want to do something about it.'

Help me? I think, but don't say; she'd want to help me.

Mark is still talking. 'I saw your text to her about things going on at school, things you wanted to talk about. Please don't. That's what I'm saying. I can't have her finding out your grubby little secret. Do you understand? It will ruin her career.'

It's the way he says 'grubby little secret' that makes my stomach churn. I want to defend myself. I want to curl up into a ball. I want to run away. It's not grubby. It's real and it's important to me. It's my life. A thought strikes me. Is that how Mum would see it? Not for the first time I wish my father was here to talk to. 'Is that all you care about? Is that all she cares about?' I burst out.

'No. She cares about you; of course she does.' He couldn't see, or chose not to see, my distress. 'But I don't want her ruining all she's done, everything she's worked for, because you started sending naked selfies to your boyfriend. And this will die down. I'm taking steps to get the site removed somehow. I know people and once it's gone we won't have to worry about it.'

I look at him and realize something. 'It's you, too, isn't it? Not

255

just Mum. If there's a scandal you're worried your moneymaking empire will be ruined.' By the look on his face I know I'm right. 'But how can a few nudie pictures of your stepdaughter do that? I don't understand.'

'Elena. I have just brokered a deal between my company and a company in the States. The Southern States. The Bible Belt of America. The company is owned by one multibillionaire, Gordon McCleod.'

'Why are you telling me this?'

He holds up his hand to stop me saying any more. 'Mr McCleod is a very religious man and we've had to sign a great many morality clauses. Do you see where I'm going with this? Any scandal about nude pictures of you, regardless that you are only my stepdaughter, will put the deal in jeopardy.'

'I was right. It is all about you. Not Mum at all. Because my mum would look after me, help me. Love me no matter what. Give up her career to help me. I know she would. But you. You wouldn't do that. You wouldn't help me because you're not my dad.'

He takes a step towards me, and for a nanosecond I think he might hit me. 'It's about your mother.' All at once I see what 'speaking through gritted teeth' means. 'That's all. We wouldn't want her hurt, would we?'

He is threatening me. How and with what I'm not sure, but he is threatening me.

I crumple. I don't feel grown-up in any way. I've been fooling myself, thinking I had it sorted, that I knew what this life was all about.

I will the tears to stay away. I swallow hard. 'No.' I manage to say. I want to say: but what about me? What about my feelings? I'm breaking up inside. Then all of a sudden I want my mum. I want to talk to her and tell her everything that's happened to me. I realize I'm overwhelmed and don't know which way to turn. Out of my depth. But Mark's voice drones on about loyalty and family and love and keeping it together and all kinds of shit and I nod and say it's fine, it's fine, it's fine.

At last he stands up.

Hello you, it's me

I don't know how to say this but I think we've got to slow down. Take a break. You know how much I love you, but you know how much I've got to lose. Those pictures. Why did you keep them? Why? We were sent a link to the website. They are out there.

Why did you keep them?

CHAPTER 32

June

The girl is standing at the top of the cliff, holding out her hand. Her blonde hair is blowing in the wind, obscuring her face. The moon is a large orb in the sky. A supermoon. Bright, almost like the sun, hanging like a picture. Alex begins to run towards the girl, shouting at her to stay, not to move because if she moves she will fall. But the wind whips the words away and into the dark sky above. Alex's legs are like lead. They won't move her forward. She has to run. Get to the girl. Run.

All at once the wind blows the girl's hair away from her face. It is Elena. And in her outstretched hand something glints in the moonlight. Elena's mouth opens. She falls backwards. Gulls screech overhead. Screech. Screech. Screech.

Alex jerked awake. Her mouth was dry and her head pounding. The screeching of the gulls morphed into the buzzing of her phone. She reached across Malone and—

Malone?

Great. Lying next to her, gently snoring, dark hair on the pillow, face relaxed and peaceful.

Oh God. What had she done?

She would have to sort that one out later. Right now she needed to answer her phone. It could be Gus ringing, not realizing what the time was. She scrabbled for it on the bedside table. Malone turned over. She held her breath for a moment, then cut off the phone's noise.

'Alex, it's Honey.'

Alex struggled to sit up in the bed, pulling the sheet up to cover her naked breasts. Naked. Oh Lord.

She screwed up her eyes and looked at the clock. 'Honey,' she whispered, desperate not to wake Malone, 'it's only half past five. In the morning.' She stifled a yawn and tried to ignore her dry mouth and the insipient headache right behind her eyes. The room was airless, and stank of stale alcohol, though that smell could have been coming out of her pores.

'We got a reply.'

'To what?' She swung her legs out of bed, grabbing a shirt that lay discarded on a chair, and crept out of the bedroom.

'To the message.' Honey sounded impatient.

Alex shut the kitchen door and sat down, rubbing her temples with one hand. She had managed to put on the shirt. It smelled of Malone. 'Just wind back a bit, Honey. It's very early, still the middle of the night for me, and I had a late night last night.'

'Oh. Yeah. Sure. Soz.'

'So?'

'I left a message in the draft folder of that email account of Elena's, do you remember? For the other person to get in contact?'

'I remember.' Clever trick, that. Set up an account and use the draft folder, and it doesn't leave a trail on the internet. Unless someone like Honey goes looking.

'Well, he has. Just got a message. He wants to meet you.'

Was she ready for this? 'When? Where?'

'Tonight. At the lighthouse. I read a book called that once.'

'To The Lighthouse.'

'Yeah, to, at, what difference? He wants you to go there.'

'I mean the book. It's called *To The Lighthouse*, by Virginia Woolf.'

'Right. Didn't she top herself? Virginia Woolf?'

259

'Yes. Walked into—' What was she doing talking about Virginia Woolf and her books? 'Never mind that, Honey. Did he say anything else?'

'Nope. Just that. At ten o'clock.'

'Okay.

'Er … look … er, you take care, yeah? Tell someone there where you're going?'

'Will do.'

As usual Honey put down the phone without any of the normal pleasantries. Saves time that way, mused Alex.

She made herself a hot chocolate: a comfort drink to try and get rid of her dry mouth and headache. It worked, sort of, though the sugar in the drink coated her mouth and teeth. But the headache receded, for the moment. Now she wanted to get her head down for a couple of hours, try to get rid of the fuzzy, muzzy feeling. And the nausea that had crept up on her.

'Where have you been, gorgeous?'

Alex stopped halfway to her side of the bed, mid-tiptoe, feeling like a bad version of the pink panther.

'Come on, I can hear you. Come back to bed.' His hand patted the side next to him.

Oh God. Now what?

'Come on, darlin''

'Malone I—'

He opened one eye and beckoned to her. 'Come here and I'll tell you how it happened.' He stretched, arms above his head.

Did she want to hear this? No, but she probably ought to. But she wasn't about to get back into that cosy, warm-looking bed with him wide awake. No way. She should have gone to the guest room.

She perched on the edge.

'Suits you.'

'What?'

'My shirt. Sexy.'

'Shut up, Malone. So. Tell me.' How she wished she could remember. There were flashes of memory, like tossing more booze down her throat after confronting … who? She screwed up her eyes. Paul Churchill. That was it. In the bedroom, then the en suite. She had found a ring—

She jumped up and looked for the dress she had been wearing last night, finding it in a crumpled heap on the floor. Picking it up, she felt around in the pocket. Yes. It was still there. She took it out and held it in her hand. But what had happened after she'd found it?

Frustratingly she could remember nothing. Nothing at all. What had happened to her? It was unlike her to drink so much that she had a complete mental block. Usually, she remembered something. Come on. Come *on*. She sat down again, trying to force her mind to remember.

'I came looking for you.'

She jumped. She had forgotten that Malone was lying inches away from her. 'Why?'

'I didn't like you going off with that rogue of a man.'

'Jonny?'

'Yes. Jonny Dutch.'

'Oh God, Malone. Get over yourself. You shouldn't even be here. Much less … ' She waved at the bed.

He grinned. Alex could almost call it a wolfish grin. God, he was irritating. 'Get to the point.'

He nodded. 'Right. I will.' He sat up in the bed and Alex had to stop herself staring at the well-defined muscles of his chest and the brown arms with just the right amount of hair and—

'Get on with it,' she said.

'I went to the pub.'

She shook her head. 'Hang on, Malone, let's backtrack here. You came looking for me, that's where we start.'

He began to stroke her bare arm. She hated him doing that;

it sent too many delicious shivers up and down her body. 'Stop it,' she said, removing his hand. 'Now.'

'It starts in the pub. I was talking to Kylie. Lord love her, but she's a flirt.'

Alex raised an eyebrow.

'Okay, okay. Kylie and me, we get on okay, and she knows what goes on around the village: an absolute mine of information. Turns out she's seen Tulip in the pub in the past with a couple of kids from the posh school.' He grinned. 'Loving the name Tulip for Jonny Dutch. Loving it.'

'Which kids? Elena?'

'She thought maybe Elena a while back, but this time it was that young kid, Max, and Naomi—'

'Bishop?'

'Yep. And Naomi Bishop. She said she thought they were arguing, but about what she didn't know. Huddled in the corner, apparently. They were joined by Felix and Theo.'

'Interesting.'

'More than interesting, Alex, you've got to admit.'

'Maybe he was being nice. Buying them a drink. Being matey.'

'Does he strike you as a teacher who gets "matey" with his pupils? Especially ones he doesn't even teach?'

Malone had a point.

'Okay. So what's this got to do with last night?'

'Probably not much. I just wanted you to know that I think Tulip isn't as nice as you thought he was.'

'Who said I thought he was nice?'

'I saw the way you looked at him.'

'Rubbish. You're imagining it.'

'He wants to get into your—'

'Malone,' she said, warningly. 'Enough.'

'Okay, okay. So anyway, Kylie—'

'Your new best friend.'

Another grin. 'Something like that. Anyway, Kylie said Tulip is all charm and winning smiles but sometimes he could look calculating and cold.'

'That's going a bit far,' she protested.

'You would think that, wouldn't you? He was out to charm you.'

'And he's Honey's friend's uncle.' She enjoyed baiting Malone.

Malone shrugged. 'We can't choose our friends or relatives. As I was saying, I didn't like the picture Kylie was painting of him so I left to come and find you at the party. And you were completely out of it. Tulip was sort of holding you up and Churchill was trying to paw you.' He mock shivered. 'Fair gave me the heebie-jeebies I can tell you.'

Alex shook her head slowly. She couldn't remember any of this. 'Holding me up?'

'Yeah.' He looked at her, his expression serious. 'How are you feeling now?'

'Right now?' She frowned. 'Muzzy. Sick. Little people using pickaxes in my head.'

'Memory?'

'Nothing.' She looked at Malone, realization dawning. 'Are you saying one of them – Jonny or Churchill – might have slipped a date rape drug in my drink?'

There was silence, then Malone laughed. 'No, you were just out of it. The booze. Babbling away about parties and children and bottles of pills or something.'

She looked at the ring in the palm of her hand and went over to the chest of drawers. There, in the top drawer, safely wrapped in a pair of knickers, was the other ring: the one she had found in the chalet on the coast path.

She turned to Malone, a ring on each palm. 'Look, two rings. Eternity rings.'

Malone cocked his head. 'Er … are you giving me one?'

'No. Don't be stupid. One of these is Elena's. I found it in the chalet on the coast road; the other I found at the Churchills' house last night.'

'What? Just lying about?'

She shook her head impatiently, and immediately regretted it as the pickaxes went to work again with determination. 'No. In Paul Churchill's bathroom. See? Look at the two hearts. They're a pair. God, I hope he didn't realize I'd taken it.'

'In his bedroom? No wonder he thought his luck was in.'

'Oh, Malone. I was exploring, that's all. Needed to go to the toilet and took the wrong turning by mistake.'

'By mistake? Right.'

'Oh, do stop it,' she said. 'And I'm starting to remember a bit more now.' She could hear the jazz music in her head; it had been background noise while she stood in the bedroom with Paul Churchill leering at her, swaying on his feet. She had not wanted to push past him, but then plucked up the courage. He'd caught her arm. 'You think you know everything,' he'd said, blowing alcohol fumes into her face. 'Well you don't. You should just trot off back to your fancy place in London and leave us be. There is no story here for you. No story at all. Do you understand?' Spittle hitting her face.

'Are you all right?' Jonny appeared at the top of the stairs. 'Come down and have a drink.'

'No, I need to go,' she said.

Jonny wouldn't hear of it, insisting she had another drink. Maybe some more food.

So she had ... just the drink, not the food. And because she was feeling so unnerved she had more than one glass: she had several. Not that she'd meant to have so many but—

'Jonny kept filling my glass,' she said.

'Bastard.'

'Yes, but I kept drinking it.'

She told Malone about going into the bedroom, finding the ring. Hiding it. About Paul Churchill trying to scare her off; Jonny Dutch rescuing her. 'I was going to come home, but somehow it didn't happen.'

264

'Tulip and his magical powers of seduction.'

'Maybe.' She remembered some more. He wouldn't let her leave, kept insisting she stayed with him. Wanted to know what she'd been doing upstairs with Paul Churchill. At the time she thought he was jealous, but thinking about it now it was like he was pumping her for information.

'He didn't want to let you go.'

'No, he didn't.'

'Then I came along.'

'Yes. Jonny was supposed to help me. Get me an interview with Zena Brewer. Tell me which school Paul Churchill had taught in. He did none of those things until I nagged him. In fact, he's done damn all to help. All he seems to have done is turn up like a bad penny at odd times. Almost as if he's keeping tabs on me,' she added, thoughtfully.

'Well, I wrestled you away from him.'

Alex looked at Malone.

'Okay, not wrestled. But we did have a bit of a debate as to who would take you home. I won.'

'Mostly because you had the excuse of staying here, I suppose.'

'Something like that.'

Alex looked at him. 'Malone? What did you say?'

'Ah, nothing but the truth.'

'Don't fob me off with your Irish lies.'

'Just told him I was an old flame come back to claim you.'

She clicked her tongue in irritation. 'I'm not a parcel, Malone.'

'No, I know that. But it worked. I brought you home and we—' He grinned.

Alex looked at him with dismay. 'Tell me we didn't, Malone. Please tell me. I could do without that sort of complication right now, I really could.'

'Am I that bad a prospect?'

'No, Malone,' she said, her anger rising. 'All you did was marry someone for the good of the job. Then you put her inside. You have a child you never see. You're a bloody good prospect.' She stood up, gathering a bundle of clothes together, hoping to God she had all she needed. 'And now I've got things to do.' She stalked out of the door.

'By the way, Gus called me last night,' Malone shouted after her.

Alex stopped. 'You? Why you?'

'He said he couldn't get through to you.'

She ran down to the kitchen and looked at her phone. Sure enough, three missed FaceTime calls from Gus. Why hadn't she seen that earlier? And a voicemail. She pressed the answerphone.

'Hi Mum.' Gus's voice. The sound of laughter and clinking glasses in the background. 'Hope you're okay. Um. Got a few things to tell you. Um. I'll try you tomorrow.'

A few things to tell her? She looked out of the window at the breaking dawn. The sky was red around the edges now. Red sky in the morning, shepherd's warning. Was this the day the weather was going to change? What did Gus want to tell her? He wasn't in hospital, definitely in a bar. If he needed money he would have said something straightaway, she was sure. How had he sounded? She listened to the message again. Tried to analyse how he sounded. Happy? Sad? Cautious? Apprehensive? That was the one. Apprehensive.

'He said he had found his father.'

Alex whirled round; she hadn't heard Malone come up behind her.

'His father?' She tried to process what he'd said.

'Don't sound so surprised. He does have one, you know. You knew he was looking for him. And I told you—'

'I know what you told me.' The words burst out of her. God, she was angry all over again. He always had that sodding effect on her. 'You did have to interfere, didn't you, Malone? Jeez. You had to stick your bloody great oar in when you had no bloody business doing that. No business. What gave you the right? Hmm? What?'

'I've already said, he asked me.'

He was so bloody calm, it infuriated her even more. 'Well you should have told him you couldn't. You should have told him—'

'I didn't want to lie.'

She looked at him, then laughed, astonished. 'That's what you do, Malone. Lie and lie and lie.'

'Do you want to hear what else he said?'

He was so calm she was unnerved. She folded her arms across her body. 'What?'

He gave a brief smile. 'You look like a teenager yourself when you stand there like that in my shirt.'

'Get on with it, Malone.'

'He said his father had been surprised—'

'Well, he would have been, wouldn't he? It was a one-night stand and I never told him about Gus.'

'And remembered you.'

'Oh yeah?'

'He described you, apparently. He's got his own family now, but wants Gus to meet them.'

'How very twenty-first century of him.'

'Come on, Alex. Get off that moral high mound you've built for yourself and admit I did the right thing. Gus was pleased. Said he had more of a sense of where he came from. Felt more settled.'

'So now I've got to say what a brilliant job you've done for my son, have I?' Her voice was cold; she was cold.

'Someone had to help the lad.'

'It should have been me.'

'But you wouldn't have done, would you?'

She glared at him, anger surging through her body, then seeping out through her toes. He had a point. 'You still shouldn't have said anything.'

'I know, I'm sorry. You're right, but—'

She held up a hand. 'Whoa. Say that again.'

'What?'

'The "I'm sorry" bit.'

He gave her one of his crinkly, dancing eyes smiles, and the anger drained away completely. She hadn't known Gus wanted to find out about his father. He had never brought it up, so she hadn't talked to him about it. But she should have guessed. It wasn't normal for a teenage boy not to be curious about his dad. She had been closing her eyes to it all. It had taken this feckless, amoral undercover police officer to do the job for her.

'I was saying, I'm sorry, you were right, but I'm glad I did, and he'll phone you again tonight. He says he has to walk quite a way from where they're staying to get a signal.'

Alex sat down. 'I want a bacon sandwich.'

Malone put the flowery pinny on again. 'Your wish, milady, is my command.'

'Oh, shut up Malone.' She gave his arm a friendly punch. 'And I'm still not having sex with you.'

'Who says you haven't already?'

She groaned and put her head on the table.

CHAPTER 33

'I didn't want to come.' Mark Munro stood on the coastal path looking out over the beach, the sea, the groynes in the distance poking out of the water. 'When she died … ' Alex saw his Adam's apple bob up and down as he swallowed. It struck her how young he was. 'Elena, that is. I couldn't come with Cat to see where she'd died.'

The day was going to be a long one. Malone had made her bacon sandwich with streaky bacon, soft white bread, plenty of butter and it had gone a long way to making her feel more human. What she wanted to do was to sit in front of her computer and type up her notes, see where she was getting to in the search for the truth behind Elena's death. She wanted to gather her thoughts, think about the strands that led to Elena falling off the cliff. The obstruction of the Farrars; the enigma that was Jonny Dutch; the strange couple the Churchills made; Theo and Felix and their involvement in Elena's life. And then there were the local kids and the nasty piece of work that was Bobby. Who had Elena been close to? Who had wanted to get rid of her? She also wanted to go and see Max Delauncey in the hospital as soon as he was well enough to receive visitors. She had managed to dispatch Malone with a shopping list with enough items on it that he'd have to go to Mundesley so that she could get him out of the way. He really did her head in, as Gus would say.

She couldn't think straight when he was around, pushing her

emotions first one way and then another until she was so twisted up she didn't know what to think. Waking up in bed with him this morning had been … what? A terrible thing? Fun? Never again? She didn't think anything had actually happened between them however many faces he made or winks he gave her. It almost made her feel disappointed. If anything had happened, she would like to remember it. And surely if she had slept with Malone, she definitely would have remembered? There. Sorted. Nothing happened. So why did she feel let down? See? She was all over the place.

She had tried to ring Gus, despite Malone telling her that Gus would FaceTime her again when he got to some Wi-Fi. But she couldn't settle. She badly wanted to know what Gus thought of his father; what he was like these days. And if he had met the rest of his family yet. He'd got his own family, Malone said. Boys? Girls? How old? Had Gus got a ready-made family for him over in Ibiza? She slapped down the worm of jealousy. It would be good for Gus to discover he had some normal relatives, that he wasn't forever the 'cousin of the murdered twins'.

Then Mark Munro had knocked on the door. He looked terrible, as if he had driven all night. He had day-old stubble and his skin was an unhealthy grey colour. He was dishevelled, as if he'd picked his clothes out of the dirty laundry basket, and he could have done with a good wash. He'd got her message about wanting to speak to him, he said. Thought it might be important so had got up very early – Cat was in France – and had driven to Norfolk to see her. First of all, she gave him a strong coffee and a bacon sandwich, reckoning it had made her feel so much better it was sure to help him, especially as he looked as though he hadn't been to bed at all, never mind getting up early. Then she felt fresh air was called for.

'Why was that?' Alex stood next to him. 'Why couldn't you come and see where she had died?'

There were clouds like puffs of cotton wool in the sky for the first time in weeks. Even the sea breeze had more of an edge to it. She wondered if the heatwave was finally coming to an end. She could almost smell it in the air, feel the change of pressure. It felt as though the heat was climbing to a point where it couldn't sustain itself any longer.

'Cat was in bits. We hadn't been married that long. About nine months. We were juggling a lot of stuff. Her job, my job, Elena. We'd moved her to The Drift because our jobs were taking us away from home more and more – Cat particularly.'

'And you didn't want to be stuck with a teenage girl to bring up.'

Mark looked uncomfortable. 'If I'm honest, no.'

'So you persuaded Cat to send her away.'

'It wasn't like that.'

Alex didn't say anything. She watched the sand martins fly in and out and around the cliffs.

His shoulders slumped. 'Maybe it was. Maybe you're right and I wanted Cat to myself.'

'But you didn't support her when Elena died, when she needed you most? And I know you were away for the inquest, but couldn't you have come back?' That was brutal, she thought. And blunt. And struck at the very core of herself. How selfish had she been when Sasha needed her the most? How concentrated on her sordid love life had she been? It had made her blind to her own family's needs. Never again. Perhaps that was why she was being harsh: she couldn't bear to see other people make the same mistakes as she had.

It was evident Mark thought so too as he looked at her like a whipped puppy. 'I suppose you think I'm uncaring. Unfeeling.'

'I don't know. Are you?' And she didn't know if she could be bothered listening to his excuses.

'It was a difficult time and I didn't know what to do for the best. Cat said she wanted to come here on her own; to see the place where Elena died, and I let her. I should have been with her, though, shouldn't I?'

Alex nodded. 'Probably. The thing is, when people are grieving they don't always think logically; they say things to try and make stuff better for other people, but they don't necessarily mean it. Sometimes you have to say I am doing such-and-such whether you like it or not.' She shrugged. 'That's what I found, anyway.'

He looked at her. 'We're the same, you and I. We've both suffered because people we love have suffered.'

Oh, how she hoped she wasn't the same as this man. But part of her, a deep down part of her, thought she might well be.

'I hold her when she can't sleep,' he went on, 'when she cries for her daughter. I am trying to heal her pain. You must have done the same for your sister.'

Alex sighed. 'Oh, Mark. Her pain won't heal. She'll learn to live with it, one day, but it won't heal.'

'I thought she was getting better, getting over Elena … ' It was as if he hadn't heard her at all. 'I wanted to be able to put it behind us. Then we had the inquest followed by that wretched thing on Facebook. That message: *Elena did not kill herself*. And she took it as gospel. It opened up all the old wounds. She became obsessed with it. I wanted her to talk to the police, but she wouldn't listen. "No," she said, "I don't trust them". So she came to you. She trusted you.'

'We're old friends. I'm glad she felt she could come to me, even though we hadn't seen each other for years. And, of course, she wasn't getting over it, as you put it; you never get over a thing like that. Christ, it only happened, what, six months ago and you're expecting her to "get over it"? I don't think I'll ever get over the murder of my niece and nephew … ' she had to take care not to let her voice break, 'and that happened more than fifteen years ago. I've learned to live with it.'

'You didn't do badly out of it.'

Alex was made of stone. 'What do you mean?'

'I saw all the articles. About how the killer was unmasked by the children's sister. You. That must have been a great feeling. Bylines everywhere. I expect you were paid a lot of money for those articles.' He was sneering now. 'Bloody journalist. Bloody parasites. Sell out your grandmothers. Or in your case, your sister.'

Alex kept her mouth in a straight line. Don't react. Don't open your mouth. She had schooled herself long and hard not to react to that sort of opinion. For her own sake, she couldn't afford to say anything. She wondered what an intelligent, sane, lovely person like Cat had seen in this man.

'Nothing to say?' His smile was cruel. 'I thought not. You lot are all the same. Poking your long noses into everything. Think you are the moral arbiters of society. Well, I've got news for you. You're not.'

She managed to get her feelings under control. She knew the best form of attack was pleasant politeness. She gave him a small smile. 'I'm sorry you think that way and if I've offended you, I'm sorry. But I am wondering, Mark, what you're trying to hide.'

He looked at her and laughed. 'Don't be so silly.'

Patronizing git.

'I think,' she began, still in her oh-so-reasonable tone, 'the reason you're being so defensive is because you have got something to hide, not just from me but from Cat, too.'

'I don't know what you're talking about.' But he did; she could see he did. 'I came to see Elena, you know. I wanted to be able to tell Cat that she was well and happy.'

'So you came to see her when?'

He looked straight out to sea. 'A couple of weeks before she died.'

'You're lying.' She could afford to be blunt.

He turned his head slowly. His features were twisted, his mouth looking as though he was chewing several bitter lemons. How

273

could she have thought he was handsome? 'I don't understand what you mean?'

'I know you saw Elena two days before she died,' she said, slowly, wanting the words to register. 'Not two weeks. The question is, why have you been lying about it? Especially a lie that can catch you out so easily? Did you have feelings for your step-daughter?'

'Feelings?' He laughed. 'Is that what you think? No, no, nothing like that.' He spread his hands as if in supplication. 'It was, I don't know. I don't know. I suppose I thought … ' He shook his head. 'I don't know what I thought. Why I lied.' Then he let his breath out. 'I suppose I thought that if people knew why I had gone to see her so close to when she killed herself that they might have blamed me for it. For putting pressure on her. Too much pressure.'

'Okay. Let's look at why you came to see her then. It was about the pictures, wasn't it? The naked pictures of Elena.'

Now his hands were warding her off. 'Stop it. Stop it. How do you know about those? How?'

'Mark,' she tried to be gentle. 'I've seen them.'

'What?' His face was a mask of horror. 'I thought … I hoped—'

'That once she was dead no one would see them ever again.'

He nodded wordlessly. 'I was only thinking of Cat. I didn't want Elena to say or do anything that might hurt her. She had to keep quiet about those pictures, otherwise she could ruin her mother. Imagine if the press got hold of them. That's why I came to see her that night. To ask her not to talk to her mother about the pictures. I would make them go away, but she had to keep quiet. I didn't want Cat's career to be harmed.'

'You were only thinking of Cat?'

He nodded.

Somehow Alex didn't think that was true.

'So if it was believed that Elena killed herself, your job was done. No one would ever see the pictures.'

'Yes. You see, you do understand.'

'And if you said she was ill and depressed it compounded the idea that Elena threw herself off the cliff?'

There was a bitter note to his laugh. 'That was the idea. But it didn't quite work out, did it? I had the site where some obnoxious prick had posted them taken down, and was assured that would be that. So how come you know about them?'

'I found them.' She didn't want to tell him about Honey. Nor that Cat had given her access to Elena's phone and computer. Somehow she thought Cat wouldn't want Mark to know quite how much she was trusting Alex.

'What do you mean you found them?' His voice was suddenly as hard as steel.

She thought quickly. 'I saw one of her old school friends and she still had some of the photos.'

'Who?'

Alex shook her head. 'It doesn't matter who.'

She flinched as Mark gripped her shoulders. 'Who?' His eyes were wild and he began to shake her.

She wriggled free. 'Stop it, Mark. I am not going to tell you. Deal with it. But those photos will not surface again. I've made sure of it.' How she wished it could be so simple, but she had thought more than once, if they were still on Elena's phone, someone, anyone, could have downloaded them and kept them. She pushed the thought away.

He looked defeated. 'Is that what you wanted to tell me? About the photographs?'

'I really wanted to talk to you about why you lied about when you last saw Elena. And how you managed to get past Zena Brewer to see her. I imagine you didn't climb up a drainpipe.'

His mouth twisted in a smile. 'No. Zena was easy to get onside. She's a sucker for a famous parent and a bit of flattery. Power and money are sexy. And now you know why I was reluctant to tell the truth. I suppose you'll tell Cat now.'

'I think it's up to you to tell Cat, don't you?'

He nodded.

She watched as he walked away. She didn't like or trust him. Not at all.

CHAPTER 34

ELENA

December: sixteen hours before she dies

So today I feel like shit.

I am going through the motions. I drag myself out of bed and throw on some clothes. I open the curtains and look out of the window. That same dark sky turning from night to grey day; rain that is running down the window. I watch the rivulets of water, playing that childhood game of guessing which one will reach the bottom first. I flatten my palm on the glass and rest my head on the back of my hand and wonder what to do now. I can barely summon up the energy to move.

The air in the room is stifling. The radiator has been on since six and I can smell the staleness of sleep, sweat, and my own despair. I chew the bottom of my lip, then fling on some clothes and my parka, pull on my trainers, grab my phone, and let myself out of the bedroom.

I gasp as the sea wind hits my face. It slices through my joggers, freezing the front of my thighs. The bare branches of the trees bow and scrape with the force of the wind. My trainers are getting wet as I squelch through the puddles left by the overnight rain. I don't know where I'm going or what I'm going to do; I just know I have to do something to get rid of the gnawing in my stomach, the whirlwind of thoughts in my head. I have to make sense of it.

I look up into the leaden sky at the dark clouds scudding by. If I look over the sea, I can still make out the winking lights of a buoy that bobs on the water warning sailors of I don't know what. I can hear the sea in the distance, the waves throwing themselves onto the shore as if they are angry with the world. I know how they feel.

It's over.

It can't be over.

I have done everything I have been told to do. I have kept it secret; I have met up in out of the way places; I have sent photos exactly as I was asked. I have loved.

I walk down to the very edge of the grounds. There is a sturdy fence where the land that belongs to The Drift ends and the field in front of the cliff begins. It would be easy to climb over the fence and find myself at the edge of the cliff. But I think of how I have already conquered my worst demons and I think of Mum waiting for the Christmas holidays so she can, as she says, 'whisk me off skiing'. I couldn't do it to her.

I take the phone out of my pocket and pull up the email account.

Can we talk? I type. *Please.*

I look at the phone.

I wait for a reply.

Meet me by the chalet on the cliff. Midnight.

CHAPTER 35

June

Alex walked back to the cottage relishing the thought of at least an hour or two before Malone got back from the shops. She needed to get her thoughts straight in her head. Thoughts about Gus and how to approach him when he finally rang. She would, of course, be supportive and interested to hear about his travels and how he had gone about the search for his father. She would praise his ingenuity and apologize for not talking to him about his father before. She would ask all about the family, his new family, and how he thought he fitted in. She tried not to think that maybe his father's wife and children wouldn't want to know him. That they would reject her gorgeous boy. If they did, she would be on the first plane over there to burn their house down. No, that was being silly. She would tell them what a wonderful person he was, and then burn their house down.

No she wouldn't. She had to let Gus lead his own life. He wasn't stupid; he would have thought all of that through and come to the same conclusion. He could be headed for rejection, but if he didn't try, he wouldn't know.

There was a definite unsettling of the air now. Waves with white horses were beginning to roll to shore and clouds drifted across the sky. She wondered if the heatwave was going to break soon. And she thought about the coming meeting with whoever had replied to Honey's message in the draft folder. She had a pretty good idea who it could be. It would be interesting to see if she was right.

A figure peeled off the wall by the front door. Her heart sank. She felt for her phone in her pocket. She could call Malone, ask him to come back as soon as he could … get rid of Dutch for her. Or—

'Jonny,' she said, mustering a smile. 'What are you doing here?'

He smiled back. 'Came to see if you were okay and to say sorry for letting you get into that state last night.'

Lord, two men apologizing in the space of a morning. What was the world coming to?

'Don't worry about that. I'm quite capable of making my own decisions, you know.' She tried to keep her tone brisk, no-nonsense.

'I'm aware of that. Just, you know, not wanting you to feel bad.'

'Right.' What was it about feelings and relationships that one day you could be quite excited by someone, think that there may be some sort of future or that you could just have a good time with them, only for that feeling to disintegrate in a split second? Before the barbecue and before she knew that Dutch hadn't been straight with her, she had thought she and Jonny might have something going for them, but after, all that feeling had gone. Was it because he'd let her get horribly drunk? So drunk that she wasn't sure what happened? Or was it because she was coming to realize that Jonny Dutch wasn't as nice as his smile. Or, God forbid, it was something to do with Malone. Put that thought in a box and pack it away.

'And I wanted to catch up.'

He fell into step right behind Alex as she let herself into the cottage. She could feel his breath on the back of her neck.

'Catch up?'

'Why not?' He leaned against the kitchen counter as she filled the kettle.

'Coffee?' Politeness instilled in her from childhood. She'd really wanted to tell him to eff off.

He nodded. 'So, not too much of a hangover?'

'No. A bacon sandwich and a walk saw any threat of one of those off, thank goodness.'

'Mind you,' he sat down, made himself comfortable, 'you were soon spirited away by … Malone, isn't it?'

'That's right.' As if he didn't know. She took two cups out of the cupboard and began spooning coffee into them, ignoring the machine sitting reproachfully on the side.

'And you don't mind that?'

'What do you mean? Sugar?' She held out the jar helpfully marked 'sugar'.

'No thanks. I mean, you seem like someone who knows her own mind so being rescued like a damsel in distress by someone on a white charger feels a bit, well, you know.' He shrugged.

She would not rise to his bait. The kettle boiled, its whistle sounding loud in the silence.

'No, I don't know,' she said, lightly. 'Tell me.'

'What I said. You're more independent than that, more resourceful.'

She poured the just-boiled water on the granules, resisting the temptation to pour some on his lap.

'You may feel I haven't helped you much. About the Elena thing. As I was supposed to be your spy in the school. But I guess that's just it, there was nothing to find out. I talked to some of the teachers and the kids that were in her year, the ones that are just about to leave, and they all said the same. Nice girl, a bit flaky.' He shrugged. 'I think that's all there is to it.'

'All there is to it?' She handed him the mug. 'What do you mean by that?'

'She was known for her depression, her eating disorders. There'd been something going on that made her miserable; she'd just broken up with her boyfriend and—'

'Any ideas?'

'What?' He sipped the coffee. She wasn't going to offer him a biscuit.

'Any ideas what happened?'

He shrugged. 'I imagine she'd had enough one day and went and threw herself over the cliff. Maybe she regretted it the second she did it but—' He banged the flat of his hand on the table making Alex jump. 'Too late. No one's going to survive that fall.'

'What about those lads in her year: Felix and Theo? And what's the other one called?' She pretended to think. 'Ollie, that's it. The ones who threatened me. You were going to put out feelers about them, remember? Do you think they had anything to do with it?'

He shifted uncomfortably on his chair.

She pushed the cup of coffee towards him. 'The ones who deal drugs.' She added, just in case he hadn't got her meaning. Her voice had an edge of steel to it, she was glad to hear. 'I know they do. I've seen it happen. And after the business with Max they aren't going to get away with it.'

He nodded. 'I see.'

'And I think you know about Felix and Theo, don't you? That they've been questioned over dealing?'

He raised an eyebrow. 'So?'

She looked out of the window at the sky, the clouds. Seagulls. All normal. 'Here's the thing,' she said. 'You're the trendy art teacher. You have had an exciting life, a frightening life, even, with all the army heroics. You dabble: a bit of cannabis here, a bit there. Medicinal, you say. Then I hear you've been getting up close and personal with some of the kids from The Drift. Naomi Bishop? Max Delauncey, now in hospital after an overdose. The same Max Delauncey who stabbed you, in case you'd forgotten. You're even pretty friendly with Felix and Theo and that lot. So friendly, I begin to wonder whether you have anything to do with the drug dealing. After all, you probably have the contacts. What with your "medicinal" cannabis and those monthly trips down to London Sy spoke about. Buying trips, were they?'

Dutch raised an eyebrow. 'That's a big leap, isn't it, Alex?'

He sat there looking relaxed, as if he didn't have anything to worry about. For a minute, Alex wondered if her conclusions had been wrong. Perhaps he was merely an innocent art teacher after all. She suddenly became aware that she was alone in the house with Jonny Dutch. A house that was miles from anywhere. She remembered how threatening the boys had been the other night. She sipped her coffee.

'Come on, Jonny, I think you're behind the drugs around Hallow's Edge. You got those boys to warn me off and I think you supplied Max. You did, didn't you?' She held her breath.

For a moment he stared at her, his eyes hard. 'Proof?'

'None.'

'So?'

Had he won? Had he bloody won? Not if George could help. Surely, somehow she must have seen Jonny Dutch and the teenagers. Perhaps she didn't realize what she had seen. It would be worth talking to her some more.

'I have proof.'

Jonny Dutch stood. He loomed over her. She hadn't realized until now how tall he was. Her heart thumped in her chest. 'You think you're so clever, don't you?' he said.

'I don't know what you mean?' She was not going to be cowed by this man.

'You come here, some half-arsed journalist thinking you're going to "get to the truth"', he made quotation marks in the air, 'behind a girl's death. Stupid. She threw herself off that path and that's it.'

'Maybe.'

'You're going around implicating everybody in her death, shouting about drugs. She killed herself, Alex. End of story. No drugs involved.'

'As I said, Jonny, maybe. And maybe the fact you peddle drugs had nothing to do with her death. But, you know, she didn't like the drugs going around in the school, what it did to her friends. To her best mate Tara. To Max Delauncey. And here's the thing. You deal drugs. Did she find that out? That you deal?'

'You'll never get that accusation to stick, Alex.'

She looked at him steadily. 'Felix and Theo will give you up rather than face time in a young offenders institution.'

'Really?' he sneered. 'Any idea who their fathers are? A barrister and a judge. You think they're going to let their precious boys go to jail? No, of course not.'

'But are they going to protect you? Won't they be looking for a scapegoat?'

She saw a flicker in his eyes. 'You don't think I'm where it stops, do you? And what proof have you got?'

He was right. He wouldn't be the end of the row. There would be others more powerful, more dangerous. Other people in a line that stretched back to Latin America or Africa where drug money was used in terrorism or to terrorize. But she couldn't do anything about that. She could do something about him. She felt the reassuring presence of the phone in her pocket.

Mistake.

Dutch's hand shot out and grabbed her arm, twisting it out of her pocket and away from her body. He pushed her hard and she fell backwards, stumbled, fell onto the floor. Her head hit the tiles hard. She blacked out for a moment. Came round. Found Dutch, knees either side of her body, holding both her wrists in one hand above her head. He had her phone in his hand.

'Do you think I'm stupid?'

She looked at him, seeing two of him for a moment. Her vision cleared. He was staring at her. She shook her head. 'No,' she whispered. She felt weak. Sick. Not again, she thought. Not again.

'No. Exactly.' With his free hand he scrolled through her phone. 'Ah, here we are.' The tinny sound of his voice reached her ears.

'*You may feel I haven't helped you much. About the Elena thing. As I was supposed to be your spy in the school. But I guess that's just it, there was nothing to find out.*'

'Very clever, recording our conversation. However, it's easily got rid of.' His thumb pressed down. 'There. Gone.' He threw the phone across the floor. Alex turned her head, watching despairingly. Now what?

Dutch's knees pressed against the sides of her torso, squeezing it painfully.

'Now then, Alex Devlin, what are we to do?' He grinned.

She shivered. 'Nothing,' she said. 'Let me go. You've deleted the recording. You're right, there is no evidence.'

'No. But it seems a shame to end our relationship here.' He cocked his head to one side.

'We don't have a relationship.'

'Hmm.'

He adjusted his position so he was kneeling between her legs now. He used his free hand to caress her face. 'Come on, Alex. You know you want this really.' His hand moved down her body, fondling her breasts roughly, down, then he brought it up hard between her legs. She squirmed, trying not to cry out. He laughed. Then slapped her face. She heard a ringing in her ears. Now he held a wrist in each hand.

Think, Alex, think. She wasn't going to be raped by this lowlife.

'We have unfinished business, Alex. You see,' he smiled again, 'I know you like me. Most women do.' He slapped the other side of her face. It was easy to make herself go limp. 'Honestly, I only wanted Theo and Felix to give you a bit of a fright the other night. Make a couple of heavy breathing calls. Couldn't have you following kids around the village, could we? You might see what they get up to. And it could have been worse. I could have set Bobby on you, and believe me, you wouldn't have liked that. Come on, Alex, where's your fight?' He had let go of her hands and was bending down low over her.

285

Where was her fight? She had allowed herself to be intimidated by two teenage boys. It wasn't going to happen again.

Alex gathered herself, then reached out, putting a hand flat on each of his shoulders keeping her arms straight. She twisted her body, managed to get her feet on his hips and push him away. Then she began kicking him. His face, his chin his groin, his stomach, anywhere she could reach. She put all her frustration and anger into the kicks. She felt her feet connect with bone and skin and soft muscle. He cried out with pain and fell backwards.

She leapt to her feet. Dutch was lying on the kitchen floor, his eyes closed.

His hand shot out, grabbed her leg.

She twisted and turned, then kicked him in the side of his head with her free foot. He went limp.

She stood, panting, her hands resting on her knees. The bruises she'd got in her tussle with Felix and Theo were beginning to hurt again. Her knee was sore. Her face was sore.

'Bloody hell, Alex. I thought you liked him.' Malone stood in the doorway, two supermarket carrier bags in his hands.

'Not so much,' she said, trying to ignore the ringing in her head from Dutch's well-aimed slaps. She rubbed the sides of her face. 'I'm fed up with people hitting me in the face. I thought I'd do something about it this time.'

Malone dropped the bags on the floor and took her chin in his hand. This was becoming familiar territory. His gentle fingers, his concerned look, his smouldering eyes … for God's sake, Alex, get a grip. Get a grip.

'It is becoming something of a habit. I'll go and fetch the arnica, if we've got any left.'

'Er, before you do that … ' Alex pointed to Dutch who was beginning to moan and groan on the floor. 'Could you do something with him?'

Malone looked at Dutch and sighed. 'What do you suggest?'

'Police?'

'Why?'

'Drug dealing.'

'Evidence?'

Alex nodded to her phone that was still lying on the tiles in the corner. 'I recorded a confession. He thought he deleted it, but I'm sure the police can get it back. If they can't, Honey will be able to.'

Three hours later and Alex was sitting in the garden, cup of tea in hand, being waited on hand and foot by Malone. The police had come and gone, taken Dutch and her phone away and taken a statement from her. She rather liked this newly concerned Malone, especially as her whole body ached.

The newly concerned Malone came out and sat down with her. 'I told you I had got some intel on Dutch, but you wouldn't listen.'

'And I suppose you're going to tell me now.'

'Just that I was right.' He smirked. 'He's certainly got form. Despite being decorated for bravery in Afghanistan, he left the army under something of a cloud. Word has it he took drugs as well.'

'Probably had post-traumatic stress disorder.' She had certainly written enough stories in her time about the effects the war in Afghanistan had on soldiers. 'So how did he get the job at The Drift?'

'Sven Farrar. His brother was killed in the Gulf War. Took pity on Dutch and leaned on the governing body. I think it helped he was only doing a few hours a week.'

Alex sighed. 'Now I don't know whether to feel sorry for him or to just hate him. He obviously needs help.'

'He'll get it where he's going, without ruining any more young lives.'

She nodded. 'I guess so.'

'Now,' Malone said, handing her his phone. 'You'd better try

Gus on this because he won't be able to contact you now the plods have got yours.' He stood. 'I'll leave you to it.'

Alex sat looking at the phone for a few minutes. Picked it up. Scrolled through Malone's rather sparse contacts and found Gus's number. Her finger hovered over the FaceTime symbol. Gus had found his father. The man she had hooked up with for one brief night while they were both high on God knows what. The first and last time she'd had anything more dangerous than alcohol. He had been the DJ in a nightclub; she'd been there as part of a press junket. Her first taste of freedom. Her shiny new job. That night had put paid to all that. She never saw the DJ again; never told him about Gus. There hadn't seemed to be any point at the time. Perhaps now, in hindsight, she had been wrong.

She pressed the connect button.

'Hey, Mum! How are you doin'? And why are you on Malone's phone?' He looked bronzed, his hair shot through with highlights from the sun. He was lying on a sunbed and she thought she could see a pool behind him. Her chest felt full at the sight of him.

'I haven't got mine at the moment … long story, my darling.' She brushed his question away. 'Anyway, I'd rather hear about you.' She smiled at him, feeling emotions well up in her throat, but determined to keep up a bright and breezy front. 'Tell me what you've been doing. It looks lovely where you are, Gus.' She tried to swallow the big lump in her throat.

'Well … '

She realized she was going to have to lead. It wasn't fair on Gus to expect him to make the running. 'Look, love, I know you've found him. Your dad, I mean. Malone told me.'

He visibly relaxed. 'Mum, I—'

'It's fine. Really. I should have told you more about him. I should have been helping you, not Malone.' She smiled. 'Tell me what's been happening.'

'Are you sure?'

No. 'Yes.'

'Well, I'm sure Malone's told you that it wasn't easy at first. He'd travelled around such a lot. At one point I thought I was going to have to tell you I was going to Latin America.' He laughed. Alex tried to laugh with him. 'But it turns out that he came back to Ibiza a few months ago and bought a bar. Anyway,' he took a deep breath, 'we found him in Es Cana. There's a real chilled-out vibe here.'

'Has he … ' she hesitated for a second without knowing why, 'got any family?'

A big smile broke out on Gus's face. 'Yeah. He met Juanita in Argentina and he's got three children. Isn't that great?'

'Yes, great.'

'Two boys and a girl. Fourteen, twelve, and ten. Camila – that's his daughter, my half-sister, Mum, can you imagine that? – she's a sweetheart, wraps everyone around her little finger. The two boys are Marcos and Caleb and they like football. Manchester United, of course. Juanita says I can stay as long as I like. She's been cool about it all.'

'It must have been a shock for them, though, Gus, when you turned up?'

For the first time Gus looked a little awkward. 'It was a bit. I emailed him first, though. I couldn't wait, you know? He told his family about me before I turned up.'

'That's good, darling.' Her face was aching with keeping up the smile.

'Thanks, Ma. And you see,' he scratched the side of his face with his thumb; a habit from childhood and a sure sign he was worried about saying something, 'for the first time in ages I'm not looking for Millie, you know? I'm not looking for a 20-year-old who looks like Auntie Sasha or like you. Not trying to see her face in the crowd. Not looking on the beach, in pubs, in movie queues. Do you understand?'

Alex nodded. Of course she did.

289

He nodded back. He smiled again. 'And it's bloody gorgeous here.' He sat up. 'Um, look, we reckoned, that is Dad, um, Steve and me, that you wouldn't want to speak to him just yet, would you?' He had a half-hopeful look on his face.

She was glad of the get-out clause. 'No, you're right.' She laughed. God, it was a strain. 'A bit too much, I think, at the moment.' She laughed again. 'How long are you staying? Because you mustn't outstay your welcome.'

Irritation flashed across his face. 'I won't, Ma, don't worry. Me and Dave are off to explore the island in a couple of days. We might come back here before we carry on. Is that okay?'

'Of course it is, sweetheart. It's nothing to do with me.'

'No.' He smiled. 'Listen, Ma, gotta go. I think we're all going to the beach to hang out.'

'All of you?'

'Yeah. It'll be fun. Look, I'll phone you in a couple of days. Will you have your phone back by then?'

'Probably. Don't know. Give it a try.'

'I will.'

She heard excited voices in the background calling Gus's name. More shrieking and shouting. He turned his head away from her, smiling and waving. His new family.

He turned back. 'Okay, Ma. Talk soon.'

'Yes. Talk soon. Bye darling.' Another aching smile.

He was gone. She touched the blank screen where his face had been, not sure how to describe what she was feeling. Jealous? Usurped? Not needed? Or was that being too selfish, too self-absorbed? This is what she wanted for Gus, wasn't it? For him to be happy. Find his own way in the world; find out who he was after living in the shadows most of his life.

CHAPTER 36

ELENA

Twelve hours before she dies

I didn't know time could drag like this.

I go to my classes. Have lunch. Everything I eat is tasteless.

I haven't been happy, and I know part of it is the pressure of keeping the whole thing secret. I have wanted to shout about it, tell people what a wonderful life I am having, and I haven't been able to. But I have done everything asked of me and now it's over, because of those stupid photos. Why did I do them? The simple answer is, because I was asked. I didn't know some perv would be able to download them and post them on some frigging website, did I? It's not my fault, is it? I didn't want to do the photos particularly, so why am I being blamed for the whole fucking thing? I shouldn't have had to do them in the first place, should I?

I know now what I am going to say. I am going to say 'It is fine to end it. I have had enough.' And I will walk away, just like that.

But can I do it? I have to admit I have enjoyed the intrigue: the excitement of the secret meetings, the thrill of possible discovery; the deliciousness of what people would say if they knew who I was seeing. Perhaps I will say something to the Queen Bees after all.

I find the Queen Bees in their usual Wednesday-afternoon-bunk-off-school cannabis-smoking hang out, huddled on the beach and sheltering from the wind by the side of the wartime concrete bunker that had been tossed and turned over by the winter storms a year ago. My heart sinks when I see Max is with them.

'Look who it isn't,' says Naomi, pulling her cashmere coat around her for warmth and sucking hard on the joint that is being passed around. 'To what do we owe this pleasure?'

I shrug. 'Wanted to see what you were up to.' I look at Max who appears positively skeletal. He keeps sniffing, wiping his nose with the back of his hand.

'Leave him alone,' says Naomi. 'He's with us.' She gestured around. 'And you can see what we're up to. Chilling. Have you heard from Tara?'

'No.'

Naomi shrugs. 'She'll be okay. She'll have a brat to look after, keep her busy.'

I stare at her. 'You know about that?'

'Come on,' laughs Naomi, 'everyone knows about that.'

Jenni wraps her scarf more tightly around her neck. Natasha takes a hip flask out of her coat pocket and swigs from it. Max stands and shivers.

'I suppose you've been busy,' continues Naomi. 'What with taking photographs and all that.' She laughs. It is not a pleasant laugh.

I can feel the blush spreading up from my neck.

'Mind you,' Naomi isn't finished yet, 'I think the trolls went too far. You're not that bad. Not good, but not that bad.' And she giggled. 'But we're bored of those pictures now, can we have some more, please?'

'Sure,' I say, reaching out for the joint. 'Why not?'

'Oooo, becoming one of us now,' says Jenni, as I breathe in, trying not to cough when the smoke hits the back of my throat.

'No,' I say, breathing out with a bit more ease. 'Just wanted to see what the fuss was about.'

Max looks at me, a puzzled look on his face, as if to say: what on earth are you doing?

To be honest, I haven't got a fucking clue. I have another toke.

I look around me. What am I doing here?

'Are you going to tell us who it is? We're all dying to know.'

I blink slowly. 'Well.' Shall I? Shan't I?

The wind makes another determined effort to whip the sand around our feet and legs.

They seem to lean forward as one. After another pull on it, I hand the joint to Nat. 'No,' I say. And laugh at the disappointment on their faces. Except for Max. He is looking at me at last and I see fear on his face, but the skunk has got to me and I laugh again.

'See you,' I say, as I walk away.

I spend the rest of the afternoon trying to do some work, but my head is muzzy and I can't think straight.

I go to the canteen for supper. Eat something laughingly called beef bourguignon. AKA stew. I hardly taste it. It is like swallowing bullets. I drink water because my head still feels thick. I don't talk to anybody and none of the Queen Bees is here. I wonder where they have gone and what time they'll be in to eat. Perhaps they are still on the beach, but surely they can't be that careless? If they are not here for supper, they'll be missed. Mentally I shrug my shoulders. Not my problem.

I wander along to the common room because I'm bored with my own company and I try to watch some rubbish on television but I can't concentrate. I go back to my room. I think of Mum. I think of Mark and of how he warned me off confiding in Mum. But I will. I want to have a proper talk to her. During the holidays.

I want to tell her how I feel. What I have done. I pick up my phone. Begin to text her.

'Mum, I don't think I can do this any more.'

But I stop, because what am I going to say in one stupid text? I throw my phone across the room and go to bed, fully clothed, to wait for the time to pass.

At half past eleven I get out of bed.

I leave the room and make my way down the dimly lit corridors through the house. I reach the back door and feel up on the lintel for the key, unlock the door, and put the key back. How great it has been since a sixth-former duplicated the back door key and left it for future students to use to escape. The door clicks shut behind me. I realize I have left my phone where I threw it earlier, but luckily the sky is clear for once and the moon lights my way.

Hello you, it's me.
Please don't go to the chalet. Please, please.
I love you.

CHAPTER 37

June

Malone had not wanted her to go, but there was no way she wasn't going to meet Elena's lover. Then he wanted to go with her, reasoning that she'd had a tough day (no shit, Sherlock) and was battered and bruised (really, no shit Sherlock) and should let him go to the lighthouse. She'd refused. Then he began to get heavy-handed, telling her, no, *ordering* her to stay behind. 'Have a bath,' he said. 'Relax. Watch a romcom or something.' She wanted to slap him. He tried to kiss her. She pushed him away.

'I am going by myself and that, Malone, is that.'

He pushed his hair away from his forehead and gave an irritated sigh. 'I can't let you do that.'

'Tough,' she said. 'You'll just have to suck it up.'

Then he'd leaned forward and kissed her hard on the mouth.

She stood still for a moment, shocked, more at what a mix of feelings the kiss had thrown up than at the actual kiss itself. 'What was that for?' She put her fingertips to her lips, which were still tingling.

His hand snaked around the back of her neck and he pulled her towards him.

She found her senses and pushed him away, stumbling backwards in her haste to get rid of him. 'No you don't, Malone. You're not going to get round me that way.'

'Shame,' he said, with that slow smile of his that always got her in the solar plexus. 'I thought I was in with a chance.'

'Well, you're not.'

And as far as she was concerned, that was an end to it.

She closed the front door behind her, patting the pockets of her thin anorak to make sure she had Malone's phone and his small but powerful torch. He had some uses. A sea mizzle snaked around her as she walked down the path, the phone lighting the way. A storm was surely on its way. If she looked across the sea she could see forks of lightning in the distance and hear faraway rumbles of thunder. The sky was darker than it should have been at midsummer: clouds scudding across it, hiding the moon and the stars. The heatwave was about to break.

She peered at her watch. She had plenty of time to get to the lighthouse before her assignation with whoever had left the message for her in the email. It had to be Elena's lover. It had to be. No one else would know about that trick. She walked on, trying not to think about how disturbed she had been to feel Malone's body hard against hers. And how she had felt a bubble of excitement as it looked as though he was going to try and kiss her again. God, why wasn't life simple? Why couldn't she fall in love with someone simple and uncomplicated? An accountant, perhaps, who could at least do her tax return. Not some guy who worked in the underbelly of society and who she never knew whether he was going to stick around or not. And who kept sticking his nose into her business.

Bloody Malone.

Turning off the track she began walking up the path between the fields of oilseed rape. It felt very lonely only being able to see the crop either side of her and the tall red and white bands of the lighthouse ahead; its three lights flashing every thirty seconds, warning ships of the dangers of the sea. There was no light pollution out here. The wind was getting up and she could hear the sea in the distance, crashing onto the shore.

The lighthouse loomed in front of her. Of course it looked different in the dark, and when she'd been here before, she'd hardly taken it in, she'd been so intent on following George and seeing what she was getting up to. Poor kid. Hopefully what happened to Max would serve as a warning to her. Why did so many youngsters seem to set out to ruin their lives? What made the difference between one being on the right road and another taking a wrong turning? It was a conundrum: nature versus nurture.

She listened. Nothing but the sea and the wind. Apart from the lighthouse and her torch, there was no light anywhere. No cars, no footsteps, no people talking. She could have been at the end of the world.

She walked up to the door of the lighthouse and pushed. It swung open.

A whitewashed stone room greeted her, and she shone the torch, lighting up the darkness. The walls were covered with laminated boards: photographs of the lighthouse and its surroundings. Information about its history. How it was saved from demolition and was now run by a trust. The air was musty with the faint tang of the sea. And there was the bottom of the spiral staircase, the steps winding up the inside of the perimeter wall. How many were there? Looked like at least a hundred. Still she could hear nothing. Was she supposed to go up? Evidently. There was nothing else around.

She began to climb, her footsteps echoing around the walls, which began to close in on her the higher she went. Looking down it was as if she was climbing around the inside of a snail's shell. She clung onto the brass banister, trying not to think of the void on her right. This was not for the faint-hearted.

At the top of the stairs she entered a room that housed a tangle of electronic equipment. This, she surmised, was the guts of the place: the equipment that operated the lights.

'Up here.'

Alex jumped at the voice. The torchlight picked up a smaller set of stairs.

'Come on.'

She took a deep breath and went up.

A huge lantern, the actual light of the lighthouse, dominated the next room. The walls were all large diamonds of glass and she could imagine that during the day the views over land and sea would be spectacular.

But not now.

'Here, let me put this on,' the voice said. The room was suddenly lit up by a far more powerful torch than hers, and, for a moment, she was blinded.

'They say this has the power of a thousand candles or something stupid like that. Whatever the power of a thousand candles means.' There was a laugh. 'Still, it does its job.'

Paul Churchill came from behind the light. Dressed in dark jeans, dark shirt, and trainers. Unlike the last time she had seen him, he was fully sober and had lost any pretence of joviality. His pale eyes blinked at her. Then he smiled. It wasn't reassuring. 'Were you expecting me?'

'No,' said Alex. 'I thought I might see Louise.'

'Louise,' he mused. 'Hmm. I don't think so.' He cocked his head. 'Come and look at the view.'

'The view?'

'It's lovely from up here you know.'

'If Louise isn't coming, then there's no point in my being here, is there?' Her heart began beating faster. 'Anyway, there's nothing to see at this time of night.' She hoped nothing had happened to his wife.

'Oh there is. Come on. Look.' He opened a small door Alex hadn't noticed before. 'We can go outside.' Then he came round behind her, blocking her exit. She had no choice.

He gave her a push in the small of her back.

She stepped outside onto what she thought must be some sort

of viewing platform that went all the way around the lighthouse. White railings came up to her middle: the only things stopping her from falling. The long trek up the stairs, the height, the muggy air, all conspired to give her a feeling of vertigo. She held onto the rail for support. The sky was heavy with clouds and threat, as if it were waiting for something to happen. Thunder rumbled all around. She could see the outline of the fields, lights from the village in the distance. If she turned, she could see the grass that led to the sea that led to the horizon.

'What do you think?' said Paul from behind her. 'I love it up here. You can feel at peace, that no one is going to bother you. No demands. No crying children, no whingeing students, no dissatisfied wife.'

'I didn't realize the lighthouse was open to everyone.'

He inhaled deeply. 'Such lovely air, don't you think? Oh, and it's not. I'm a volunteer, you see. It's open one Sunday a month and we show people around, give them a bit of history about the lighthouse, the area, the shipwrecks, the drowned sailors. Tourists love it. Especially when we tell them about the lighthouse keeper who threw his wife off this very platform in the nineteenth century.' He chuckled. 'It's a long way down. Of course, the public aren't allowed out on here. It's a special privilege I have reserved for you, Alex.'

'I was expecting Louise.' She made her voice sound level and clear. It was a hard act.

Paul Churchill sighed. 'Of course you were. What made you realize?'

'That she was the one Elena was in love with? A combination of things, I think: the way Louise looked when she spoke to me about her; the way you looked when I mentioned Elena. Finding the ring in your bathroom. And the ring was so delicate, more for a woman than for a man. And what the head of Stratton School said when we spoke to him.'

He sighed. 'Ah yes. Dear old Nigel. He couldn't keep his mouth shut, could he? After all I did. Not that he ever knew that I saved his poxy school.'

'How did you do that?'

'I took Louise away from it before any scandal could break. She was getting far too interested in a sixth-former there – a girl, naturally – so we had to move. I didn't particularly want to, but it was for the best, for me and that girl, poor bitch. And in fact, at the time, it seemed like quite a shrewd move. Going to The Drift. Better school. More prestigious, more influential. I saw it as a good place for the kids. Sea air. Healthy. Sports. Good results. High in the league table. All that.'

'But Louise fell in love with Elena.'

His lip curled. 'Love? I don't know whether I'd call it that, not really. Infatuation, more like. Control, even. Says she's "gay". Says I "stifle" her.' He moved closer to Alex. 'I don't stifle her. I just want a wife.'

Alex wanted to move; he was crowding her, pushing her against the barrier. She could feel the metal digging into her stomach.

'You can understand that, can't you? You've got a boy, a teenager, haven't you? And you know what it's like to lose those you love. I mean, look at your sister's kids. She lost them. I guess it affected you as well. And I can't lose my children.'

Alex felt as though she was being crushed: it was hard to catch her breath.

'They're my children. And I told Louise she had to stop this nonsense or I would take them away from her. Oh, I didn't want to do that, because then people would know. Know what sort of woman she is. Seducing young girls. Elena Devonshire.' He laughed. 'She couldn't have chosen the daughter of a more influential person, could she? I had visions of high-ranking policemen coming around, detectives, digging, digging, digging. I didn't know what to do.' His breath was in her ear. 'But the Devonshire woman sent you.'

He took a step backwards. She was free and could breathe again.

'A washed-up journalist with a past she's running away from. Alex Devlin. Do you think I didn't look you up? Found out all about you and the part you played in sending your brother-in-law down.' He grinned. 'Your family must love you.'

Alex kept her mouth shut.

'And then, I wanted to get to know you. At the barbecue. Jonny said he was bringing you and I was pleased. I thought, maybe we can talk. Maybe you would understand.'

'Understand what?'

'How you can love someone and hate them at the same time.'

She did. She knew how to do that all right. Her sister was someone she had protected all her life. Always tried to be there for her, however much she'd been pushed away. The times at school when she had protected her from bullies and from thought-less teachers. And during Sasha's illnesses, her depression, anorexia, and self-harm, Alex had always been there to patch her up. Sometimes, though, she had hated her too: hated her for ruining her teenage years, then sucking the life out of her and Gus. But she hadn't been there when Sasha had needed her most. And that's why she was here for Elena. For Cat. If she had failed Sasha and her children, she wasn't going to fail Elena and Cat. 'Where's Louise?'

'Where she belongs. At home with the girls.'

'No. I'm here.'

Louise Churchill stepped onto the platform, and at the same time forks of white lightning lit up the sky and threw her pinched face into sharp relief. She was dressed in a pair of leggings and a tee-shirt. She wore flip-flops on her feet. There was a sudden thunderclap almost overhead.

'Louise. What are you doing here? What about the children?' Paul asked, suddenly anxious. 'You haven't left them alone when there's a storm coming, have you?'

His wife was calm. 'They're all right. They're at home with a babysitter. I called her after you left. I knew you were coming here. It's your favourite place, after all.' She turned to Alex. 'I did love her, you know. Elena. I did love her.'

'But not enough,' said Alex. 'You're a teacher: you're supposed to be the one in charge. She was just seventeen when she died, sixteen when you first began to groom her. If you had really loved her, you wouldn't have done anything about it. She was the child. You're the adult.'

'I did not groom her!' Louise shouted, her words almost drowned out by another clap of thunder. Then the rain started. Soft at first, it quickly became more intense. Alex felt it soaking through the flimsy anorak she had on.

'Grooming sounds so, so seedy and nasty,' said Louise. 'What we had, Elena and I, was not like that. I told her some people would think it was wrong, but our love was pure. Unadulterated. No one could understand.'

'What kind of woman grooms a child, Louise? Especially one in her care? And asks for naked pictures of her?' Alex couldn't get through to her.

'I did not groom her,' she insisted again. 'I loved her. Really loved her. I was lonely.' She shot a glance at Paul. 'He's so cold; he thinks about himself, that's all. Himself and how he can further his career. I didn't want children. I wanted out. But do you know what, he raped me. Our two beautiful girls are the results of his rape.' Rain, or maybe tears streamed down her face. 'And now he uses the children against me. Says if I leave I'll never see them again.' Her hair was plastered against her head.

Alex felt rather than saw Paul sag. 'Louise, you know I love you. I've been trying to do my best for you and now you do this. Humiliate me.'

'You never loved me. You loved the idea of me.'

'You married me.' There was genuine bewilderment in his voice. 'I thought you'd keep me safe. I thought I'd live a happy life:

as happy as I could, if I married you. I never wanted to fall in love with girls. I never wanted that. I wanted to be normal.' She rubbed her hands over her face as if she was trying to wake herself up. 'Normal, that's all.'

Alex didn't understand. 'But Louise, it's the twenty-first century. Gay or straight, it doesn't matter.' She reached out her hand, touching the woman softly on her arm.

Louise shook it off. 'It matters if you were brought up in my house,' she spat. 'Anyway, I didn't do anything about it, not until I met Annabel at Stratton. She loved me, but Paul took me away from there. And then I found Elena. God, she was beautiful. And smart. And funny.' She smiled, a faraway look on her face. 'We talked about everything, she and I. We planned to be together. We might even have run away together and then nobody would have been able to touch us. But then those pictures came out. Our beautiful, tender pictures. And people laughed at her. Called her names, horrible, horrible names like slut and whore, and worse. And I thought I should end it so it wouldn't all come out. Because of the children. My children. And now she's dead and all I have left are the emails, and it's all because of you.' She pointed at her husband.

Then, without any warning, Louise flew at Paul, hands outstretched, nails raking down his face. She began to pummel his chest. 'I never loved you. Never. Do you hear me? Never. I loved Elena and you killed her.' She banged her forehead on his nose. Again and again until the blood flowed. For a moment, Alex stood frozen to the spot. Paul got hold of a hank of Louise's hair and yanked her head back. 'You mad bitch.' He pulled her off him and, before Alex could react, began banging her head on the railings. Bang. Bang. Bang. Bone crunched on metal. Alex ran at him, tried to pull him off. She had her hands full of his tee-shirt, her palms slippery with blood, then she elbowed him in the side. He gave a yelp of pain, but didn't let go of Louise.

But Louise found strength from somewhere and lifted her foot, bringing it down on Paul's instep. Then she whirled round, face a death mask of blood and flesh, and brought up her knee. But Paul was too quick for her and pushed her. Hard.

Another flash of lightning. Paul holding a knife in his hand. Paul, nose streaming blood, bringing the knife up and stabbing Louise in the stomach, once, twice, three times.

Louise, surprised, looked down, then put her hands over her wounds, before sinking gracefully to the floor, eyes staring up at the dark clouds.

More lightning streaked the sky, lighting up Paul. Thunder boomed directly overhead, but he didn't flinch. He stood, panting, fists clenched, a look of triumph on his face.

'There. You saw it. She tried to kill me. She made me do it.'

Alex shook her head. 'No,' she whispered. 'A knife. You had a knife.' She couldn't move. The knife had been meant for her. Rivulets of Louise's blood ran across the concrete, dripped over the side into the air. The rain began to wash it away.

'I didn't mean to kill her.' He looked at the knife as though he'd never seen it before. It clattered onto the concrete. He wiped his hands down his jeans, again and again and again. He looked at Alex, but didn't see her. 'I love her, you know. I always knew she didn't love me, not really. But I thought it would grow. And I thought if we had children it would tie her to me.' He rubbed his face with his hand like someone rousing themselves from sleep. Blood and mucus was smeared all over his cheeks. 'I love her. I caught her looking at those pictures, those disgusting pictures, one day on her computer. She told me she wanted to leave me. That's when I told Theo Devine about them.'

Alex held out her hands to try and appease him. 'Paul, we can sort this out.'

'I didn't mean to hurt her.' He shook his head. 'Not Louise. Not my Louise.' He began to cry, great snivelling, snotty tears that mingled with the blood from his nose.

She stepped forward and put her hand on his arm. 'Let's go down the stairs.'

He pushed her off. 'No!'

She tried to swallow her fear and began to back away, feeling behind her for the door that would lead inside the lighthouse. She had to get away before he turned on her. She felt the handle. She couldn't quite grasp it. Her hands were slippery with rain and blood.

Paul shook his head slowly, his eyes far away. 'I know you think I pushed Elena. But I didn't.'

Alex stood stock still. 'Who did, Paul?'

'I tried to reason with her, to ask her not to break up our family, that what Louise felt for her was merely a passing thing; we could get her help and no one would need to know. But she wouldn't have it. A 17-year-old bitch was holding me and my family to ransom. She was going to destroy our lives. Ruin my children's future. Wanted to tell everyone about the great love they shared. I had to do something. I knew the scandal would break us.'

'What did you do, Paul? Did you kill Elena?' She was so close, so close to getting answers.

He looked at his hands as if he couldn't believe what he had done. He peered at his palms, then the backs of his hands, then his palms again. 'Louise made me do it,' he said. 'She made me so angry sometimes. I used to go outside and punch the wall of the house in the alleyway. Punch. Punch. Punch. Do you know where I mean?'

Alex nodded, remembering his grazed knuckles at the party.

'I had to keep a lid on it because of the girls, you know? Sometimes I would run for miles. Miles and miles along the beach to run away my anger. But when those pictures of that girl were posted on the website, I thought it was only a matter of time before everybody would know about her sordid, ugly affair and we would be ruined.' He lifted his head and looked at Alex. 'But we're ruined now, anyway, aren't we? Louise and me? There's no future for us.' He looked down at his dead wife's body. 'No future. The children will be better off without us.'

'Who pushed Elena, Paul? Was it you?'

'No, I told you, it wasn't me.' There was anger in his voice.

'Who was it?' She held her breath.

He was staring beyond her when he suddenly vaulted over the railings.

He made no sound.

CHAPTER 38

However much they tried to make hospitals look welcoming – bright lights, different shades of white and green on the walls, garish posters warning of frightening illnesses, chairs upholstered in jolly shades of grey – they never lost that antiseptic smell or the echo of footsteps down the maze of corridors. They always made Alex feel nervous, too. It hadn't helped that, when they were searching for the lift, a trolley with the body of a little boy was wheeled past surrounded by a gaggle of men and women in white coats. Wires, drips, and an oxygen tank completed the picture. Alex felt tears come to her eyes, until Malone pointed out the child was a dummy and the doctors were in training.

Alex marched on ahead. Bloody man.

At least, she thought, as they came out of the lift and turned left onto another identical corridor, the situation with her sister Sasha was better. The new treatment was working. Heather McNulty from Leacher's House had phoned her that morning to say they were pleased with her progress, although there was still some way to go. The delusion about being the killer of Jackie Wood was still in her head. Nevertheless, Alex was looking forward to visiting her.

But as soon as she'd had that thought, another followed quickly behind. Perhaps it was time to stop running from her past? Time to go to back where she really belonged and where she had, in the most part, felt safe. Give up the anonymity of London and embrace the place she loved so much – Sole Bay. She could build her life there once more; build a safe place for Sasha when she came home. And Gus would love to go back there, too, whether it would be to live or merely to visit. She wasn't so naive as to think that now Gus had found his independence he would want to give it up again, but she was sure enough of his love to know he would come back to her. Maybe he would want to stay in Ibiza for a while. She would have to accept it. All she wanted for him was to be happy.

And Malone? She glanced across at him as they walked side by side. He grinned, took her hand. Perhaps it was time to go with the flow where he was concerned. Not worry about the future, but take each day as it came. One day at a time. The last few days with him had been magical. After he had found her at the bottom of the lighthouse kneeling by the broken and very dead body of Paul Churchill and on the phone to the police, he had called in favours, got hold of the right people, did whatever undercover cops like him did to smooth things over so that she found herself back at the cottage without having to spend hours giving a statement over and over again.

Afterwards, Malone had made it his business to try and erase the terrible events of that night from her mind, and to a great extent, he helped. She smiled as she remembered the day and night in bed making love, and the care he took not to hurt her any more than Dutch or Churchill had done, either physically or mentally. Neither of them spoke of the future.

'What are you thinking?' asked Malone.

She shook her head, the glimmer of a smile on her face. 'Nothing for you to worry about.'

And then there had been Bud, ringing her up, wanting more details for the exclusive she had sent over, delighted with the story and offering her as much work in the future as she could handle. On a freelance basis, of course. She had spoken to Cat, and had her agreement in what she wanted to say. The compromising pictures would have to be written about, and Cat agreed that was necessary if only to highlight what went on online. And she also said she would give Alex an interview over the next few days. Mark had categorically refused.

But they still didn't know whether Elena had jumped or was pushed.

'Are we ever going to find out?' Cat had said to her, despairingly.

'Cat, I haven't finished yet. I'm not going to rest until I have found out the truth, I promise you that.' But there were times when she wondered if she could really keep that promise.

'Look, we're here,' Alex said.

There was the sign for Cley Ward, and they pushed through the double doors.

Max was in a bed in the corner by a window, propped up by pillows. He looked small and pale and managed a watery smile when he saw them. A man was sitting on the hard plastic chair beside his bed, reading a newspaper. The man folded up the newspaper and stood as they approached the bed.

'Yes?' he said, frowning.

'Uncle, it's okay. She's a friend of mine,' said Max.

Uncle. Alex stuck out her hand. 'My name is Alex Devlin. You must be Edward Delauncey?'

'Yes.' His face cleared. 'You're the one that found Max.' He coughed. 'Thank you so much. I mean it. There must be some way to repay—?'

Alex shook her head. 'No. There's nothing to repay.'

'Thanks for coming,' Max said, then looked at Malone. 'Who's he?'

'Don't worry about him, he's only Malone. Doesn't want to let me out of his sight.' She rolled her eyes. 'He thinks he's helping me, so I'm letting him think that, but don't tell him.'

This raised a small smile from Max.

'Here, sit down.' Edward Delauncey offered Alex his chair.

Alex sat. 'How are you, Max?'

He gave a wan smile. 'I've been better, but also a lot worse. I'm determined to give it a proper try … coming off the drugs. I know it won't be easy, though.' His fingers plucked at the hospital blanket.

'We're going to get you the best care we can, rest assured, Max,' said Edward Delauncey. 'How could I not have known about this? I thought that school was one of the finest in the country. It was one of the finest in the country when I was there. And now I find there are drugs and goodness knows what going on.' He sighed. 'Look. I was going to get myself a coffee. Would either of you like one?'

'That would be great, thank you,' said Alex. Malone shook his head.

'I'll be back soon, Max,' said Edward Delauncey.

Max nodded as his uncle strode off.

'He seems to care for you, Max,' said Alex.

'You think?' Max's eyes were bright with tears.

'I know so.' Alex's voice was firm.

'He says … he says I'm going to get better and then go to a school nearer to home.'

'That's good.' Alex put her hand on Max's cheek. 'Look, Max, you wouldn't want this to happen to anyone else, anyone else's child, would you?'

He chewed his lip. 'No.'

'So can you tell me who gave you the smack?'

He lifted his chin. 'Felix.' No hesitation. 'I think he knew it was too strong for me. He watched as I injected it. Then left.'

'Bastard.' This from Malone.

Alex nodded. 'Another tick against him. Don't worry, Max, him and his mates and Jonny Dutch—'

'We thought Mr Dutch was cool, you know? Able to get us a bit of skunk for parties.' His voice was small.

'So why did you stab him?'

Max couldn't look at them. 'One day,' he began, his voice hardly a whisper, 'we were in the pub, you know, the one in the village?'

Alex nodded.

'Mr Dutch and some of the others said it was a good job Elena was dead. That she knew too much. And then he laughed. I lost it. And the next day I went to Mundesley and bought a knife – said I needed it for fishing – and then, then I stabbed him.' Max looked up at Alex. 'I'm sorry.'

'Look, Jonny Dutch was running a very lucrative business in dealing drugs. You name it, he got it. He used to make a trip to London once a month for supplies and Felix and Theo used to sell it – for a cut – of course. He gave Felix the drugs for you. It wasn't very difficult to create the demand in Hallow's Edge. And that's far worse than giving someone a nick in the arm. Though you shouldn't have taken the knife into school. Someone could have got badly hurt.'

'I know. Bit of a shit place, really, Hallow's Edge,' said Max.

Alex shook her head. 'No, it's some of the people who are shit, not the place.'

He took a deep, shuddering breath. 'You want the truth about what happened that night with Elena.'

Alex became still. 'Do you know what happened, Max?'

Max turned his face to the window, eyes brimming with tears. 'After she died – Elena, I mean – I used to go to the school chapel and pray that one day I would be strong enough to think about what happened that night. Because for a long time I wasn't. I didn't know what to do.' The tears began to fall. 'I was in a bad way. The drugs were killing me, I knew that, but there seemed to be nothing I could do about it. I thought: "just one more hit and I'll stop. Just one more." But I never could. And Felix kept getting me better stuff. Wanting me to try this and that. And then I hadn't got any money left.'

He took a deep shuddering breath and closed his eyes. Alex thought he had gone to sleep. Malone's phone began to ring.

Alex looked at him, annoyed.

'I'm sorry,' he said, glancing at the screen, 'but I have to take this.'

He leaned over and kissed Alex before walking away from the bed towards the nurses' station.

Later Alex would wish she had watched him as he walked out of her life again.

Max opened his eyes.

'Elena's funeral was awful. The girls – Naomi and Nat and all that lot – were all crying, clinging onto each other as if they had lost one of their greatest friends, when in fact they'd all been plain jealous of her. She was funny, smart, knew her own mind. I wished I'd had half her guts. I loved her, you know. Really loved her.'

Alex stroked the hair away from his forehead. 'I know you did.'

'Her mum was so composed. Pale and thin but kept herself together. I felt, I dunno, heartbroken, I guess. Then I really began to go out of control with the drugs and shit. I was cutting classes, couldn't care less about school. All I could think about was Elena's mum whose world had ended.' He stared at a blank space on the wall. 'Eventually I stopped dreaming about Elena. I thought it would get better. Then there was the inquest, and all the talk started up again in school about why she'd jumped: that she'd been depressed, not eating again, that she'd been jilted by a boy in the village. And I wanted to scream: "no, it wasn't like that!" But I couldn't.'

'That's why you sent that message as Kiki Godwin,' said Alex. 'And then you sent one to me and we met in Mundesley. But you told me then that you were there: you'd gone to talk to her but she went over the edge. It was deliberate.'

'I lied.'

'Why, Max?' Were they getting to the truth, finally?

'Mrs Farrar,' he whispered.

Alex closed her eyes briefly. The Farrars. 'What about her, love?'

'She found out about that Facebook message to you.'

'How?'

His face crumpled with misery. 'Felix saw me. In the library. When I was at the computer. That's how Mrs Farrar found out I was Kiki Godwin. And she said I would be expelled from school if I didn't tell you Elena killed herself. She said there would be a big scandal and my uncle would throw me out of his house. Then I'd have nowhere to go. Nowhere.' A tear trickled down his cheek. 'So I did what she asked.' His voice was barely a whisper. 'I didn't have the guts to tell you—'

'Tell me what,' Alex asked quietly.

Max turned his head and looked directly at Alex. 'What really happened that night.'

CHAPTER 39

ELENA

The night she dies

'Should you be out at this time, miss?'

I sink lower into my parka and try to give the old man and his mangy carrier bags a wide berth. Bit difficult up here on the cliff path, especially as I think he lives in the tatty old caravan that looks as though it's about to fall into the sea. And he stinks worse than anything I've ever smelt. I mumble something as I pass, but feel his eyes on my back. When I risk a backwards glance I see he has carried on walking, shaking his head. Probably muttering something about the youth of today or some such crap.

He rounds the corner out of sight.

Although it is cold, the wind has dropped. I can smell the brine of the sea. The moon and the Milky Way make the sky look like a carpet of stars and light my way, and I see the old man's caravan and further on, the abandoned chalet.

What a place to come to. Far worse than the old summerhouse at the school. By day it looks dirty and decrepit, totally abandoned. By night it is sinister, somewhere that is hiding secrets. I always avoided coming here. I know some of the kids from The Drift and the local ones used it as some sort of hideout, but I have never been tempted.

'Ow.' I rub my shin, not having seen the stone wall that surrounds the chalet. I hop over it, trying to avoid the smashed glass and empty crisp packets littering what passes for a garden. I go to the door and push it open.

I let my eyes get used to the dark before I step inside. How I wish I had my phone so I could shine a light in the dark corners.

The place stinks. It stinks of piss and vomit and general shit.

What am I doing here?

'She doesn't love you any more.' A hoarse voice comes from the corner of the room.

I screw up my face as the light from a torch shines into my eyes.

'She doesn't love you any more and she wants you to leave her alone.'

'Who?' I try to sound brave, but I know my voice is wobbly.

Suddenly he comes towards me and grabs my arm. 'Louise,' he hisses into my face. 'Louise.'

I try to wrench my arm free but Paul Churchill holds it fast. 'Just listen, you stupid girl. Louise and I have it good here, and we don't want you to spoil it, understand?'

I nod, too terrified to do anything else. My legs are shaking and I can feel the sweat pooling at the back of my neck. I am stifled.

'Leave me alone.' My voice breaks and I think I see tears in his eyes. It makes me brave. 'Please.'

'Keep away. Louise doesn't want to see you any more. I thought she'd made that clear?'

I remember her messages: how she had tried to finish with me, then how she said she loved me, and I feel defiant. 'We love each other.' I am not going to let her go without a fight.

Paul Churchill lets go of my arm. He shakes his head. Even in the gloom I can see tears in his eyes. 'No, you don't. She never really loved you. And anyway, you don't know the meaning of the word. You're just a silly little thing who's got caught up in something she doesn't understand.' He rubs a hand over his face. 'Christ, I could understand if it was one of those druggy creeps like Theo or Felix. But a girl?' His shoulders slump. 'She always goes for girls.'

'What do you mean?' I understand it now when people say their heart stops. Mine came to a complete halt. My chest feels crushed. I hold my breath.

He laughs. It sounds harsh in that broken-down building. 'You don't imagine you're the first? Her only love, do you? She's done this before, in our last school, but I managed to stop it before it went too far. Here, look.' He scrabbles in his pocket and brings out a dog-eared photograph, which he pushes into my face.

I almost gag. It is Louise, my Louise, with her arms around a girl with long blonde hair and clear skin. She looks a little like me, I think. But it is the look on Louise's face … I have seen that look so many times. She looks at me like that. 'I thought … ' I whisper.

'That you were the first? The only one?'

' "You are my one and only": she said that. She said that to me.'

'No. But she was cleverer with you: hid it all well, and I really thought she was looking after the kids, doing her job at the school. But I found out eventually. I always do.'

Is this how it feels when your world comes crashing down? When all your hopes and dreams turn to ashes in your mouth? I think of Louise, our secret meetings; the words of love we have exchanged. How I gave myself to her freely.

'I don't believe you,' I say. Then I shout: 'I don't fucking well believe you.' My cheeks are wet; my nose is running.

He looks at me with something like sorrow reflected in his eyes. 'I'm sorry.'

And it is those words and the sadness behind them that convinces me what he said is true.

He walks away.

I stand for a minute, numb. I cannot feel my body. I lift up my hand and see the ring she gave me on my finger. I wrench it off and throw it away. It rolls away into a corner, then I run outside and I hear loud sobs and realize they are mine. I stumble over the glass, the rubbish, the small stone wall. I lurch down the path like a drunkard. I veer off the path and down the road that leads nowhere.

The sky is dark; the cloud has come in. There is rain in the air. It begins to fall on me. Slowly at first, then quicker and quicker.

I can't go any further. I crouch down, tears dripping onto the earth, mingling with the rain. I don't know what to do. My heart feels as though it is tearing itself apart and I can see no future.

'Elena?'

I look up. Max is standing in front of me. He is shivering. Blinking rapidly. His tongue flicks in and out of his mouth. 'I'm so tired,' he whispers. 'I hurt. All over.'

'Leave me alone.' I try to wipe the tears away.

'Elena?'

I stand up, ready to shout at him – to tell him to fuck off, to stop following me around – but he looks so small and cold. 'What is it, Max? What do you want?' I am cold now, too. The rain is soaking my clothes, running down the road, making puddles here and there.

'You and Louise—'

I flinch. 'There is no me and Louise. Not any more.'

'I know you've been shagging her. I know you're … ' He hesitates. 'Like that.'

'I'm just someone who loves someone. That's all.' I shake my head. I don't want the love I have felt all these months to be reduced to those words. I am loved. I was loved. But now my life is ending.

'You're a dyke. A carpet muncher.' He is crying too. 'All those pictures were for a woman. That's disgusting. I'm glad Theo put them around.' I could hear him trying to sound brave and shouty, but it doesn't ring true.

'Theo.' It was good to have it finally confirmed. I want to laugh but feel myself crying instead. 'Couldn't bear the rejection, I suppose.'

All at once I get my strength back. I walk towards him, fists clenched. His eyes widen and he takes a step backwards, then another. 'We were in love,' I say. I stop. I don't want to go any closer to the edge. And this was Max. Little Max. 'We are in love.'

Max licks his lips again. 'I'm going to tell everybody. Everyone will laugh at you. It'll be in the newspapers. The dirty cow'll lose her job.'

'No. Don't. Please.' Even now I want to protect her. My lover. 'Why shouldn't I?'

I look up at the sky, the rain on my face. 'Because.' I can't think. 'Because you love me?'

Max shook his head. 'He said … ' he swallowed. 'He said, if I pushed you, he would get me the drugs I needed. He knows where to get them. To make it all go away.'

'What?' Disbelief. Horror. Sympathy. All rolled into one. 'What are you talking about? Push me? Where?'

'Over the edge. He says you've ruined everything. He wants to keep the life he has. And you're never going to love me, are you?' He looks around, eyes wild. 'I haven't got any money. I need some shit. He said he would get it for me.'

I turn and he is there, some way away from us, standing. Looking. Blocking my way back up the road.

Paul Churchill.

I stand very still, hoping the fear doesn't show on my face. All I can see is the end of the road and I know it's a long way down to the rocks below. I shudder at the thought of the height. I lick my lips. 'Max. This is me, Elena. I can help you.'

He shakes his head, again and again and again. 'No you can't, nobody can.' He giggles, and that is the most frightening thing of all. The drugs have sent him mad. Then his face falls. 'But I can't do it, Elena. I can't. You were all right, you see. You didn't laugh at me. You were kind to me. I was, I am, angry with the whole world but you, you were kind to me. You know your own mind. I've got nothing.'

'But Max,' I say, taking a step towards him.

He shakes his head. 'You wouldn't understand. Not in a million years. Do you want my advice?' he laughed bitterly. 'No, I don't suppose you do. I'm just a kid and a kid with a crush on you, but I'm going to give it to you anyway. You're just an outlet for Louise Churchill. Someone to lean on. She's done it before and Paul had to rescue her. That's why they moved here.'

'I know,' I whisper, but Max doesn't hear me.

'Don't throw your life away, Elena. You'll do well in your exams. You'll make something of yourself. Whereas me? Well, I don't amount to much.' He is gabbling now.

'You do, Max. You do.'

Max smiles sadly. 'I love you,' he says. And then he begins to run, not at me, but around me, towards the edge of the cliff. I try, but I can't catch him as he runs past. I know what he is going to do. Then he seems to change his mind and he tries to stop at the edge of the cliff. He tries to keep his balance. Forwards. Backwards. Forwards. He teeters on the edge and I run, catch one of his flailing arms. The moon goes behind a cloud. I hear the water crashing onto the rocks below. The winking of the buoy on the horizon. The wind in my hair. His other arm comes up to grab me to help him get his balance back. But he pulls and pushes me.

He pulls at me.

We slip and slide on the wet tarmac and shale.

The rain falls faster.

I push him backwards, away from danger, away from the edge, and he falls onto the ground.

My feet slip and slide on the wet tarmac and shale.

I see Paul, watching. Silent, still. A small smile on his face.

I see Louise in the distance, face contorted, mouth open.

I can't hear her.

The sea is grey. White foam around its edges. Seaweed on the rocks.

'No!' I hear screaming, but I can't tell if it's Max or Louise.

I think of Mum. Of the life I am never going to have.

I am in free fall.

Hello you, it's me.

I am so sorry.

I am so sorry.

But it had to be this way.

CHAPTER 40

CATRIONA

October

'I wasn't sure where to do this,' Cat said, as she sat down on a bench in the tiny churchyard overlooking the English Channel. It was a bright, sharp autumn day with blue skies and shifting clouds. A breeze blew the red and gold leaves off the trees. 'You always loved the seaside, and I know you loved that woman.' After all these weeks, she still couldn't bring herself to utter Louise Churchill's name. 'But I didn't think Hallow's Edge would be where you'd like to stay.' She leaned her head back, clutching the urn tightly. 'I reckoned you'd like to be where your dad is. You always loved him so much.'

She thought about Elena as a child, always waiting for Daddy to get home, for him to pick her up and whirl her around until she pummelled him with her little fists, begging him to stop. She smiled at the memory, trying not to cry but it was so hard. She had made herself promise she wouldn't cry when she came here to see Patrick with their daughter's ashes, but knew it was a promise that was hard to keep.

Nearly a year since Elena had died trying to save Max and, slowly, so slowly, the edges of Cat's grief had begun to soften, leaving behind a regret that she hadn't cherished her daughter enough when she was alive. That was the heaviest cross to bear. The guilt of not giving her enough time. It was something she was just going to have to get used to living with. Alex told her it was possible, and that eventually, you did learn to live with it; the guilt faded and the memories remained.

Memories: like Elena's laugh and how she would fling her head back and laugh with abandon. How brave she had been to overcome her anorexia and depression, and how she had been a rock when Patrick died; a source of strength when really she, her mother, should have been a source of strength to her daughter. Looking further back, she could remember creeping into Elena's room, watching her breathing as she lay like a starfish in her cot. She and Patrick laughing with wonder at this scrap of new life. Then Cat thought about Elena as a teenager, when she had come out of the dark times, and had been sweet and loving. The times when Elena had confided in her about a boy she fancied, or how a boy was hitting on her and she didn't like it.

Though there were some memories that were proving harder to capture as time went on. She could no longer remember what Elena had smelt like. However much she held an imaginary Elena in her arms and buried her face in her hair, Cat couldn't find the essence of her. She couldn't remember either whether Elena liked Harry Styles or Niall Horan? Rihanna or Katy Perry? Who was her favourite author? And how old had she been when she first began to talk? Worn her first bra? Perhaps these were milestones that passed her by as she was so busy with work.

'I missed such a lot,' she told Patrick. 'After you died and she'd been ill, I flung myself into work. I lost my way with her.' She stared out over the grey water of the Channel. 'I didn't know she was gay. She must have been so lonely. So very lonely.'

She put the urn down on the grass and went over to Patrick's grave and knelt down, putting her hand on the cold earth. 'I miss you too, Patrick. I could have done things differently, I know that.

But I did what I thought was right at the time. And I have to hold onto that, not dwell on what I might have done differently. Alex is right about that. Those are the thoughts that would send you mad.'

A robin flew in and perched on the top of Patrick's headstone. It looked at Cat with a beady black eye, making her laugh.

'I'm going to resign,' she told Patrick. 'As an MEP. I thought I would set up a charity in Elena's name to help teenagers with problems. I'm taking advice as to which way to go. Alex is going to help. She says the paper will give it plenty of publicity. I haven't told Mark yet.' She sighed. 'We're separated. I don't think we'll stay together. He's not who I thought he was. He lied to me about our daughter. Maybe we could have got over that, I don't know. I suppose the thing is, though, he's not you, Patrick.' She blinked away tears. She was all cried out.

She looked up and saw Alex walking towards her. One good thing had come out of all this horror, and that was her renewed relationship with her childhood friend. Alex had got to the truth behind Elena's death and, as with everything in life, the truth was not simple and straightforward. And without Alex, she would never have known the extent of Elena's kindness and sacrifice.

Alex sat beside her and took her hand. 'I've just heard that they're throwing the book at the Farrars – drugs, fraud, neglect, dereliction of duty – they'll never work in a school again.'

Cat nodded. 'I'm glad.'

The robin began to sing. The wind had dropped.

'Time to let go.' Cat stood and picked up the urn. Alex stood beside her. 'I want to meet Gus, Alex. Soon. Please.'

Alex squeezed her arm.

Cat nodded, then turned to the grave. 'Here, Patrick, I'm giving you our daughter back. Take care of her, won't you?' She shook Elena's ashes around his grave. The robin carried on with his song.

As the last of Elena went onto the ground, the breeze got up again, and the sound of it through the remaining leaves on the trees was like a voice whispering in her heart.

THE END

ACKNOWLEDGEMENTS

Many, many thanks to my agent Teresa Chris for her unwavering support and belief in me – may we have many years of shopping ahead of us. Thanks also to Sarah Hodgson – a fantastic and insightful editor – and all the team at HarperCollins.

Of course, I must say thanks to all my friends and colleagues whose names I have shamelessly borrowed, particularly Laura Devlin for the use of her surname for my main character.

Thanks to Julia Champion for constantly coming up with cunning plans to spread the word. Your enthusiasm is boundless.

And to Susan Rae, always a cheerleader, Jenny Knight, because you rescued me more than once from plot holes, and Sarah Bower for your tireless support and friendship.

Huge thanks to all you readers, reviewers and book bloggers. Your thoughtful comments and support have been invaluable.

A special thanks to Melanie McCarthy. Your unstinting encouragement means so much. The rest of the family isn't bad either.

Finally, I must say thank you to Emily Riley, Jenni Cooper and Nick Childs who have done much to bang the drum. As have all the Swaffers.

And to Kim, Edward, Peter and Esme. I couldn't have done it without you.